DEATH AND HARD CIDER

DEATH AND HARD CIDER

Barbara Hambly

SEVERN
HOUSE

First world edition published in Great Britain and the USA in 2022
by Severn House, an imprint of Canongate Books Ltd,
14 High Street, Edinburgh EH1 1TE.

Trade paperback edition first published in Great Britain and the USA in 2022
by Severn House, an imprint of Canongate Books Ltd.

severnhouse.com

British Library Cataloguing-in-Publication Data
A CIP catalogue record for this title is available from the British Library.

ISBN-13: 978-0-7278-5074-4 (cased)
ISBN-13: 978-1-4483-0897-2 (trade paper)
ISBN-13: 978-1-4483-0898-9 (e-book)

All Severn House titles are printed on acid-free paper.

MIX
Paper from
responsible sources
FSC
www.fsc.org   FSC® C013056

Typeset by Palimpsest Book Production Ltd.,
Falkirk, Stirlingshire, Scotland.
Printed and bound in Great Britain by
TJ Books, Padstow, Cornwall.

For Everett and Sara

ONE

September, 1840

New Orleans on a hot September night. A rank stink of gutters and piss.

Benjamin January, during the height of the fever season when he'd work the wards of Charity Hospital, habitually walked home along Rue Burgundy rather than the wider – and marginally better-lit – Rue des Ramparts. There had been a time when the Rue des Ramparts had been mostly lined with the small, neat cottages bought by bankers and sugar brokers and planters for their mistresses: free women of color, quadroons and octoroons and musterfinos nearly as fair as white women. Soft candlelight in French windows. Sometimes a piano played, or quiet voices talking.

But times were changing.

With the cathedral clock striking one and gluey heat stifling the town, January preferred the dangers of dark and silence in the smaller street to the near-certainty of trouble each time he should pass one of the grog shops or gambling dens or brothels that had come, more and more, to establish themselves in those cottages after their owners went broke. Grog shops, gambling dens, and brothels paid good rent. In the harder times since the bank crash three years ago, landlords couldn't pass up the money. The result was that at this hour of the night, a homegoing black surgeon was likely to meet white teamsters and stevedores, and men from the riverboats and the ships, all of them drunk and many of them looking for a fight. Any black man who defended himself ran the risk of being beaten to death for the crime of being 'uppity'.

The darkness among the shabby cottages of Rue Burgundy, one street closer to the river, had its own perils.

The man that attacked him was silent and fast. Had January not been straining to hear the smallest rustle in those abyssal little passways that led into the cottage yards – had he not been walking, for safety, not on the brick banquette but in the middle of the street itself – the man would undoubtedly have reached him in two strides and driven his knife between his shoulder blades before he was even aware of the danger.

He wasn't expecting the knife. He was ducking, turning, to take the blow he expected – a club or slung shot – on the heavy-muscled curve of his shoulder; the knife ripped down along his ribs and he stumbled, shocked.

He'd been expecting slave stealers. Six foot three and built like a cottonhand, this wasn't the first time somebody had tried to kidnap him to sell in Missouri. But as he slapped the weapon aside, turned away from the blow, he saw that his attacker was as black as himself, coal-black, African-black. The distant glow of a street lantern showed him 'country marks' scarred into the glistening face.

The African didn't even pause in his lunge. He just kept coming, with the desperation of a man who must succeed or die. He knew how to fight, hooked January's foot with his heel in an attempt to trip him, and almost succeeded, in the slippery mess of horseshit and puddles in the street. January took another knife-cut on the thick leather of his medical bag, then wrenched the bag sideways, to twist the knife free. The attacker grappled him, inches shorter and thin, emaciated under rags that smelled like a privy.

Then suddenly the African twisted free, dashed into what he probably thought was an alleyway between the cottages.

January knew it was only a passway, leading into somebody's yard. Knew, too, that it was in all probability barred across by a gate. He stood for a minute, panting, blood running hot from the gash in his side. He looked down at the knife still sticking out of his bag. It was the kind of long-bladed fighting-knife that river pirates and sailors carried. Blood, a few days old, caked the hilt.

His attacker had been alone.

All he needed to do now, he knew, was to turn and head down-river to Rue Esplanade as fast as he could stride – glancing behind him all the while – 'til he got to his home. He felt a little giddy from the bleeding but knew the wound wasn't deep. His wife – the beautiful and indomitable Rose – would stitch him up like a split shirtsleeve (actually a lot more efficiently than she could sew shirtsleeves), and that would be that.

That would be that.

He walked over to pick up his hat where it had fallen in the first impact of the attack. From the black rectangle of the passway – barely blacker or deeper than the darkness of the street – he could swear he heard the man's breath.

The pounding of the man's heart.

He walked toward the passway, hand outstretched.

The country marks told their story. And the smell of his attacker's rags.

He knew who this was. Who it had to be.

'Don't be afraid.'

Silence. He remembered how the man had attacked, not backing off to reconnoiter but tearing in desperately. Succeed or die.

Succeed or die.

'*No tengas miedo.*' The crews of the ships that still worked the slaving routes from the Guinea Coast to the Caribbean, in defiance of the British ban on the trade, were often Spanish or Portuguese. His attacker might not have learned any French.

Silence.

January had been bought, and freed, when he was nearly eight, by the sugar broker who had bought and freed his mother and taken her for his mistress. After that date, almost forty years ago, he had not had any of the African tongues spoken around him. Few enough spoke them in the quarters anyway. When he was a small child, a dozen men and women on Bellefleur Plantation – including his father – spoke Yoruba or Mandingo or Ibo, but of necessity they had used a kind of cane-patch French among themselves. He tried to remember the few words his aunties had told him, words they'd spoken to their children . . .

He said, '*In awdhik,*' haltingly, stepping toward the passway. He hoped it actually meant, *I will not harm you*, as he remembered (or thought he remembered), and not, *I'm going to chop you up and eat you for breakfast.*

Backed up against the tall iron-faced gates that led into the cottage's yard, the man was little more than a gleam of eyes, a sheen of sweat on a thin unshaven face. Breaks in that sheen showed more clearly the ritual scarring carried by so many of the older slaves on Bellefleur. His friend Mohammed LePas the blacksmith bore it, and old Uncle Bichet who played cello – beside January's piano – at the white folks' dances in the winter season.

His father had worn such scars.

January touched his chest, said, '*Ore,*' and hoped the man

understood . . . But why would he understand the language of another tribe? Africa was a land of hundreds of tribes and tongues. Then, touching his chest again, he said, '*Sadiq.*'

The African's expression still did not change. The whole body, tensed to flee, to spring, to do whatever it took to escape, did not relax.

He wanted my clothing, thought January. *Anything, to help him get away.*

He set down the bag – and the knife – and spread out his hands. Then, when this got no response, he held one cupped hand before his chin and made signs of eating.

Slowly, the African tapped his own chest – his eyes never leaving January's – and he said what sounded like, '*Akinto.*'

January gestured to him – 'Akinto' – and to himself, 'Sadiq.' *Let's don't confuse him with changing what I call myself. If he knows any Arabic at all* – and many of the tribes did – *'friend' will serve for a name as well as any.* Again he made the sign of eating, and very simple signs for: *I will walk . . . You follow me . . . Food.* Then reaching down, he picked up the knife, and skidded it along the bricks of the passway to his attacker's feet.

Akinto picked it up quickly, put it into the sheathe at his belt. Then held out his hands, showing them empty.

January gestured to him to follow, picked up his battered medical bag, and walked away down Rue Burgundy.

The whole distance down that street – not quite three-quarters of a mile – January heard not a sound behind him in the darkness. Nothing, save for the keening of mosquitoes, the many-voiced chorus of frogs in the gutters. In the trees behind the cottages, the rattling drone of the cicadas, like some hellish machine. Away to his left from Rue des Ramparts came snatches of piano badly played. Now and then a man's voice yelled drunkenly in English: *He's a fucken hoor I tell you, kissin' white folks's asses . . .* Heaven only knew to whom the speaker referred. But no footfall, no breath of movement, behind him. He did not look back.

The penalty for helping an escaped slave was five hundred dollars and six months imprisonment. Enough to ruin him, and his family, for life, even if some venal jailer didn't make a side deal with a slave trader and then report him 'escaped'. He knew, too, that kidnapping gangs worked the streets here at the back of the French town these days, and that field hands went for upwards of twelve hundred dollars.

In Texas, Missouri, Arkansas and Mississippi, cotton planters cried out for labor: the mills of England and Massachusetts devoured all the cotton they could purchase, and begged for more. Despite US law and the British navy, men still made fortunes smuggling in Africans through Cuba.

Once a man's free papers were torn up and he was away from white businessmen who knew him by sight, he was anybody's nigger.

Walking, listening, January ticked through possibilities in his mind. A man named Ti-Jon, whose master let him 'sleep out' and work with the stevedore gangs on the waterfront, knew pretty much everybody in the unfree side of New Orleans life. He would know men who spoke the language of the tribes . . . *But which tribe?* Mohammed LePas had been born in Africa but had been taken from his village there nearly fifty years ago. Uncle Bichet, nearly forty.

The thought intruded despite all his instincts of compassion. *The man has a knife. He doesn't know the town. What do I do if he runs from my house, is pursued and tries to return there?* In the five years he'd been hiding fugitives in the storerooms below his house's main floor, January had lived with that fear: that somehow one of those he'd helped would lead white pursuers back to him.

Back to Rose, and his sons.

Back to the hostages – as Bacon had said – that he had given to Fortune.

God had given him the windfall cash that had let him buy the crooked old Spanish house on Rue Esplanade, and to the atoms of his bone marrow he knew that God had done this for a reason. He himself was a free man, and not still cutting cane in some white man's fields, not through any merit of his own, but because of his mother's beauty. Because of the spell she'd cast over St Denis Janvier, and because that man had had the decency to buy her children when he'd purchased her. He was well aware that he owed God a lot.

Feed my sheep, the Lord had said to St Peter, and he hadn't asked whether doing so would put that sturdy fisherman's wife or children in danger. When he'd first spoken to Rose about working with the Underground Railroad, as it was nowadays called, she had simply said, 'Of course!' The niece and the nephew who shared their home had alike (and gleefully) sworn their help and their silence.

But how was he to explain this to a stranger who had neither French nor English nor Spanish? Who knew nothing of this land and its laws? Who didn't know that *nothing* – no breath, no hint, no whisper – of the hiding place must be revealed?

He stopped, at the glimmer of a far-off lantern hanging where the Rue Burgundy crossed Rue St Pierre and the dim light fell on movement too big for a rat. In the distance it was hard to tell, but by the scaly glister, he guessed it was a half-grown gator, making its way back to the Basin where the boats from the canal turned around.

I'll deal with THAT when the time comes.

First things first, Rose often said.

And the man behind him – if he *was* still behind him – was hungry, and exhausted, and almost certainly terrified. *Let's take care of that, before all else.*

The old house on Rue Esplanade stood on a seven-foot foundation, the relic of the times before the levees kept the streets of New Orleans from flooding every spring. Nowadays the houses in town stood up only a few feet above ground level, though as a rule anybody who could afford it, left the ground-floor rooms for storage, or purposes that weren't essential. All those little cottages – dark and shuttered up tight here along Rue Burgundy and the other rear streets of the French Town – were built low to the ground.

Wide doors – like the doors of a barn – broke the street frontage of the Spanish house, large enough for its original owners – whoever they had been – to unload freight into. They were shuttered and locked tight, and January turned into the narrow passway that led between the riverward wall of the house and its nearest neighbor. The pitch-black slot was barely wider than the span of his powerful shoulders. Only there did he take a candle from his pocket, and a tin box of phosphorous matches. A rat whipped away past his foot at the sudden flare of light. Three immense frogs belched at him, goggled disapprovingly as he moved along the mossy bricks to the locked iron gate at the passway's end.

A dark rustle of banana plants as he stepped into the open again.

The thick scent of jessamine and sweet olive. He left the gate open behind him, crossed to the kitchen, lit a lantern. Kneeling, he lifted the lids of the buried clay oil jars that contained, in their cooler depths, the little crocks of beans, rice, and sausage left from dinner and supper. These he scraped into a glazed bowl, fetched bread from the tin-sheathed breadbox, and carried these out to the table under the kitchen's deep, projecting eaves. In a clay pitcher he fetched water from the big yellow filter jar, and a tumbler. Then he crossed back to the main house, and unlocked the barn-like door that opened to the yard.

When he turned back from doing this, Akinto stood beside the table, poised like an animal to flee.

Exaggerating his movements, January pointed in the four directions: river-ward, swamp-ward, upriver and down, after each indication miming a cringe of abject terror. Then, pointing to the earth at his feet, he folded his hands on his breast, shut his eyes, and heaved a sign of relief and peace. *You're safe here*. He pointed into the black rectangle of the door under the house, cocked his head down onto his pressed-together hands, closed his eyes and gently snored.

Never taking his eyes from him, Akinto took the bowl, and the tumbler of water, sat on a bench near the kitchen door and devoured the rice and beans and bread: neatly, but very fast. A starving man, not a starving beast.

In the low gleam of the lantern light January guessed his age at somewhere between thirty and forty. He had outgrown a boy's weediness, and though thin, had the body and the movements of a man. January wondered if he had children, back in Africa or – God help them! – on the ship that had brought him here. Through what little was left of his shirt he saw now that the ritual scarring marked his chest as well, pinched lines of scallop, like an alligator's back.

When Akinto had eaten, January motioned him to come, and, warily, the African followed him into the darkness under the house. January moved aside the false wall that concealed one of the two tiny rooms at the swamp-side end of the cellar, revealing the narrow space – eight feet deep by twelve wide – with its two beds, its clean tin latrine-bucket, its pitcher and basin for water. Clean, worn sheets were folded on the end of the beds; January spread one, moving stiffly with the pain in his gashed side, and, leaving the lantern beside the door, went to the yard again and fetched water from the cistern. Akinto stood all the while beside the outer door, watching him, his hands still empty but his knife at his side.

January beckoned him to the hidden room, showed him how the door opened from within. The dark eyes moved suspiciously to the doors that led to the yard. January showed him the padlock, and the key, then took both and laid them on the floor of the little sleeping-room. It was past two in the morning and he was exhausted, and, he reminded himself, he had a piano lesson at nine thirty. Little Flora McCullen, the daughter of one of the few Americans who had returned to New Orleans this early – most of his pupils wouldn't be back until mid-October, when the weather finally started to cool. He mentally damned the little golden-haired cherub to Hell, and patiently mimed again: the four directions, danger in every direction. Here: *silence. Secret.*

Akinto repeated the gesture. *Here. Silence. Secret.* In his eyes, January saw he understood.

He took the lantern, left the door of the cellar open a crack behind him, and climbed the steps to the house.

TWO

Rose was sitting in the darkness of the little rear parlor. Her hazel-gray eyes widened behind her spectacles as he set the lantern down and she saw the blood. 'What happened?'

'Just a gash,' he said. 'Not deep . . .'

But as the heat and shock of the struggle, and the tension of the walk here – listening to every sound in the night – began to wear off, he realized he was trembling. He dropped into the chair she brought around for him. 'Christ almighty, it hurts.'

She was already on her way to the pantry, where there was a spirit lamp and water. 'Who was that with you?'

She spoke softly as she always did – the more so now, with (*thank God!*) the first two of her boarding-school pupils asleep in one of the attics upstairs. As always, she seemed unsurprised. It was far from the first time she'd been waked by the soft creak when he opened the door into the storage cellar, or felt the slight scrape of the false wall being moved on its hinges. It lay directly beneath their bedroom. Under a light robe of faded silk she wore her nightdress, and her brown hair, soft and curly as a white woman's, lay in a thick braid between her shoulder blades.

'He's an African.' He kept his voice, like hers, to barely more than a breath. A candle went up in the pantry and he heard the whisper of water poured from pitcher to pan. Then the smell of alcohol as she charged the spirit lamp, and the brighter glow of its flame. Carefully – since every muscle in his body now seemed to be connected to his right shoulder and side – he opened his medical bag, and brought out alcohol, basilicum powder, a needle and thread. 'Escaped from one of the slavers up from Cuba, I think. I *think* his name is Akinto, but he doesn't speak a word of French or Spanish.'

Briefly he recounted their meeting in Rue Burgundy, while Rose eased coat and shirt off him, then went back into the pantry and came out with half a dozen beeswax candles, a tumbler of rum, and a small glass globe such as lacemakers used, filled with water, to magnify the light. By that time the water in the pantry veilleuse was bubbling softly, and January, after draining half the tumbler, shut his teeth hard. She washed the cut, first with water and then with stinging alcohol, her hands light and cool. Very little disturbed Rose.

As she threaded up the needle he went on, 'Tell Gabriel and Zizi-Marie' – these were his nephew and niece, asleep now in another attic chamber – 'to keep the young ladies away from the cellar, and stop the boys from playing there.' His oldest son, at three, wasn't called Professor John in hope or speculation. The child would have investigated the Midgard Serpent or Cerberus the Hound of Hell had he encountered them.

And though he was fairly certain that the two boarding students half-guessed that their schoolmistress' husband sheltered runaways in the cellars – both girls were returnees from previous years – he was also certain that their mothers would withdraw them at once, if even a whisper got out.

'I'll talk to Ti-Jon tomorrow about finding someone who at least knows a little of his language, and how we can get him out of town.'

He drained the rest of the rum, curled his big hands tightly around the back of the chair which he now straddled, and bent his back to give her the best angle to work. 'God only knows what we can do for him beyond that. There isn't a shipmaster south of Boston who'd take him on as a hand. He's obviously a runaway, and doesn't know a word in any tongue. I'd be willing to bet he doesn't even know the name of the place he sailed from, or how to return to his home from there . . . if his home still even exists.'

But when he woke in his bed, a few hours later – little Flora McCullen's piano lesson was at nine thirty and at this season of the year he needed the money too badly to be late – and padded barefoot down the back-gallery stairs, it was to find the padlock, and the key, both lying neatly in front of the cellar's shut rear door. He pushed the door wide for better light and went inside, to find the hidden door closed but the room behind it empty. The water in the pitcher was gone. Crossing to the kitchen he found Rose, with Gabriel, a youth of seventeen with the slim bone structure that recalled both January's mother and his sister, Gabriel's mother.

'He's gone,' said Gabriel. Past the young man's shoulder January saw into the kitchen, where a couple of empty bowls and assorted crumbs on the table proclaimed that their guest had helped himself to all the yams, all the apples, and probably the entire contents of the breadbox.

'He took a pillowcase.' Rose nodded toward the washroom next door. 'And your green calico shirt and Gabriel's trousers.'

'And the sausages, the bacon, the cheese, and the eggs. Zizi's already gone down to the market . . .'

January sighed. 'He was starving.'

'I know,' agreed Rose.

Gabriel added, 'I'd do the same thing, Uncle Ben, if I was on the run and somebody left the kitchen door open. The kitchen string is gone, too, and the tinderbox. He was thinking ahead.'

'"Inasmuch as ye have done it unto one of the least of these my brethren",' said January, '"ye have done it unto me".' And he felt the sting of shame, to find himself mentally calculating how large a hole would be gouged in the household's slender finances, once the food was replaced so the boarders wouldn't notice anything amiss at breakfast – not to mention shirt, trousers, and the tinderbox. 'I'm sorry, Rose.'

She tiptoed to kiss him. She was as tall as many men, but January, she often said, would have made Hercules look puny. 'That's why I love you.'

All of this – and the additional time it took to cook breakfast once Zizi-Marie returned, breathless, from the market – meant that it was almost nine forty-five before January tapped gently at the back door of the McCullen house on Bayou St John. 'Why, Ben,' cried Mr McCullen, slapping him jovially on the (fortunately) left shoulder, 'we'd just about given you up!' His pupil's father was a sturdy, pink-faced Virginian who managed the offices of a steamboat company, redolent of macassar oil and chewing tobacco, his watch chain a laundry line of seals and fobs. 'Flo's been askin' for you since she had her breakfast. All over herself, she is, to show you that little piece you asked her to learn; an' don't she play it a treat!'

January beamed. 'Excellent!'

He followed McCullen through the kitchen – attached in the American fashion as part of the house itself – and into the wide front hall. From the back parlor he heard someone picking out the tune 'Little Pigs' on the piano: a light and rather hesitant touch that he recognized as the child Flora's. McCullen nudged him in the ribs – January had taken the precaution of walking on the man's right – grinning with pride. 'Ain't it the cutest thing you ever heard? She's already got herself a Tippecanoe sash, too, a little one she begged Mrs Farmer to make her – Mrs Farmer's in charge of the refreshments for the Ladies for Harrison Committee . . . Oh, and that reminds me . . .'

They entered the parlor. Flora McCullen turned on the piano bench, five years old, honey-golden ringlets cascading down her back and dark eyes wide and serious. Despite his unkind thought of last night, January was fond of the child, who was, he had observed, as polite to the household slaves as she was to him or to the white governess who came to fetch her back upstairs when her lesson was done.

'That was very pretty, Miss McCullen,' said January, and her face lighted with the compliment.

'Sing him the song, sugar,' urged her father, and then jabbed January in the ribs with his elbow again. 'It's just the cunningest thing! Sing it for him!'

Obligingly, Flora turned back to the keyboard and picked out 'Little Pigs' once more, and sang in the sweet treble of smallest childhood:

> What's the cause of this commotion, motion, motion,
> Our country through?
> It is the ball a-rolling on,
> For Tippecanoe and Tyler, too.
> For Tippecanoe and Tyler, too.
> And with them we'll beat little Van, Van, Van.
> Van is a used-up man,
> And with them we'll beat little Van.

'Tippecanoe,' she explained gravely, turning from the keyboard, 'is Mr Harrison, that's running for president. He beat the Indians at Tippecanoe. Mr Van Buren' – she pronounced the name with care – 'is the president now, and he's rich and lazy and spends all Papa's tax-money on gold spoons and fancy gardens for the White House. Is your master going to vote for Mr Harrison?'

January was rescued from having to explain – not for the first time – that he didn't have a master, by McCullen clapping him on the arm again and saying, 'And that's what I wanted to ask you, Ben. Now, I know you're heard about the Great Rawhide Ball that's being rolled south from Natchez to New Orleans—'

He broke off, to sing in his booming voice, '"It is a ball a-rolling on/ For Tippecanoe and Tyler, too . . ." The Whig voters of Natchez put it together, six feet across of solid rawhide—'

'I have indeed, sir,' agreed January, trying to look like a man who didn't consider this one of the stupidest schemes he'd encountered outside of *Gulliver's Travels*.

And indeed, the Whig gentlemen who had hired him to play at a reception on the coming Thursday (for the wealthy Whig planters, bankers, and merchants of the town), and at the mayor's dinner at the beginning of next week (for the truly wealthy Whig contributors), had talked of little else. By this time January had had considerable practice in nodding, with an expression of grave approval, and saying, I have indeed, sir . . .

'Contains twenty thousand signatures so far!' McCullen fairly coruscated with delight at the thought. 'It's a phenomenon – like Old Tip himself! Like the whole motion in this country, for the common man's voice to be heard at last!'

January nodded again and kept his reflections to himself concerning common men of color, common men – white or black – who worked on the docks for fifty cents a day, and common men who happened to be Catholic, Jewish, Irish immigrants, or Freemasons.

And women – common or uncommon – of course . . .

'Well, sir,' the American went on, 'that ball's gonna reach New Orleans, we calculate, a week from Friday – that'll be the eighteenth. And the Whig Club of New Orleans aims to give it a reception that'll make every voter in the state sit up and take notice! Yes, sir! We aim to roll it right down Nyades Street to Tivoli Circle, with the militia marchin' in parade, and flags wavin', and log cabins comin' right into town on wheels, and Mayor Freret himself and representatives of all three city municipalities there to greet it. What do you think of that?'

I think it's the stupidest idea I've ever heard, sir . . .

'I think it'll make the newspapers from here to New York, sir.' McCullen beamed. 'And that's where you come in, Ben!'

Oh, good.

'Martin Duralde tells me he's hired already you and your boys to play at his reception on Thursday – he says you're the best in town.'

'That's extremely kind of him to say so, sir.' January inclined his head a little in gratitude – gratitude the more heartfelt because the tail-end of summer, before the wealthy started to return to New Orleans with the first cool weather, was the hardest time for musicians and until the rest of the boarding students arrived next month, he and Rose were struggling to stay out of debt. 'We are playing, yes – six of us, some of the best musicians in the state, if I say so myself.'

'Can you pick up another couple – say, bring it up to ten? Because the thing that parade needs is a band playing in Tivoli Circle, before the ball rolls in. There'll be a hell of a crowd all along Nyades Street and a bigger one in the Circle itself, and we want to keep folks there and keep 'em entertained. Get 'em clappin' their hands, get 'em stirred up . . . Can you do that, Ben? Get your boys together . . .?'

'I can do that.' The men January usually played with – his friend the fiddler Hannibal Sefton, Cochon Gardinier, Philippe duCoudreau, Jacques Bichet and his frail old uncle – owed money to every grocer in town and would greet the prospect of another engagement with as much enthusiasm as McCullen displayed for twenty-five tons of ambulatory rawhide. Mentally he ticked off the other musicians he'd have to track down for a larger venue in open air . . . clarionettists, maybe someone to play a drum . . . Open air would require him to play cornet instead of piano, and Uncle Bichet to trade his cello for a bass fiddle . . .

'Dandy!'

January gritted his teeth as McCullen slapped him on both shoulders.

'And,' the American went on in triumph, 'in addition to that – I just heard this morning' – he pulled a folded piece of notepaper from his pocket and waved it as if it were a summons to court – 'from Marshal Duralde that his father-in-law . . .'

Only a childhood's worth of beatings – and half a lifetime of caution around white men – kept January from interrupting with: Henry Clay?

But his startled eagerness must have been clear on his face, because McCullen's smile widened still further, as if giving permission for January to exclaim, 'Henry Clay?'

'In the flesh.' The big man was almost hugging himself with pride.

'Coming *here*?'

'Coming here.' By his tone the American could have been speaking of one of the major saints, if not an archangel straight from God. And indeed, the emotion January felt at the thought of hearing the great politician speak came close. (*Though naturally if St James or St Peter arrived to make a speech in favor of General Harrison for president I should certainly attend . . .*)

On the whole, January had little use for politicians. He knew the names of the country's leaders, and followed events in the newspapers as he would have daily inspected the boundaries of his property, had he happened to live in close proximity to a jungle inhabited by lions. Though excluded from the vote, he kept a wary eye on those who made the laws of the country and the state, and didn't trust most of them as far as he could have thrown his own piano.

Henry Clay was one of the few exceptions.

'The Marshal says his father-in-law should be arriving Wednesday – the day after tomorrow – on the *Vermillion*. He tells me he's got you booked to play for his reception Thursday – that's the tenth – but he's got pamphlets being printed up, calling all the Whigs – all the Whig clubs up and down the river, all the voters, all the general's supporters and every good man who believes in reform – to rally at Duralde plantation Saturday evening, to hear Senator Clay speak. Can you and your boys be there?'

Saturday's the twelfth . . . January did a hasty mental calculation of the dates upon which he and 'his boys' had been hired to play for the opposing party. Louisiana Democrat Club reception Friday night at the Aubin plantation just downriver of town, Democrat Club musicale on Sunday night (moved from Saturday owing to the delayed arrival of the wealthy Madame Trepagier from Mobile) . . . Democratic Planter's Club cotillion out in Milneburgh Wednesday the sixteenth . . .

He hoped he wasn't forgetting something. Saying, 'I'm sorry sir, we're playing for Van Buren's supporters that night' would *not* make a good impression . . .

'We'll be honored.'

'I knew I could count on you!' McCullen smacked him yet again on the arm. 'The rallying will be outdoors at Duralde – Martin Duralde tells me he'll have the piano moved out onto the gallery for you. With Clay coming, it'll be the biggest thing in the state! The committee's bringing in two log cabins – two of 'em! – on wheels, and all the hard cider the town can drink!'

Flora said, with a glance for her father's approval, 'Mr Harrison was born in a log cabin. He's the people's friend.'

In fact, January was well aware that William Henry Harrison had been born on a very large and very wealthy tobacco plantation in Virginia. But he was aware, too, that the Whig party had been seeking for years to find – or manufacture – a Whig replica of Andrew Jackson, who had, like Harrison, been a military hero and had, so far as anybody knew, actually been born, if not in a log cabin, at least on the remote frontier. When the Democrats had mocked Harrison during his previous presidential run, as appealing only to frontier bumpkins, the Whigs had seized the image and magnified it.

Log cabins.

Hard cider.

Indian fighter.

The people's friend.

Instead of Old Hickory Jackson, Old Tippecanoe Harrison. (And who the hell Tyler was, January – and pretty much everybody else – had only the vaguest idea.)

And everyone – to judge by the newspaper reports – loved the story. Accurate or not.

He smiled a little, said, 'You realize, sir, that if you're pouring out hard cider you're going to have every Democrat in Orleans parish at your rally, as well as all the Whigs.'

'Doesn't matter! What everybody will see is that it's the biggest rally this state has ever seen. There'll be dancing – all the ladies will come, in their Tippecanoe sashes!' He framed the imagined scene with his outflung hands, eyes sparkling as if the crowds (and the six-foot ball of rawhide covered with signatures) were before him in fact. 'Fireworks over the river! Henry Clay himself speaking for Old Tip – and maybe some of those Democrats that come for the cider'll have their minds changed, when they hear what a strong American can do for this country, after four years fiddle-farting around with that weakling Van Ruin.'

January – who had in fact admired the little New Yorker's reliance on diplomacy rather than Jackson's fire-breathing threats – doubted this, but said, 'Stranger things have happened, sir.' *Like saints flying through the air and the Devil appearing in London a few years ago spitting blue-and-white flames from his eyes . . .*

McCullen laughed again. 'You boys'll get fifty dollars for the reception,' he promised. 'Sixty for the rallyin'. And all the hard cider your men can drink.' He winked, and held out his hand. 'The Whig Club put me in charge of the entertainment – and entertainment it'll be!' As January shook his hand, McCullen added, 'I'll draw up a contract, if you can come by tomorrow or Wednesday.' Then, as January moved to bring up a chair to the piano, McCullen's brow contracted. 'Say, are you all right, Ben? You're lookin' a bit peaked.'

January straightened up, and shook his head. 'Thank you for asking, sir. That's kind of you to notice. Carrying a trunk upstairs for one of my wife's boarding students I overbalanced myself, like an idiot, and fell. I think I may have sprained a rib.'

'Oh, ow!' exclaimed the American sympathetically. 'That's no joke! You be all right to teach?'

'Just fine, sir. Miss McCullen doesn't run me around too bad.'

And Flora McCullen giggled.

Her father was whistling, 'Tippecanoe and Tyler too/ and with them we'll beat little Van . . .' as he strolled out the door.

*   *   *

'Henry Clay,' said Rose that evening, as she lighted the smudges along the railing of the rear gallery. The smell of burning tobacco, gunpowder, and lemongrass did little even for such excellent cooking as Gabriel's, but it was better than trying to eat inside the house with the shutters closed against the mosquitoes. After giving a piano lesson to Rose's two students after lunch, January had spent much of the sweltering afternoon on the levee, trying – unsuccessfully – to locate Ti-Jon. At the moment he wanted nothing more than to sit where the river breeze could fan him, mosquitoes or no mosquitoes.

He had tried, on several occasions, to rig curtains of mosquito-bar all around the rear gallery, on the principle of an enormous curtained bed, but it hadn't answered as well as the smoke pots did. The whiney little monsters always managed to get in. With rain falling almost daily, from noon until two or three, the entire city became a giant mosquito ranch from Easter to St Luke's Day – one reason that the other three boarding students would not arrive for several weeks. Moreover, the candles on the table drew insects larger and less savory, which entangled themselves to loathsome effect in the netting.

Gabriel, still in the white jacket he wore to help at young Michie Alcitoire's new eating-house, crossed from the kitchen through a yard already filling with indigo shadow. 'I thought it was that Indian fighter who was running,' he said, mounting the steps. 'Old Michie Tippy-toes . . .'

'Old Tippecanoe.' January grinned. 'A nickname I'm pretty sure he never had until the Whigs decided to run him for president. And yes.'

'I've never heard of him,' protested the young man. 'Why isn't Mr Clay running himself?'

'Because *everybody* has heard of *him*,' returned January, leaning back through the pantry door for a stack of plates. 'Personally, I think he's worth ten of Old General Tippy-toes – if not twenty. But the Whigs are scared to run him again. He's come out with too many opinions that too many people don't like. He favors the National Bank, and tariffs to protect American industry. He's come out and said that slavery should be forbidden in the new territories. He even managed to talk the Southern senators out of pulling out of the Union, not once but twice. They call him a compromiser – the Great Compromiser. Nobody wants a compromiser.'

He laid the plates neatly along the ten-foot table, smiled a greeting as fairy-like Germaine Barras and sturdy, earnest Cosette Gardinier came out onto the gallery and dipped curtsies to him. Their mothers – like Rose's mother, and January's – were placées. Their fathers, well-off white gentlemen, had recognized in their offspring a hunger and a capacity for learning beyond what was universally expected of the daughters of the free colored demi-monde. Such girls – and such parents – were rare as hen's teeth, in New Orleans as in the rest of the United States. The young ladies who were sent to Rose, came to be educated as boys were educated – in history and science and languages – rather than simply to 'learn accomplishments' like sketching and music and how to please white gentlemen who would support them as mistresses.

With such a curriculum, reflected January with a rueful smile, it was no surprise that Rose's school perpetually teetered on the brink of insolvency: *Who the hell wants an educated woman?* And his smile widened with joy as she followed the girls in, a gawky, bespectacled Don Quixote, tilting valiantly at the biggest windmill of them all.

'Most of all,' he went on, glancing back at Gabriel, 'people drag up that old lie about Clay making a deal back in 1824, when he was Speaker of the House of Representatives: that he'd throw the votes he got for president to Mr Adams, in exchange for being made Secretary of State when Adams won. He threw his support to Adams because Adams was smarter than anybody else running in that election, and Clay was smart enough to know it. And because he didn't think that killing two thousand five hundred Englishmen in battle qualified Andrew Jackson to make decisions for the nation about treaties with Britain or the National Bank.'

'Didn't you fight in that battle, Uncle Ben?' Zizi-Marie came onto the gallery, Baby Xander balanced on her slender hip and Professor John toddling purposefully behind.

'I did – and I still don't think Jackson would admit the country needed a bank if George Washington himself came up and hit him over the head with one.'

Germaine Barras frowned a little as January held her chair for her. 'Why do you care, M'sieu Janvier? What difference does it make to people like us who the *blankittes* elect?'

'That's right,' Gabriel agreed. '*We* don't have any say in it.' He brought up a high chair for Professor John – who immediately took the nearest fork and tried to disassemble the hinge of the bar that held him in it. Zizi-Marie – at nineteen, echoing something of her grandmother's stunning beauty – sat at her elder nephew's side, the baby on her knee.

Gabriel set the dish of greens and bacon in the middle of the table, and held the chair for Cosette, then took his own seat. January folded his hands, and after a moment's silence, thanked God – with the whole of his heart – for the roof over their heads (mosquitoes and all) and the food before them, only slenderly augmented from the market after their guest's depredations of the night before. In his heart, he included Akinto in that blessing, wherever he might be. He guessed the African needed the help far more desperately than any of them did.

'Even if these Whigs talk about how slavery is bad for the country,' Gabriel went on, as plates were passed, 'you really think anybody's going to listen? Or vote for them? It's not bad for the rich folks, and that's all they care about.'

The two boarders listened avidly, absorbed in topics that were never discussed in their well-bred homes.

'That's why they're running on a lot of different arguments.' Rose poured out the rather watery lemonade. 'It's not just, "slavery is bad for the country". They're promising reform – which I think means giving a voice to more of the factory workers in the North – and they're promising to bring back a National Bank, so businesses can get credit again without worrying that their bank will go bust. They're promising to promote federal support for things like roads and railroads and canals. And I think they're hoping that between the railroads and the factory-hands and the anti-slavery societies, and people who just believe it when they hear songs saying Van Buren is a sissy and a scoundrel, they can scrape together enough votes to get Jackson's men out of office.'

'And *blankittes* really *believe* all that?'

'Why not?' teased his sister. '*You* believe that Trina LaBayadere's smart because she laughs at your jokes.'

Gabriel opened his mouth to retort, then closed it, blushing to the tips of his ears.

'Be that as it may,' said January firmly – he had shaken his head wonderingly over his nephew's admiration for the giggling

Trina for months – 'Senator Clay is going to speak Saturday at Duralde Plantation downriver, when the Whigs rally in support of Harrison, and I'm very much looking forward to hearing him.'

'And Michie Duralde is – what?' Zizi-Marie – whether because she was the granddaughter of the best-informed gossip in the New Orleans demi-monde or the daughter of a voodooienne who lived by secrets – had a lifelong fascination for family connections. January smiled to see how she ticked possibilities off on her long fingers, exactly the way his own sister – Zizi's mother Olympe – did. 'Senator Clay's son-in-law? Nephew?'

'Marshal Duralde' – like Will McCullen, Gabriel gave the middle-aged planter the title he had once held, as Federal Marshal in Louisiana's days as a territory – 'is Senator Clay's son-in-law and his brother-in-law. His older sister Julie married the senator's brother Tom. They were in Michie Antoine's restaurant just last week,' he explained to the boarders, as if this knowledge of the details of other people's personal lives was somehow unmanly. 'Michie Duralde and his sister, I mean. They were talking about who in town was Whigs and who was Democrats, and Michie Antoine – Michie Alcitoire,' he corrected himself, 'said that anybody who runs a restaurant needs to know these kind of things, so he doesn't sit Democrats like Charles-Louis Trepagier down next to Mayor Freret or Captain Tremouille of the City Guards who're Whigs.'

The two girls giggled at the thought.

Zizi-Marie rolled her eyes, and spooned up a little porridge for Xander. 'Yeah, and I'll bet half the people at that reception you're playing for . . . Is it the Whigs Thursday and the Democrats Friday, Uncle Ben? Or the other way around? I'll bet you're going to see the same people at both those charivaris, promisin' your senator they're good Whigs an' turn around promisin' all those Jackson men like Michie Mouton and Michie Trepagier they're good Democrats, so they'll get contracts and government jobs no matter who wins.'

'Well,' said Rose, 'if General Harrison wins, he's bound to make Senator Clay Secretary of State again, since I think the only job the general himself has had – at least for the past ten years – is county clerk in Hamilton County, Indiana.'

Gabriel shook his head. 'And your Whigs think all the people in town who own slaves are just going to forget about what Michie

Clay says about slavery, just because they wave flags and sing songs and yell "Tippecanoe and Tyler, Too!"?'

'And give them hard cider,' January pointed out.

THREE

The assembly gathered at the Duralde townhouse three nights later, reflected January, would have confirmed his nephew's worst suspicions about the susceptibility of *blankittes* to flag-waving and choruses of 'Tippecanoe and Tyler, Too!'

He and the other musicians had arrived at seven, and still had to pick their way through a snarl of carriages waiting to either drop their passengers in front of the covered carriageway, or simply to move on down Rue Chartres after the French Creole sugar planters – or the American bankers and brokers and steamboat-company owners – got disgusted with waiting and abandoned their vehicles to walk the thirty or forty feet of *banquette* to the door.

'I thought summer's supposed to be the quiet time in New Orleans!' protested the new clarionettist, a young Charleston man January hoped would strengthen Philippe duCoudreau's somewhat pedestrian concept of rhythm.

Cochon Gardinier widened a piggy eye at the newcomer and exclaimed, 'This *is* the quiet time, Griff!'

Griff Paige joined in the laughter, and January shook his head. 'This election, I don't think there *is* a quiet time. It wasn't like this four years ago.'

'I don't think it was like this at any time since the French Revolution,' remarked Hannibal Sefton, and paused to doff his hat to a pair of market-women edging through the crowd in the other direction. 'Or the ancient Roman Saturnalia, for that matter: *Iam Cytherea choros ducit Venus . . .*'

The ground-floor shop that faced the street was shuttered and dark, but the arch of the carriageway which led to the main door and the courtyard beyond was lit with cressets like the Hell-mouth in a medieval triptych. The gallery above the shop was astir with servants, lighting mosquito-smudges and fetching lemonade, punch, and champagne to those who'd been invited to dine with the Great Man.

In an hour – when the reception would officially begin – the street would be impassable, and the huge double parlor that occupied the whole 'premier étage' (which Americans persisted in calling the second floor) would be jammed.

As Zizi-Marie had prophesied, even the French planters, and the Americans who owned the cotton presses and lumber-mills which depended on slave labor, would be there, guessing that Harrison might win and eager to have Senator Clay know their faces.

As it happened, January had seen the senator on a number of occasions, when he himself had been in Washington City three years previously. As he and his little orchestra – violins, a clarionet, flutist, oboe, and old Uncle Bichet on his sweet-voiced cello – took their places around M'sieu Duralde's splendid English pianoforte, January easily picked out that unmistakable head of fading red-gold hair, taller than most of the men in the room. His lean, handsome face bright with genuine welcome, Clay greeted the men who'd pledged their support to the old war hero from North Bend, Indiana.

January knew perfectly well that he himself wouldn't speak to the politician. Musicians – particularly men of color – simply didn't. Even when he'd played in Paris in the twenties, *liberté*, *égalité*, etc. notwithstanding, guests didn't address the hired help unless it was to request something. But he found himself looking forward to Saturday night, when he hoped he'd hear the man speak before a crowd. Clay's voice – which he heard in snatches through the muted murmur of those around him – was a warm baritone, pleasant to listen to, with the gentle drawl of the upper South. The young man beside the senator was obviously his son: same red-gold hair, same long-legged height. Looking for someone, January thought. Turning towards the doorway every time it opened, with the slightly smitten expression that January recognized, having seen it on Gabriel's face every time he was someplace where Trina LaBayadere was likely to turn up.

The thought of his nephew's first love made him smile as he settled on the piano bench and led the way into the 'Cracovienne'.

Playing at receptions was different from playing for balls or the opera. The music was meant to be heard but ignored, never to conflict with or distract from conversation. The old Austrian émigre who had taught him had said, 'They want to know you're playing but they don't want to listen. You understand that, and all will be well.' He was glad to observe that Griff Paige seemed to know this, too. For receptions – or for the early portions of the evenings at which he would later play for dancing – he and the other musicians would choose popular ballads like 'Kathleen Mavourneen' and 'The Moon' or the flowing sweetness of Mendelssohn and Chopin.

And let the *blankittes* talk.

That's what they were here for.

He recognized them as they came in, and the reception line formed up. The line was a bit somber in its lack of feminine brightness, for Martin Duralde's wife – Clay's daughter – had died shortly after the birth of their second child. Duralde's older sister Julie acted as hostess, short and sturdy like her brother Martin and gracious in the half-mourning of long widowhood. Henry Clay himself stood beside his sister-in-law and his son-in-law, shaking hands and smiling, and January thought – though they were across the room and in candlelight – that despite the effort to hold himself up, the politician looked traveled to death.

No surprise, he reflected. The man had been making speeches, attending political 'rallyings', and shaking hands with every man of property and influence from Washington City to Nashville and then all the way down the river to New Orleans: Tippecanoe and Tyler, Too!

January felt a pang of sympathy.

He'd spent yesterday, and much of today, on the levee in his quest for Ti-Jon, and had only ascertained – *finally*, that afternoon – that Ti-Jon's owner, Michie Dessalines, had rented out the whole gang of his slaves to a lumber contractor in the swamps of Plaquemines Parish. 'Ain't be back 'til Sunday night,' one of the loading crew at the steamboat wharves had informed him. 'Maybe Monday.'

Officially, Ti-Jon was the property of Philippe Dessalines, who also owned three steamboats, several town store buildings, and shares in two brickyards and a cotton press. But Ti-Jon and the dozen other young men whom the French Creole contractor had bought – and could sell – like so many mules, didn't work in the cane fields that surrounded the city, nor did they live beneath their owner's roof, as house servants did. Instead, they rented their own lodgings – with free colored families or in the cheap rooming-houses of the 'back of town' in the Faubourg Tremé. They bought their own food and clothing, kept themselves out of trouble, held jobs on the wharves or in the cotton presses or driving freight out to Bayou St John. They managed their own affairs, and stopped by Michie Dessalines' office once a week with a set sum, renting their bodies and their freedom of action as hack-drivers rented their cabs. Whatever they earned above and beyond their rental, they could keep.

The arrangement drove the city fathers crazy – especially the Americans. But it was a common one in cities like New Orleans, Mobile, Savannah and Richmond. January's mother owned six slaves, over and above her household staff, and she rented them out to all and sundry, and considered her son a fool for not having followed her example when he'd gotten the windfall cash a few years back, with which he'd bought the house. January prayed that Sunday – or Monday – wouldn't be too late, for a man hiding in the marshy ciprière between the town and the lake, and though he knew the likelihood of hearing any word of the runaway was slim, he had spent the rest of that afternoon patiently canvassing the Third Municipality – downriver from his own house on Rue Esplanade – and the grimy neighborhood around the canal and the turning basin, listening for news.

Not Old Django at the grocery in the 'back of town', not Tyrell Mulvaney the Irish cabman, not Parnassus Sam down on the wharves, not the coffee-sellers in the market-place nor Cora Chouteau at the Buttonhole Café nor any of the voodoos – Mamzelle Marie or Queen Regine or his sister Olympe . . . None of them had heard of an African taken by slave catchers. No such African had shown up in the long, grim line of slave jails on Baronne Street. January doubted that Akinto would go upriver – his goal after all was to get back on a ship – and prayed also that he was right in his guess: the bayou country around New Orleans would be safer than the Natchez Trace going north. Even a giant rolling ball of rawhide wouldn't discourage the river pirates and slave stealers that haunted the river landings.

Nor had any of his acquaintances, friends and chance-met gossips known of anyone, anymore, who spoke the old African tongues.

Only to Olympe had he told the truth. To the others he'd spun a tale of an old man in the market-place . . . *God only knows why, but he's been coming up to me for days now, trying to tell me something. He shows me what I think has to be a gris-gris, made out of bones and string. But I can't understand a word he says . . .*

An escaped slave, even one illegally in the country, was worth at least eight hundred dollars to somebody. And times were hard.

Someone *has to speak his language . . .*

And from that tiring, sweating, cautious quest, he'd returned, yesterday and the day before, to his house to wash and shave and go back out to the Second Municipality – the American section, when the town had been divided four years ago into three independent dominions (*And whose bright idea was* that*?*) – or to take the steam-cars up to Carrollton to teach children – white or colored, French or American – the hard, patient disciplines of musical scales. The key to unlock the heart of beauty.

Now he saw Philippe Dessalines shaking hands with Henry Clay, assuring him that he was wholeheartedly in favor of the American Colonization Society, of which Clay was president. 'Because you are right, sir! The proper place for the children of Africa is *Africa*. When you look behind all these revolts and rebellions, you'll always find, it's the free coloreds who start them. And they start them because their natures are incompatible with the natures of white men. Those who are freed here in America must be returned to where they will be happy and at peace . . .'

Not that Michie Dessalines has ever freed a slave in his life . . .

Beside him, January heard Griff Paige mutter, '. . . Said no man of color in America, *ever* . . .' and Jacques Bichet snickered as he flipped through his music in quest of 'Beulah Spa'.

'Oh, *sir*,' squeaked Jacques in cane-patch gombo French, 'I's just *dyin'* to leave America where I got a good home an' family an' go live in a jungle swattin' flies . . .'

'You keep on like that and you're gonna leave *this* good home and be out on your butt on the street swattin' flies,' January warned him, though they all spoke in murmurs beneath the rising clamor of the room. Michie Dessalines' partner – a man named Wachespaag and one of the most generous contributors to the New Orleans Democrat Club – nodded sagely and declared, 'Why, the pastor at my church told me only the other day of a free colored family who came to him . . .'

Then Cochon Gardinier – the second violin – glanced across the salon and said, 'Oh, lord!'

Following his gaze, Hannibal Sefton, without a pause in the lacy beauty of his lead-in to 'Beulah Spa', murmured, '"O, she doth teach the torches to burn bright!"' – Romeo's words upon first beholding Juliet. 'Five cents says he calls somebody out before midnight.'

January – who like all the others could have played 'Beulah Spa' backwards and in his sleep – turned his head to see who they were talking about. He had learned long ago that his fellow musicians were worse gossips than any of his wife's demure pupils.

He saw, and rolled his eyes. *Somebody* was going to get called out before the evening was over, anyway.

Young men were *always* calling each other out over Marie-Joyeuse Maginot.

There she stood in the doorway, pretty as a half-opened rose jeweled with dew. The prettiest girl in the room. You could have put her in a chamber the size of St Peter's Basilica in Rome, packed to the walls with maidens from every land from Portugal to China, and she'd *still* be the prettiest girl in the room.

And she knew it.

The young man gazing at her with his heart in his eyes was James Clay.

January sighed. *Oh, lord! indeed . . .*

Marie-Joyeuse returned young Mr Clay's gaze with those extraordinary eyes, blue-green as tourmaline under lashes like black velvet. The slight pucker of her brow, the hand pressed to her bosom, the tremor of that sweet, pink mouth, all cried out across the width of the room. *Thank God you're here! The evening would have been desolation, without sight of you.*

Back in June, when January had briefly given Marie-Joyeuse lessons on the piano at the summer cottage her father had rented in Milneburgh by the lake, he'd seen her practicing that particular expression in the parlor mirror. When she'd started rehearsing it on him – the melting glances under the lashes, the tremulous, come-hither smiles – he had found a convincing reason to terminate the lessons. ('I think your daughter has learned all I can teach her, Monsieur Maginot. A talent like hers needs greater skill than mine . . .') Whether she enjoyed teasing a man who would be lynched for responding, or simply wanted to work on her technique, he didn't know, and didn't want to know.

Hannibal was still giving her harp lessons. January wondered whether his amorous friend – who at least was white – would come out of the experience with a whole skin.

But young Mr Clay, like a man in a dream, took two steps towards her, and Marie-Joyeuse moved as if she would reach out to him with one exquisite little hand. Her cousin, the dark-browed stallion Damien Aubin, caught her arm and led her back through the crowd to where her father stood talking with the other French planters. It may only have been coincidence, but at almost the same moment, Senator Clay appeared at his son's side with white-haired old Augustin de Macarty, former mayor of New Orleans and one of the most influential planters and businessmen in the city. James Clay – according to William McCullen – had recently gone into law partnership with his father and was expected by all to enter politics. Falling in love with the daughter of a semi-impoverished sugar planter in New Orleans was probably not what his father intended for him.

And dancing, or flirting, or making sheeps'-eyes at any American whatsoever was clearly not what the members of the vast inter-locked Aubin-Maginot-Mabillet-Bossuet clan had in mind for one of their damsels, no matter how badly her father needed money.

And as January and his companions played, Henry Clay, tall and smiling despite the echo of weariness in his face, moved on through the crowded ballroom as if nothing had happened. In between Scots ballads and tunes composed for the New York theaters, January admired the way the senator stitched together the disparate factions of New Orleans society: not just French Creoles and Americans, but the enmities to the knife among the French Creoles themselves. Napoleonistes who hated royalists, Legitimistes who would not speak to supporters of the original Revolution . . .

Much as he considered the American Colonization Society an idiotic – and at root, pernicious – venture, January looked up to the man as he looked up to few other whites he could think of.

At least he admits there is *a problem, rather than automatically siding with the slave owners.*

'Tis Home Where'er the Heart Is . . .'

'The Harp of Love . . .'

And Clay listened to them all. For a man famed for quick wit and sharp retorts, he had the great gift of attention to the words of others before opening his own mouth. When he'd glance up from the golden flow of the music, January most frequently saw the senator absorbed in what someone else was saying to him. He nodded with genuine interest to banker Hubert Granville's suggestions about linking independent banks to Clay's proposed National Bank; to little Bernard de Marigny's encomia of his racehorses; to coffin-jawed Melchior Aubin's plans to improve sugar production with the purchase of the newest models of vacuum pans and enclosed furnaces . . . 'You must have heard how these new methods increase the crop yield, sir, if one could only afford the expense! Yet half the plantations on the river – and, I'm ashamed to say, my own place at Aurore – are still milling the cane with mule teams and burning up hundreds of cords of wood in a day!'

January half-smiled at the senator's tact. Clay couldn't be ignorant of the fact that there was a Louisiana Democrat Club reception at Aubin's Aurore Plantation, a mile and a half downriver, the following night. Yet he nodded as sympathetically as if Aubin had pushed a giant ball of rawhide into the salon single-handedly and contributed ten thousand dollars to General Harrison's campaign.

With equal attention, the senator listened to Anne Trulove's concerns about credit – her planter husband couldn't have told a bill of lading from the Bill of Rights and had no idea why a state bond from Missouri wasn't worth the same as one from New York – and was charming to Mrs McCullen and her little group of Ladies for Harrison, bright-colored sashes and all.

His son followed him, not much older than Gabriel, like Gabriel at Alcitoire's observing and learning from a master. And, like Gabriel, young James Clay would periodically turn his head towards one bright, small figure in rose and green on the other side of the room, his heart palpitating visibly on his sleeve.

'Flow Gently, Sweet Afton . . .'

'The Light of Other Days . . .'

Donizetti barcarolles and Mozart waltzes, mingled with snatches of conversation: 'Absolutely dotes on her, you know – Why, he sold *three field hands* to buy her those pearls she's wearing . . .' 'Tippecanoe and . . . who the hell is *Tyler*, anyways?' '. . . in broad daylight! On the carpet! With her *husband* of all people . . .!' 'Damn uppity yeller French niggers don't know their place . . .' '. . . can outrun anything in this parish – or this state!'

Schubert's 'Erlkönig' and 'Picking Up Sticks'.

'. . . Mabillet married one of the Viellard sisters, so he's actually brother-in-law to Florentin Miragouin *and* second-cousin to Charles-Louis Trepagier, and you *know* how rich the Trepagiers are . . .' 'What the hell you expect, from a man whose vice-president's been keepin' a tavern in Kentucky an' livin' with a colored woman . . .?'

''Course we'll beat that pussified little scoundrel!' Tom Spanish, a bluff and paunchy planter from the other side of Donaldsonville, lifted his voice over the general din in the room. 'And everybody knows, Senator Clay, that the general'll have you to thank for his victory. With you as Secretary of State again—'

'Now, at this point, sir' – Clay raised an admonishing finger – 'my old mother would flick you on the head with her thimble, and tell you that story about the girl with the basket of eggs on her head, who counted her chickens before they were hatched and ended up with an omelet in the road. Only God knows who's going to come out the winner in this election—'

A disparaging chorus.

'And . . .' Clay effortlessly rode over the noise, like a trained actor quieting a rowdy house. 'And . . . win or lose, I won't be Secretary of State again.'

More shouts, shocked and disbelieving. Melchior Aubin frowned like a glowering saint. 'Won't . . .? Sir, you have more experience, more talent than the rest of Congress put together—'

'And more years on me,' sighed Clay, half-comical, 'than the whole of the House of Representatives, at least. Gentlemen,' he went on, as the noise threatened to rise again, 'I am sixty-three years old. I have crossed back and forth over the mountains between Kentucky and Washington City more times than my old bones care to count—'

More shouting . . . ('Beat any man in Washington in a fist-fight . . .!')

'—and the climate in Washington itself makes New Orleans in the summer – if you will forgive invidious comparisons – seem like an Alpine meadow. To say nothing of the company,' he added, with his schoolboy grin, which got a general laugh. 'In the words of the Duke of Wellington after three days at the Battle of Waterloo, I am gettin' too old for this shit.'

At nine, as agreed, the musicians retreated across the courtyard

to the kitchen for beer and discreet visits to the slaves' outhouse
next to the laundry. Cressets threw nervous shadows among
the banana-plants and trellised jasmine, but barely illuminated the
darkness. Duralde's cook Simeon and his assistants roiled in quiet
frenzy preparing quenelles, turkey galantine, and a *double cascade
des pommes* for the supper that would divide the two halves of
that evening's festivities. Beer for the musicians was set out on a
worktable outside the open folding-doors of the kitchen itself,
superintended by a tall, slim woman named Lottie.

'Mrs Julie Clay told me to time you all,' she informed January,
with a glance towards the upper-story gallery, and then at the large
steel watch that hung from her belt. 'God forbid Mr Duralde's
guests don't get in their fair share of dancin' before supper's laid
out.' Her French, though good, was extremely American and
January guessed she'd been one of the slaves that Clay's daughter
Susan had brought with her from Kentucky at her marriage.

'They will if nobody calls anybody out,' he remarked, thinking
of Marie-Joyeuse Maginot.

In the flame-light, Lottie's teeth flashed in a grin.

'I swear to God, Mr J, I never seen white folks so all-fired ready
to kill each other.' She shook her head. 'I thought they were bad
in Washington City, when Mr Jackson was runnin' for president
– Lord, I never heard men use language like that in my life! Never
mind goin' after each other with pistols an' knives! But half of
Congress was straight out of the backwoods so you'd kind
of expect it. Here—'

On the gallery, young James Clay escorted Marie-Joyeuse out
of the long double-parlor and into the cooling gloom above the
courtyard. He cherished her little kid-gloved hand in his, bent his
head down to listen to her words; then clasped her other hand.

'Like my mama says,' replied January, 'handsome is what handsome does.' Old Jules Maginot, he recalled, was a Democrat,
whose father had fled the rebelling slaves in Sainte-Domingue in
1791 and had married his Louisiana cousins. January guessed that
he – and the rest of the Aubin-Mabillet crowd – had come to the
Whig reception intent upon garnering Clay's support for the handsome Damien Aubin. Damien – the grim Melchior's younger
brother – was currently an assistant secretary in Washington City,
with an eye on running for Congress himself in two years . . .

'Don't you think it!' Griff Paige called down from the other end of the table. 'I bet you'd have just as many black men as white getting into brainless duels if we didn't know we'd end up in jail for it.'

'Not *as* many,' disagreed January, after a moment's feigned calculation. 'Not as long as we can't vote or run for office.'

The musicians around the table laughed, joined by Lottie, but there was a wry note to the mirth. On the balcony, sure enough, Damien Aubin appeared in one French door just as young Mr Clay – whom the girl had sent off to fetch, presumably, punch a few moments before – returned with his offering. There was a brief pantomime as Marie-Joyeuse either recalled some rendezvous in the parlor or heard someone calling her, because she rustled back indoors, leaving the two gentlemen to glare daggers at one another . . .

The girl's going to get one of them killed. January tried to feel only disgust, and not anger. His sister Olympe would have shrugged and said, *What do you expect of blankittes?*

The fact that Damien Aubin had to bow and scrape a little to Senator Clay if he wanted to keep his position after a Whig victory couldn't have sweetened his view of Clay's son.

He might feel called upon to speak words that could only end in blood.

And the girl, January guessed – remembering those teasing eyes – would be hugging herself with delight at the mischief she was causing.

The talk turned to the Grand Rallying of the Whigs on Saturday evening, downriver at Duralde's plantation. 'If they really bring in two log cabins on wheels to dispense hard cider to the populace at large,' commented Hannibal, 'that's when you're really going to see a re-enactment of the Battle of New Orleans.' Reaching across, he took Lottie's hand and kissed it. 'Do you require that I fall on my knees before you, beautiful lady, to coax you for a cup of tea, or would abject pleading and tears suffice? I have sworn off alcohol of any kind for the duration of my life, but tea is life to me. "The grace of heaven/ before, behind thee, and on every hand/ Enwheel thee round" . . . do not cast me into outer darkness.'

The woman gave him a glance of mock hauteur, in the manner of some of the *grandes dames* in the reception room, and the fiddler promptly dropped to his knees and kissed the hem of her skirt.

'Oh, get up,' she said, laughing. 'Crazy white man . . . I had men beg me for liquor before this, but never for tea—'

'I'd go into the kitchen and grovel before the cook,' he explained, rising and dusting off his knees, 'but frankly I'm afraid he'd brain me with that ladle of his—'

'He would.' She stepped away into the lamplit hot-box of sous chefs and waiters, still chuckling.

When she came out again, with tea – the cook was so preoccupied with arranging candied angelica, redcurrant jelly, and apples of various sizes for the *cascade des pommes* that he didn't even see her raid the tea caddy – January asked her, in a lower voice, 'Might I trouble you for another favor, ma'am? I'm looking for someone who might know some of the guinea languages . . .'

And he spun for her the tale he'd already circulated along the waterfront, of the old man and his gris-gris.

Lottie pursed her lips disapprovingly at the mention of a voodoo charm, then considered the matter. 'I'll ask Simeon' – she nodded back toward the cook, enormously fat and glistening with sweat in the lamplight – 'when he's not about to go into a palsy-stroke over how bendy the angelica is for that dessert he's making. Simeon's a lunatic in the kitchen, but lord, his family's been in this town since seventeen-whatever and he can tell you the name of your great-grandmother's pet canary-bird. If I do hear of anybody like you're asking for, where can I find you?'

'The big Spanish house on Rue Esplanade, just down from Rue Burgundy—'

'The girls' school?' Her face brightened with interest.

'My wife runs it. And looks like,' he added, hastily polishing off his beer as the Duralde butler appeared in the rear doors of the downstairs dining room, looking in their direction, 'someone is about to come out and ask you if your watch has stopped.'

He clapped his hands – though by his own watch it was only five of nine – and the men drained their beer (and Hannibal returned the teacup to Lottie with a profound bow) and trooped across the yard, speculating again about who was going to call out who before the supper interval.

'Ten cents says it's politics,' offered Philippe duCoudreau.

'Tippecanoe and Van Buren,' inquired Jacques Bichet. 'Or some French bullshit about Napoleon?'

'Fifteen says it'll be over Marie-Joyeuse Maginot . . .'

It turned out to be both.

Scarcely had Mr Clay led his sister-in-law into the opening set of quadrilles, than Jed Burton, a square, red-faced planter, cornered Martin Duralde to demand whether Harrison was going to pusillanimously knuckle under to a bunch of Papist Mexicans and abandon the brave American Republic of Texas, or whether he was going to stand up like the man he claimed to be. Duralde, after looking quickly around for either Clay or Clay's son, tried to smooth over the situation, but Will McCullen demanded whether that slick Dutch weasel Van Buren had any plans to prove *his* manhood by admitting Texas to the Union . . . 'An' it ain't like we've heard one word about Texas from *him* . . .'

At the other end of the room, January noted Marie-Joyeuse Maginot making a great play with her fan and her dance-card as James Clay – nothing daunted by his earlier dismissal – bowed before her. This time it was her father who descended upon them, almost visibly trailing stormclouds in his wake. According to January's mother – who knew pretty much everything about anybody in New Orleans – the elderly planter was on the verge of bankruptcy, due to unwise investments immediately before the bank crash three years ago. January's first wife, Ayasha, having been a seamstress, he could see confirmation of this rumor in the outmoded cut of the man's swallowtail coat, the rubbed places on the heels of his shoes. But Marie-Joyeuse, he observed, wore a gown which would have cost – he estimated with a taste of sour anger in his mouth – the price of an eight-year-old child at the Merchants' Exchange, ten blocks from where he sat.

And probably did.

It's not your business, he tried to tell himself. And failed.

There's nothing you can do about that . . .

And would that child be better off, plunked back on the shores of Africa?

Another thing he didn't know.

Fifteen couples on the dance floor did a graceful little series of hops, first to the right, then to the left, arms extended in a rustle of silk and fine linen. January's hands flicked lightly over the piano keys, ear and eye following the music of Mr Haydn, the way Ayasha had been able to mend lace while carrying on a conversation. The music eased, for a time, the despairing anger in his heart, at what he could not change.

Old Jules Maginot gesticulated. Young Clay drew himself up and clearly tried to explain, obviously under the impression that because he'd grown up hearing people whisper as he walked by, 'That's Henry Clay's son!' Frenchmen in New Orleans would overlook the fact that he was American.

Yes, there was Cousin Damien again, broad-shouldered, powerful, kingly and handsome, like the hero of a Byron ballad. He took Marie-Joyeuse by the elbow again and steered her firmly away, as voices were raised at the other end of the salon.

'. . . damn abolitionist Whigs in Congress . . .'

'. . . a man doesn't have to be an abolitionist to want to stay out of war with Mexico . . .'

'No, only has to be a fucken coward—'

Marie-Joyeuse cast a doe-like glance back at young Mr Clay – whose view was blocked from the look of adoration she raised, moments later, to her cousin's glowering face.

'Who you callin' a coward?' bellowed McCullen.

'Nine twenty.' Hannibal didn't even pause in his light fantasia on the *chaine des dames*.

Cochon Gardinier followed his glance to the case-clock at the far end of the salon. 'Hasn't called him out yet—' His violin didn't miss a stroke.

'And he won't.' January flourished the whole complex figure into the *demi-promenade*. 'At least not yet. Here comes Ma'am Clay—'

The hostess, panting a little from her exertion on the dance floor, edged through the growing press and laid a conciliating hand on Burton's arm. At the same time her glance summoned young James to her side, just as he prepared to sally to Marie-Joyeuse's rescue. January returned to the quadrille with the whole of his attention, letting himself be seduced by its lightness as he'd have been seduced by a girl's kisses. *Don't think about what woman is crying because her child was sold to pay for Marie-Joyeuse Maginot's new dress. Don't think about the fact that politicians are shrieking about each others' eating-habits and table-manners and not mentioning slavery or the men who'll die if we go to war with Mexico. Don't think about Akinto, hiding in the woods, starving, if he's still alive at all.*

The couples on the floor swept past one another, kid-gloved hands guiding kid-gloved hands, silk swirling bright in the candlelight.

There is nothing you can do about any of it.

If you let anger consume you, there will be nothing left for joy.

'Take your hand off that girl, sir!' The young man's furious voice cut through the thickening uproar around Duralde, McCullen, and Burton like the chop of a knife. All eyes turned to the French doors that led onto the gallery. James Clay had thrust aside the curtain that half-covered the glazed panels, to reveal Damien Aubin gripping Marie-Joyeuse by the arms, bending his face down to hers.

January didn't hear what she said, but he saw her lips move as she cast a swift, pleading glance toward young Clay – undoubtedly something along the lines of 'Oh! M'sieu Clay . . .!' gasped in the tones Andromeda would have used to greet Perseus.

He heard what Aubin said, clearly enough. Everybody in the overcrowded salon did.

'Get away, American! This is no affair of yours!'

Clay almost shouted back at him, 'I reckon it is, Aubin! If you can't leave that girl alone for your poor wife's sake, then have a thought for the girl herself! But I guess a damn Democrat who steals the government's money has got no more shame than a dog.'

'Curse,' said Hannibal mildly, as the music jolted to a complete halt. 'And here I'd bet there wouldn't be a fight over the girl until ten.'

FOUR

But in fact, neither January nor Hannibal lost money on the evening's proceedings.

Instants after Melchior Aubin and Henry Clay descended upon the two potential combatants – Aubin grabbing his brother's wrist as Damien raised his gloves to swat James Clay across the face, Senator Clay seizing his son by the arm – Julie Clay turned a basilisk glare on the orchestra and January immediately dropped back into the Haydn quadrille, as if nothing had happened.

Nobody in the salon seemed to notice the slightly distracted quality of the music, with all the musicians inconspicuously craning their necks and straining their ears to follow the events at the upriver end of the salon. Nobody danced, or even attempted to. For the next forty-five minutes January selected the most familiar and least demanding tunes that he knew, playing them like an automaton to the vacancy in the middle of the big room, while everyone clustered around the walls furiously exchanging political opinions and gossip about all the parties involved. Griff Paige, whose chair was half-hidden behind a potted palm-tree, listened, struggling not to grin, and didn't even pretend to follow along.

January could scarcely blame him, though he wondered if the gentry of Charleston – Paige's home city – were so much better mannered than those of New Orleans, that he wasn't used to such carryings-on.

'Stop this at once!' Fifteen years Damien's senior, with his thinning hair and jagged, prematurely lined features, Melchior Aubin could easily have been mistaken for the young politician's father. 'Dueling is the height of stupidity and I forbid it. No!' he added, as Damien opened his mouth to protest. 'I will not have it!' And, more quietly, 'I did not place you where you are for you to engage in puerile imbecilities.'

White-haired Jules Maginot and the deaf, elderly aunt who served Marie-Joyeuse as a companion were already leading their charge to the door.

James Clay tore his arm loose from his father's grip and would have followed them out, but his aunt Julie, and Martin Duralde, blocked his way.

The end of the immediate scene, however, didn't mean that anyone returned to the dance floor. January, Hannibal, Cochon, Jacques, Philippe duCoudreau, Uncle Bichet and supposedly Griff played their light waltzes and mazurkas, cotillions and quadrilles, to a room full of furiously talking men and women until the supper gong sounded and everyone went downstairs.

'So, was that a challenge or wasn't it?' asked Jacques, as Lottie and one of the kitchen-boys brought gumbo, bread, and rice to the table outside the kitchen where the beer had earlier been served. 'And was it over politics or the girl?'

'And does Aubin really have his hand in the till?' DuCoudreau's blue eyes – bright against fine-boned African features – sparkled with interest.

'Aubin's in the State Department.' Cochon – second cousin to Rose's pupil Cosette – spread a napkin like a tablecloth across the spotless acres of his white satin waistcoat. 'So he'd know about things like what's going to happen to the Seminole land once the fighting gets settled in Florida. And you know there's land speculators from here to Boston like cats at a mousehole, wanting to jump on that.'

'And whether he's stealing money or not, that's exactly what politicians always say about each other.' January dropped a dollop of rice into his gumbo. 'Thank you, ma'am Lottie.'

'And maybe they always say it,' put in Griff Paige with his crooked grin, 'because it's always true.'

'That don't mean the senator's gonna let that son of his up and shoot a member of the State Department.' Uncle Bichet settled down at the other end of the table, the smoky flare of the cressets gleaming in his spectacles and making dreamscapes of the scarring on his face. 'Brother Melchior's been fixin' to do favors for whoever'll keep his boy in Washington once the election's over. He's not gonna let that happen.'

'I will say,' remarked Hannibal, 'that this isn't the first time Mamzelle Maginot's had a duel fought over her. That was back in July, Benjamin, when you were in New York. She was just back from France, and staying in Milneburgh with – I think it was the Mabillets, but it may have been the Aubins. Cousins, anyway. I played for two weeks at the Elysian Hotel and was treated to the sight of her, on five occasions, setting the young gentlemen off against each other, apparently for her own amusement – including young Aubin, by the way.'

January made a noise usually written *Hmph.*

'Was he married then?' Griff asked. 'The Clay boy said he's got a wife . . .'

January gestured with his spoon to the musicians around the table. 'We all played at his wedding last November. Just before he went back to Washington for the Congress.'

'I take it Mrs Aubin didn't accompany him.' The young clarionettist regarded January with half-closed eyes. Blue-gray, like Philippe duCoudreau's – a color common among the *gens du couleur librés.* Like duCoudreau he was what the dealers called 'bright', meaning he had at least three white grandparents, if not seven. His French, though very American, was good.

'Men in the government generally don't take their wives,' January answered shortly.

'He take his mistress?'

'I think so.' In fact, January knew that Aubin had done just that. The men joked about this, but January kept silent. Damien Aubin's mistress – his *plaçée*, in the parlance of New Orleans – was the daughter of his own old friend Catherine Clisson.

Catherine had been sick with worry the whole time Zandrine had been away, and with good cause. Washington City, and its nearby neighbor Alexandria, Virginia, were hubs for the slave trade for the entire Atlantic coast. Kidnapping gangs worked almost openly in those and other large cities, and the big dealers paid cash, no questions asked.

Because of his friendship with Catherine, January had taken more note of Damien Aubin than he would of other young bucks of the French Creole society in town. He had never been able to tell whether that passionate, volatile, young demi-god had entered politics at his older brother's bidding, or because he didn't want to be dragged into the exhausting business of making a rundown plantation a going concern again after decades of parental neglect.

For a man who gave the impression of physical prowess combined with an instinctive air of command, January knew from his mother and sisters that the younger Aubin was much more interested in horses, waistcoats, and cock fights than in a planter's responsibilities. It was Brother Melchior, January had heard from Catherine, who had raised Damien, had him educated, and had prepared him for a place in the halls of power. And according to Catherine it was he who had negotiated the seventeen-year-old Zandrine's contract of plaçage and who paid (grudgingly) for Zandrine's little cottage on Girod Street, even as he paid for his brother's fancy waistcoats.

January also suspected it was Melchior who had arranged his brother's marriage to the daughter of Charles-Louis Trepagier as well. He'd certainly paid for the reception.

Listening to the men describing the wedding to Griff, he remembered the Trepagier girl . . . *Woman, rather*, he reflected. She was twenty-five, superannuated by French Creole standards, tall and thin, with a long nose and a tight-pinched mouth. She'd been rouged to within an inch of her life and festooned in a hundred-dollars worth of ivory silk and point-lace. Not once had she looked at her new husband, neither during the ceremony nor the reception afterwards. During the winter he'd seen her twice, at Twelfth Night parties in the company of the widowed Melchior, while her husband (and Zandrine) were in the capital, and had noted in passing that she kept the length of the room between herself and her father, her brother, her stepmother, and her stepmother's brother and his wife.

'Oh, she's crazy,' his sister Dominique had told him shortly after the wedding. 'She's been practically locked in a convent for *years*.'

And now Damien Aubin was stepping out onto balconies and behind curtains with a beautiful little flirt who had every man in the room expiring with love at her feet.

Hannibal went on to relate the story of a duel he himself had participated in, as the second to a friend, between the local priest of an Irish village and the Protestant clergyman who was the landlord's cousin – 'Little bantam about Uncle Bichet's size, but took the notion of putting on the whole armor of the Lord and going into battle for his faith very seriously indeed' – and beneath their laughter, January heard, in the darkness beyond the glow of the kitchen's lamplight, the unmistakable velvet baritone of Henry Clay.

The senator spoke in English, and probably louder than he intended. With the whole table of the musicians, and the hubbub in the kitchen, all chattering in French, it would be easy to believe oneself unheard. 'I won't have you making your name in politics as a man who gets into fights over girls in the houses of his supporters!'

'And what kind of a name would you have me make, Father?' retorted James Clay hotly. 'That of a man who lets his father pull him out of affairs of honor?'

'Do you not think your mother and I have had enough heartbreak? The man's a crack shot over any distance! Do you think I'd look forward to writing her that you got yourself killed over a girl—'

'Stop calling her "a girl", Father! She's Mademoiselle Maginot, not some lightskirt in a bawdy-house. And I love her.'

'And you are engaged!'

'Not yet I'm not! It's *you* who decided I was going to be engaged to Miss Jacob! You and her father and her father's business manager—'

'This is the first I've heard you had any objection to the match!'

'This is the first I've met someone I truly wish to wed! Maybe the first time I've truly wished to do *anything* that *you* didn't come up with for me to do!'

Evidently, January reflected, Damien Aubin wasn't the only young man being used as a political tool.

He barely had time to turn his head back toward Hannibal ('—the duel to be fought with military broadswords, contestants to each remain standing behind lines drawn six feet apart—') before the broad-shouldered figure of James Clay strode out of the darkness at the side of the kitchen, and stormed off down the carriageway that led out to Rue Chartres, the direction taken by the Maginot party forty-five minutes previously. A moment later a shape that had to be Henry Clay – tall and whip-slim and straight as a soldier – stepped forth, and stood for a time, looking after his son.

Had circumstances been different, January guessed the man would have gone after James. The young man was twenty-three, the age at which it is perilously easy to do stupid things after altercations at parties. But as a politician – as guest of honor at a reception with a presidential election at stake – there were things that Clay himself couldn't be seen to do. His shoulders were bowed as he crossed the yard back towards the house, little more than a shape in the darkness.

Looking after him, January saw him lay his hand to the handle of the door, then pause, his face set, as if for the moment he could not bring himself to open it. Then he straightened his shoulders, tossed back his head, pulled the door open and smiled brilliantly as the lamplight streamed out onto him. Like an actor stepping back into character before putting his foot on the stage. Or a general who knows he has to show courage to his men.

The Spartans, January found himself remembering, wore red into battle, so that their enemies would not see them bleed.

As the last guests were departing and the musicians waited, once more, in the courtyard for Martin Duralde's butler to bring the final installment of their pay, January stepped over to the kitchen door and remarked to Lottie, 'I know it's none of my business, but I heard someone speak tonight about Senator Clay having heartbreak in his family – and not needing any more of it, should Aubin actually have called his son out. What happened?'

An odd tightness pulled for a moment at the woman's lips. 'Of his five boys, the oldest is in an asylum for the insane at Lexington,' she replied, after long thought. 'The youngest looks to be going the same way. Another is a drunkard. And all six of his daughters are dead. Heartbreak enough.'

Someone called to her from the kitchen, and she turned away, her face without expression.

Heartbreak enough, reflected January. Enough for a white man, anyway, who hasn't been torn from his entire family and taken to a land where no one speaks his language, where he has no way of feeding or clothing himself or finding his way home again, ever. He wondered again – as he had for three days now – how hard it would be to locate the fugitive African in the ciprière.

But he only said, as his companions pocketed their pay, 'And the Democrats tomorrow! Gentlemen, at six? Philippe, Jacques . . .'

'Ten cents says Clay's boy turns up in disguise,' offered Jacques.

'Michie Aubin's reception is at eight – plenty of time for us to walk down there.'

And thank God, he reflected as their steps echoed damply in the brick tunnel of the carriageway, *for the election*. Money enough to make good his unexpected contributions to a stranger's welfare without rousing the suspicions of Rose's pupils. Money enough and more, to see everyone safely through the remainder of the sweltering fall.

It was unheard of, to work so many nights in the summer, and in town, too. But an election like this one had never been heard of before, with 'rallyings' and parades and log cabins being wheeled into town with hard cider for all comers. The wealthy owners of plantations and steamboats and town rentals might hold their noses at it, but to the musicians, it was as if the sky had suddenly rained soup.

Tippecanoe and Tyler, too . . .

'If he does turn up he'll run smack into a dozen other Whigs that're here tonight,' pointed out Cochon. 'And I wouldn't put it past Mamzelle Maginot's father to peach on the boy to his daddy.'

It was relatively early – the reception had never recovered its momentum and most guests had departed before midnight, another thing unheard-of in New Orleans. But it was summer, and Rue Chartres was empty and dark. Despite the bricking-over of the gutters a few years previously, the air whined with mosquitoes, from a thousand cisterns and rain-barrels, and huge brown palmetto-bugs beat the glass of the street lamps with roaring wings. From the direction of the river, January heard the faint din of the gaming-houses, and the voices of the men still unloading freight by torchlight on the wharves. The damp air smelled of privies, and mold.

'Aurore Plantation's right across the fields from Duralde,' added Jacques. 'You think old Melchior's gonna do somethin' before the rallyin' Saturday night, like sneak over an' dose all that hard cider with jalap?' The flautist named one of the most powerful purgatives on the market.

'He'll poison half the Democrats in the parish if he does,' opined January with a grin. 'For free cider? Every Democrat in Louisiana's going to be there, as well as all the Whigs. Anyone want to bet how soon somebody'll get called out tomorrow night at Aubin's?'

'Americans invited as well as French?' inquired Cochon, digging in his pocket.

'They have to,' said January. 'The Democrats need all the votes they can get. The way the Whigs have gotten everyone all whipped up about Tippecanoe and Tyler, too, and all that hogwash about "It's Time We Elect a Man of the People" – like Harrison's ever set foot in a log cabin in his life – Van Buren's up against the wall. Most of the voters believe whatever the handbills and the songs tell them.'

'Like that fool lie about how wonderful Africa is,' sniffed Griff. 'An' why don't all we free colored go there and quit takin' white men's jobs?'

'They'll tell any fool lie,' said Cochon, who like January interested himself in politics despite the fact that he was forbidden to vote, 'if it gets the abolitionists up North to think that a vote for Old General Tippy-Toes is the same thing as a vote for getting rid of slavery. They like to pretend their Colonization Society is a way of getting men freed. But it's really only a way to get rid of librés . . . which is what the blankittes have wanted all along.' He shrugged. 'Only abolitionists don't want to admit that.'

'So what's Clay?'

'Senator Clay,' Griff answered Jacques, as the men made their way along Rue Chartres, headed downriver, in the direction of the Faubourg Marigny, 'is one of the founders of the American

Colonization Society. The Send 'Em Back To Africa Club. As if anybody in their right mind would want to go live in Africa, after bein' born here, payin' taxes an' livin' here, not even speakin' the language. It's all a way of tellin' their neighbors how good they are – they want freedom and all that All Men Are Created Equal crap – without ever really having to come across with anything.'

They paused at the corner of Rue Esplanade, where their paths would part: Cochon and Griff continuing downriver into the Faubourg Marigny, the others turning north to January's house and the shabby dwellings of the Faubourg Tremé beyond Rue des Ramparts.

'But I'll bet you anything you like,' put in Cochon wisely, 'that even if there isn't a single Whig within ten miles of Aubin's place tomorrow night, if there's Americans there as well as French, somebody's gonna call somebody out before eight thirty.'

Hannibal produced a half-dime from his pocket. 'Given Melchior Aubin's entire disapproval of dueling, I'll make it nine.'

'That old sourpuss may disapprove of dueling . . .' Again, the young Charlestonian's voice had that bitter edge. 'You mark my words, though; give Brother Damien a chance to put a bullet through James Clay, wife or no wife, and he's gonna do it. And *I*,' he continued, 'will put *my* money down on *that*.'

FIVE

Like many of the old Creole sugar plantations along the lower Mississippi, Aurore – named for the long-deceased mother of the Aubin brothers – had functioned for years simply as a business headquarters rather than a home. 'Home,' to the French Creoles, was the family townhouse in New Orleans.

But the townhouse January knew – again, from Catherine Clisson – had been sold years ago, thanks to old Gauthier Aubin's gambling and his brother Yves' stubborn belief in a gold mine in Turkey that he had purchased, through a plausible agent in Paris, that simply needed periodic infusions of 'investment' to make the family rich. For ten years, Yves' son Melchior, dry and tough as a leather strap, had lived full-time on Aurore, and the stout, bustling

Frenchwoman he'd married had assisted him in pulling the over-cropped lands into production again, and in raising his handsome younger brother to get ahead in the world by insinuating himself into the government in Washington City.

Melchior Aubin had barely come out of mourning for his wife last November, when he'd presided over Damien's wedding to Olivia Trepagier.

Grouped awkwardly in a corner of what had originally been a bedroom – and later a sort of pantry off the dining room – the musicians could still be heard through the double doors that opened into the Aurore dining room, which had been cleared to function as a sort of back parlor for the Aubin clan's gathering of the Louisiana Democratic Club. It was as uneasy a coalition as the Louisiana Whigs. As January and his partners frolicked through much the same repertoire as last night's – with the exception of tunes like 'Little Pigs' and 'Auld Lang Syne' which had been co-opted for Harrison campaign songs – January could see through the open door into the dining room how the planters, brokers, contractors and cotton-press owners separated themselves like the elements of a badly-made béchamel sauce. Contrary to expectation, this smaller gathering – without the cachet of Senator (and it was still hoped, Secretary) Clay – boasted no trimmers from the other side of the political fence. But as usual, Royalistes talked only with Royalistes, Orléanistes huddled with Orléanistes, Bonapartistes kept to themselves . . . and everybody snubbed the Americans.

Not the best way, he reflected, to unite men in support of a single candidate. Particularly one who was being blamed for the financial panic which had so swiftly followed his inauguration four years before.

He recalled playing here three years ago, and how deftly Cécile Aubin had smoothed over these age-old enmities: how she had drawn the wives of the American planters into conversation – if only on the subjects of servants and fashion – with the French Creole matrons. How she had made periodic forays into the masculine groups to lead out the more argumentative – or more inebriated – gentlemen into company where they were less likely to end up shouting, swearing, or challenging one another to duels. Stout, bossy Euphémie Miragouin (a cousin of the Mabillets, January's sister had informed him) was performing this function this evening, heavy-handedly, to judge by the expressions on the faces of all concerned, the present Madame Aubin – Damien's wife Olivia – having taken refuge in a corner of the musicians' room. She stared around her from partial concealment behind a window-curtain, an expression like a spooked sheep in her round, gray, near-sighted eyes.

Despite his deep distaste for even the accepted 'customs' of adultery in New Orleans and Paris, January could understand Damien Aubin's flirtation with the prettiest girl in the room.

Through the doorway into the dining room, January could see Marie-Joyeuse, exquisite in yet another silk gown of the newest Paris mode – this one yellow – pearls glowing against her rose-petal skin like the tears of a woman whose husband has been sold. She was laughing with young Adrien LaFrennière, the dandified son of a well-off importer, raising those extraordinary eyes to his as if just discovering new and wondrous facets of his personality. When he clasped her hand she turned her face aside, overcome – and January caught the glance she flung to some other man in the room, that same look of relieved joy she'd used last night. *Thank God you're here . . .!*

Sure enough, when young LaFrennière – whose waistcoat rivaled Chinese imperial robes in splendor and must have cost the price of a carriage-team – hastened into the musicians' room to fetch the girl a lemonade, Damien Aubin appeared at Marie-Joyeuse's side, gripped her hands.

'Five cents on Aubin and LaFrennière in the next fifteen minutes,' offered Cochon, ruffling 'My Heart and the Lute' to a close. Then: 'Curse it, here comes old Melchior—'

The musicians lilted into the graceful strains of 'Beulah Spa'.

The older brother checked his progress through the dining room as Marie-Joyeuse turned playfully from her would-be lover, but Damien caught her hand when she would have slipped away. Melchior strode grimly on, caught the sleeve of Basile Aubin, the brothers' cousin twice removed and head of the interlocking family of clans, who had been watching Madame Miragouin's efforts at conviviality with glowering impatience. Words were traded. The wealthy, white-haired merchant pointed Melchior in the direction of the musicians' little side parlor; Melchior strode in, caught his brother's wife by the elbow, and almost shoved her out into the dining room to do her duty as hostess. The American men barely glanced after them. The American women whispered, 'Well, they *said* it was to a convent in Paris but *I* heard it was to a mental institution . . .' '. . . Trepagiers practically supported Secretary of State Livingston's wife before he married her, and are *dear* friends to Senator Nicholas . . .' '. . . attacked some poor French girl with a pair of scissors . . .'

By the time Melchior reached the dining room, neither Marie-Joyeuse or Damien were anywhere to be found.

Meanwhile, the men, like a sullen bass counterpoint, were carrying on: '. . . just a God-damned excuse for making us slaves of the Congress . . .' 'And where's the money going to come from, for all those bridges an' turnpikes an' railroads? If Massachusetts wants a railroad, let 'em built it themselves! . . . Next thing you know, those abolitionists in Congress are going to be tellin' us what we can do with our own property!'

Lemonade in hand, Adrien LaFrennière looked about him helplessly. 'Still on for a challenge?' whispered Hannibal. '"Rightly to be great is not to stir without great argument . . ."'

'Hell,' retorted Griff, 'Mr Pretty-Waistcoat doesn't look like he's got the sand to defend *himself*, let alone Little Miss Heartbreaker.'

'Bunch of damn mountebanks,' boomed Jefferson Butler, the owner of (among other things) the largest emporium of laces and silks on Nyades Street in the Second (or American) Municipality. 'What the hell does it matter whether Old Granny Harrison leaves the latchstring out of his door or not? *If* he does, which I'll go bail he doesn't. The man hasn't held public office in ten years, unless you want to count being a county clerk. And who the hell is Tyler?'

'And them women!' Jed Burton shook his head, with his braying laugh. 'What business do *women* have wearin' Vote for Harrison ribbons an' singin' stupid songs at political speakin's? If I ever caught my wife with one of those damn sashes I'd . . .'

January returned his attention to the pianoforte.

'The Landing of the Pilgrims'.

The aria 'Whiter Than Ermine' from *Les Huguenots*.

Old Jules Maginot put his head through the door, looked around, withdrew . . .

'You see that lame-brained log cabin they're puttin' up on Duralde's front lawn,' jeered steamboat owner Harry Fry, 'for this "rally" they're holdin' tomorrow night? *And* I hear they're bringin' in another one, twenty-feet high, on wheels . . .'

That, at least, January had heard. Will McCullen had given him instructions ('We'll be bringin' it in from the path that leads out past the cane fields at nine.' His grand gestures had seemed to summon the procession from the air. 'Torchlight, ladies' choir singin', a wagon haulin' the biggest barrel of hard cider in the state! So at nine, I want you and your boys to stop and make sort of a pause – then bust into "Tippecanoe and Tyler, Too!" with everythin' you got!')

Walking along the shell road from town that afternoon, the wind blowing mercifully tepid off the river over the levee, January and his fellow minstrels had seen the preparations as they'd passed Duralde plantation, a quarter-mile downriver from the first of the wharves. It was a neighborhood where many of the original sugar plantations remained, green monochrome acres of cane stretching back from the river to the darker-green monochrome of the marshy ciprière. Sugar was a hard crop on the soil, as well as on the men who worked it. The growth of the town was already prompting many families to dispose of their outworn acres, as Bernard de Marigny had done in establishing the Faubourg Marigny. Half-built tracts of houses, abandoned with the bank crash, alternated with brickyards, tan yards, woodlots to serve the steamship trade.

Duralde was among the first plantations one encountered, walking downriver from the Faubourg Marigny and the Third Municipality. January, Philippe, Hannibal and the others could see the frames for the fireworks already being set up on the plantation wharf, the banners stretched between the gallery pilasters of the house.

TIPPECANOE AND TYLER, TOO!
HOORAY FOR OLD TIP!

The field path was being cleared and leveled, dividing the Big House and the overseer's cottage.

In front of the house, men were assembling a log cabin, two stories high and larger than any frontier cabin January had ever heard of. Lumber piled the wharf amid the fireworks frames (*Rose will shoot me if I don't bring her out here tomorrow morning to have a look*) and men were carrying it back along the field path as well, to where a second, gigantic cabin was being assembled on a wagon-bed clearly built for the purpose. A third work gang (*Do they have* anybody *out in the fields today?*) was nailing planks in front of the gallery steps to make a podium, and laying down more lumber for a dance floor. (*Who is* paying *for all this? And what are they hoping to get in return?*) In the shade of the trees, three women worked making flambeaux of lemongrass, tobacco, and gunpowder to keep mosquitoes at bay. Others were assembling trestle tables, where the Ladies For Harrison would lay out acres of beans and rice, coleslaw and barbequed pork and chickens, for the good Whig voters of New Orleans. Beyond the overseer's cottage, half-hidden where the cane fields crowded close, barbeque pits were being dug.

McCullen was right, January had reflected, as they'd helped steer the little handcart on which Uncle Bichet transported the bull-fiddle he'd chosen to play for the evening, down another half-mile of levee to Aurore. This was indeed going to be the biggest rallying of the Whigs that the state had ever seen. He wondered how many of the Aurore slaves were going to sneak away tomorrow night, to walk the half-mile through the edge of the ciprière beyond the cane fields, and avail themselves of free hard cider and barbeque.

'Ching-a-Ring Chaw' flourished to a close. Basile Aubin came in, looked around, scowled – *His handsome Congressional cousin still missing?* Philippe murmured to Hannibal, 'Ten cents on Brother Damien and *anyone* before supper.'

'Done.' The fiddler sounded slightly surprised. 'But given Brother Melchior's views on dueling . . .'

'*Napoleon?*' Melchior Aubin's harsh voice cut the buzz of talk in the front parlor like the stroke of a cleaver. 'Napoleon was the cause of these troubles.'

Silence dropped over the entire company as if a soaked blanket had been flung on them.

'None of these troubles over slavery and land-grabbing and banks – *and* corruption – would have come about, save for that cowardly Italian pimp selling our land – *our* land, Louisiana, our home – for pennies to those animals in Washington. And for what?'

'Sir.' Craning his neck, January saw through the door into the dining room, and got a glimpse of Charles Brunneau stepping forward. He knew the tubby, middle-aged businessman from half a dozen Fourth of July parades, when January would march with the Free Colored Militia and would see Brunneau, in his old, discreetly re-tailored, blue uniform of the Emperor's Light Infantry, bearing his musket among the Orleans Parish militia with glowing pride. 'I am sure you do not mean what you say.'

Old Basile Aubin, caught off guard beside the refreshment table, tried to push his way through the crowd in the doorway, but couldn't manage it. January wanted to tell him to go around through Melchior's bedroom, but knew it wasn't his place, and in any case it was far too late.

'With all my heart,' said Melchior. He looked ill, craggy features drawn with strain in the candle-glow, but the pale-blue eyes held Brunneau's, cold with contempt. 'Napoleon deserted his own troops in the field – twice – and pimped his sister to his entire general staff. For selling us like Negroes to those' – his gesture swept, not the Americans clustered uncomprehendingly in the parlor doors – most of them understood little French – but northward, towards the American cotton lands above Baton Rouge and the far-away American capital – 'only to increase his own power . . . That I will never forgive.'

Hannibal whispered, 'Is he drunk?'

'Has to be.' Cochon dug hastily in his pocket for bet money.

Face likewise drained of color in the candlelight, Brunneau pulled off his gloves, stepped close, and smote Aubin across the face with them.

Pushing towards him through the crowd in the doorway, Basile Aubin yelled, 'Don't be a fool!'

Damien, as if trying to swim through the press of spectators before the French doors to the rear gallery, cried, 'Mel, no!'

Behind him, January thought he glimpsed the straw-colored silk of Marie-Joyeuse's new dress. Madame Brunneau sprang from her chair among the matrons, gasped, 'Charles!' terror in her voice.

With good reason, reflected January. Charles Brunneau, for all his former membership in Napoleon's Grande Armee, was easily the worst shot in Orleans Parish.

Aubin stood staring at Brunneau, as if he barely saw him, while Charles-Louis Trepagier and Damien grabbed his arms and both started talking at once, and Basile Aubin caught the broker by the sleeve.

'Don't be a fool, Charles!'

In a corner of the parlor, Olivia Aubin burst suddenly into raucous laughter.

Damien released his brother, thrust his way towards his wife.

For a moment January thought he was going to strike her. But he merely seized her by the arm – as he had seized Marie-Joyeuse Maginot the previous evening – and hustled her from the room. Moving like a man in pain, Brunneau dropped his gloves at Aubin's feet, and turned to his own wife, who was now weeping with fright. 'You knew our Emperor,' he said to her simply.

And turning back to Aubin: 'Name your friends.'

'Two nights in a row,' marveled Hannibal, as the musicians devoured the supper – laid out as last night's refreshment had been, on the worktable just outside the lighted kitchen – that followed an hour of dances played to another empty floor. As had been the case last night, all around that floor, every Democrat in the parish had been either arguing politics or trading scandal about the contestants in the upcoming duel – or about Olivia Aubin. '"All strange and terrible events are welcome, but comforts we despise" . . . Makes me wonder what's going to happen tomorrow night at the rally.'

'You know damn well what's going to happen at the rally,' returned Cochon, heaping his bowl with rice, beans, and sausage with finicking care. 'I'll bet five duels arranged, not counting fights on the spot between Americans. Six duels, if Michie Fancy-Pants LaFrennière turns up there. Eight, if Aubin kills Brunneau tomorrow morning.'

'All Aubin and Brunneau's friends is Democrats,' objected Jacques. 'They won't even *be* at the rally.'

'Don't you think it!' Griff Paige waved his spoon at the flautist with a grin. 'Half the people at that rally gonna be Democrats – either looking for free hard cider, or for fights, or both.'

'I'll bet two duels,' temporized duCoudreau to Cochon. 'Three, if LaFrennière shows up, which I'll bet a fip he won't. You hold the bets, Ben?'

'What about the Democrat Club musicale Sunday night? That's at LaFrennière's uncle's . . .'

'Depends on whether Aubin kills Brunneau or only wings him.'

'And whether the father of LaFrennière's fiancée puts in an appearance . . .'

'The whole duel's nothing but murder! Brunneau couldn't hit his own foot!'

'Anyone want to lay two cents on old Melchior sending us home after supper?' inquired Hannibal, looking across the wide yard to the back of the Big House. Like most French Creole plantation houses, Aurore's two wings stretched back toward the kitchen buildings, enveloping the rather ill-kept vegetable garden between. Thus the kitchen, thirty feet beyond that, had only a poor view of the lantern-lit rear gallery of the main house, and none at all of its parlor.

All the musicians were surreptitiously craning their necks nevertheless, trying to glimpse what was going on inside.

The last French door on the downriver wing – the traditional women's wing – glowed with the light of several candles. *Madame Aubin?* January wondered.

It would make sense, by what he'd heard, to give her a room far from the main house. He did wonder a little that they'd leave her with flame in the room.

Other rooms were also lit. As the chief Aubin plantations lay upriver in St James and Ascension parishes, Basile Aubin, his son and daughter-in-law, and assorted other kin would be staying the night, taking an upriver boat in the morning.

'Half his guests have left already,' the fiddler pointed out. This included, January had observed, Marie-Joyeuse, her father, and her deaf Aunt Francine, Jules Maginot undoubtedly feeling that the family had had scandal enough. 'And this way he can argue he only owes us half our fee.'

The men laughed, a trifle sourly. This was exactly the sort of thing Melchior Aubin was known for. There had been a general exodus immediately after the challenge: Brunneau was a well-liked man, and every Bonapartiste in the room had followed him out. Most of the Americans had gone as well, once Aubin's words had been translated for them. When the orchestra had filed from the little side parlor and down the rear steps, the planter and his brother had been locked in a furious, low-voiced altercation at the downstream end of the room.

Damien Aubin, who had seemed silent and strained all evening, had raised his fists and cried, 'Can't you just once let me live my own life?'

The Aubin cook – a tall man named Andy, with the bone structure of a Fulani – now emerged from the kitchen and set a tray-load of beer mugs on the table. 'I'm guessin' Michie Melchior up there's gonna be too busy to notice what's in these mugs. And

I'm tellin' you, gentlemen, if that supper hadn't been already cooked and laid out I expect he *would* have closed the whole shebang down then and there.'

Beyond the kitchen in the darkness, voices drifted from the quarters, a hundred yards further away. A string of mule-barns and woodsheds stretched between the kitchen and the wagon-trace that led back to the fields, but the cane came almost up to the walls of the cabins, the kitchen, and the Big House itself, utilizing every foot of arable ground. January was aware of the stealthy movement in that dark wall that grew so close: it seemed to him that twice the usual number of flying ants, palmetto bugs, and flies speckled the kitchen's whitewashed walls. A childhood at Bellefleur had taught him more than he wanted to know about the assorted vermin that throve in this world of heat and sugar.

And how does Madame Olivia like having that kind of wildlife, so close to her bedroom?

Is that the real reason Damien would rather escape to Washington? Or spend his days with his mistress in town? To live his own life?

In the absence of courtyard walls, the green smell of the half-grown cane mingled with the distant, marshy pong of the stagnant Bayou des Ouaouarons, far back in the ciprière. More insects rattled in clouds around the flames of the cressets, and somewhere an owl screeched in the fields.

'I'll lay two cents on us being dismissed early,' offered January.

'I'll cover that.' Uncle Bichet produced the coins. 'Even odds?'

'I wouldn't even give even odds.' Cochon took a beer from the tray – Melchior had a reputation of 'water only for the help' – and added another spoonful of beans to his plate. 'And here she comes,' he added, as the dark shape of a woman came down the gallery steps from the back of the house. He quickly produced his two cents.

All the men stood. It was Euphémie Miragouin. Like her brother Henri Viellard, the 'protector' of January's youngest sister Dominique, she was tall, podgy, and near-sighted, peering through the murky flare of the cressets for a moment before homing in on January. 'M'sieu Janvier.' She beckoned peremptorily.

'Anybody touches my beer I'll drown him on the way home,' January promised in an under-voice, and followed the big woman a little distance away, to another cresset set beside one of the woodsheds within a few yards of the cane field.

'Will you take a dollar,' asked Madame Miragouin, without preamble, 'to act as surgeon tomorrow morning at this imbecilic duel? M'sieu Miragouin swears that Melchior is drunk and won't shoot Brunneau once he sobers up, but poor Charles couldn't hit the side of a barn if he was inside it with the door shut. And Melchior doesn't drink. I want someone on hand who knows what he's doing.'

'I'd be pleased, ma'am.' January bowed, not really surprised. The woman would have known of his surgical training through her brother, but he hadn't thought she'd paid attention. 'Where will they meet?'

'Here.' Madame sniffed. 'Of all places. Back in the ciprière – you know the old landing on what used to be Bayou des Ouaouarons?'

'There was a woodlot there, yes.' In January's first years in New Orleans, half-suffocated by the walls and houses after his country childhood – and by the instructors at the St Louis Academy for Young Gentlemen of Color – he'd explored a great deal of the countryside beyond the city's boundary walls. In those days the danger of being kidnapped had been slight. It had still been legal for planters to buy slaves straight from Africa . . . and there had been far fewer Americans.

He recalled the bayou in question as barely more than a ditch, an almost currentless arm of Bayou Gentilly, cut off by some long-forgotten crevasse. His sister Olympe had used one of the old sheds in the woodlot there as a sort of hideout, to cache her gourds of mouse-bones and graveyard dust. 'I think I can find it,' he said. 'First light?'

She nodded briskly. 'Melchior just sent one of his boys off to town with a message – to Dr Barnard on Rue Royale, I daresay. But Barnard works at the Charity Hospital these nights because of the fever, and like as not he'll be only half awake. Personally, I wouldn't have Barnard to take a splinter out of my finger.'

'I'll be there, ma'am.' January bowed again, not by the flicker of an eyelid implying how heartily he concurred with her opinion of his white colleague.

'Shirt-drooling idiots,' she added. 'Both of them.' In the gold flare of the cresset she looked extraordinarily like her overbearing mother. 'Poor Paulette was nearly frantic when she and Charles left. I daresay that's what set Olivia off, though Charles stands more of a chance of hitting himself than he does of shooting Melchior. Though,' she added thoughtfully, 'he might very well hit Damien by accident. Damien is Melchior's second, of course.' She slid her hand into her reticule, produced a silver dollar, which she slapped into January's hand.

'I've never seen Melchior angry like that,' she added, as January gave her a third bow of thanks. 'I knew he hated Americans, but—'

She shook her head, then shrugged. Then she fished forth a small leather purse, from which she counted out twenty-one dollars, even as, from around the other side of the house, January heard the clink of harness, as carriages began to move from the river road toward the house. Torchlight from the front gallery reflected suddenly on the nearby wall of cane. 'I've told Melchior it's probably best if he simply sent everybody home after supper,' she announced. 'This is for the part of the evening you've played so far.'

It was slightly less than two-thirds of the amount Aubin had offered for their services that evening, but January was well aware that arguing wouldn't do him any good. Most planters would have paid the whole sum even if the evening was cut short.

'I suppose we're lucky we got supper,' remarked Hannibal, when January returned to the table with the news and the money. Various two-cent sums were passed back and forth all around. 'My Uncle Elliswrode would have booted us out an hour ago and saved the whole meal, cooked or not, for the servants the following day. "Thrift, Horatio, thrift . . ."'

Uncle Bichet handed January two cents. 'Or you want to bet that Ma'am Miragouin gonna be at the duel in the mornin', kin or no kin to the family?'

In spite of the fact that no lady ever attended a duel, January grinned and shook his head.

As they trundled Uncle Bichet's little fiddle-cart back along the drive to the shell road that followed the river back to town, behind him he thought he heard, distantly, from that last, lighted chamber of the women's side of the house, a keening unhuman wail, like an animal caught in a trap.

*   *   *

Before he got into bed that night, after walking Cochon and Griff to their doors in the Faubourg Marigny, he checked the lantern-clock on the wall of his bedroom to make sure it was still running – sometimes it decided not to bother – and estimated how many hours of sleep he'd get before he had to wake, wash, shave, and dress for the duel.

There may even be time to take Rose and the girls down to Duralde in the afternoon to see the frames of the fireworks . . .

He wondered if Paul – Olympe's husband – would be willing to sneak Rose into the rally, under cover of darkness, to watch the pyrotechnic display. Or if Germaine and Cosette would try something that hare-brained.

Along with everyone else in the parish . . .

A light sleeper in any case, he was usually aware of the clock's chimes even without waking: *Three should be plenty.* The days were already beginning to shorten.

And at three, he reflected, any slave stealer in town would be asleep . . .

But he still dreamed of taking a circuitous route to Bayou des Ouaouarons, dodging through the clumps of cypress and palmetto that still grew wild on many lots at the back of the *banlieue*, evading possible kidnappers among the crotch-high weeds. Looking for someone, he thought, but he couldn't remember who. *Olympe?* But her hideout shack was dark, overgrown with scuppernong and swamp laurel. No moon shone, and the lantern he carried in his dream burned too brightly – it was one of the new patent Argand lamps; why hadn't he taken the dark lantern? Someone would see him . . .

Someone was there, he thought in his dream. Someone creeping through the abandoned houses with a rifle, someone hunting . . .

Hunting who?

Not him.

Akinto, he thought. *Akinto is hunting the men who took him from his children . . .*

His children are dead in Africa. His wife is dead – in his dream he didn't know how he knew that, or if it was true – *and he will have revenge.*

Pounding on the French doors nearly startled him out of his skin. He rolled, seized the knife that was always under his pillow and dropped straight out of bed, sliding underneath it almost before his mind clicked to full wakefulness. Rose's bare feet hit the floor at the same instant and she reached little Xander's cradle in two steps, calling out as she moved, 'Who is—?'

'Michie Ben!' a woman's voice cried from the gallery outside. 'This here Gazoute, Ma'am Catherine's Gazoute—'

Catherine Clisson. January shot from beneath the bed, was on his feet and at the French door and was aware of Rose retreating to the door that led to Professor John's nursery – *Just in case*, January reflected belatedly, *that wasn't really Gazoute at the door . . . or that the servant-woman wasn't alone . . .*

'You got to come!' sobbed the woman's voice. 'You got to come! She took poison, an' Ma'am Catherine says she gonna die!'

SIX

The cottage was in the Faubourg Marigny – the Third Municipality when the city had been physically divided up between American and French sectors. It lay half a mile from January's own house on Rue Esplanade; only minutes to walk. Rose, ruffled and alert and tying her headscarf as she strode at his heels, had gone up to wake Zizi-Marie in the attic while January was dressing – to tell her to stay downstairs with the children – and in those few minutes Gazoute had given January the whole story.

Zandrine's cook had beat on the door of Catherine Clisson's cottage on Rue Dauphine barely forty minutes ago. Ma'am Zandrine was vomiting, shaking with spasms, calling for her mother. Calling Damien Aubin's name. *I'm sorry*, she kept crying. *I'm sorry, I'm sorry . . .* There was a bottle of medicine she'd got last November, when she'd been caught with a baby, just as her protector was preparing to take her to Washington City with him. She'd got shut of the baby, then . . .

The bottle lay empty beside her bed.

Quinine, January thought as he walked. That was usually what was in patent abortifacients. Whoever had sold it to her had almost certainly warned her not to take more than the prescribed small dose.

'Anyone send for Michie Aubin?'

'I don't know, sir,' Gazoute replied. A thin, small woman, she was African black, almost as unusual in a house servant as it was in a plaçée. More unusually still, her face was crisscrossed with 'country marks', and she was old enough to have been brought over from Africa, like old Uncle Bichet, as an adult. Catherine Clisson, herself of near-pure African blood, like January himself, had picked her out for her maid when the middle-aged Francois Motet had taken Catherine under his 'protection' when Catherine was eighteen, nearly thirty years ago.

January was well aware that Gazoute would have done murder for her mistress.

As he would himself. When she'd become Motet's plaçée he'd thought his sixteen-year-old heart would break.

And she was still beautiful. Her hair done up in a rag and her uncorseted body thickened a little with middle age, when she opened the door of Zandrine's yellow-and-blue cottage at the sound of his foot on the low step, she still took his breath away. But it wasn't a young man's lust or a lonely youth's passion that he felt for her now, but the golden sweetness of a thirty-year friendship. When she flung herself against him, gripped him with those strong arms, what he felt for her was pity, and the other kind of loving. The first thing he said was, 'How is she?'

Catherine shook her head, caught Rose in a grip as strong and as desperate, then led them through into the bedroom. 'I got her to vomit,' she said. The cottage, though small and plain, was pretty. It was expected that young men of standing would have plaçées, and that cottages, annuities, and generous gifts would be part of the payments negotiated for them, usually by their mothers.

But the stuffy darkness within smelled of vomit, and of blood, though the bedroom chamber-pot had been rinsed clean. The mosquito-bar was tied back, the sheet thrown aside from the girl's dusky body. Zandrine's nightdress had been pulled up and what looked like every rag and mended sheet in the house folded under her bottom, soaked now with blood.

'I hadn't known she was carrying,' said Catherine quietly.

January nodded, and Rose put the long rosewood tube of his stethoscope into his hand. Gazoute appeared in the doorway with towels. Behind her, Zandrine's maid Nessie appeared, a pitcher of steaming water in either hand. She set these down, took a clean slop-bowl from the simple French dresser, as January said, 'Good girl!' and poured a little water, and a little alcohol into the bowl to wash his hands. 'What happened?'

And in his mind he saw again Damien Aubin arguing furiously with his older brother in the corner of the parlor at Aurore as the last guests departed. Remembered how strained and silent the younger brother had been all evening. How he'd sought out Marie-Joyeuse Maginot, disappeared with her onto the rear gallery.

'If you can't leave that girl alone for your poor wife's sake . . .' James Clay had shouted.

'Michie Damien, sir.' Nessie's gray-green eyes glistened with anger and pity, and she went to the door into the parlor, where Solla the cook had appeared, her arms full of three pillowcases stuffed with straw. 'He came this mornin' – yesterday mornin' . . .' She glanced at the camelback clock visible on the parlor mantlepiece, then at the French doors that led out onto Rue Girod, still dark. 'He told Mamzelle he wasn't gonna see her no more. Mamzelle said, Is it that girl? 'Cause she told me, back in August, that he's in love with some white girl. That they was childhood sweethearts, a couple years ago . . .'

She shook her head, a soft, plump girl barely older than Zandrine herself. 'He's got a wife, Michie J! It isn't right – if he wanted this other white girl, why didn't he marry her in the first place?'

She, and the cook, stood back as January poured a little more water into an invalid's spouted cup, mixed in the most minuscule trace of powdered foxglove, to strengthen the beat of the heart. Then he turned to gently lift Zandrine, so that Rose and Catherine could change the bloodied sheets for clean linen, and Nessie could arrange the pillowcases with their absorbent padding beneath her. The straw, January guessed, had come from Nessie's own pallet, and Solla's.

'An' what's that got to do with Mamzelle and him, anyways?' the girl went on, her voice still low, as the cook carried the soiled sheets away. 'He just said again, "I love her, an' I can't see you no more." An' he left, just like that. Mamzelle dropped down on the couch an' cried 'til I thought she was gonna be sick. I asked her, "What about this house? It's still yours, ain't it?" Because . . .'

Her eyes went to Zandrine, and then, in apology and shame, to Catherine. 'Ma'am Catherine,' she said softly, 'I am sorry I thought like this, I swear I'm sorry . . . but it's what I thought. I know

Michie Melchior bought this house for Mamzelle – for Michie Damien an' Mamzelle. An' I know it's Michie Melchior who's got the bank accounts. An' . . .' She fetched a chair for January, as he laid Zandrine back down, and straightened the sheets.

'Ma'am, I'm sorry, but I know it was Michie Melchior who bought *me*, an' Solla, an' give us to Michie Damien to give to Mamzelle . . . Only maybe he didn't, really. Not on paper. Mamzelle's friend Berengare Doux, that was plaçée to Michie Richard Forstall, when Michie Richard married for that second time to that woman from France, he found some way to get the house back from Berengare, an' said he couldn't afford no longer to be givin' her money, an' she's got nuthin' now – nuthin', 'cept two children. You know how it is, these days, since the banks all crashed. I'm sorry—'

Catherine shook her head, raised her daughter a little from the pillows, so that she could sip from the cup in January's hands. 'Child, I know. You don't need to be sorry.'

'It's not easy like it was,' finished Nessie. 'Cresside Morriset, when Michie Valcour's family lost so much money, an' Michie couldn't send her no more . . . These days she sort of runs what she calls a boardin' house, in the cottage he bought her. Only it's just for one man at a time, for a couple-three weeks . . .'

January's mouth pinched hard. Had he been American he would have spit.

Rose asked quietly, 'Did she love him?'

Catherine answered. 'I think so. But Zandrine . . .' She hesitated, trying to speak the truth without judgement or cruelty. 'Zandrine is eighteen,' she finished. 'She cares . . . a little too much, about too many things. When they came back from Washington at the end of summer, and Michie Damien met Marie-Joyeuse Maginot again . . .'

In the parlor, the clock struck three. Charles Brunneau, January reflected, would have to get shot without his assistance – and he'd owe Euphémie Miragouin her dollar back.

He wondered if that stout young matron would sneak away from her stout middle-aged husband to watch the fireworks at Duralde tonight – and winced at the thought that by seven, he'd have to be on Duralde's front gallery, playing 'Little Pigs' for all he was worth as a twenty-foot-tall log cabin was hauled into the torchlight and all the Ladies for Harrison waved their flags and broke into three cheers.

So James Clay was right. Damien Aubin was being more than a possessive French Creole cousin, indignant that an American – be he never so upcoming a politician – would so much as touch the hand of a French damsel.

Aubin wanted the girl for himself.

Last night's sticky darkness returned to his mind, and the distant keening of the young woman locked in her room at Aurore. *When they came back from Washington at the end of summer . . .*

When, as Hannibal had recalled, the girl had been 'setting the young gentlemen off against each other . . . including young Aubin . . .'

Doubtless using all those come-hither looks she'd been practicing on himself – and the parlor mirror – only a few weeks before.

'I take it he's going to apply for an annulment on the grounds of his wife's madness?'

Nessie, lowering the mosquito-bar over her mistress' head and shoulders, said with indignation in her voice, 'He only married her not even a year ago! He musta known she was crazy then!'

'Surely he can't think the Trepagiers would let him go through with it,' put in Rose. 'Or that Jules Maginot would let his daughter marry a divorced man . . .'

'God knows what he thinks,' murmured Catherine. 'What any man thinks, when he wants a girl. Will she be all right, Ben?'

In the soft blur of the mosquito-bar's gauze, Zandrine stirred. 'Damien?' she whimpered. 'I'm all right, sweetheart, I'm well—'

'She'll lose her baby before morning,' said January quietly. 'How far along is she, Nessie?'

'Four months. She carried small last time, too.'

Dammit. Her cheeks were flushed, under tears she'd begun to shed in her sleep, her face and hands hotter now than they'd been even a quarter-hour ago. *Dammit, dammit, dammit . . .*

'I'll send for Olympe.' The small ovals of Rose's spectacles flashed in the candlelight as she turned to the French doors, to gauge the approach of dawn. 'You can get some sleep, Benjamin. He's playing tonight at that silly Whig political rallying at Duralde—'

'Screw the rally,' January gritted through his teeth. 'I'm not going to any political rallying while—'

Catherine laid a hand on his shoulder. 'You tell me what to do for her, Ben. And your sister will be here. And if you tell me *she* doesn't know what to do,' she added, 'I'll tell her you said so and you'll find yourself turned into a toad eating flies for breakfast—'

'My sister has never turned anyone into a toad in her life!'

Nessie, he noticed, looked scared nevertheless.

'That you know about,' retorted Catherine, half a smile struggling against tears. 'Is there anything you could do, that your sister can't?'

January knew there wasn't. When the miscarriage came he knew Olympe would prepare exactly the same herbal wash that he was going to make. The fever compound of willow-bark and yarrow in his satchel was Olympe's recipe. 'Other than take a horsewhip to Damien if he shows his face here . . . no.'

And he suspected that Olympe could, and would, do that as well.

Nessie was sent to the kitchen for more hot water, Gazoute dispatched with a sheaf of notes, not only to Olympe but to Zizi-Marie and to the musicians – Hannibal, Cochon, Philippe, Griff, and the Bichet household – warning them that there was at least the chance that January himself would be unable to play at the rally that night. January knew that both Hannibal and Griff were competent pianists – the only real loser would be January himself. Gazoute evidently stopped at Catherine's own cottage as well, for long before she herself returned from delivering the messages, Ricky – the son of Catherine's cook – arrived with a bundle of Catherine's clothes, her hair- and toothbrushes, and a tin pail containing bread, butter, sausages, and cheese.

Zandrine miscarried her child shortly after sun-up, as the day was growing hot. She clung to her mother's hands, asking cloudily, 'What am I gonna do, Mama? What am I gonna do?'

Shortly after that her fever began to rise, and Nessie, Rose, and January took turns sponging her with cool water. Her eyes drifting, she spoke Damien's name again and again. 'I'll be all right,' she whispered once. 'I swear you I won't cause you trouble . . .'

Once January asked Nessie, 'Did Damien love her? Before Mamzelle Maginot came along, I mean.'

The girl said, 'I thought he did. She thought he did. He'd spend four nights a week here, an' he didn't act like it was just 'cause he couldn't stand to be home with that sourpuss brother of his. At the first he was passionate about her, Michie J – he'd go wild if Mamzelle even spoke to another man. "You're mine," he'd say. "You're mine." I don't think he ever slept with his wife.'

January remembered those harsh peals of laughter. The keening from the locked bedroom, and the woman's spooked, scared look at her wedding. *No*, he thought. *No*.

'In Washington he was. Later – when he met Mamzelle Marie-Joyeuse again – he changed.'

Mid-morning, Hannibal came by, asking if there were anything Catherine, or January, or Mamzelle Zandrine needed. 'You behold in me "Immortal Hermes of the golden rod/ in human semblance" . . .'

'You can walk with me to St Vincent's,' said Catherine, 'if Ben doesn't need you. I'll need to arrange burial, for the child.'

Her grandson. He recalled what Nessie had said, about Zandrine's friend Berengare Doux, left with nothing except two children whom her former protector claimed he was not in a position to support. But having used quinine before, Zandrine would have known the dosage, had abortion been her goal. She wouldn't have drunk the entire bottle.

When Catherine returned she asked him again, 'How is she?'

'The fever's no higher.' He sat back. The room was hot now, the French doors – which had been open earlier behind their jalousie shutters, to admit what coolness was possible – closed, guarding that coolness like a miser's treasure. January's back ached, from the repetitive movement of sponging Zandrine's fevered body, and the exhausting, constant pain of his stitched-up shoulder. 'Her heart sounds stronger. Olympe sent word she'll be here soon.'

'Thank you.' Catherine went to pour a little more water into the wash-bowl, to splash on her face. Hannibal's voice came faintly from the parlor, getting instructions about something from Gazoute: January heard a hardware business mentioned, where he knew they sold Spanish moss, to replace the straw and flocking the servants had sacrificed earlier to absorb blood. For an ex-opium-eater who fairly exuded fecklessness, the fiddler had a surprising turn for seeing what needed to be done next.

'Rose says you're getting good money for this political uproar tonight,' the woman went on. 'You need rest. Olympe knows to send for you if she needs you.'

'If you're sure—'

'I am.' Again she touched January's wide shoulder, and though her face was ashen with fatigue and grief, she sounded a little more like her old self. 'Thank you, Ben. Rose told me also you lost a dollar, to act as surgeon for that silly duel of Michie Melchior's with poor Charlie Brunneau . . . At St Vincent's I heard Michie Melchior was shot—'

'Shot?' January straightened up in surprise, and winced at the stab of pain. 'Charles Brunneau actually *hit* something at twenty paces?'

'Ball went straight through his hip, Père St Clement says. I'd have bet against it.' She shook her head, the generous square of her lips tightening to a bitter line. 'And I'll have to go back Wednesday to confession,' she added, 'and ask forgiveness for the first thought that went through my mind when I heard it. Everything Zandrine ever told me, I can't believe Michie Damien would take the house away from her, and cut off her pension, if that brother of his would let him alone. No matter what that spoiled brat whispered to him about how she just *couldn't* marry him if he had a mistress . . . which is exactly what girls that age *do* whisper . . .'

'But Melchior Aubin would never agree to his brother putting his wife aside,' January protested. 'The scandal would be horrific. And Damien's going to need the Trepagier political support – more than ever, if Harrison wins. Especially since Senator Clay says he won't accept it, if Harrison offers to make him Secretary of State again—'

A shadow passed the French doors. A brisk knock sounded on the rear door of the house a moment later, and Rose's soft alto answered the silver-grit briskness of Olympe's questions. January stood, and rolled down his damp sleeves.

Catherine sniffed. 'I wouldn't believe Henry Clay if he gave me the time of day.'

January looked at her, startled at the contempt in her voice.

'Henry "Slavery Is A Moral Wrong" Clay,' she added.

'I know he's a slave owner,' said January. 'But I think he's sincere about—'

'He's like all white men.' Catherine's anger surprised January, for like most plaçées, Catherine tended to divide whites into those who were related to her protector's family, those who were descended from the Spanish and French, and Americans: three different species. The hatred that glinted suddenly in her dark eyes wasn't like her. 'He's sincere up to the minute his own toes get stepped on. But it's all a fairytale, to get people to believe what he says, and vote. He goes on about getting the government to buy out men who own slaves, and then sending them all back to Africa . . . You know what he did when he was Secretary of State under Adams?'

January shook his head.

'He had a woman in his household, Charlotte. She sued him in the Washington courts for her freedom, because her mother had been freed. She stayed on in Washington while the case was in the courts, she and her daughter, while Mr Emancipator Clay went back to Kentucky. And when the courts finally decided no, she was actually his property, she refused to go back to Kentucky. And at that point Clay paid men to kidnap her and her daughter, throw them in a Washington jail, and then ship them down here to New Orleans to work in his daughter's husband's house. That was ten years ago,' finished Catherine. 'She's been here in town ever since.'

Lottie, thought January.

He felt no real surprise. Only a deep and weary disappointment. Fairy-gold turning – as such gold does – to dry leaves and pebbles in his waking hand.

'I didn't know.'

'It's not anything he wants in the newspapers. Not if he's trying to drum up votes in the North for his friend General Tippy-Toes.'

No, thought January. He knew he had no business being either surprised or disappointed, and that his mother, and Olympe, would both laugh at him for feeling what he felt. *Disillusion is what you get*, he reflected, *if you have the illusion that a politician – even one who has saved the country from breaking in two – is going to act like anything but a politician.*

But he still wished it could have been otherwise.

SEVEN

They say that he lived in a cabin,
And lived on hard cider, too.
Well, what if he did? I'm certain
He's the hero of Tippecanoe,
He's the hero of Tippecanoe!

If the intent of the music at a reception was to be heard and ignored for its softness, January guessed that the intent of the music played for the 'rallying' in front of Martin Duralde's plantation house Saturday night was to be loud. Presumably, so that the thousands of farmers, shopkeepers, bankers and householders gathered between the house and the levee wouldn't be able to think.

The open barrels of hard cider that dotted the space between cressets and oak trees probably helped with that.

Harrison's campaign, he realized, was not about thinking.

Maybe that's why so many people love it.

It wasn't something you thought about – Harrison very carefully avoided specifics beyond 'reform'. (And, 'I'm not a sissy like Martin Van Buren.') It was something you sang about, something you *felt* . . . Something you 'knew was right' without being able to say exactly how you'd arrived at that conclusion.

Lanterns hung from every tree-branch. Lamplight splashed the ground outside the log cabin that had been erected halfway between the Duralde house and the shell road that bordered the levee on the landward side; the moving lights of steamboats jostled above the levee as they put in at the plantation landing, to discharge yet more potential voters. Banners gaudy in the torchlight: HARRISON AND REFORM; HUZZAH FOR OLD TIP; TIPPECANOE AND TYLER, TOO!

If anybody shared the conviction of Washington and Jefferson that a candidate for office – if he was a gentleman – had no business blowing his own horn, nobody was saying so tonight.

'You common cry of curs!' Shakespeare's Coriolanus had shouted at the voters of Rome, 'whose breath I hate . . .'

January hadn't expected to see Euphémie Miragouin this evening, and had sent back her silver dollar, wrapped and sealed in paper, late that morning. He'd gone again to the blue-and-yellow cottage on Girod Street after he'd waked, washed, and gotten himself dressed in the long-tailed coat and subdued silk weskit he wore for performances, and had been inexpressibly relieved to find the young woman sleeping more easily, her fever down. His sister Olympe, in the bedroom, was packing up her medicine-satchel and clearly working hard to control her temper. In the parlor, Catherine sat in a corner, holding the hands of her younger daughter, fifteen-year-old Isobel, under the disapproving eye of two Ursuline nuns.

Catherine looked up quickly when January came in, made herself smile. 'You remember Isobel, Ben? And these are Sister Dolores and Sister St Anne, from the convent . . .' Meaning, the convent where Isobel was enrolled as a boarding student, like the daughters of so many other plaçées. The two nuns – white Frenchwomen who inclined their heads to acknowledge January's bow – had the air of a priest and a Levite binding up a wounded traveler's hurt on the road to Samaria under protest. But they couldn't, January guessed, very well forbid one of their charges to visit a sister who might be dying, even if the sister was well and truly a Fallen Woman.

Smiling, he said, 'I remember a little girl I taught piano when first I came back to this country, but this grown-up young lady can't possibly be her!'

And Isobel gave him the bright, shy smile he remembered.

Taking Catherine's hand, he said, 'Rose brought some dirty rice and sausage – she's taking it to the kitchen—'

'God bless you! Solla's just about asleep on her feet—'

The back door opened and Rose slipped in, followed by Nessie, who had the drawn look of one who hasn't slept in days. She and Catherine embraced briefly, before Catherine led January to Zandrine's bedroom. While he consulted with the disgruntled Olympe ('Those two magpies out there sure got a low opinion of the kind of people their Savior went out to dinner with . . .') and checked Zandrine's heartbeat and eyes, he heard Rose's soft voice in the parlor.

Once he even heard Catherine laugh.

But as he was leaving to meet the other musicians, Catherine had taken him aside, and all her strength and calm had fallen from her like an ill-fitting mask. 'It's not the fever I'm worried about, Ben,' she'd whispered. 'Not even about . . . about what she did. It's what she'll do next. What she'll do the first time she sees Damien walking out with that spoilt hussy of his. What she'll do when she reads in the papers of their marriage.'

And to that, he had had no reply.

As he and the other musicians had walked down the river road in the brazen, slanted light of late afternoon, he'd asked Cochon for the details of the duel between Charles Brunneau and Melchior Aubin. 'Did I hear right, that Brunneau actually managed to *hit* Aubin?'

'You did,' the stout violinist affirmed. 'Somebody could have made a fortune betting on it, but nobody in town would put so much as a sou on Charles Brunneau hitting *anything*, much less someone wrapped up in a driving coat six times too big for him – the way men do, to fox their opponent's aim. And Brunneau got him in spite of it, smack through the joint of the hip.'

'Ow!' January had shuddered at the thought of even a minor pelvic fracture. 'They get the ball out?'

'No idea.' Cochon shrugged. 'But there was blood everywhere.'

'Fellow named Bascomb was the surgeon,' provided Hannibal, walking on Cochon's other side.

'Bascomb? Who's he? I thought he was going to get Barnard.'

The fiddler shrugged. 'Maybe he heard Barnard had money on the duel. I daresay some of Aubin's house servants will be present this evening, and we can ask for details.'

Hannibal was right. It was a walk of half a mile, through the cane fields and ciprière, from the swamp end of Aurore and the swamp end of Duralde, and the waxing moon shone bright. As the evening progressed, January did indeed see most of the Aurore kitchen staff he recognized from last night, faces glimpsed in the crowd and then gone. Between songs Andy – the Aubin cook – clambered up the steps to the gallery where the band was set up and confirmed this. 'Bullet went right through, that English doctor said. Doctor said, for a miracle the bone didn't shatter like a pie plate. But Michie Melchior damn near bled to death an' he laid up good.'

Remembering Zandrine's feverish whispers – the numb grief and rage in Catherine's tired eyes and the haggard faces of the exhausted servants – January reflected with regret that like Catherine, his first thoughts at this news probably disqualified him from receiving the Host at Mass tomorrow morning . . .

Andy's ox-like gaze skimmed the torch-lit crowd below the gallery and across the lawns; then he ducked behind one of the pilasters that held up the gallery roof. 'There goes Pernet – Michie Aubin's overseer. Shoulda figured he'd be here, for all he thinks Andrew Jackson an' old Van Buren is the Father an' the Son . . .'

'Looking for strays?' Hannibal's glance sought out the trim, broad-shouldered, little Frenchman in the skirmish around the nearest cider barrel. Andy grinned.

'Likely that's what he'll tell Michie Damien, if they come face-to-face.'

'Damien's here as well?' January vamped chords on the Duralde piano – brought out onto the gallery for the occasion and already losing its tuning – and raised his brows.

'Well, he sure sneaked out quiet the minute it got dark. An' with the both of 'em gone, you can bet every man, woman, an' child from the quarters is gonna be here too . . . 'cept maybe Jerry. Jerry's Michie Melchior's valet. An' I'm bettin' Jerry ain't gonna be sober longer'n it'll take for him to pick the locks on the liquor cabinet.'

Even with the memory of Zandrine Motet's despairing whisper in his ears – *Mama, what am I gonna* do? – and the ache of the pity he felt for Catherine, January flinched from the thought of a man lying alone – weak and drained and almost certainly feverish – in that dark echoing house, with no one near but a drunken valet snoring in a corner.

Nor could he push from his mind a deeper foreboding. If anyone should take it into their head to do the master of the house a harm, it was the slaves who would be blamed . . .

The slaves who could, tonight, give no good account of their whereabouts.

The entire black population of Aurore had clearly been joined by most of the slaves from every plantation within walking distance, appearing and disappearing at the edges of the torchlight or gathered beyond the kitchen. Michie Duralde had set up the barbeque pits there, not only for those voters 'rallying' for Harrison, but for his bondsmen as well.

And not only the enslaved, January observed, were appearing and disappearing. Andy had been quite right: that was definitely Damien Aubin, got up in a cheap tweed roundabout like an overseer would wear, flat steel buttons flashing in the torchlight. Still no sign of Adrien LaFrennière – not that he thought for a moment that exquisite dandy would risk scuffing his lacquered pumps in a crowd like this one, to meet Marie-Joyeuse Maginot or Helen of Troy for that matter . . .

But for a fleeting moment he thought he glimpsed, lurking in the shadows beyond the torches, a tall, skinny woman muffled up in what used to be called a riding cloak – woolen and undoubtedly suffocatingly hot on a muggy September night like this one – small round spectacle-lenses glinting in the shadows of the smothering hood.

She'd worn such a cloak, he remembered, at her wedding in November.

And, he recalled, like Rose, she was near-sighted.

Looks like everyone in the parish is taking advantage of the crowds and the darkness.

When he expressed this thought – in more general terms – Will McCullen cried cheerfully, 'Doesn't matter! What the newspapers'll print is that this is the biggest "rally" this state has ever seen!'

Cheers resounded from the landing, where the barn-like bulk of a steamboat, coruscating with lights, had just put in. A torrent of men and women poured over the levee and across the road, brandishing lanterns, torches, banners: BUFF AND BLUE, TRIED AND TRUE, OLD TIPPECANOE. In addition to a large painting of a much-younger General Harrison in uniform astride a white horse, they bore in their midst a gruesomely life-sized gallows on which dangled the effigy of what was clearly the current president of the United States, red side-whiskers and all, face realistically contorted, red flannel tongue protruding, and blood gushing from his eyes.

'Tippecanoe and Tyler, too!' shouted Tom Spanish, marching at the foot of the gibbet in the uniform of the Donaldsonville militia.

The crowd howled with appreciation, and then swarmed close around the log cabin, onto whose roof Spanish scrambled to make a speech. While the whites mobbed closer to listen, January was aware of dark forms slipping in closer, from the trees, or from the darkness around the house. These gathered surreptitiously around the cider barrels and the long trestle tables of Brunswick stew and cornbread reserved for the whites. He smiled, and wondered if Akinto – clad in his own green calico shirt and Gabriel's trousers – was among them, taking advantage of the bounty of the gods.

'. . . an' no sooner did that old fool Van Ruin get into office,' Tom Spanish yelled from his rooftop rostrum, 'than he crashed every bank in the nation an' made paupers of us all . . .'

A chorus of boos, notwithstanding the fact that it had been the policies of America's hero Jackson that had crippled the whole structure of American banks, not Van Buren.

'. . . Are we gonna take that kind of shit from that pussified Dutchman an' his rich friends?'

After what Catherine had said about Henry Clay, January had been of two minds about listening to the man speak. He hadn't expected the senator to condemn – or even criticize – the American practice of slave-holding. Not with voters listening. But he still felt the sting of chagrin, that one of the few men to seriously address the issue, who appeared to recognize future tragedy in the practice, had a very different approach when he felt his own ox was in danger of being gored.

But in fact, Clay didn't speak. January saw the man briefly, the fading mane of red-gold hair bright above the men around him. In the torchlight he thought the senator moved slowly, as if fatigued or ill, and wondered if Clay wouldn't have been just as pleased to stay in his son-in-law's house in town with a hot toddy and a good book. After Tom Spanish sprang down, Martin Duralde climbed up onto the cabin roof and declaimed – as Federal Marshal of Louisiana Territory before the arrival of statehood, he still commanded attention. Then Governor Roman climbed up, and lauded General Harrison's zeal for reform and love for the common man, without ever getting too specific about details.

And James Clay, in the torchlight just below him, fervently pressed the hands of Marie-Joyeuse Maginot to his breast.

January felt little surprise at seeing her slip from the darkness. He launched into 'Anacreon in Heaven' and scanned the crowd – tight-packed now around the log cabin – for the deaf aunt who usually stood as the girl's chaperone. Or had Marie-Joyeuse told the poor woman some lie about where she was going this evening, as he guessed she habitually lied to her father?

'Pity there won't be any way of telling when one of them challenges the other,' murmured Hannibal, taking advantage of Congressman White's impassioned call for unity against effete champagne-sipping non-entity Van Buren . . . (*Still no mention of any actual issue . . .*) 'Because I'd bet on it within the next fifteen minutes, given that Melchior Aubin's laid up downriver and Senator Clay seems to have disappeared.'

January looked around – the senator was indeed nowhere to be seen – and checked his watch. Nor could he see those flashing steel jacket buttons. 'I'd bet that way myself. I wonder if Damien got wind that his little sweetheart would be here tonight, or if he just guessed she'd sneak off for a tryst with young Clay—'

Hannibal's fiddle soared on a succession of triplets around the unsingable melody. 'Little minx probably told him herself. Arranged to meet Clay at nine and Aubin at ten . . . Look, there she goes . . .'

January turned his head in time to see Marie-Joyeuse – elfin in a green-striped silk dress whose skirt was already fouled with dirt and cane sap – step back from young Clay as Will McCullen emerged from around the corner of the house and gave January the agreed-upon sign. The girl's bright skirts vanished into the dark beyond the torchlight. January signaled to the other musicians, and as Congressman White brandished both fists and cried, 'Let's keep that ball *rolling*, for Harrison and Reform!' the band burst into their most stirring rendition of 'Tippecanoe and Tyler, Too'. The Ladies for Harrison – tricked out in colored ribbons, banners, and cockades – began to sing and wave their flags, and the second log cabin appeared from around the corner of the house, drawn by an eight-ox team and surrounded by a cheering mob with torches and yet more banners: MARTIN VAN BUREN, YOU WON'T DO, THE PEOPLE'S CHOICE IS TIPPECANOE. Two distressed-looking raccoons and a dilapidated eagle were chained on top of the cabin. To add a backwoods touch, January supposed, not to speak of preventing impromptu orators from using it as a podium, at least as long as they were sober.

Fireworks erupted like Vesuvius over the river, crystal streams of bursting stars, thunderclaps of smoke and the stink of gunpowder.

Deafening cheers. *Can Catherine hear them, a mile away in Marigny? Can Zandrine?*

From the corner of his eye he thought he saw torchlight flash on steel buttons, just beyond the stationary cabin. In his mind he heard Nessie's voice, relating what Damien had said to his mistress, *You're mine. You're mine . . .*

> Old Tip's the boy to swing the flail,
> Hurrah, hurrah, hurrah!
> And make the locos all turn pale,
> Hurrah, hurrah, hurrah!

A knot of very old men marched in the ambulatory cabin's wake, clothed in the uniforms they'd worn sixty-odd years before when they'd fought behind George Washington. They bore a banner depicting Washington (also astride a white horse and looking very like General Harrison). A larger squad of militia followed, men of January's age, some of whom he recognized in the pyrotechnic flash – men who'd fought England a second time, in 1815.

Frenzied cheering. Other militiamen behind them, in scarlet uniforms and cream-colored shakos, rifles on their shoulders. Someone flung a dead bird at the dangling effigy of Van Buren. Three men got into a brawl near one of the cider barrels. 'Oh, good,' approved Hannibal. 'Let's knock over one of the cressets and set the whole place on fire . . .'

In the crowd by the original cabin-cum-podium, Martin Duralde caught James Clay by the arm to ask him something. Young Clay wrenched free of him as a dark shape emerged from behind the cabin and strode purposefully away into the darkness, in the direction Marie-Joyeuse had just scampered . . .

> His latchstring hangs outside the door,
> As it has always done before;
> The people vow he will be sent
> To Washington as President!
> Hurrah, hurrah, hurrah!

Governor Roman sprang up into the doorway of the moving cabin, leaned down with a dipper to fill the brandished cups of voters (and a lot of non-voters as well) with hard cider that spilled and

splashed in the lamplight from within. The smell of it mingled
with the unwashed stink of sweaty men, the errant clouds of powder
smoke.

More fireworks, like the rattle of infantry guns on a battlefield.
Colored stars exploded over the river. It crossed January's mind
to wonder if Damien Aubin – if that had in fact been Damien –
was armed.

Haven't your mother and I had enough heartache? Senator Clay
had asked. The man's a crack shot . . .

And January recalled Catherine's face in the harsh afternoon
light as she looked down at the body of her daughter. *It's not the
fever I'm worried about. It's what she'll do next . . .*

You're not the only one whose heart has ached, Michie Clay . . .

It wasn't until an hour later – with the pandemonium continuing,
wild cheers nearly drowning Mayor Freret's encomium of General
Harrison, True Friend of the American People – that January
glimpsed James Clay again, prowling through the lamplight
between the log cabins and clearly the worse for drink.

And what does General Harrison think about all this, anyway?

Or Michie Clay, for that matter? The man who'd asked, sixteen
years before, how killing 2500 British soldiers qualified Andrew
Jackson to make decisions about the finances and diplomacy of
the United States. Who couldn't even run for president these days
because he had plans and opinions and beliefs, instead of slogans
and songs and giant balls of rawhide.

The man who, whatever else he had done, approached the
problems of the Republic with a scalpel-clear intelligence and a
long view of the future.

The man who'd said, I'd rather be right than president. And had
his own party take him at his word.

TIPPECANOE AND TYLER, TOO!

The gathering lasted until nearly three in the morning, January
heard later. He and the other musicians left at two – paid by the
Tippecanoe Club of New Orleans and then lavishly tipped to play
on for two hours after their previously agreed-on time, and given,
in their rest breaks, ample beef and burgoo and cornbread and pie
to make it worth their while, not to speak of all the hard cider
they could manage. The fireworks ended at midnight – 'Lack of
ammunition, belike,' murmured Hannibal – but there were enough

men in the crowd with firearms that the noise continued for another hour. 'Does *everybody* in this country go about armed?'

There were five more fights, one of them triggered by a very drunk Tom Spanish who staggered up to Henry Clay – who reappeared around one in the morning, more haggard than ever – to demand, 'What the hell you mean, sayin' we should send all the niggers back to Africa? You know how much that would *cost*? You can't make white men cut cane. They'd all walk off, or demand more money, an' then where'd we be?'

'My dear Mr Spanish' – January marveled again at the senator's ability to remember names and faces – 'you yourself must agree that the American system is basically incompatible with the African temperament. The American Colonization Society wishes only to . . .'

At least, reflected January, watching the senator drape an arm around his accuser's shoulders to lead him back to the nearest cider barrel, whatever his actual beliefs Mr Clay knew better than to argue with a drunk.

Beside him, Griff Paige jeered. 'Ain't that just like a damn politician. Founds his damn society an' then lies about it.'

At one point early in his search for Ti-Jon, it had crossed January's mind that as President of the Colonization Society, Clay – or one of his friends – might be able to provide information about ships actually going back to Africa. The thought had not survived the drawing of two breaths, but still he had a sour taste in his mouth at such naiveté.

Damn them, he thought, deeply and profoundly sick of the whole vital, inescapable, tragic question.

Damn them.

He went back to the Duralde piano – now audibly out of tune – and they played for another two hours. January went home feeling he would take Hannibal's fiddle and beat to death the next person who asked him to play 'Little Pigs'.

Behind him, against the torchlight, the effigy of little Martin Van Buren dangled from the gallows, and drunken voices lifted in song.

It is the ball a rollin' on
For Tippecanoe and Tyler, too,
For Tippecanoe and Tyler, too!

Returning home only a few hours before first light, he stood for a time with his arm around Rose's waist, in the dim thread of the veilleuse's light, looking down at Xander in his crib. 'Only two more nights of this,' he sighed, as much to encourage himself as to reassure her. 'There's the Democrat Club musicale tomorrow night – tonight,' he corrected himself with a groan.

'Can't let the Whigs get ahead, now, can we?' Rose, night-gowned and with her soft, light-brown hair braided down her back, smiled up at him, those gray-hazel eyes altered by myopia and sleepiness.

'Not to speak of the dinner Mayor Freret's giving for every Whig planter and merchant in the parish.'

'Good Heavens, he'll have to hire a hall! That townhouse of his isn't nearly big enough . . .'

'Hubert Granville has very kindly offered him the use of his townhouse.'

And Rose giggled at the thought of that ostentatious, turreted palace on the Rue Conti, with its gilded ironwork and Italianate bronze door-handles. 'Well, *that'll* make an impression . . .'

'*Salus populi suprema lex est.* The money's nice, but I'll be very glad when that ball comes rollin' rollin' rollin' into town on Friday and we can be done—'

'You're forgetting the Democratic Planters' Club cotillion at the Hotel Pontchartrain in Milneburgh Thursday . . .'

January expressed an unkind and anatomically unlikely wish concerning the Democratic Planters. 'How's Zandrine?'

Rose sighed, her head resting on his shoulder. 'Still unconscious,' she said quietly. 'Catherine said she'd sit up with her tonight – the poor servants are asleep on their feet. I don't think Nessie's so much as lain down since Friday evening. Will she be all right?'

And January shook his head. 'That I don't know.'

The silence in the shuttered bedroom was like the peace of Heaven; the stillness, like the wisdom of God. Far off, he could hear the crack of rifles and pistols still being fired off over the river. *Tippecanoe and Tyler, too . . .*

He stripped, crawled under the mosquito bar, and reveled for one second in the knowledge that a few hours from now Rose, bless her, would wake silently, take Xander, and leave the room shuttered, so that he could sleep until his body was rested or the smothering heat drove him to wakefulness.

When he opened his eyes at noon, to the sound of the bells of every church in town summoning lazy bedfast sluggards (like himself) to Mass for the good of their souls, he smelled coffee, and heard through the shut bedroom door the clink of silverware. Then Zizi-Marie's voice said, 'That's what they say. With all the cancan and artillery going on, nobody heard the shots. They found her in the cane field, shot through the back of the head.'

??!!??

January rolled out of bed, pulled on shirt and trousers, and opened the door, to see his wife and his niece in the closed-up cool of the dining room with coffee cups and fragments of brioche and butter on a plate between them.

'What happened?' he asked, as they turned. 'Who was shot?'

Rose said, 'Marie-Joyeuse Maginot.'

EIGHT

'Oh, God forgive me.' Zandrine covered her face with her hands. 'Virgin Mary, forgive me. I wanted her to die.' She began to cry again, the desperate grief of one weakened and already in torment. And, as her mother had said, only eighteen years old. 'I prayed for her to die, and now I'm blind . . .'

'Hush,' whispered January. 'Hush. It won't last. Quinine sometimes does that.'

Catherine – her own face drawn with lack of sleep – gathered her daughter into her arms. January retreated to the parlor.

Gazoute shook her head as she closed the bedroom door, listening with one ear, in case of need. 'I was like to wear that stupid maid of hers out with a whalebone, goin' in an' sayin'' – her voice whined up to a young girl's tone, with the maid's American inflection – '"Well, that bitch Marie-Joyeuse got what was comin' to her anyways. Somebody shot her through the head last night." I hope Ma'am Catherine massacres her hide good.'

January, who understood Zandrine's prayer for vengeance as well as her horrified agony of guilty grief, was inclined to agree. 'What happened?' he asked. 'To Marie-Joyeuse, I mean.' Arriving at the cottage, he had barely begun to read Zandrine's pulse and check her eyes, when Catherine had come into the room and taken him aside, to whisper what he already knew. Though her voice had been too soft for her daughter to hear, Zandrine had known – *And what else*, January reasoned, *could have required such discretion?* But for her part he understood why Catherine felt she had to make sure he knew, before he unwittingly mentioned the dead girl's name.

'The work gang weedin' the field saw the crows comin' down.' Gazoute still looked wrung with sorrow, for her beloved mistress and the girl she had nursed and helped to raise. But she seemed the better for the night's sleep Catherine had insisted the servants take. 'Mamzelle Marie-Joyeuse was layin' on the headland at the end of the cane rows, 'tween the ciprière an' the crop. She'd been shot through the belly an' through the head, an' blood all everywhere. I will confess it as a sin but I say, it served her right.'

The memory of torchlight and darkness. Of James Clay grasping the girl's hands, and the coquettish way she turned her face aside from his desperate entreaties.

And one quick vision of the flash of steel buttons disappearing into the darkness in the wake of that striped silk skirt.

He remembered, too, Marie-Joyeuse's lowered eyelashes and bosom-lifting sighs as she slid closer to him on the piano bench. And the childlike sweetness of her voice, as he'd packed up his satchel to go, coaxing her father for a new mare ('Oh, Papa, Dancer just has no *style* . . .').

Had Zandrine asked herself – as he had immediately done – whether Damien Aubin had heard of her attempt at suicide, and the death of what would have been his child?

He returned to the bedroom. Taking Zandrine's hands, he resumed his examination, assuring her again that the blurring and impairment of her sight was a very common effect of an overdose of quinine, and that it would pass in time.

Later, as Catherine walked him to the door, he asked, 'Would you like me to walk over to St Vincent's and arrange to have a priest come here, to speak with Zandrine? Or ask Pere Eugenius from the cathedral to come, and listen to her confession? I don't think I've ever heard the good Father shocked about anything people have done, or felt, or thought. It almost makes me wonder what he did before he became a priest.'

And Catherine, who looked like a woman burning up inside, was surprised into a chuckle.

From the bed, Zandrine murmured, 'Would you do that, Michie J? Get Pere Eugenius?'

Catherine kissed him as he left – the first time she'd done so since he was sixteen.

Walking back to the French town through the moist winds that presaged the afternoon's rain, January wondered if, in the chaos and crowds of the rally last night – the cancan and artillery, as Zizi-Marie had put it – anybody else had seen Damien Aubin, after the fireworks had started and Marie-Joyeuse Maginot and James Clay had disappeared into the darkness beyond the cane.

At that night's Democratic Club musicale at the LaFrennière town-house little else was talked about, mostly at the top of everybody's lungs. Conflicting accounts of the finding of the body, and specu-lation about the circumstances of the crime, far outstripped the indignation about Tom Spanish and the Donaldsonville Boys and their gruesome effigy of Martin Van Buren. For every scheme put forward – and there were a lot of them – to attack the Whig parade on Friday and rescue the dummy president, he heard a dozen fragmentary theories, including the query half-heard in passing, didn't that yellow gal of Damien's, that tried to kill herself, have a cousin down at Wills Point . . .?

I'll have to warn Catherine about that . . .

And if Pierre LaFrennière and his wife announced once that their nephew Adrien had been at his parents' townhouse on Rue Royale in the presence of ten other family members, they announced it a hundred times in the course of the evening, generally in tones that could have been heard in Natchez.

Everyone in town apparently had heard about Zandrine. Those few who had come to the musicale ignorant of the rumor that Damien Aubin was courting his beautiful cousin, and in addition to dismissing his mistress had talked about divorcing Olivia, were not long left in that condition.

'Myself, I don't blame Aubin in the least,' declared young Galen Peralta, to a cluster of French Creole blades grouped around the punchbowl. 'Trepagier and Old Skinflint Melchior together tricked poor Damien into marrying the woman.' He glanced over his shoulder, scanning the crowded room for sight of the coldly formidable Charles-Louis Trepagier, and visibly relaxing when he saw the man had not yet arrived.

'Dieu, yes, I couldn't take her.' Burly Hercule LaFrennière shuddered. 'Looks at you with those eyes . . .' He stretched his own eyes with his fingers, in an expression of idiot intensity. 'And never says a word. Spends all day in her room with the door locked, then goes wandering around the house at night . . .' His younger brother Adrien was conspicuously absent, and like his aunt and uncle, the young merchant made a point of disclaiming his cadet's attachment to the slain girl to whoever would listen.

'You ever partner her in dance class when we were tadpoles?' Gilbert St Roche looked around at the younger members of the group. But what that experience had been like was lost in Jed Burton's sudden outburst about how those Donaldsonville Boys needed to be taught a lesson, and by God, they would be . . .

'Damn shame about Mamzelle Maginot . . .'

'Damn pretty girl . . .'

'Damien called my cousin out over her back in '38 . . .'

'I wonder if M'sieu Pierre LaFrennière requested Trepagier not to come,' mused Hannibal, over lemonade in the townhouse's courtyard between the reception and the main business of the musicale itself. January suspected that this latter program was going to be even flatter than usual, given that most of the wives and daughters of the prominent Democrats would still be away in Mandeville or Milneburgh on the lake where it was cool. 'If word's all over town about poor Zandrine trying to kill herself because Damien was courting Mamzelle Maginot, that's not the sort of excitement one wants while trying to organize a campaign.'

'Myself, I don't see why Damien would throw Zandrine over anyway,' put in duCoudreau. 'She's a good girl, and beautiful. And Aubin couldn't really *believe* Brother Melchior'd let him divorce the daughter of Charles-Louis Trepagier, for God's sake . . .'

'Don't be so sure about that.' Susanne, the LaFrennière house-keeper, paused on her way back into the kitchen with the empty lemonade pitcher. 'My niece Maisie was Mamzelle Maginot's maid, back two years ago when Mamzelle was fourteen and fell in love with Michie Damien. He was just back from college in Virginia, an' for near on to a year they were frantic for each other, Maisie says. But Michie Damien, you know how he is: crazy

jealous if she even looked at another man. They had a fight, an'
she got sent to a convent to go to school in France for a year, and
the good God knows where her papa got the money for *that*. That's
when Michie Damien proposed to Mamzelle Trepagier.'

January was silent, recalling Damien and his brother two nights
before, at Aurore. *Can't you just once let me live my own life?*

How much had that sour-faced planter had to do with his
brother's proposal? Trepagier was wealthy, and had powerful
connections. He saw again the frantic look in Olivia Trepagier's
short-sighted eyes as she had walked down the cathedral aisle to
meet her bridegroom. Saw how Charles-Louis Trepagier had held
her arm tight against his side, his face the face of a man ready to
clap a hand over his daughter's mouth the moment the priest asked,
'If there is anyone here who knows of any reason why these two
people should not be joined . . .'

It could of course have been only apprehension that she'd burst
into another paroxysm of laughter . . .

Further back, too, he half-remembered his mother sniffing,
'Hmph. Trepagier'll never get that girl of his off his hands.'

'Maisie says' – Susanne lowered her voice with conspiratorial
relish – 'Mamzelle Trepagier wouldn't let Michie Damien into her
bed after the wedding. That's why, when he came back from
Washington, an' Mamzelle Marie-Joyeuse came back from France
back in June, Michie Damien figured he had grounds to get an
annulment, an' marry Mamzelle Marie-Joyeuse, like he'd always
wanted to do.'

With a self-satisfied nod, she collected the tumblers from January,
Hannibal, Cochon, duCoudreau and the two Bichets, glanced around
for Griff Paige (who had disappeared in the direction of the slaves'
outhouse) and added his glass to her tray. 'Maisie says, him an'
Mamzelle Marie-Joyeuse took one look at each other when they
met again an' it was like pourin' oil on the embers of a fire. What
was between 'em just roared right up again like the flames of Hell.'

'That was still a cheap turn to put onto Zandrine,' insisted
duCoudreau. 'She's my cousin – well, Catherine's brother married
my mama's sister – an' all Aubin had to do was lie, anyway.
Lots of white girls says to their men, Hey, you gotta give up that
woman of yours. An' the men just say, "Oh, yeah, Sugar, I swear
she's out of my life". Yet the Salle d' Orleans keeps fillin' up with
the same men an' the same ladies, every winter.'

'"Oh gentle Romeo",' quoted Hannibal, '"if thou dost love, pronounce it faithfully . . ."'

'Yeah.' Griff Paige appeared from the darkness, straightening his coat. 'And we all know what happened to Juliet.'

As January had suspected, the actual musicale – the recital for which the wives and marriageable daughters of the prominent Democrats of New Orleans had been rehearsing for weeks – fell flat. Nobody challenged anybody to a duel, though Charles Brunneau got a certain amount of ribbing from the men about his savagery and courage. January's own experience with such events had always been that the quality of the singing ranged from quite good to excruciatingly bad, but that wasn't the point. The ladies – young, middle-aged, and a few surprising oldsters – enjoyed enormously standing up in front of a real orchestra and singing 'My Faith Looks Up to Thee' for their friends (and social rivals); January had long ago learned how to adjust the pacing and presentation of a song so as not to show up the flaws in the voices.

But the notion of raising money for the Van Buren campaign with a musicale had not been a good one to begin with, and the death of Marie-Joyeuse Maginot laid a pall on the gathering that could be neither overcome nor ignored. Most of the men disappeared from the parlor to discuss either the shortcomings of General Harrison, the plans to punish the Donaldsonville Boys for their iniquity, or the murder itself, and returned only to watch their own womenfolk perform. The absence of the programs usually printed for such occasions only underlined the fact that there had not been time to have them reprinted, with Marie-Joyeuse's name taken out: she was to have played a solo on the harp, and sung 'The Moon'. The evening broke up early, most of the Americans departing as soon after supper as manners permitted and only a few of the French Creoles staying for a dance or two, whether related to the Maginots or not.

Jules Maginot, Charles-Louis Trepagier, and the Aubin brothers had all been absent, as well as Adrien LaFrennière.

January was grateful for the shortness of the evening. After speaking to Pere Eugenius at the cathedral – and attending Mass himself – he had gone to the New Cemetery, the only mourner to walk behind that tiny coffin, barely larger than a shoebox, that had been placed in the wall-tomb rented by Catherine's mother.

The day's rainstorm had ceased by then, and the cemetery had been at its worst: sodden, steaming as the renewed heat of the afternoon drew back the water into the sky, and stinking darkly of mortality. On Tuesday – he had already seen the black-bordered handbills pasted to walls in the French Town – Marie-Joyeuse Maginot would be interred, doubtless with a great show of black carriages, sable plumes, mourning gloves and rings. He thought of that exquisite pink-and-green silk dress she'd worn Thursday evening, the equally lovely yellow silk of Friday. The pearls around her throat. The adoration in her father's eyes.

Even a brief visit with Olympe – and the news that she had heard no tidings yet of a runaway African taken in the ciprière – had failed to raise his spirits.

Music alone had the power to do that, for a time. While he was playing – while he was following the dancers with his eyes, the bright threads of melody behind him with his ears – he was able to lose himself in joy, as the writers of the tunes had intended. But walking home among his fellow musicians, gold-slatted rectangles of cottage windows burning softly through the lapis heat of the night, sadness and pity returned to him.

When he slept, he dreamed he was playing the piano – as indeed he had originally been scheduled to do that evening – to accompany Marie-Joyeuse on the harp. In his dream there was blood on her new silk dress, and glistening in the black curls of her hair.

He was waked at noon, first by the desperate knocking at the French doors of his study, then by Rose's quick, slightly awkward step on the boards of the parlor floor, crossing to the bedroom door.

He was sitting up when she opened it. He knew she wouldn't wake him, save for a desperate situation. 'What is it?'

Akinto? Olympe had said she'd send news if she heard.

Then over her shoulder he saw Gazoute, hands clasped before her, scarred face streaked with tears.

Zandrine . . . Damn it . . . I thought she was better. Damn it . . . Fear squeezed his heart, knowing what it had to be. But he had to ask. 'What is it?'

'They've arrested Catherine,' said Rose.

NINE

'*What?*'

Rose handed him his shirt.

January pulled on that garment, then his trousers and his boots, a red tide of anger swamping his heart.

He knew exactly what was going on.

At last he said, 'She was sitting up all night with Zandrine Saturday night. Yesterday morning she looked like she'd dragged rocks from Natchez to the Belize in a wheelbarrow. They can't believe—'

'No one saw her,' pointed out Rose quietly. 'Gazoute, Nessie, and Solla were all asleep. And Girod Street is a half-hour's walk from where Marie-Joyeuse's body was found.'

'That's ridiculous.' Only he heard in his own voice that he didn't sound disbelieving at all.

Only deeply angry.

Four people sprang to his mind, who would have shot Marie-Joyeuse – not including the incapacitated Melchior Aubin and whatever other profoundly jealous swains the girl might have collected over the past two years.

All of them were white.

Gazoute was sitting at the dining-table when January and Rose emerged from the bedroom. January gestured her to stay that way, when she would have risen. 'I think probably it would be better if you stayed here. Zizi—'

His niece emerged from the pantry, with coffee and a small plate of his nephew's pralines. These she set on the table beside the maidservant's elbow – a tallish girl, the double, January always thought, of what his sister Olympe would have looked like at eighteen, only with straighter teeth and gentler eyes.

'Will you see Ma'am Gazoute has everything she needs while we're gone? We won't be long. Thank you.'

Rose leaned through the door of the little room behind his study, spoke to the two girls poring over their history lessons – 'That's stupid!' January heard the outspoken Germaine exclaim.

'It is,' agreed Rose, with that quiet calm that always acted on him as an anchor, steadying his thoughts. 'But you let Ma'am Gazoute alone unless she wants to come in here and talk to you. She may want to just sit quiet for awhile. I should be back in an hour or so.'

She followed him across the gallery, down the steps to the street. The rage in him still felt as if he'd swallowed red-hot iron.

He said, as they strode down Rue Burgundy, 'I can see young Clay shooting Aubin, but Marie-Joyeuse?'

'You don't think it might have been an accident? That she tried to get between them?'

He started to answer from his anger, his belief that Marie-Joyeuse Maginot cared far too much for herself to endanger her own precious skin by stepping between two men about to kill each other over her, then closed his mouth again. She'd been sixteen. Even children not spoiled rotten from infancy by doting parents considered themselves immune to death at that age.

And she had been – at least according to the LaFrennière housekeeper Susanne – passionately in love with Damien Aubin.

He said, 'I don't know. I'll have to see the place.'

Which has been trampled over by every field hand on the Duralde place and for six plantations around. And rained on yesterday. And will probably be rained on again before I can get out there, given Mayor Freret's dinner tonight . . .

It wasn't even a case where he could absent himself. Tonight it was just himself, Hannibal, and the Bichets. If he dropped out, they'd all go unpaid.

The stone-floored watch room of the Cabildo was quiet when he and Rose entered. Lieutenant Abishag Shaw – a stringy Kentucky gargoyle with dirty hair and eyes like an amiable wolf – sat at his desk in a corner, sorting through a pile of scrawled memoranda to which he periodically added from a heap of scrap paper at his elbow. As January and Rose crossed the room toward him he set down his pencil, looked up, then stood and fetched a wood kitchen-chair from the line of them along the wall, holding it for Rose as she sat.

'Just fixin' to send you round a note, Maestro.'

January shut his teeth hard so as not to say, *Were you, now?* He considered the Guards lieutenant a friend and more than a friend – had saved his life more than once, and owed his own life to him. And he knew the burning hatred of all white men that now swept through his very bone marrow was unreasonable.

There had already been another chair beside his desk, and at Shaw's gesture January took it. The guardsman then spat his wad of tobacco in the direction of the sandbox in the nearby corner – it landed with a splat on the flagstones – slouched his long height into his own seat behind the desk once more, and folded his hands on the papers.

'About Marie-Joyeuse Maginot and Catherine Clisson?' January's voice sounded flat in his own ears.

'Friend of yours, I recollect?'

'For many years.' He had a momentary vision of Catherine at eleven, already halfway to womanhood. Her mother had dressed her even in those days as a grown woman, in the high-waisted, narrow-skirted gowns of Napoleon's heyday, her hair smoothed and shining with pomade and a line of tiny pearls at her throat. Even then, she had not played with the other children on Rue Burgundy. She was destined, her mother had implied, for better things.

'You take care of her daughter Saturday?' The gray eyes were expressionless in the narrow face. Friends were friends, but Abishag Shaw – though he sensed his friend's anger – followed truth like a shark on a blood-trail.

'I did.' With medical conciseness, January related the events of the day of the rally, including what Catherine Clisson had told him about the termination of her daughter's relationship with Damien Aubin. 'It was her opinion that Aubin had dismissed her daughter because he had some idea of having his marriage to his wife annulled, and marrying Mademoiselle Maginot. I told her this was absurd. I don't know the strength of M'sieu Aubin's faith, or of Mademoiselle Maginot's, but the Church doesn't hand out annulments like Vote for Harrison pamphlets. For one thing, I don't believe M'sieu Aubin's brother would stand for it, nor the father of Madame Aubin. And the loss of their support would end M'sieu Aubin's hopes of a political career, no matter who wins the election.'

Boys' voices, shouting in the Place d'Armes. The rattle of an iron hoop being rolled. Shaw's eyes flickered to the big doors of the watch room, then returned to January.

'She believe you?'

'I don't know.' January spread his hands. 'What you believe when you've been twenty hours without sleep, have just lost a grandchild and fear your daughter may be dying, and what you believe two days later, when you've rested, are different things. Madame Clisson was angry, yes, and very bitter – and terrified for her daughter. But I literally cannot imagine her harming anyone. And in any case, I simply cannot picture her disguising herself to go to a rambunctious political rally, so she could lie in wait for a girl whose only sin – in truth – was flirting. Flirting and maybe saying what every girl says to a man she thinks is going to marry her. I've known Madame Clisson for most of my life. That is not something she would do. Ever.'

Shaw didn't sigh, but January thought something relaxed in the gray eyes. But the Kentuckian only asked, 'When'd you see Ma'am Clisson Saturday?'

'At about four o'clock. I stopped at Mademoiselle Motet's cottage on my way to Duralde's. Her fever was less, her heartbeat stronger and more even. But she was still unconscious, and would require constant nursing through the night. Madame Clisson knew this. In addition to heart arrhythmias and convulsions, quinine poisoning can produce temporary blindness, which would be terrifying to the girl, should she wake up. If Madame Clisson cared about her daughter enough to do murder, I can't see her leaving her alone for several hours with everyone else in the house asleep.'

'No,' agreed Shaw quietly.

He said nothing more for a time, and January's fists closed on themselves beneath the level of the desk, as his mind ran through all the things that, as a black man facing a white officer of the law, he couldn't say. *Why did you suddenly decide it was she? Because it was only yesterday afternoon that somebody mentioned that Catherine had been up nursing her daughter by herself, with the servants all asleep? Are you looking at anyone else? Say, Damien Aubin or his mad wife or his wife's father . . .?*

It was Rose who asked, in a reasonable tone, 'I take it you've been out to look at the ground where she was found, sir?'

'That I have, m'am. Only it was after it had rained yesterday – 'bout four in the afternoon. You could still see where the blood had soaked into the dirt – from 'bout the middle of the headland back towards the house almost to the edge of the cane, where she'd crawled after that first shot, tryin' to get away.'

He opened the drawer of his desk, brought out an irregular wad of lead roughly the size of a chickpea, and set it on top of the papers.

Rose immediately picked it up, removed her spectacles to study it closely. 'It's rifled.' She touched the faint scratches on the gray surface.

'That it is, m'am. Duellin' pistols sometimes is, an' the shot for one'll work as well in a long gun with the same caliber. I couldn't find the ball that went straight through her body, but her killer must have been pretty close to her. Moon was near full, if you recall, an' the night clear. Second shot looks to me as if her killer stood over her an' shot her again to make sure. This was in the ground, just under where her head was.'

January remembered his dream. Remembered Marie-Joyeuse's sweet voice, and the glittering arpeggios on her harp. He'd seen gunshot wounds.

He said, 'That's not a shot you could make with a rifle.'

'It ain't,' the Kentuckian agreed. 'I did look round Miss Motet's house for clothes or shoes that was wet or muddied up, an' didn't find nuthin'. But with a day to get rid of 'em, that don't mean nuthin'.'

January swallowed back the words, *You mean if your suspect is black it don't mean nuthin', you cold bastard?* He forced himself to remember this man was his friend.

Fireworks had been going off over the river for hours. If Marie-Joyeuse Maginot had screamed for help, it wouldn't have been heard.

'Was there a gun in the house?'

'Shotgun.' Shaw took the ball from where Rose had set it down, turned it over in bony fingers. 'Powder an' ball for a duelin'-pistol. This looks to be about the same size. Ma'am Clisson know how to shoot?'

Again January forced himself not to shout at him, *How dare you?* He knew Shaw was only doing what Shaw did.

'That I don't know. She never spoke of it. And it is illegal for a person of color, of either sex, to handle firearms, as you know, sir.'

For a moment the Kentuckian's gray glance lifted – as if he knew perfectly well about the rifle January had hidden in the rafters of his attic – but he said only, 'An' yet they's plenty that do.'

January nodded. In a voice less harsh, he went on, 'I've been back in town for eight years, and I've never heard anyone else – including my mother and my sisters, who know Madame Clisson well – speak of it either.'

''Tain't usual,' Shaw agreed. 'An' you can bet your Mama or Ma'am Viellard' – he gave Dominique her lover's name – 'woulda flapped some about how un-ladylike it is.' His glance shifted in the direction of the wide stairs that led up to the offices of Captain Tremouille. 'I did point that out,' he added, his tone flatly matter-of-fact.

January felt his shoulders relax. 'Jules Maginot is a Democrat,' he went on after a moment. 'Why would Madame Clisson even have thought to look for Mademoiselle Maginot at a Whig gathering?'

'Oh, come on, Maestro, a good quarter of the folks at that shindig was Democrats. Democrats or pickpockets, not countin' what I made to be about a half a regiment of field hands from every plantation from Bayou Gentilly to Wills Point.'

'You were there? Sir,' he remembered to add.

'I was. Other'n bein' a Whig myself, I sort of thought, with nigh on to seven thousand people slaverin' around for free food an' hard cider, it'd be a good idea to keep a eye on things. But as for Miss Maginot, she'd be there 'cause she'd a knowed Senator Clay'd be there, with that lovestruck boy of his. An' it may be she figured with Old Tip set to beat Matty Van all hollow in the election, Damien's gonna be out of his State Department job by Christmas, an' young Clay's daddy runnin' Washington for the next four years, Secretary of State or not. 'Course she'd be there.'

January glanced at the litter beneath Shaw's hands. In the Kaintuck's sprawling scrawl – and half a dozen other scribbles as well – he read notes like: *Firewrks – Pernet by gallery . . . cabin entry Granville w Harshaw + Trulove . . . Cournand + Forstall . . . cbn entry A. Trulove + A/M Mayerling . . . gallows T-J . . .*

Shaw, he understood, was laboriously reconstructing the mosaic of who had been seen by whom, and when.

'An' I think Ma'am Clisson's smart enough to figure that out. You see young Clay that night?'

'I did.' January related, in as much detail as he could recall, the little vignette of flirtation and jealousy he'd observed from the gallery in the torchlight. 'That was just as the second log cabin came in and the fireworks started. I saw young Michie Clay again an hour or so later, and I thought he looked drunk – though I could have been wrong,' he added, out of consideration for the fact that it wasn't any black man's place to have an opinion about a white man's sobriety. Not if he was in the headquarters of the police and knew what was good for him, at any rate.

'I remember thinking that I wouldn't be surprised to learn that he'd shot Michie Damien. By that time of the evening there were fights starting all around the grounds, from what I could see.'

'You saw pretty good, Maestro.' Shaw scratched absent-mindedly under his faded old jacket. 'You see the senator, any time of the evenin'?'

'Early on.' January considered the question. 'I thought he didn't look well. In fact when he didn't make a speech, I wondered if he'd gone back to town early. Then I saw him again around one in the morning, trying to explain to Tom Spanish why founding the American Colonization Society didn't mean that he actually wanted to free any slaves. Why—?'

'Where is the captain?' roared a voice from the outer doors. January had seen from the corner of his eye two men come striding in from the Place d'Armes, and turned his head now to see Martin Duralde and James Clay planted in front of Sergeant Boechter's desk. Duralde looked exactly as one would expect a man to look, who had been dealing with the police and the murdered body of one of his neighbors, but his cheeks were blotched red with anger. He shook the crumpled sheet of notepaper he held and went on, 'This is outrageous . . .'

'It has been taken care of, m'sieu,' said Boechter. 'M'sieu Freret—'

'It damn well better have been taken care of!' stormed Duralde, and wheeled, to stride off up the stairs that led to Captain Tremouille's office.

January was aware of the tilt of Shaw's head, the way he watched the furious man out of sight.

'Maestro,' said the Kentuckian quietly, 'why'n't you go on around to the jail an' see Ma'am Clisson. You give this to Stookey at the jail' – he pulled one of the scraps of paper on his desk over in front of him, and scrawled on it in pencil – 'an' make whatever arrangements she needs you to.'

Voices floated down the stairs. Angry shouting.

'Freret's up there now with the cap'n,' Shaw continued. '*An'*
Cap'n Barthelmy from the Third Municipality, where the crime
took place, argufyin' over whose jurisdiction the whole thing
belongs to – not that them idjits in the Third Municipality could
figure out that Cain killed Abel when they's two of the only three
men alive on Earth.'

January glanced at the block-printed missive in his hand. MAM
CLISON VISIT A SHAW.

'You happen to know where this Mr Motet – M'am Clisson's
friend – could be reached?'

'I believe he's visiting his son's family near Mobile. I'll write
to him this afternoon.'

'If'fn I stopped by round about four, I could make sure that
letter got on a boat goin' out tonight.'

January paused, and met the policeman's eyes. Then he only
said, 'All right,' and Shaw nodded.

'Good.' He handed January the scrap of paper. 'There's a few
words I needs to say to you, Maestro. Quiet-like.'

TEN

The new parish prison – shared by all three 'municipalities'
of the divided city – lay about a half-mile behind the Cabildo,
and immediately behind the fenced ground alternately
known as Circus Square (its official name) and Congo Square. This
was the part of the First Municipality, where the land sloped backwards towards the part of town known as The Swamp – after which
came the real swamp, and then the marshy ciprière with its mosquitoes, alligators, squatters and slave stealers. Though the building
was only a few years old, it already wore a look of grim neglect:
three tiers of barred windows; a shabby mass of bricks like a trio
of massive goods' boxes laid end to end along Rue Orleans.

The only reason it couldn't be smelled clear from Rampart
Street, reflected January, was that the rest of the neighborhood – of
saloons, bordellos, warehouses and cheap lodgings clustered
around the canal's turning basin – provided too much competition
in that department.

'Stookey at the jail', who reminded January forcibly of a semi-anthropomorphized weasel, glanced at Shaw's note, squinted at January and Rose as if suspecting them of fraud, then led them through a short hall to a room about the size of the pantry back on Rue Esplanade. 'Wait here,' he said. 'I'll fetch her.'

He was half an hour doing so, and the room was like an oven. 'Nonsense, Benjamin,' said Rose, 'what woman would let her oven smell like this?' Walking to the door, January could look down the hall to the heavy iron doors that opened into the first of the prison yards – that of the white men, as he recalled. The white men, that is, who didn't have the money to pay for less crowded rooms, and better water and food, on the second floor.

Two men in blue uniforms sat in front of that iron portal, chewing tobacco and playing cards. The floor-bricks all around their chairs were boltered with expectorant. From somewhere in the gloomy corridor away to the left, January could hear a man screaming. Neither guard so much as turned his head.

Once a man whom he recognized as a well-known slave dealer tapped at the door of the office, put his head in, asked politely, 'Mr Stookey in, boy?' And then gave both January and Rose a long look of speculative calculation, as if asking himself how much he'd have to pay Stookey to hand them over to him, if they were by chance going to be incarcerated.

With equal politeness, January replied, 'He should be back soon, sir.' And didn't dare look the man in the face for fear he'd go over and break his nose for him – and then he *would* have been incarcerated.

And he knew the dealers came to the jail regularly, bribe-money in hand.

The man seemed to debate whether he wanted to come back, or share a ten-by-ten room with two people of color for an unspecified length of time, then withdrew.

Rose closed her hand over January's. January looked at the wall.

'Ben, oh God!' Catherine almost flung herself into the little room, and January caught her hands.

'I'll be out here in the hall,' said Mr Stookey from the doorway. 'Can't let you stay more'n a few minutes, an' this door gotta stay open.' His French was even worse than Shaw's. 'You c'n take my chair there, ma'am – you need I should git you a chair too?' He looked at Rose.

'Thank you, sir.' She smiled at him. 'I'll be fine.'

January gave him a quarter – he seemed to be waiting for it – and held the chair for Catherine to sit. In the hall he heard Stookey call out cheerfully, 'Hey, Hewlett' – Hewlett was the dealer – 'been meanin' to send for you. Got me a couple bucks in here says they're free, but I got my suspicions . . .'

He could almost see the man execute a laborious wink, and hold out his hand.

'Are you all right?'

She gestured the words aside. 'Zandrine—'

'I'll go there after I leave here.' He folded his big hands around hers, and felt them trembling. Her eyes, velvet African-dark like his mother's, flooded with tears. 'Everything's going to be all right. Lieutenant Shaw says he can get a letter out to M'sieu Motet in Mobile this afternoon. He won't let them keep you—'

She steadied her breath. 'They don't set bail for murder.'

'Not if you're not related to every wealthy planter and family in town, they don't,' said Rose, and Catherine gave the ghost of a laugh. The Motet family, of which old Francois Motet was now the head, owned half a dozen sugar plantations and three cotton plantations in the so-called Delta of the Yazoo River in Mississippi, and was, as Rose hinted, connected to every other influential French Creole clan in New Orleans. Francois Motet was a cousin to Captain Tremouille of the New Orleans City Guards, and probably to Mayor Freret, Martin Duralde, and Henry Clay as well. 'I'll bring over some food later – is there anything else you need? Are you safe up there?'

'It's just . . . It's just dirty.' She twitched her skirt surreptitiously, as if fearing something had crawled up between the layers of her petticoats. But January could see already that she wasn't rumpled or bruised, and didn't bear herself like a woman who has been bullied in the yard. 'There's only one real roughneck in the cell and she managed to get the other women mad at her,' she reported shakily. 'And you've already given me the one thing I need, just coming here.' She swallowed hard, lifted her chin. 'I didn't . . . I swear I didn't . . .'

'Good God, Catherine, I never for one second thought you did!'

'There's somebody important who can't account for himself, isn't there?' Tired wisdom hardened in her eyes.

January remembered Shaw's questions, and the way Martin

Duralde had stormed into the Cabildo with James Clay at his heels. Remembered the gossip and speculation of the men last night. 'Whoever actually killed that girl,' he said softly, 'I'll find him.'

Even as he spoke the words he saw the way Catherine sighed, and looked away. She didn't say, *And you think that'll do any good?* She didn't have to.

'I take it nobody came to the house Saturday night?'

Catherine shook her head, something he had already guessed. If anyone had, Shaw would have found it out. 'And the other women were all asleep all night?'

'I had to order them to bed.' She sighed, rubbed her eyes. 'They'd been up caring for Zandrine, running back and forth on errands . . . And I could never have slept anyway. I remembered what you said about her eyes being affected. If she *did* wake up, that's the first thing she'd think of. That it was God's punishment.'

January nodded. The only voice that could reach through shock and shame and horror would be a mother's. The only hands that could pull Zandrine back towards the world of light.

He gathered the woman in his arms – his first love, his dear friend. He felt her weeping against his shoulder, soundless. Felt the pride in her that wouldn't be seen shedding tears in this place. 'I'll find who did it,' he promised again. 'Michie Motet won't let anything happen to you – or to Zandrine.'

She managed to say, 'It's all right. The guards'll take money away if you give it to me, but Rose, if you could bring a little extra food, for me to share round with the other women in the cell . . .?'

'Of course.'

'And I'll speak to the jailer,' said January quietly, 'and let him know that you have a white gentleman friend who'll be *very grateful* to find you well – and *here* – when he arrives in a few days. If a letter goes out tonight—'

'M'sieu Motet is at his son's place.' And again, he could feel the sigh that shuddered through her. One more monster, if not killed, at least driven back.

Rage stifled him again. Rage at white men. Rage at Hewlett, Stookey . . . Clay . . . Shaw . . .

All of them. Complicit in what could happen to this woman . . .

Closing the door on it was like trying to shut a trap-door onto
Hell.

'Yellowhammer Plantation. Baldwin Country, Alabama.' For a
moment, those strong arms cinched tight around him. *My friend.
My dear friend* . . .

She swallowed hard, and forced her voice cheerful. 'Then I
guess all I need is a clean pair of drawers, a fly-swatter, a comb
– a cheap one, because somebody'll steal it – and some soap.
Though I think any soap'll just dissolve, from the river water they
got comin' out of the spigot in the yard . . .'

'We'll come tomorrow,' he promised. 'We'll be here whenever
you need us.'

Standing on her toes, she kissed him again, then turned, to grasp
Rose in her arms. 'Thank you,' she whispered. 'Thank you.'

It was one dollar a night for a 'private' room on the upper floor
('Less'n we has some other gal of color come in able to pay,'
apologized Stookey), which included an actual bed rather than
simply a blanket on the floor, and rainwater bought from a vendor,
rather than river water from the common pump in the yard.
''Course,' added the jailer, 'if we gets a couple white women
wantin' real private rooms and able to pay for 'em—'

'You send word to me, sir,' said January, and wrote his address
on the back of his visiting card. 'And I'll better whatever price is
offered.' (*And thank God for the Whig rally and Mayor Freret's
dinner tonight and that Great Ball Rollin' into town Friday . . .
Tippecanoe and Tyler, too!*) He knew, as he knew his name, that
Francois Motet would pay him back.

Mr Stookey spit (politely turning aside from Rose) and nodded.

January left the place quickly, lest the rage he felt show in his
face. Mr Hewlett was still in the corridor and he felt the man size
him and Rose up again as they walked past.

He said nothing until they reached the market arcade off the
Place d'Armes. When the gombo-vendor's pretty daughter brought
them tin bowls of shellfish and rice he felt almost too ill with
anger to eat, but knew he might not get another chance for hours.
And he did, he found, feel better for the food. Rose was her usual
matter-of-fact self, but, he thought, very quiet. While they ate,
clouds gathered for the inevitable afternoon rainstorm, and when
Rose left him at the corner of Rue Esplanade to return to her

students, he quickened his pace into the Faubourg Marigny, and reached the cottage on Girod Street just as the first drops began to fall.

In spite of himself, he was conscious of the camelback clock on the faux marble mantleshelf in the parlor as Nessie let him in. He was meeting Shaw at four, and at seven thirty would be at Hubert Granville's townhouse for the mayor's dinner.

Which barely gives me time to shave and change . . .

He wondered if James Clay would be there.

Or the senator – who had dropped out of sight early Saturday evening . . .

But in all honesty, January couldn't imagine even a stupid politician committing a crime that foolish – and in circumstances so obvious – much less one as intelligent as Clay. (*Well, maybe Andrew Jackson would have . . .*)

He found Zandrine awake, clearer in mind and calmer in spirit than she had been. Catherine's friend Bernadette Metoyer sat beside the girl's bed, a handsome former plaçée who these days ran a chocolate shop on the Place d'Armes. 'It was Pere Eugenius, who helped her,' Bernadette murmured to him, setting aside the novel she'd been reading to her (Scott's *The Fair Maid of Perth*). January felt the pulse in the fragile wrist, angled his small mirror to the window-light to better see the girl's eyes.

'I can't see, Michie J!' Zandrine swiped her hand in front of her eyes, tears staining her cheeks. 'Everything's all crazy! Mama . . .'

'It'll be all right, mamzelle.' He squeezed her hand, guessing that in the mental confusion caused by the poison she'd forgotten his earlier reassurances. 'Your sight will come back.'

'Your mama can't be here right now, honey,' added Bernadette, with a motherly gentleness that surprised January. In business affairs the woman was hard as granite. 'But I'm here, and Gazoute, and Nessie, and we'll all stay right here by you . . .'

After he had made sure of Zandrine's progress, he crossed the little yard to the kitchen, where Nessie and Solla were washing up lunch things and boiling another batch of the herbal febrifuge Olympe had brought the previous day. From them, January gathered their account of the morning's events. Shaw had searched the house immediately and thoroughly, had questioned the three servants separately – Gazoute had spent the night sharing the women's room, to be near her mistress – before he'd even mentioned the murder. This was precisely what January himself would have done, though he shook his head a little at the cook's shock and surprise. It evidently hadn't occurred to any of the three women that questions about Saturday night *had* to have something to do with Marie-Joyeuse Maginot's death.

'It broke my heart,' said the maid, as she poured the herbal infusion through a strainer into a clean pitcher. 'Watchin' Mr Damien drift away from Mamzelle. After how he'd loved her, takin' her to Washington with him . . . He didn't keep her in some little hotel down by the Navy Yard, either, like a lot of the assistants did with their lady-friends. He got her a nice little house, just off Judiciary Square. An' he'd bring his friends there – congressmen, an' other secretaries from the department where he worked. She'd put on suppers there, champagne an' all that, just the way he liked things. There wasn't anything she wouldn't do for him, nor he for her. She said to me more than once, that he was the only man she'd ever love.'

January recalled the number of boys Zizi-Marie had fallen in love with, before she'd settled (it seemed now, at least) on young Ti-Gall L'Esperance. Saw again how Gabriel – self-assured to the point of cockiness – stammered and fumbled and lost the thread of his conversation when the lovely Trina LaBayadere happened to pass them in the market. If Damien Aubin had taken Zandrine under his protection before he went to Washington – When? The summer of 1838? He and Rose had been in the Caribbean, on the business of the white side of her family . . . Zandrine would have been barely seventeen.

Of course she'd believe that the man who loved her with such possessive fervor was the only man she would ever love.

The semi-tropical summer rain drummed on the banana plants in the courtyard, hissed down the kitchen chimney. Solla, stout and pretty in yellow calico, paused in wiping the last of the coffee cups, said sadly, 'Mamzelle said, even in Washington, he'd sometimes call out Mamzelle Maginot's name, when he was in bed with her. When they came back here, an' he met the girl again, she said she knew she didn't have a chance.'

Drying silverware at the worktable set before the kitchen's wide folding doors – January hated to sit idle while other people worked

– he thought about that for a time. Putting together in his mind that broad-shouldered form in evening dress Thursday night, pulling the dark-haired girl from the salon. Remembering that doe-eyed glance she'd given the man.

'You don't think Michie Damien would have harmed Mamzelle Maginot, if he'd heard that your mamzelle had drunk poison on account of his putting her aside? If it *was* Mamzelle Maginot who told him to dismiss her? If maybe he'd heard that your mamzelle had died?'

Solla said nothing for a long time. Seemed to be concentrating the whole of her attention on a gold-trimmed cup-handle – the finest Limoges china, blue and yellow like the cottage. On the towel before her she adjusted the positions of tiny German-crystal finger bowls, making all perfect, buying herself time.

He saw that this was something the two servants had asked one another.

'I don't know, sir,' Solla whispered at last.

'Mr Damien . . .' Nessie turned from the shelf that the cannisters of coffee, tea, and sugar shared with the neat stack of blue-backed household account books. 'He was always gettin' into trouble, doin' an' sayin' things that later he said he didn't mean. But seemed to me, he meant 'em at the time.'

She thought about it for a moment more, then added, 'Just 'cause he was crazy in love with Miss Maginot, doesn't mean he didn't still think our mamzelle was still *his*.'

'He looks so big an' strong,' said Solla slowly. 'Like there's nuthin' he can't take care of. Like he could handle anythin' from a British invasion to a pack of lions. My old Michie was that way, down in Plaquemines Parish. But I seen Michie Damien with his brother, an' he's like he's back ten years old. It's like when their daddy died, Michie Melchior stepped in an' became the daddy, because he's smart, an' he knows what to do with money, which is somethin' Michie Damien never could figure out. Michie Damien's a fine figure of a man,' she concluded. 'But it's all on the outside. Inside, he's still a little boy. A little boy who just wants to be happy.'

Happy with who? January wondered. *With the mistress who traveled with him, kept house for him, organized entertainments for his guests? For whom he was the only man she'd ever love? Or with his beautiful, exasperating, flirtatious first love?*

'Did he keep a gun here?' he asked at length.

'Yes, sir. A shotgun. That American guard that came here took a look at it. Mr Damien would sometimes leave pistols here, too, if he was in town for the afternoon an' goin' to be shootin' with his friends at Mayerling's gallery.'

Dueling pistols, probably. Rifled? Like the ball Shaw had found?

The rain, brief and violent as first love, was easing. From across the yard, through the French doors open to the evanescent cool, January heard the camelback clock chime the half-hour, and knew it was time and past time to go. *And another day gone by that I didn't go down to the levee to ask if Ti-Jon is back . . . Where was Akinto sheltering, during the rain? At least he's still free . . . If he isn't dead . . .*

He said, 'Thank you, Nessie, Solla.' He gave them each a quarter, not having ever met any enslaved person anywhere who didn't keep some little cache of coin. 'I'll be sending off a letter to M'sieu Motet this afternoon. In the meantime, either Rose or I will be going to the prison every day, to make sure Ma'am Clisson has what she needs. Are you all right here for house-keeping money?'

He was counting out three of his last five of Will McCullen's silver dollars (*Tippecanoe and Tyler, too!*) when Bernadette appeared in the French doors across the yard.

'Virginie's coming at dinner-time.' The chocolate-shop keeper named her sister, when January crossed to join her. 'Babette will be here later tonight.' Another sister.

'Thank you.' January spoke from the bottom of his heart.

'You give my love to Rose, now . . .'

As he walked back towards the French Town again through the thinning rain, he turned in his mind what he had learned . . . *if anything*, he reminded himself. A gleam of steel jacket buttons in darkness. The come-hither glance Marie-Joyeuse had darted at young Mr Clay in the torchlight . . . identical to the one she'd thrown to Damien Aubin, to the one she'd practiced in front of the parlor mirror at that Milneburgh cottage.

Her funeral was tomorrow.

He wondered if James Clay would be there.

Or Damien Aubin.

Monsieur Francois Motet
c/o Xavier Motet
Yellowhammer Plantation, Baldwin County
Alabama

Benjamin January, fpc
Rue Esplanade
New Orleans, LA

September 14, 1840

Dear Monsieur Motet:

I am writing to inform you that our mutual acquaintance Madame Catherine Clisson has had the misfortune to be wrongfully accused of the murder of Mademoiselle Marie-Joyeuse Maginot. She is being held in the parish jail, while her daughter Alexandrine is severely ill.

I have been acting on her behalf since her arrest on Monday morning, September 14, and will continue to do so until I hear from you. Because this is a matter of some urgency, I will take the liberty – asking your pardon – of contacting your attorney, M. Marcel DuPage, at the earliest possible moment. As a surgeon myself, I can attest that Alexandrine is in no immediate danger, and is of course receiving the best of care.

Until I hear from you, or receive instructions from M. DuPage, I will take it upon myself to make sure that Madame Clisson receives clean clothing, appropriate food, and what-ever else she may require, during her incarceration. I have arranged for preferential quarters for her at the parish prison, and I will continue to visit her daughter and do everything necessary to oversee her welfare.

Respectfully,
Benj. January, fpc

January dusted sand across the paper, tapped the excess back into the shaker. The visit to Zandrine had calmed some of his anger, though he felt drained by it, almost hungover.

More deeply, he could still taste the decades-gone cocktail of despair, rage, and utter revulsion he had felt when Catherine had informed him – as kindly as she knew how – that Francois Motet had asked her to 'place' herself 'under his protection', as the custom of the country termed it. To become his mistress, with a house of her own, an annuity of six hundred dollars a year, and the assurance that all her housekeeping bills would be sent to him. At that time, January – aged sixteen – had not yet begun to play for public or private balls in New Orleans, but he had seen Francois Motet: a stout, balding, married sugar planter in his forties with seven children and bad teeth. According to January's mother, Motet had paid off his previous mistress when the woman had run up unconscionable bills at the milliners' and five thousand dollars worth of gambling debts. 'You can't!' he had shouted at Catherine, sickened at the thought of the white man's hands on her body, his mouth on her mouth. Nasty, brown, half-toothless mouth . . . 'I won't let you!'

Catherine had been eighteen. Catherine's mother, he recalled – beside herself with delight that she'd managed to arrange the contract – had come in and thrown January out of the house. January hadn't spoken to Catherine for two years.

He remembered, too – sitting now at the desk in his own little study on Rue Esplanade, with all the French doors thrown open to the murky post-rainstorm heat, looking back at his younger self – the first time he'd played at a Blue Ribbon Ball in the Salle d'Orleans, and had seen Catherine come in on Francois Motet's arm.

She'd been modishly attired in the slim-fitting French costume so popular then: rust and rose that complemented her near-African blackness. He'd looked aside, unable to bear the sight of them.

Then he'd looked back, and had seen with what careful affection the older man escorted Catherine to a chair along the wall, before going to fetch her some negus. And he had been struck almost speechless by the expression of peace on Catherine's face, and her smile when Motet came back to her.

Not a gaze of smoldering desire, but a smile of genuine affection. Of pleasure in the man's company.

He'd watched them laugh together before the planter disappeared through the velvet curtains into the passageway that connected the Salle d'Orleans with the ballroom of the Theatre d'Orleans next door, where a subscription ball was in progress attended by the wives and daughters of the wealthy New Orleaneans and (officially, anyway) those wealthy New Orleaneans themselves.

She cares for him.

And, his eyes for a time burning with tears, *And he for her.*

Without even anger, it was as if his heart broke all over again . . . but he felt happy for her.

Happy in her happiness, Motet's brown teeth and widening tonsure notwithstanding.

It was the first time he'd understood that the aching passion he felt for her wasn't the only kind of love there was.

There were things a black man couldn't write to a white one, which included that their 'mutual acquaintance' was in fact Motet's mistress or that Zandrine was Motet's daughter. But he knew that the old man – in his seventies now, and a dozen years a widower – would waste not a moment in returning.

He had just folded the letter and stuck wafers at both ends and the middle, when Shaw's voice said, 'Maestro?' from the gallery. Though the French door was open – in the vain hope of a whiff of river breeze – January rose to greet him, motioned him to one of the room's worn Spanish chairs.

'Can I get you something?' he asked. Here in his own house, the anger he'd felt at noon was gone. Not dissolved, but put away in its place, beside many other things.

Shaw was white, but Shaw was his friend, the brother he'd never had.

'There's ginger water in the pantry.'

'I take that kindly in you, Maestro. Thank you. You playin' tonight?' the policeman asked, when January returned from the pantry with the refreshment. January thought he looked tired, though the dense heat after the rain would be enough to crush anyone.

'I am.' January handed him the thick Mexican tumbler, laid the sealed letter on the table beside him. 'Thank you for seeing to this.'

'I can't say as how any of this entire fandango, start to finish, is my pleasure.' Shaw tucked the envelope into his jacket pocket. 'You seen Miss Motet? How is she?'

And after he'd listened to January's account of his visit – including the servants' estimate of Damien – Shaw pulled a folded paper from his hip pocket and held it out to him.

It was yellow and cheap (and tobacco-stained), a handbill such as had inundated New Orleans for weeks now with blazing slogans

such as VOTE FOR OLD TIP and VAN IS THE MAN – THE
PEOPLE'S CHOICE.

This one was headed with the stylized image of a coffin. Beneath
it the headline said: HENRY CLAY – MURDERER.

ELEVEN

J anuary – still standing as he'd been when he'd set down the
tumbler of ginger water – slowly took his desk chair again.

Without a word, Shaw brought out and handed him two other
papers.

> Beloved,
>
> I must see you. Since our words last night I can't get you
> out of my thoughts. I beg you on my knees, come to me at
> the end of the fields by the ciprière, when the fireworks begin.
> There is something I must say to you.
>
> My love burns within like a magical flame,
> And my soul takes wing at the sound of your name.
> Each moment is darkness while we are apart.
> I wait for you, darling, with the whole of my heart.
> Adrien LaFrennière

January unfolded the second sheet.

> Mr Clay,
>
> Papers have come into my possession regarding your
> connection, in 1806, with Mr Aaron Burr, whom you defended
> against charges of treason. If you do not pay me $10,000 for
> these proofs of your own involvement in his conspiracy to
> involve the United States in a war with Spain, I am already
> in touch with those who will.
>
> I will be waiting for you on the Gentilly Road, directly across
> Bayou Gentilly from the St Gemme sugar house, just after
> sunset on the evening of Duralde's rally. Tell no one of this
> meeting. Come alone. My son will be watching the road and
> if you are accompanied – or if there is any trouble whatsoever

– I will not hesitate to send these proofs of your complicity to the newspapers in New York, Philadelphia, and New Orleans, as well as those in your home state of Kentucky.

    For your own sake, do not fail me.

    Margaret Blennerhassett

'Blennerhassett . . .'

'English feller what's supposed to of plotted with Aaron Burr.' Shaw walked out through the French window to the gallery again, blew his wad of tobacco over the rail and into the street, then came back in to sip his ginger water. 'Plan was to rob every bank in New Orleans, an' use the money to fund conquerin' Texas. Supposedly they was gonna get troops from that feller Wilkinson, that was territorial governor at the time, an' set up Burr's own empire an' maybe go on to conquer Mexico the followin' day if'fn it didn't rain. Margaret's his wife. Blennerhassett's, I mean. An' I guess his niece into the bargain.'

'I remember.' January had been ten at the time, and well recalled the uproar among the older boys at the St Louis Academy when the story broke in the newspapers. 'I didn't realize Senator Clay had defended Burr.'

He remembered, too, hearing Bella, his mother's servant, talking with Jimbo the yardman about Burr's trial. The former vice president had attempted to escape, he recalled, and evidence against him had been obligingly produced by the same General Wilkinson, who had clearly thought better of the whole scheme.

'He did,' affirmed Shaw.

'And didn't some of the evidence against Burr turn out to be doctored or tampered with or something?'

'Rewritten, so my daddy told me. Daddy had clippin's of every newspaper in Lexington, not that he could read his own name. He'd get my brother Tom to read 'em out, when he got into a argument with the neighbors over it, years after, whenever they's drunk. The court came damn close to chargin' Wilkinson on the strength of it. *An'* turns out the whole time he was also spyin' for the Spanish . . .'

President Jefferson – January also recalled – and his hand-picked successors Madison and Monroe had thereafter taken damn good care of Wilkinson for the rest of the man's life.

He turned the paper over in his hand. A half-sheet of coarse yellowish foolscap. 'Is this genuine?'

'Beats hell outta me.' The Kaintuck cradled the tumbler between his hands. 'The senator genuinely received it. An' given the tales the Whigs is makin' up about Van Buren bein' a aristocrat, an' them the Democrats is makin' up about General Harrison not actually ever havin' won a battle in his life, he genuinely thought it was a good idea to ride out to Bayou Gentilly from Duralde's Saturday night, an' see what he was up against.'

'I take it, no one showed up at all.'

'That's about the size of it. He give me this note hisself, last night.'

The two men sat for a time, regarding one another in the fading afternoon light.

At last January said, 'Well, damn it. And where does Madame Clisson come into it?'

Shaw looked aside, and sighed. 'Somebody – an' I ain't sayin' who 'cause nobody told me, but I will mention that Mayor Freret's a Whig – started countin' up who might have wanted this girl not to go around getting people either married to her or killed in duels over her. Then somebody said, "Didn't Damien Aubin dump his mistress on account of Miss Maginot's pesterin'?" an' somebody else pointed out that Zandrine Motet tried to kill herself an' was laid up an' in no shape to go around shootin' nobody . . . So Captain Tremouille sort of suggests I go ask what Miss Motet's mother was up to Saturday night. An' a lot of people think that sounds a lot better'n that Henry Clay shot a sixteen-year-old girl 'cause she was sparkin' his son.'

'It does.' January opened out the handbill again, and read.

HENRY CLAY
MURDERER
This is the question that the mayor and the City Guards of
New Orleans seek to answer.

(This line, January observed, was typeset in the tiniest available font. The headlines occupied a third of the broadsheet's space.)

The citizens of New Orleans were shocked and scandalized with the discovery of the body of the beautiful sixteen-year-old Marie-Joyeuse Maginot, found Sunday morning in the fields behind Duralde Plantation, brutally shot through the head.

The daughter of a prominent Democratic planter, M. Jules-Henri Maginot, Mademoiselle Maginot had been courted by James Clay, son of the visiting Senator Henry Clay, who is in New Orleans campaigning for his political boss, General Harrison. Senator Clay, best remembered for the shady bargain he struck in 1824 to sell his presidential votes to losing candidate John Q. Adams in exchange for the office of Secretary of State, was scheduled to attend a political meeting at the Duralde Plantation Saturday night, but did not arrive there until the early hours of the morning. He was represented at the meeting by his enamored son James, and by Martin Duralde himself, Clay's son-in-law whose sister married Clay's brother.

Clay, whose personal debts total at least $10,000, attests that he was in fact at the Whig 'rally'. He further claims that his son – currently engaged to marry the daughter of James Jacob, the wealthiest man in Kentucky – had no interest in Mademoiselle Maginot.

Mademoiselle Maginot's heartbroken father begs for justice for his daughter. All other suitors of the beloved Mademoiselle Maginot have definitively established their presence either at the riotous political 'rally' at Duralde's, or elsewhere, and Whig mayor William Freret has the city guards diligently inquiring for others who may have done this frightful deed.

WHO HAS THIS INNOCENT GIRL'S BLOOD ON HIS
HANDS?

'Is that true?' January set the handbill down. 'About all other suitors being accounted for? Did someone keep a list?'

'That,' said Shaw, rising, 'is what you an' me's got to find out, Maestro. The LaFrennière boy really was home that night, with about a dozen cousins *an'* his fiancée, a Miss DuBose from Ascension Parish—'

'So his relatives made sure to tell everyone at the Democrat Club musicale last night.' January sighed. 'Repeatedly. So I assume they knew about the note.'

'Pretty much the whole parish knows. It was in Miss Maginot's pocket when she was found.' From the same distended pocket in his coarse corduroy trousers, Shaw produced another paper, this one a list of names. 'I made a pretty good start on t'others, but there musta been close on seven thousand folks there that night. Whoever wrote that handbill, I don't see how they could have knowed where "all other suitors" was, this quick.'

'You think anybody – Whig or Democrat – is going to *care*?'

'Not really.' Shaw leaned across the table, tapped the list in January's hand with one bony finger. 'Them names on the left is them as her daddy said had asked his permission to pay her their addresses. I'm guessin' there was more.'

'Oh, God, yes.' January glanced over the paper in his hand. There was a second, shorter list at the bottom of the page, with question marks beside the names. 'Madame Aubin was at the rally,' he said, and Shaw's brows went up.

'You saw her?'

'Keeping to the darkness at the edge of the crowd. She was wearing a hooded domino cloak – she'd worn it after her wedding last November – and spectacles. She must have been suffocating in it—'

'Oh, *her*. I did see her. I figured she was some woman keepin' a eye on her husband, like they do sometimes when they sneaks into the Blue Ribbon balls. Them gig-lamps on her face was hard to miss. That was early on in the evenin'—'

'I saw her, I think it was early as well. Her room's at the back of the house at Aurore, at the far end of the women's wing. The cane fields are less than thirty feet from her window. The house was practically empty that night, with the servants all sneaking away to the rally. Damien was gone, Pernet the overseer was gone, Brother Melchior would have been plastered to the eyebrows on opium . . . I gather Damien doesn't sleep in his wife's room.'

And he gave him a brief outline of what he had heard, and overheard, of Olivia Aubin in the past five days.

'Any idea why he married her?' Shaw slouched back into his chair, and scratched absent-mindedly under his shirt. 'That story true, 'bout Brother Melchior pushin' him or trickin' him into it?'

'I don't know. He'd quarreled with Mamzelle Maginot – who was supposedly his first love – and after losing her he may simply not have cared who he married. I understand from Mamzelle's servants that though he looks like Jove's oak-tree he'll do whatever his brother tells him to. But whether, in between being kept an eye on most of her life, and being sent to a convent in France for seven years, Madame Aubin's had the opportunity to learn to shoot well enough to hit a small woman by moonlight at twenty yards . . .'

'An' get her on the first shot.' Shaw considered the matter with narrowed eyes. 'You didn't happen to see either Charles-Louis Trepagier or that son of his at this hoo-rah Saturday night as well?'

January shook his head, and tapped with his finger another name on the list. 'And you know Brother Melchior was in no state to follow anybody through the cane fields by moonlight . . .'

'He may have been in a state to pay somebody else to do it, though.'

January thought about that. 'Melchior Aubin isn't a stupid man,' he said at last. 'Or a careless one – except about getting himself into that brainless duel in the first place. I don't know about the Trepagiers, but I suspect Melchior Aubin wouldn't put himself in a position to have the actual killer come around a second time, and a third, and a fourth, with his hand out asking for more. If he was going to do murder, I doubt he'd risk a confederate, except possibly his brother, who I understand is a crack shot. What' – he gestured with the shorter of the two notes – 'did Adrien LaFrennière have to say about this?'

'Not a thing, 'cept it wasn't him what wrote it. He was crazy in love with Miss Maginot, but his daddy wouldn't hear of him makin' her a offer, seein' as how he's already engaged to Miss DuBose. The DuBoses own about two thousand acres in sugar up in Ascension Parish an' more in cotton in Mississippi. An' by what I understand, the Maginots ain't got a pot to piss in. Jules Maginot showed me 'bout a hundred poems LaFrennière'd wrote to his daughter. Handwritin's close enough, but the paper's nuthin' like.'

'Is the poetry any good?'

'Hell, Maestro, I ain't no judge – but I don't think Mr Shakespeare got anythin' to worry about.'

'Ink looks the same.' January held the two notes side by side. The love note was on thin, probably French, laid notepaper, the letter to Clay on yellowish foolscap.

'Different pens,' said Shaw. 'LaFrennière's other poems is all wrote with a quill, like that love letter. That'd make the handwritin' look closer than it might if'fn it was wrote with a steel nib, like Miz Blennerhassett uses. You think Sefton would care to take a look at these?'

January glanced at Shaw and wondered if the Kentuckian knew of Hannibal's second trade as a forger, primarily of high-quality freedom papers for January's clients in the Underground Railroad. But Shaw was absorbed in examining the two notes, and didn't enlarge on the thought.

'How long did Senator Clay wait at the rendezvous,' he asked, 'before he said to hell with it and came back to the rally? I saw him just about when the fireworks ran out and they started shooting guns.'

'That's about when he said he come back.' Shaw picked up the handbill. 'Feller at Gosser's Printin' on Magazine Street says Jeff Butler brought this in this mornin' about ten.'

Dimly, January heard Rose's voice as she came in from the yard – she conducted the chemistry lessons in her workroom above the laundry. Heard Germaine's light banter, and the gruff voice of Olympe's eleven-year-old daughter Chou-Chou asking a question about vacuum pumps. Chou-Chou had recently started as a day-student of the school, in exchange for helping Rose and Zizi-Marie in the kitchen and laundry. Over the course of the past few years, Chou-Chou had gone through periods of insisting that she was a boy, wearing breeches, cutting her hair short, and demanding that she be described as her Uncle Ben's *nephew* . . . and that she be given a boy's education. She'd been back in tignon and skirts for nearly a year now, but her determination to master the secrets of science and chemistry (chiefly explosives) hadn't altered, and she was fast overtaking the older girls in their studies.

Both her grandmothers were horrified. Both her parents glowed with pride.

A few moments later china-ware clinked in the pantry, reminding January that it was nearly five and he had to be at the Granville palace on Rue Conti at seven.

'I'll see what I can learn.' He pocketed the list of names and both notes.

And maybe, after Marie-Joyeuse's funeral, I can finally steal half an afternoon to find Ti-Jon . . . Damn Tippecanoe, AND Tyler – whoever the hell he is – too . . .

Because of the Whig Club dinner, supper on Rue Esplanade was early, Hannibal arrived for it, shabby and indigent as ever, ten minutes after Shaw's departure. On the rear gallery, in the small, hot parallelogram of sunset light that came through between the buildings around it, the fiddler examined the two papers with a succession of Rose's magnifying lenses, while January helped set the table and Zizi-Marie brought *étouffée* and rice over from the kitchen. After two years of providing Olympian feasts for his family, Gabriel had left his work in the kitchens of the Hotel d'Iberville and taken employment at young Antoine Alcitoire's new restaurant on Rue St Louis, and was seldom home of an evening.

'Without seeing samples of young M'sieu LaFrennière's actual poetry – if one can so term it – I can't say for certain.' Hannibal returned to the table and handed the notes back to January. *'Non effugies meos iambos* . . . But I'd guess from the irregularity of the pen strokes, that the love note, at least, is a forgery. See how the ink blots slightly where the writer stops mid-word to double-check the shape of the letters against an original? You'll sometimes see the same blotting when a semi-illiterate tries to write, because they're struggling with the angle of the pen.'

He obligingly handed the love note to the two girls, who were, again, avid to learn of matters they'd never have heard discussed at home. 'Mama's *dog* could write better poetry!' Germaine exclaimed.

January could only hope they didn't share their enthusiasm in letters to their parents.

'But the wording of the note is educated,' Hannibal went on. 'I doubt a sixteen-year-old would catch the difference. Madame Blennerhassett's is written more evenly, probably because the writer isn't trying to fool a reader who knows the original hand.'

'Would you say the same hand wrote both?'

The fiddler considered for a time, picking at the crawfish in his étouffée. 'I think so,' he said, as Cosette handed the missive back. 'Look at the long letters in the love note – how the up-strokes on the 'l's and 'f's are so uneven – and how that characteristic 'I' is shaped. Our forger is struggling to shorten the long strokes, to match those of his sample. You see where the ink blots just a little where his hand flinches. And you see the places where he didn't succeed or wasn't concentrating.'

Only after the girls had left the table, and Zizi-Marie and Chou-Chou bore the dishes back across the yard to the kitchen, did

Hannibal draw his chair closer to his hosts, and produce the foolscap from his pocket.

'Now look at the long letters on the Blennerhassett screed. They're like trees. That Italianate 'I' turns up in the LaFrennière note, where it doesn't really fit.'

'Any idea whether the writer was a man or a woman?' Rose asked.

'I'd say a man.' His skinny finger tapped the opening lines. 'See where the letters cramp up, trying to be smaller and more ladylike? I don't think an actual woman – even a woman with a bold, big hand – would do that. And you can see where the letters keep getting bigger towards the end of the sentences, when our writer is thinking more about what he's saying than about being dainty. I wonder if the good senator suspected something?'

'If he did,' pointed out January, 'he still didn't have much choice about keeping the rendezvous. Being linked with Burr's conspiracy – if there actually *was* a conspiracy – particularly now, would not only sink him politically, but would almost certainly harm General Harrison's chances of election. He *had* to find out what was going on – and he *couldn't* let anyone know where he was.'

'I'm a little surprised' – Rose poured out some rapidly-cooling tea – 'that he even admitted it to Shaw.'

'He probably wouldn't have,' guessed January, 'if the Democrats hadn't printed up those handbills.'

'So who else made it onto the list?' inquired Hannibal. January handed it over. 'A bit skimpy,' remarked the fiddler. 'She tried her best to interest me – for practice, I think,' he added. 'But I had no desire to receive unfriendly visits from the likes of Hercule LaFrennière and Arnaud Cournand, to say nothing of being thrashed by her father. *Procul hinc, procul este . . .* There were times when I wanted to spank the girl – or more prudently, hire someone else to do it. Still,' he finished, sadness darkening his eyes, 'this wasn't something she deserved.'

From within the house floated the music of January's piano. One of the girls was playing 'The Moon', like the passing rustle of silken skirts.

'Those are only the ones who addressed her father,' said January, re-folding both notes and stowing them in his pocket again. 'Or maybe the only ones her father would take seriously. I would say, Beggars can't be choosers, but she seemed quite capable of kicking over the traces and raising a fuss if her will was crossed. My mother – or Dominique, or Olympe – should have more information. They're on my list to call tomorrow.'

'Followed immediately, I presume, by Miss Maginot's maid?'

'I think Shaw has spoken to her,' January replied. 'Before anything else, I want to have a look at the place where it happened. There won't be anything left out there, after Sunday's rain, and today's. But I still want a look. Thank God nobody's giving a ball for anybody tomorrow night.'

The New Orleans townhouse of the banker Hubert Granville was, as January had said, more like a Medici town palace than merely a wealthy man's dwelling-place. Three stories high – not counting the attic story beneath a fashionable Mansard roof – it boasted the newest style in balconies above the banquette, elaborate with the new cast-iron railings and trim that gave the pink-stuccoed edifice the look of a lace-trimmed Valentine card. Above the ground-floor shops, the second floor – what in France would have been called the 'bel étage' – gave infinitely more scope to a gathering of the wealthiest of the local planters, bankers, merchants and property-owners of the surrounding parishes than was possible at the mayor's own handsome (but non-palatial) townhouse.

For one thing, reflected January, only in this ostentatious urban Versailles could all of them have fit into the same dining room.

Mayor William Freret and his dark-haired English wife received in the main parlor, together with Granville and the plump Mrs Granville, her round pink face seeming an afterthought within the gorgeous splendor of her gold lace gown. The musicians were installed behind discreet screens across the back of the wide central hall. 'Heard but not seen,' murmured Hannibal, adjusting the pegs on his violin. 'Like the bad children that we are.'

But since they all knew that none of the politicians and planters were paying the slightest attention, January and the others could at least play Mozart and Haydn and Rossini, and not – *thank God!* – yet another rendition of 'Little Pigs'.

Now and again fragments of talk drifted to them, about enlisting the militia not only to march in the 'Grand Parade' Friday to welcome the Great Natchez Ball but to make sure that Coal-Oil Billy and the boys from Jefferson Parish didn't attack Tom

Spanish's Donaldsonville Boys – who were insisting upon the effigy of the slaughtered Van Buren as their standard.

'Hell, let 'em!' boomed Granville, a massive Philadelphian who, with his golden beard and red-gold hair, rather resembled the king in a packet of playing cards. 'It'll look good in the papers. If Van Ruin's corpse has got to be rescued by a bunch of skulking Irishmen, that's proof the man's on the skids.'

The night was brutally hot, all the windows open to admit the frantic, persistent barking of a dog from the yard across the street. Martin Duralde and James Clay arrived last of all, with apologies to the two hostesses for Senator Clay's absence. 'My father hasn't been well,' said the young man.

Later in the evening, when young Mr Clay passed the door of the hall, January wondered that the young man had come himself. His voice had barely been heard, and his face seemed to have aged ten years. He kept close to his brother-in-law's side. January wondered if there had been a scene at Duralde – or wherever the Clays were staying: 'You'll go in my place and like it!'?

'He looks like the Spartan boy who hid the fox under his cloak,' Hannibal commented, as the four musicians were shown from the courtyard gate at the evening's end. 'The one who let the thing chew out his liver rather than reveal his pain. Although I rather think that in this case the organ being masticated is his heart.'

The street was quiet, save for the still-hysterical barking of the dog. As January shook hands with the impassive English butler and stepped out onto the brick banquette, a carriage clattered around the corner. The street lantern, hanging from its crossed chains over the intersection, threw little enough light, and most of the windows along the street were dark. But he thought he saw a shape slip out of the carriageway of the opposite townhouse, moments before someone within that yard came out, torch in hand, to open the gates.

And he thought – though Uncle Bichet and his cello case blocked his line of sight down Rue Conti – that whoever that was, was carrying a rifle.

When he stepped around the little group on the banquette, the figure was gone.

TWELVE

Before setting forth for the mayor's dinner Monday night, January had written a note to his younger sister Dominique, at the moment enjoying the relative cool of the lake-front in Milneburgh, asking if he might visit on the following afternoon. Zizi-Marie had undertaken to carry it to her sweetheart Ti-Gall, with instructions that it be taken out to Milneburgh on the steam train.

When January woke in the fugitive cool of Tuesday morning and checked the front gallery, no reply had yet been received.

'Well, God forbid you should run into that fat *lavette* of Minou's in her own house.' Olympe – to whose cottage on Rue Douane January repaired for coffee – set cup, beignet, and a little dish of molasses-dark sugar chunks on the worktable before him, and continued her own task of chopping onions for that evening's stew. In the yard behind her house the dawn mildness lingered, but within an hour, January knew, heat would settle again. The kitchen behind them already radiated with the scorch of the open hearth.

But Olympe's tone was tolerant. Henri Viellard – the *lavette*, or dish-rag, in question – had been Dominique's 'protector' for almost ten years now, and had shown himself not only a faithful and ardent lover, but a good friend to January and Rose. 'I expect,' Olympe added, her eye on baby Zéphine – crawling enthusiastically in the circle permitted by a length of cord tied around one ankle – 'you'll be seeing what Maman knows as well, while you're out at the lake?'

'That's why I need coffee.' January held out the list Shaw had given him.

His sister dried her hand on her apron. Tallish and thin, Olympe Corbier had big hands like January's, and in her faded calico skirts and plain white blouse she looked like any *bonne femme du couleur* in the French Town, save for the pattern of the tignon that wrapped her hair. Few white men would have read at a glance the meaning of the five points that emerged from its dark-red folds, but any person of color in the town would have known them for the mark of the voodooienne.

'You think a jury's gonna convict any white man – or woman'
– her eye touched the name of Olivia Aubin – 'if they can pin this
on a black woman instead? Or that any court in the country's
gonna listen to what a black man – or woman – has to say about
who they saw at this ruckus they had goin' Saturday night?'

'No,' said January simply. 'But any name – any detail – is going
to be a track or a string or a trail that may lead someplace else,
someplace we can find witnesses the courts *will* listen to. Like
when somebody tells you some little detail about somebody's old
love coming through town when you happen to know that the
girl he used to be in love with, just had a baby about nine
months after Mr Used-To-Be came by . . .'

And Olympe smiled, because he was right. She dealt in magic,
and the divination of the gods whom the whites thought had all
been left behind in Africa. But she dealt also in secrets. Any
of the 'queens' who dispensed gris-gris and magic candles, who
'put the cross' on people's shoes or stashed juju-balls of black
wax and pins under front steps or kitchen floors, had their network
of contacts: among the unfree, among the washerwomen and hair-
dressers and market-women who saw the whites when they got
up in the morning, and weren't on their guard.

'Well.' She turned Shaw's list over in her long fingers, and her
brows went up, as Hannibal's had. 'Somebody wasn't keeping
track of little mamzelle's sweethearts very close.'

'What do you know about her?'

'She was a prick-tease.' Olympe shrugged. 'She came to me
a year and a half ago, begging for a ouanga to make Galen Peralta
love her. I asked her, did she know he had a mistress, and she
said yes, could I give her juju to make Marie-Anne turn ugly
and sick? I said, That's not what I do, but I sold her the love-
ouanga. About two months later I hear from Queen Regine over
in Marigny, that Marie-Joyeuse been to her, too, for a ouanga to
make Pierre Forstall crazy in love with her.' A wry smile suddenly
brightened her face, white against a complexion ebony-black as
January's own.

'And then Queen Regine tell me, Marie-Joyeuse asks, can this
ouanga be used for any man, if she just change the name she write
on the paper, or use a different piece of paper? And can she sell
her a big bottle of it, like those American stores that try to
sell you a quart of what you only need a gill of?'

January laughed in spite of himself. 'Maybe she was stocking up for her trip to France?' And just as quickly, his laughter faded.

In an hour, he would see her buried. And no girl of sixteen deserved death for being a prick-tease.

'She came to me again just this past July,' Olympe went on. 'Like she thought I'd forgot the last time. She asked for a ouanga to put on Damien Aubin. When I said he was married, she said, "It was me he's supposed to have married. It was me he asked first. I'm the one he loves."'

'Did you sell her a ouanga?'

Olympe nodded, like a shopkeeper queried about pins. 'The ouanga calls the spirits, brother,' she said. 'Erzuli, and La Sirène. They know who a man's supposed to love, and all the white feathers in the world aren't going to bring a man to the woman the spirits know is wrong. From what I hear, Olivia Trepagier's got no use for a man in her bed anyway.'

'Tell me about Olivia Trepagier.' He tore a fragment from the beignet, trickled honey on its warm heart. 'How crazy is she?'

'Crazy as any dog is, if you beat it all its life.'

'Crazy enough to kill?'

'Depends on how she feels about bein' held up as worthless in front of the whole town an' shipped back to that hell house of her daddy an' brother an' stepmama, with no way ever of gettin' out again.' Olympe's tone was casual, but her dark eyes glittered with compassionate rage. 'So you tell me.'

'Can she shoot?'

The voodooienne's eyebrows nearly disappeared into the edge of her tignon.

'Shoot well enough to hit a girl in a striped dress at night, forty feet away?'

'That's what I love about you, brother.' Her white, slightly protuberant teeth sparkled in a grin. 'You look at how things are, not how things should be if everythin' was proper. I don't see where she'd learn.'

'Me neither.'

'But she was out of the country seven years, an' stranger things have happened.' She swept the chopped onion into a pottery bowl, went to where a big clay oil jar was buried in a corner of the yard, pushed the lid off it and brought out a little rush basket, dripping cool water. She spread newspaper over the worktable, emptied out a couple of catfish and about a quart of shrimp. 'Go in the kitchen get me that leftover chicken from the jar on the counter, would you, Ben? There should be sausage in there, too . . .'

'What about the others?' he asked over his shoulder. 'The other young men?'

'Not so young, some of 'em.' Olympe dried her hands again, and took a kitchen pencil from her skirt pocket. 'Pierre Forstall's a widower, and got to be forty. She's had Philippe Cournand runnin' after her like a lovesick kid, and Martin Clos—'

'All men with money.'

'I said she was a prick-tease, not that she was stupid. Martin Clos called out Arnaud Cournand over her in July, and I hear from Marie-Toussainte Valcour that Arnaud threatened to kill himself, *or Marie-Joyeuse*, if she wouldn't be his . . .'

January paused beside the table, brows raised.

'His papa packed him off to Cuba last month. He's still there.' She took the gourd bowl of meat from his hands. 'Oh, and Jean DuBose got in a duel with Arnaud over her too.'

January dug out his notebook, jotted down the names. 'I'll ask Shaw about them,' he said. 'DuBose and the Cournands are Democrats, like Maginot himself and the Aubins. I'll ask Ti-Jon, too, if I can ever catch up with him. I didn't see him at the rally, but I'd lay money he was there.'

'He was.' She tidied the glistening heap of shrimp on its bed of clean newspapers, the shreds of chicken and slices of sausage. Under the banana-plants beside the kitchen wall, Zéphine was making magic passes with a stalk of resurrection fern, with the active assistance of one of Olympe's cats. When the banks had crashed three years before, Paul Corbier, an upholsterer, had taken what work he could find in the cigar factories along Tchoupitoulas Street; the few dollars he made at this a week, added to what little the poor men and women, slave and free, at the back of town could pay for Olympe's spells, barely bought food for the little household on Rue Douane. Only the fact that January and Rose had taken the older children into their household – Gabriel and Zizi-Marie, and these days Chou-Chou ate most of her meals at their table as well – let Olympe and Paul salvage enough money to place eight-year-old Ti-Paul in the small school run by two refugees from St Domingue over in Marigny.

We'll get through this. January watched the baby swat around her with the fern, dodging the cat's inquiring paw. A young man, a young woman, making their way in the adult world . . . a girl given the freedom to find her own eccentric identity . . . *Family.* Peace seemed to fill the little yard, like the scent of fresh fish and wet leaves and kitchen smoke. *This is the thing that's worth keeping, when all else disappears.*

He wondered, not for the first time, whether Akinto had left family behind him in Africa. A baby girl playing with ferns. A wife chopping onions.

'And you've heard nothing so far, about the African being taken? Or where he might be hiding? I think he has to be in the ciprière—'

'If he's smart.' Olympe scooped the onion shreds into a small pottery dish. 'I cast the beans for him every night, and I ask around. M'am Araignée' – she named the spirit that lived in the black-painted gourd on her parlor shelf – 'she say he hid good an' safe. They watch over him. Ogun, Papa Legba, Ezili.'

The loa, thought January. The African gods, who heard the voices of their exile children, here in this terrible land.

Over thirty years of Christian teaching and deep belief told January that nothing lived in that little tar-black gourd bottle on his sister's shelf. That nothing whispered to her, when she looked into the ink bowl, or cast dry beans into their tray of graveyard earth.

But he believed her, and was glad.

The bell was tolling in the little mortuary chapel as he approached the gates of the old cemetery at the back of town, near the turning basin of the canal. From across Rue des Ramparts, he saw the carriages approach, nearly a dozen of them, the first four the undertaker's black coaches, at ten dollars apiece for the morning. Four times four black horses, black plumes nodding above black manes groomed like silk.

Like that green-and-pink dress she wore Thursday night – only Thursday! Guilt stabbed him, for grieving that saucy, spoilt girl whose desire for a new turn-out had quite possibly cost some woman her husband or her son. *A dress worn once . . .*

This extravagant display of sorrow would ultimately be borne by the slaves as well.

An elderly couple helped Maginot from the carriage behind the hearse: the woman retained enough of Marie-Joyeuse's beauty to mark her out as the old man's sister. The deaf chaperone was absent, probably back at the rundown Maginot plantation at Shell Point. In general, women did not attend funerals. Old Maginot clung to his sister, weeping helplessly, and, awkwardly, his brother-in-law laid his hands on his heaving shoulders.

How can I look on that grief and think about the people in the quarters weeping for those sold to pay for those plumes and coaches and the mutes walking alongside?

How can I not?

From across the street, January noted the others descending from the carriages that followed behind. He knew most of them by sight: Jean DuBose, Philippe Cournand, and Martin Clos because their mistresses were Dominique's friends. Adrien LaFrennière in mourning so deep it might have been for a wife, even to a veil on his tall silk hat. Stout, bespectacled Henri Viellard, like an immense black pudding, sweating in the heat – *He must have come in from Milneburgh . . .*

White-haired Basile Aubin and his son Evard. Mayor Freret, whose mother was kin to every French Creole family in the state. Martin Duralde – presumably also a cousin – and with him his fifteen-year-old son in almost identical adult mourning. Henry Clay and his son James, both men looking white-faced and ill. January wondered how many of the men present had seen the handbill Shaw had shown him yesterday, with its insinuations about the senator's finances and movements on Saturday night.

Just stepping into his carriage must be like running a gauntlet . . .

But Clay's son, January guessed, had begged to attend, and whatever he thought of the match, the senator wouldn't leave him to attend alone.

The Clays, father and son, hung back as the silent procession wound its way among the whitewashed sepulchers, so as not to meet the grief-shattered Jules Maginot. Like all New Orleans cemeteries, this oldest burying-ground did not and could not host actual burials: any grave would fill with water faster than it could be dug. Tombs like miniature houses crowded the walled enclosure, brick or plastered or faced with marble. Some were railed in iron. Most simply jostled almost shoulder to shoulder, with only feet between them. Here and there brick bench-tombs made breaks in the rows – masonry crumbling away, from the depredations of rainy summers and riotous resurrection fern. Thumb-sized black roaches and finger-long crawfish crept from the cracks, obscenely replete.

Now and then he saw voodoo marks chalked on the tombs. Petitions to the dead.

It was easy to follow unnoticed.

Three other men of color walked at the tail of the line. *Maginot house servants?* Coming to support the master they may have served for the whole of their adult lives, or to bid farewell to the girl they had possibly known from her babyhood. Like everyone else they wore black armbands, and long black 'weepers' tied around their hats.

In the silence, the harsh jag of Maginot's weeping seemed to echo off the tombs. January always found white folks' funerals strange for their lack of music – the noise of traffic along Basin Street, the shouts of river-rats and Kaintucks on the other side of the wall, seemed like the cries of unknown birds.

No sign of Damien Aubin.

Unless . . .

Movement caught his eye. Someone else was following the cortege, farther away. A dark shape, springing from the cover of one tomb to that of another, carrying . . .

Is that a rifle?

Carrying something.

Recollection flickered through January's mind. A dog barking wildly in the hot night. Someone slipping out of the shelter of a carriageway, disappearing into the dark of Rue Conti.

There are few things, he reflected uneasily, *that look like a rifle, that* aren't *a rifle. Are we mistaken about this whole thing? Was Marie-Joyeuse the intended victim at all? She has to have been. The moon was bright. Nobody could have mistaken her for a man . . .*

He was moving even as he thought, dodging between the tombs. Another brief sight of a man, and yes, that looked a lot like a rifle . . .

And then he was gone. January counted tombs – which all looked pretty much alike – but when he came up to the place where he thought his quarry had been, there was of course nothing to be seen.

Grass grew between some of them. Mud, between others. Fresh tracks, a man's boots, long, squared, narrow toes like a dandy's . . .

If they're his.

Mud tracked across the pale aprons of pavement before some tombs. Tall fronts with three compartments, stone vases for the flowers, wrought of wire and black beads, placed by the families on the Feast of All Saints. Here and there, a rare statue of a saint, gray stains running down the white marble like tears.

No sign of his quarry.

January felt no particular fear – a hunter was not going to spook his intended target, whoever it might be, by shooting an inquisitive passer-by. But uneasiness drove him back – after a certain number of false leads – toward the funeral itself; an obscure feeling that whoever was the hunter's prey, the knowledge that someone was watching might well drive the threat away.

If it is a threat. If it isn't just a gardener, or someone come to put a . . . A what? A something *that looks an awful lot like a rifle to someone who hasn't had enough sleep now for five nights and whose mind is on sudden death . . . Put a* something *on a tomb that has nothing to do with any of this.*

January didn't believe that explanation for a second.

The Maginot family had been old inhabitants of New Orleans when George Washington and Thomas Jefferson were still playing patty-cake on their fathers' plantations in a British colony. Maginots had buried their dead in the original cemetery beside the city's moated walls. Theirs had been one of the first tombs when the Old Cemetery on Basin Street was new. The stucco had been renewed three times, and the marble slabs that covered its six compartments, stained and worn and inscribed with scores of names. Uncles, aunts, children dead before they'd learned to walk. Grandparents, great-aunts who had never wed. Like all tombs, the floors of its compartments ended several inches short of the backs of those 'ovens' as they were called, so that in the fulness of time, Granmère Louise's or Uncle Tobit's desiccated bones and fragments of broken coffin could be shoved back, to fall through to the sepulcher's central hollow, yielding room for the next family member who happened to die.

They're all still there, reflected January. *Just not in their original configuration.*

John Donne's poem circled back through his mind:

At the round earth's imagined corners, blow
Your trumpets, angels, and arise, arise
From death, you numberless infinities
Of souls, and to your scattered bodies go . . .

From between the tombs he watched the pallbearers – uncles and those ubiquitous male cousins that made up the network of any French Creole girl's life – come forward, with that small white coffin, gently manhandling it up a ladder to the open 'oven' door on the tomb's second level.

At least all their dust is in the same place . . .

In spite of himself, he saw the girl's tourmaline eyes gazing up into his, her mouth pouting to be kissed.

A few yards from him, nearly hidden behind another tomb, James Clay looked aside, pressed his gloved knuckles to his lips. His father glanced sidelong at him, then turned back towards the tomb and the girl his son had begged him to accept as daughter-in-law.

Was she shot by mistake? January's mind scrambled through fragments of answers, shards of questions. *Is there something here I'm not seeing? Did the killer expect someone else, after sending her that note? Was the note meant for someone else?*

Was the man he'd seen – or thought he'd seen – now in pursuit of the true quarry, the person whose body was originally intended to be the one entombed today?

All whom war, dearth, age, agues, tyrannies,
Despair, law, chance, hath slain . . .

For whatever reason that man thought that someone had deserved death.

Or woman, he thought, recalling Chou-Chou in her trouser-wearing days. He knew at least two other women who had masqueraded successfully as men . . . one of them had been at Duralde's Whig Club reception Thursday, with his discreet French Creole 'wife'.

Or was the man – or woman – he'd seen – or thought he'd seen – like himself, the would-be avenger of Marie-Joyeuse Maginot's death? And that being the case, how did that would-be killer know who to pursue?

He looked around him at the maze of stained walls, rank grass. The crowding, miniature houses of the city of the dead. A long-toed boot-print in the mud . . .

And like a second maze, the faces of the men beside the tomb: Jean DuBose with tears running down his apple cheeks; Adrien LaFrennière, face invisible behind his fantastic veil, arms wrapped around himself as if he feared he would fall to pieces from excess of grief. His heavy-featured brother loomed at one side, and patted his shoulder. January wondered if the young man knew that the girl to whom he'd written so much passionate doggerel had flirted with his brother before him.

Denis St Roche, stooped and saturnine, face expressionless as stone. Evard Aubin, fair and dandyish and one of the deadliest duelists in New Orleans. The widowed Pierre Forstall, and Philippe Cournand looking half-sick with guilt, as if he feared someone would tell his wife he'd gone to the funeral of the girl he'd loved.

Whigs and Democrats. Planters and merchants and those who'd invested in steamboats or real estate or slaves . . . He even glimpsed Michie Dessalines, Ti-Jon's master, and a small cluster of well-dressed men whom he recognized from the Faubourg Tremé Free Colored Militia and Burial Society – Maginot cousins 'from the shady side of the street'.

One of them? Someone else? Someone knows something . . . Requiem ætérnam dona eis, Domine; et lux perpétua lúceat eis . . .

His mind went back to the tiny coffin, slipped into the rented wall-tomb in the New Cemetery. To the girl lying in a blue-and-yellow cottage on Girod Street, who would have been denied even that, had her attempt to end her own despair succeeded. 'Michie Damien, you know how he is: crazy jealous if she even looked at another man . . .'

'What am I gonna do, Mama?' Zandrine had whispered. 'What am I gonna *do*?'

At the foot of the ladder, Jules Maginot covered his face with his hands, shaking with sobs, like a tree in the storm that will uproot it before the night's end.

THIRTEEN

It was a walk of a little more than a mile along the top of the levee, from the Place d'Armes to Aurore Plantation. The river breeze mitigated the worst of the forenoon's brazen heat. This was the stretch where the ocean-going ships put in, the iron steam-packets and the big three-masted merchantmen, flags of England, Russia, France and a half-dozen of the larger Germanic principalities splashes of color against a cloud-spatched sky. Carriages rattled along the shell road just inland of the grassy rise, and from the bustle of the wharves below to the right, the mutter of voices was both sharp and indistinct, like Babel on the day after the Lord had laid His hand upon its hubristic populace.

Shaw listened to January's account of that morning's funeral, his only comments the occasional spit of tobacco into the weeds that grew along the footpath. 'You mark which of them swains was at the graveside?' he asked at length.

'LaFrennière, Philippe Cournand, DuBose – that I know about,' answered January. 'Mayor Freret was there, too, and half a dozen Aubins and Mabillets. Any of them could be our rifleman's target.'

'Or none.' Shaw tilted his hat a little further, against the sun-glare from the water below. 'Who's left over, who mighta thought this poor girl worth killin' over even after she's dead?'

'Arnaud Cournand – his father thought it wise to send him off to Cuba so he wouldn't get himself killed in a duel with Jean DuBose over the girl. Martin Clos. My sister's friend Phlosine is his plaçée and from the little I've heard of him, the man's always falling in and out of love with wealthy white girls and always finding something disappointing about them within a month.'

'Don't sound to me like a man who'd go crazy with passion.' The policeman paused, to spit at a frog in the rank grass. 'But humankind always sort of keeps on surprisin' me.' The frog regarded the expectorant with surprised disdain, but didn't bother to move. The attack had missed it by feet.

'James Clay,' concluded January, 'If anyone could have sent

his father off on a wild goose chase, it would be he. Or Damien
Aubin.'

'Damien Aubin,' Shaw agreed. 'By my notes, the timin' on
young Clay would be a tad close.'

'And his father?'

'If'fn you believe a man as smart as Clay'd kill a girl – at a
rally where seven thousand people are lookin' to see where he is
– over his son's fool puppy love.'

The first time I've truly wished to do anything that you *didn't
come up with . . .*

He heard the young man's despairing cry.

And yet, he thought, *that* crime, *that* way of murder – without
even searching her pocket for the note that had lured her there –
was indeed the act of a fool. And whatever else Henry Clay might
be, he wasn't a fool.

Olympe would sneer at him. But he didn't believe it any more
than Shaw did.

'*An'* whoever-all else we don't know about,' Shaw went
on, ticking the point off on his long fingers. 'Which it sounds like
there coulda been a whole glee-club of 'em.'

To their left, the cottages and building lots of the Third
Municipality petered out, amid swampy pasturage dotted with
cattle, lumberyards, brick kilns, warehouses and woodlots. Though
much of the land was exhausted by over-cropping, here and there
the dull-green cane fields and brightly painted houses of small
plantations still spoke of older days.

'But by what you tell me about the handwritin' on those two
notes, whoever it was sent the one to Miss Maginot that night, it
was to set up Senator Clay.'

'How'd she get the note, by the way?'

'Colored boy left it with a servant. Can they describe the boy . . .?'

'Of course not,' January finished resignedly.

'Same story with Clay. Coulda been the same boy. Either it was
to get him really arrested for murder, or to scare him into headin'
home an' not attendin' this ruckus they's havin' Friday when their
Great Rollin' Ball comes a-rollin' into town. So who among
our friends back there at the boneyard would have killed a girl
that age, to get a senator to go home without makin' a speech?
What was the main point?'

'That's *if* – January shook his head – 'the person who shot

Mamzelle Maginot is the same one who lured her out there with a note. We could be looking at two different events entirely. And *if* my friend with the gun really is hunting her killer and not someone else for some other reason. And if he seeks vengeance for Mamzelle Maginot, how does he know who he's hunting? Did he see something Saturday night? Learn something later that we need to know?'

'Consarn it.' Shaw spit again, and walked on in silence, hands jammed in his pockets and elbows hanging out of the holes of his threadbare coat sleeves.

Clouds moved up from the Gulf, marble mountain-tops above a slatey roof that breathed rain.

At Duralde, men were dismantling the log cabin beside the trees. The lumber they stacked behind the overseer's tiny dwelling, and as January and Shaw clambered down off the levee and crossed the open ground to the Big House, cleaned now of debris, he glimpsed the bare chassis that had supported the mobile cabin, parked behind the kitchen and surrounded by a welter of woodchips and trash. He wondered what had become of the raccoons and that poor eagle.

Shaw hailed a woman sweeping the steps up to the gallery and asked, was Mr Duralde to home? And being told, no, asked after the overseer, or anyone in charge.

'I'm here from the city guards, ma'am.' He removed his miserable hat. 'Come to have a look at the place where poor Miss Maginot was killed.' He knew enough to completely ignore January, whom everyone – January knew – would take for a servant of some kind. On the way from the levee to the house, he'd fallen several steps behind the Kaintuck, and made himself look humble.

The woman crossed herself. 'Michie Carpenter out in the field, sir.' She gestured toward the footpath January well recalled: the rear yard; the stables; the quarters – barbeque pits now cold and covered over. The mill, the woodstores, and beyond them the cane.

The field nearest the house – as he had seen on Friday from the road – had been dug that summer. It was a back-breaking job, and such men as weren't dissecting General Harrison's putative dwelling-place were out burying cut sections of stalk in the hillocks of earth between the soggy ditches. The field beyond had been ratooned – harvested last December and left to re-grow cane from the previous planting – and the one beyond that stood head-high, ready to be cut when the cold weather came. Michie Carpenter sat his heavy-boned bay mare on the footpath beside the first field, a big, rangy man in his forties with an Indian's brick-dark complexion and an African's nose and cheekbones, and a mouth that could have bitten the heads off nails. Shaw explained who he was and asked Mr Carpenter's permission, to see the place where the young miss had been shot.

'That was a hell of a thing.' The man whistled to one of the planting gang. 'Gus, show this gentleman the place where the poor girl was killed,' and Gus saluted him and laid down his spade on the cart where the cane sections lay.

'This way, sir.'

January followed like a good servant.

As Shaw had said, the place was a narrow strip of land at the far end of the last field, where the ground finally became too squishy for cultivation. January noted where the ditches alongside the cane had been extended a little ways and a number of the nearer cypresses felled, clearly with the intention of opening more land. Hackberry and elephant-ear still tangled the ground.

'She was layin' here.' Shaw had cut a stalk of maiden-cane from the edge of the ratooned field, and used it to mark a spot a few feet from the wall of cane that bounded the riverward edge of the little headland. Two afternoons of rain had left barely a stain on the weeds. 'Blood trail ran back this-a-way, to 'bout here, so she musta been standin' here when the first bullet hit her.'

January tried to imagine the spot by moonlight, with the clatter of fireworks a mile away, the gaudy flare of color on the sky. Had that helped the gunman's aim? 'And she crawled towards the cane,' he said a length. 'Even with a full moon, I doubt she'd have seen someone at the edge of the woods, especially if they were far back.'

'They coulda been nearer.' Shaw swiped with the cane at a king snake, slithering through the trampled weeds at his feet. 'Them ditches come right up about to where the blood starts, an' that upstream one there's deep enough to hide a man.'

'Not a man who wanted to be seen at the rally afterwards,' January pointed out.

'Woman in a cloak coulda got away with it. In the dark, if'fn she didn't hang around too long after.'

From his pocket he produced the ball of deformed lead he'd

shown January at the Cabildo the day before. 'Has to been a pistol,' he said. 'An' he has to have had it on him at the rally. Leavin' it out here earlier, he runs the risk of one of the hands comin' on it.'

'And no sign of powder from re-loading?'

'Not after a day an' a half.'

Notwithstanding, Shaw worked his way around the edges of the headland again, bending and stooping his rangy body to study the ground. January retreated a few respectful steps, as if to let him get on with an incomprehensible job. To the field hand Gus – who as January had figured would much rather linger 'to be of help, sir,' than go back to planting cane – he said in an undervoice, 'Was you one of them as found her?'

The slave nodded. 'Next mornin', that was. Seneca – that's the gang driver – said as how they was too many birds comin' down, for just some little triflin' thing like a rabbit, an' Michie Carpenter sent two of the hog-meat boys to see. They come runnin' back, scared bad, sayin' they's a dead lady back there layin' on the ground, a white lady. An' there she was, just where your massa say, with blood all leadin' back to the center of the open ground. She'd had a fan, I guess, in her hands, an' had dropped it there, but you didn't need that to see where she'd fell.'

'Damn,' January whispered. 'I was here Saturday night – out by the front, I mean. You coulda shot off a cannon back here an' not heard it.'

Gus managed a crooked grin. 'You an' everybody else in the parish. You saw how Michie Duralde gave us our own barbeque pit, so long as we took turns to work the other pits an' help move that blame silly cabin of theirs on wheels. It true General Harrison born in a log cabin? But I swear I saw just about everybody – house servants an' field hands – from every place from here to Chalmette, out there watchin' the fireworks an' snitchin' food when nobody was lookin'.'

January shook his head. 'Bet there was some sore backs Sunday mornin'.'

The field hand chuckled. 'I tell you, you never saw so many men dodgin' an' lookin' the other way' – he demonstrated someone exaggeratedly pretending to avoid notice – ''cause pretty much all the overseers in the parish was here, too, whether they'd vote for General Harrison or not. There was plenty moonlight, but if you're in where there's just torchlight – not up close to the bonfires – unless you're right up next to somebody, you couldn't tell George Washington from the King of Prussia.'

'Guess that was lucky for me,' said January with a grin, ''cause Michie Shaw told me yesterday' – he nodded towards the Kentuckian, still bent double and walking in a sort of squat as he investigated the ground – 'how he was here as well, an' I never saw him.'

'Folks like Michie Forstall over to Bayou des Prêtres, or Ma'am Picard at Louveciennes, they don't care.' Gus shrugged. 'They just laugh an' say, "Don't get caught by the pattyrollers on your way back". An' just about the whole quarters, an' the house servants too, snuck over from Aurore, 'cause Michie Pernet – that's Michie Aubin's overseer – was here meetin' that slutty Ma'am Floride that's got a husband runs a grocery in Marigny, so he wouldn't't'a noticed if you'd knocked his hat off. An' with Michie Aubin still laid up from that duel – an' wasn't that a stupid thing, after all his goin' on for years about how duelin' is a sin an' a waste!'

'It's a sin an' a waste when somebody else does it,' agreed January sagely. 'But when somebody calls your favorite Emperor of France a pimp, well, that's different.'

'Was *that* what that was about?' His companion shook his head wonderingly at the vagaries of *les blankittes*. 'Far as I'm concerned, they's all pimps . . . An' Ma'am Olivia didn't got a word to say 'bout any of it, 'cause she was there herself. Seen her with my own eyes, all got up in a cloak, an' spectacles like a bug's eyes, duckin' back from the torchlight when the parade come in, hopin' nobody seen her. Lookin' for Michie Damien, I'll bet. An' small wonder he'd be off holdin' hands with a gal who *don't* lock her door against a man, or throw all her dresses out in a pile behind the kitchen an' light 'em.'

'Which don't do us a whole lot of good,' remarked Shaw, tilting his dilapidated hat forward on his head as they climbed the levee once again, 'seein' as how even a middlin' lawyer could tear to pieces when she was seen an' how close to her husband an' his lady love . . . always supposin' you could find a court south of Boston that'd listen to a black man's testimony an' a slave's testimony at that. No surprise Damien wouldn't take her to Washington with him. Wonder they'd keep her on a place so close to town as it is.'

'I think,' said January, 'it's the only plantation their father had left, once his debts had been paid off. They sold the townhouse, I know that. The other Aubin plantations are all under the management of Uncle Basile or his son.'

He glanced out across the Aurore lands, now spread out below them to their left. The contrast with the well-kept Duralde acres was dismal. January caught the glint of the sky's reflection in a flooded field. In another, cane ratooned too many times grew in straggling clumps, like a beggar's hair, every which-way and none of it thick enough to yield sufficient sugar to justify the work of milling and boiling. *Too few hands*. He winced at the thought of the labor that would fall on those who remained.

He remembered Melchior's words, overheard – how many nights ago? – when he'd spoken enviously to Senator Clay about the more efficient vacuum-pan boilers, the steam-driven grinders that could make all the difference between painful subsistence and the sort of wealth that still poured into the pockets of the Forstalls, the Destrehans, and the Viellards.

No wonder Brother Melchior had been – as Cochon had remarked – all but wiping Henry Clay's boots at the Whig Club reception, in the hopes of keeping young Damien in Washington. Politics would pave the road back, for that branch of the Aubin family.

Well worth it, he reflected, *for Brother Melchior to urge his unwilling cadet to propose marriage to a madwoman.*

He just wanted to be happy, Solla had said sadly.

Not with a girl who has no money. He could almost hear Melchior's harsh retort.

The stately, middle-aged man who opened the farthest upstream door of the Aurore plantation house was darker than most planters would buy for a house servant, though he greeted them in perfect French and with manners that half the planters January had encountered would have done well to imitate. The office into which he led them still had the scrupulously untouched aspect it had borne Friday night: obviously nobody had done work at the desk for the four days since Melchior Aubin's injury and the death of Damien's beloved. A bit to January's surprise, the butler said, with a bow, 'If you will excuse me, sir, I'll ask Michie Melchior if he's well enough to see you,' and left the study, not through the door that would have led into the bedroom immediately behind it, but through the parlor door.

Sickroom, thought January. *Back in the men's wing.*

He must be badly hurt. He'd heard such rooms called, 'born an' dyin' rooms' away from the activity of the main house.

Shaw whispered, 'Watch the door,' the moment the butler left.

The office desk, like all the furnishings of the plantation house, was plain, local work, well made but without even the chaste embellishments one would see manufactured in town by such artists as Rousseau or Glapion. Most importantly, it did not boast a lock. The drawers that Shaw opened moved smoothly and silent, well-made and well-waxed. From one, the Kentuckian drew a sheet of coarse, yellowish foolscap and a note-sized piece of cream-colored French laid paper. From another he took a steel-nibbed pen, and – again to January's surprise – a quill, the tips of both stained brown with traces of ink. Shaw stepped over to January silently as a cat, nodded towards the desk, and whispered, 'Write somethin'.'

January understood. There was still no sign of the butler's return. In fact, as he wrote *Margaret Blennerhassett* on the foolscap with the pen, *Adrien LaFrennière* on the notepaper with the quill, he reflected on how silent the house itself was. Noon was always a quiet time, especially in the summer in South Louisiana. In houses where there were children one would hear their voices at their lessons or their play; in a house with growing daughters, there would be the soft voices of mothers or aunts instructing the girls in needlework.

In this house there was nothing. The servants would have finished their work as early as they could because of the heat, and retreated to their own quarters, to eat before the white folks wanted their dinners at three or four. Through the door he'd seen that the merged parlor and dining room retained the empty, rather stiff aspect of a makeshift ballroom, the parlor furniture pushed back around the walls. Only the braided straw matting had been unrolled once again on the floors, the dining table returned from the small pantry which he and his orchestra had shared with the punchbowl and cheeses. The mirrors and pictures had been draped again with gauze against the spotting of the ubiquitous flies. But no books, no newspapers, no evidence that anyone had entered or used these rooms since the furious exodus of Charles Brunneau and those who supported his cause.

The ink in the office standish, he noted, seemed exactly the same color and consistency as that on the two notes Shaw had showed him yesterday.

Shaw scooped up both sheets, fanned them briefly dry, then folded and shoved them into his pockets. January wiped both pens on the inside of his shirt-tail, and replaced them in the drawer. On a shelf, beside the plantation ledgers, lay the sort of fancy wooden casket that expensive gunsmiths sold with pairs of dueling pistols, and sure enough, when Shaw flipped it open, January saw it contained the whole kit: two pistols; a small silver powder-flask; a tiny bottle of oil; patches, gun worm; brushes, each in its own compartment; ramrods; and a wash-leather pouch of balls. And, significantly, a petite silver-mounted hammer.

This ball is rifled, Rose had said.

The Englishman who'd run the shooting gallery that January had frequented in Paris had showed him the delicate touch needed, to tap home a ball into a tight-fitting barrel whose grooves would so vastly improve the weapon's aim.

'Some gentlemen regard it as cheating.' Colonel Rory had shaken his head. 'No *true* gentleman would defend his honor with a rifled weapon. It simply isn't *done*. Myself . . .' He had spread his brown, calloused hands, three fingers missing – left behind, like his left leg, on the field at Waterloo. 'I daresay I could survive the shame of it, to stand at the grave of my opponent and hear all his friends whispering behind my back, "Rory Hallam doesn't fight fair."'

Shaw pocketed two pistol balls, folded the pouch exactly as it had been, closed the casket, and replaced it, as the door to the gallery creaked at the back of the dining room, and the butler's measured tread pressed the floors.

With January a few paces behind like a good servant, they followed the butler through the parlor and dining room, out the French door to the rear gallery, and thence along the gallery on the upstream wing that stretched back from the house.

The two chambers between the main house and the sickroom at the end of the wing were shuttered. Outside the French door of that last chamber, a valet sat on a wooden stool, on hand should his master require anything. *And if his master's too weak to call out*, January reflected, *I hope he has a good, loud bell at his bedside*. The man appeared to be asleep. (*I'm bettin' Jerry ain't gonna be sober*. January could still hear Andy the cook saying the words, in the flame-lit hubbub Saturday night.)

In the opposite wing, the rooms on the women's side of the house were likewise closed, as they had been Friday night. In his mind he heard again Olivia Aubin's thin howling.

That room was shuttered now. No maid waited outside.

'What the hell do you want?'

Well, at least we don't have to worry that he's too weak to make himself heard . . .

The little table beside Melchior Aubin's bed supported a handbell, as well as a carafe of water and a glass. Presumably the medicines had been cleared away. The mosquito-bar had been tied back, and the man himself was sitting up, half-dressed in shirt, waistcoat, and cravat, sheet and counterpane drawn up over his knees. His head thrust forward aggressively, anger glinting in his eyes.

Despite the memory of Zandrine weeping as she felt her child slip from her womb, despite the memory of Catherine clinging desperately to his arms in that pestilent little office at the jail, January was physician enough to breathe easier. Even from where he stood in the French door to the gallery – even with the dimness of the shuttered room – he could see that Melchior Aubin's color was good.

Ball went right through, Andy had told him Friday night.

Dr Bascomb, whoever he is, must be good.

'I do beg your pardon disturbin' you, Mr Aubin.' Shaw made a little bow and stepped up close to the bed, where, after a grudging moment, Aubin signed to the butler to fetch the room's single wooden chair for him. 'They's a couple questions you maybe could clear up for me, that been asked about your brother an' Miss Maginot.'

'My brother and I' – Aubin's voice was cold as a dull razor on a chilly morning – 'are kin to the Maginots. We've known the girl all her life. And, not to speak ill of the dead' – a remark which January knew invariably preceded speaking ill of the dead – 'I personally found Miss Maginot a spoilt and undisciplined child. I understand my Uncle Jules doting on her as he did. He doted on his wife in just such a fashion, and Madame Maginot died only two months after Marie-Joyeuse's birth. I don't think the old man ever got over it. But that's no excuse for letting the girl have and do everything and anything she pleased. It's certainly no excuse for spending on her money which could have gone – should have gone – to . . .' He stopped the rush of his words with an almost audible snap, turned his face sharply aside.

'So there was nuthin' more than cousinry,' Shaw continued mildly, ''tween your brother an' Miss Maginot?'

'Nothing.'

Head tilted a little to one side, Shaw made no reply.

'Oh, I believe there was some kind of calf-love nonsense when Damien returned from university.' The planter made an impatient gesture with one hand. 'But my brother is a married man. I consider the vulgar insinuation made by young Mr Clay at Duralde's reception to be only envy – the envy of an American upstart when a door is closed in his face by the family of a girl he fancies himself in love with.'

'You think – bein' Miss Maginot's cousin an' all – she was serious about young Clay?' January could almost see the policeman sorting bits of information like a hand of cards. Lies with lies, facts with facts. Questions with other questions. 'I only asks . . .' Aubin's head had whipped back around and his mouth half-opened to retort. '. . . 'cause there mighta been some other young blade, got jealous enough to cause trouble.'

'Miss Maginot didn't confide in me.' Aubin settled back into his pillows, his shoulders suddenly slumping. His voice, when he spoke again, had dropped to the scratchy weakness of a man in pain. 'Or in my brother. My impression was that Senator Clay would never have stood for the match. He told me – and he was very vehement about it – that his son is engaged already to a Miss Jacob, of Louisville. In any case, he said, the last thing a young man needed, setting out for a career in politics, was a wife who cannot be trusted not to involve him in scandal – a position with which I have to concur. Now please,' he added, his voice sinking further, and he pressed his hand to his forehead. 'If we are finished here . . . Jerry!'

He raised his voice feebly, and, when he got no response from this, groped for the handbell.

'I'll fetch him, sir,' January volunteered, and stepped out onto the gallery, where the valet dozed in his chair.

He looked up with a start when January touched his shoulder, his gasping breath a swamp of expensive French cognac. More typically of house servants, the valet was light-complected, quadroon or octoroon, January guessed – fair enough in any case that the veins broken in nose and cheeks by decades of alcohol abuse showed clearly under the ivory skin.

'You Jerry, sir?' asked January, in his most humble cane-patch French. 'Your michie callin' you—'

Jerry said, 'Shit,' ran quick hands through his hair, straightened his disordered cravat, and ducked into the chamber.

January heard Aubin murmur, 'Show the gentleman out, Jerry—'

''Fore I goes,' said Shaw apologetically, 'you think there's any chance I could have a word with Mr Damien Aubin? It'd save me comin' back out here,' he added, with a patient persistence that was in itself a warning to those who knew him, ''cause I know Captain Tremouille, an' Captain Barthelmy from the Third Municipality, got questions for him, too.'

There was a moment's silence. Then: 'My brother is . . . prostrated by his cousin's death.'

January schooled his face not to show his thought: *Prostrated by nothing more than cousinry and calf-love years ago?*

Though Shaw obviously thought the same, he only said, 'I understand, sir.' But the inflection of his voice was clear, and his stance unmoving. *I understand, sir,* but . . .

'Jerry' – Aubin's words were barely more than a feeble whisper – 'please fetch M'sieu Damien here.'

'Michie Melchior,' protested the valet – and January could only assume that the cognac was responsible for the temerity of an objection, since Melchior Aubin was clearly not a man to cross – 'you know Michie Damien—'

'*Fetch him!*'

Jerry emerged from the bedroom and trotted off down the gallery toward the main house, glancing behind him and bumping twice against the gallery railing. Damien, presumably, occupied a bedchamber in the front part of the house. *Because of his status as a married man?*

As January turned back towards the bedchamber, movement caught his eye in the kitchen building, past the shabby line of mule-barn and woodsheds, and he saw the cook, Andy, beckoning him, a friendly glass of lemonade in hand.

FOURTEEN

'An' here I thought you's a musician, Ben.' Andy brought around a chair to the worktable under the abat-vent, the deep overhang of the kitchen roof that provided shade in the summers – and at least a moderate chance of intercepting the river breeze – and protection against the oncoming afternoon rain. In an old-fashioned kitchen like Olympe's, the fire was built up on the hearth first thing in the morning, so that the coals would be settled into the proper incandescence when it came time to cook dinner. To judge by the smells, and the bundle of wet newspaper and onion-tops at one end of the table, like Olympe, Andy had already prepped his vegetables. Neatly as a gambler shuffling a deck, the cook cut flour and butter together for a pastry casing; the kitchen behind him had an atmosphere like the Seventh Circle of Dante's Hell, but much better-smelling. 'You a friend of the police?'

'The lieutenant,' said January significantly, 'is a friend of *mine*. I asked him, could I come along this afternoon. The police are accusing the mother of Michie Damien's plaçée of killing Mamzelle—'

'The girl what tried to kill herself?' Andy's face puckered in concern, and January nodded.

'She's a friend of mine, a dear friend. And of course since she was sitting up all night at Mamzelle Zandrine's side, since she'd let the servants go to bed—'

'*Damn!*' The concern turned for a moment to disgust, and a dark anger. 'They do say no good deed goes unpunished—'

'The cook, and Mamzelle Zandrine's maid, had been up all night the night before, when she took the poison. So when the police showed up—'

'Double-damn.' The big hands paused in the mealy mix of flour, then started again, unthinking as a machine. January reflected that like Gabriel, he could probably mix pastry in his sleep. 'Like a girl's mother would be anyplace else – an' bless her, for not thinkin' her cook an' the maid can just go on like a steam engine, like some folks I could name. Bet the man thinks Mama left her girl lyin', stuck a pistol in her pocket, an' walked all the way down here, 'cause gettin' revenge on a white girl's *way* more important to her than carin' for a black one . . .'

'That's pretty much what they do think.' January drained the lemonade. 'Anything here I can help you with? My nephew's a sous-chef at Alcitoire's,' he added. 'So I know which end of the knife to hold.'

Andy grinned. 'That's kind of you, thank you, Michie J. But *nobody* in this house touches pastry but me.' And he waved him to the chair again. 'An' your friend's the only black person accused, ain't she?'

'I'm sure they'd accuse her daughter too, if the poor girl wasn't too weak to stand an' still half-blind with the poison she drank, but yeah. Her sight'll come back,' he added, seeing the shocked expression on the other man's face. 'That can happen, when you drink most of a bottle of quinine. She's better today than she was.'

Andy crossed himself, knife still in hand. 'Bastards.' And the anger flickered again, fathoms deep, in the dark eyes. 'But you know, for all his ravin' an' stormin', Michie Damien wouldn't have touched a hair of her head. Since it happened, the man ain't been out of his room. Ain't changed his clothes, keeps his door locked – cussed like a crazy man when Park – that's his valet – tried to go in an' get him a clean shirt or shave him or get the mud off his boots. An' him that used to be so pernikkity 'bout the way he looked an' dressed . . .'

He shook his head, kneading the flour and butter into beads the size of seed pearls, as January had – a thousand times, when he lived in Paris – watched his first wife, the beautiful Ayasha, knead couscous.

'An' it never occurred to any of 'em that it'd make more sense for Mama to kill Michie Damien, if like I heard it was 'cause he turned her off? Like he really thought his brother, an' Ma'am Aubin's family, are gonna let him just turn Ma'am Aubin out of the house to marry that girl. A man don't turn his plaçée out unless he wants to.'

'It'd make more sense to me,' agreed January quietly. 'But I've never had a daughter of mine try to take her own life' – in spite of years of careful education in logic, and discussions of good and evil with his confessor, he still crossed his fingers to avert evil, as old Auntie Jeanne had done in his childhood – 'so I really don't know what I'd do, or who I'd blame. I think it more likely, myself, that one of Ma'am Aubin's kin would have shot that poor girl, if they really thought there was danger that Michie Damien would put her aside. But you never can tell with *blankittes*.'

'That's for damn sure.' Deftly, the cook dusted the pastry-board with flour, rolled out the pale dough. 'Reach me that bowl there by your elbow . . . Thanks, Ben. I'd think so, too. 'Cept Isaiah the mule boy seen old Charles-Louis Trepagier, an' his son Michie Alain, pretty much in an' out of that crowd at Duralde most of the evenin'. Isaiah, an' Tina, an' Cuffee . . .' He rattled off the names of a dozen fellow slaves. 'See, we started puttin' our heads together when we heard – 'cause we thought like you're thinkin' – tryin' to see, when poor mamzelle was shot durin' the fireworks, which I think she has to have been, if it coulda been madame's kin. Both of 'em – an' that prissy-mouth brother-in-law of hers, too – was in the crowd most of the evenin', because we was all tryin' to see where they was, to stay out of their way. Pretty near everybody here was there, even old Monroe – he's the butler – who wouldn't dance a jig if you was to pay him twenty dollars to do it. When Cindy an' I – Cindy's my wife – got back at God-knows-when, the whole house was empty, 'ceptin' for Jerry. An' Jerry was laid out on the parlor floor with a bottle of Michie Melchior's brandy. I guess the thought of all that hard cider he was missin' was too much for his fortitude.'

He shaped the dough neatly into the Dutch oven, fetched and unwrapped the towel-shrouded corpses of a chicken and a duck from the end of the worktable.

'Includin' Ma'am Aubin . . .' January lowered his voice as he handed over the covered dish of sauteed onions, garlic, peppers. 'So I heard.'

Andy sighed, and shook his head. 'Yeah,' he agreed, and wiped his hands. 'Cindy an' I, we came back late. The moon was just above the trees over the river, so it wasn't but a few hours 'til dawn. We came back through the cane, in case Michie Pernet had got back early – though *that* wasn't likely, given that woman he's sparkin'. An' we seen her – Ma'am Aubin, I mean – slip out of the cane herself, in that long cloak of hers, an' run across the open ground an' up the gallery steps to her room. Michie Damien locks her in at night,' he added quietly. 'Sometimes we'll hear her, sort of wailin', for hours.'

It had begun to rain, with the tropical swiftness of the summer afternoons: a few patters, a minute or two of fleeting, warm squalls, then gray sheets, pounding down on the abat-vent, on the dark cane that crowded so close around the house, on the shingles of the quarters' roofs and the glossy leaves of the slaves' provision grounds. Droplets hissed down the chimney as Andy carried the Dutch oven to the hearth, and January followed, and scooped aside the heaped coals so that the cook could set the thick iron pan among them. Both men shoveled the coals onto its lid, streaming with sweat, then retreated to the worktable outside the doors again, where a bob-tailed kitchen cat was already licking the plate.

'But she can get out.' Andy didn't even glance towards the house as he poured them both more lemonade and moved the cat. He knew Michie Melchior wouldn't be watching. 'She sleepwalks. I think she has a key hid someplace in her room, though Michie Damien's searched the place a dozen times since he come back this summer.'

He picked up the cat again as it leaped back onto the table, cradled it in his arms. 'I've caught her myself, walkin' in the full moon along the field path back toward the ciprière – an' it's usually full moon, when she walks. I went an' got Cindy – 'cause I know you don't wake a sleepwalker – an' we sort of steered her back to her room, carefully like. She told us all the way about this reception she gave for the ambassador of the Shah of Persia, an' what she'd had to have cooked for him, an' what she'd worn . . . Betsy, who maids for her when she's not helpin' here in the kitchen, said later Ma'am Olivia asked her, how come she had to clean her shoes again next mornin', when she'd done it only the day before.'

Shaw listened with interest to January's account of this conversation, when the rain thinned away enough to permit them to head back toward town. Monroe the butler had come to the kitchen for a pitcher and a glass of lemonade, and had carried them back towards the house beneath an umbrella, his entire body stiffly announcing, I am only doing my duty but you wouldn't catch *me* inviting such a person to linger . . .

And for nearly an hour January, sitting under the kitchen abat-vent while Andy cleaned greens and made up a vinegar sauce, had observed Shaw, sitting in lonely white state on the back gallery drinking his lemonade, ignored by all, until the rain let up. There were things, January was well aware, that white men just didn't do, and going over even to his own kitchen to gossip with the slaves – much less to another man's, and a planter's at that – was one of them.

'Not like to do us much good,' remarked the Kaintuck, when they stopped – the moment the rain had definitely ceased – where a rough bench had been constructed at the head of a path that led down to a woodlot, opposite a dilapidated landing. January pulled his memorandum book from his pocket, and swiftly jotted everything he'd been keeping in his own mind of what Andy had said, about who saw whom where and when Saturday night. Shaw rested a boot on the side of the bench and looked down over his shoulder, chewing the tobacco he'd taken from his pocket before they were even off Aubin land. 'Like when an' where young Clay was seen in the crowd at Duralde, an' your sayin' as how you saw Ma'am Aubin snoopin'. Ain't a judge in the state that'd even let it into court.'

'No.' January made a final notation, closed his eyes for a moment, casting his mind back. *Have I forgotten something? Of course I have . . .*

'But it can save us time later. And maybe lead us somewhere.'

'Like to your friend with the rifle, whoever he is?'

Far off, the cathedral clock struck three, the sound queerly muffled in the waterlogged air. Time enough, January calculated, to get home, change clothes, and take the steam train out to Milneburgh to see what his mother and Dominique had to say about the Aubin family finances and how crazy madame might actually be, full moon or otherwise. *And with luck*, he thought, *maybe I can actually spend an evening with my own wife and my own sons, and not have to play 'Little Pigs' for the two thousand seven hundred and fiftieth time this week. Or listen once again to how many Indians General Harrison killed . . .*

'You seein' Sefton this evenin'?' asked Shaw.

January nodded. 'He's playing at the Turkey Buzzard. I think that's where he's sleeping these days. Jefferson Butler's hosting Coal-Oil Billy and some of the less refined Democrats in town there to organize an ambuscade to rescue President Van Buren's

effigy, when the Giant Rawhide Ball comes *rollin'* into town
Friday—'

'Yeah.' Shaw sighed wearily. 'We heard all about that. Captains
of all three municipalities – *an'* Mayor Freret – been at Tom
Spanish to leave that fool thing back in Donaldsonville. We don't
need nobody gettin' theirself killed over a damn scarecrow.
But they won't hear it. It's their right as Americans to hang the
president in effigy an' their forefathers didn't freeze barefoot at
Valley Forge to have a bunch of politicians tellin' 'em what they
can an' can't do.'

He took from his pocket the two sheets of paper he'd stolen from
Aubin's desk. 'These won't prove nuthin' neither,' he said. 'Least
we can get an idea if'fn we's lookin' in the right direction.'

'Michie Damien say anything interesting?'

Shaw stood silent a moment, chewing. His gargoyle face bore
no particular expression, but sadness, and pity, darkened his eyes.
'Only as how he'd stood between his young cousin an' a slick
American politician like any good Frenchman would,' he said at
last. 'Said he'd heard his young cousin was like to tell some lie
to her daddy an' go with deaf old Aunt Francie just to watch the
fireworks, an' off he went to protect her, knowin' just how much
use Aunt Francie would be in the circumstances; an' that it was
none of my damn business why he'd dismissed his lady friend an'
no gentleman would even ask that kind of question anyways.'

'Did you expect anything different?'

'With Brother Melchior layin' there watchin' him like a
snake? No.'

He sighed. 'He looked bad,' he added. 'He'd been drinkin'
heavy. Weepin', too, looked like. His brother told him to straighten
up an' be a man.' In his voice January heard a trace of what was
almost embarrassment, to see another man so broken before him.
'They both say they's gonna report me to Captain Tremouille for
bein' a dishonorable American, but—'

His head snapped sharply around. January had heard the scrunch
of footsteps on the shell road below the levee, but had thought
nothing of it, save that people were out and about again after the rain.
But the footfalls had changed, and looking down the grassy slope
January saw a woman climbing the short distance to where they sat.

A woman wearing the old-fashioned, billowing, hooded cloak
he'd seen in the darkness beyond the log cabin, Saturday night.

And at her wedding in November.

Octagonal spectacles flashed, thick as the bottoms of wine bottles. 'M'sieu,' she panted, as she came up to the bench. 'M'sieu . . . Shaw?'

'Ma'am.' Shaw took off his hat and bowed like a damaged limberjack.

'Please.' She looked aside, as if fearing to meet the eyes of either man. 'I know it's terribly forward of me' – she thrust a visiting card at Shaw, engraved with rigid correctness: *Madame Aubin, Aurore Plantation, Orleans Parish, Louisiana* – 'I know we have not been introduced—'

'I knows who you are, ma'am.' He bowed again, and moved to help her to the seat on the bench that January had instantly vacated the moment he'd seen her climbing up.

She shook her head in quick denial. 'I must get back soon.'

Closer to, in daylight, and out of a crowd, she looked more relaxed, less likely to go off into hysterical laughter or tears. She wore spectacles, he guessed, only because she knew she'd need to recognize them, as she'd worn them Saturday night. By the way she squinted he also guessed they were old and no longer completely effective. Her frock was slightly too elaborate for day wear, and slightly too girlish for her awkward height, flat bosom, and wide shoulders. January suspected it was one her stepmother had had made for her when she'd married, an advertisement for the Trepagier wealth and influence rather than a garment made to flatter an un-pretty old maid.

'But I wanted to-to apologize for my-my husband.' She brought the word out awkwardly, as if not quite sure she should use it of him. 'He is . . . as you saw, he is not really himself . . .'

Gently, Shaw asked, 'Did he love her?'

For a moment the huge eyes touched his, then dodged away again. 'Yes.' The small mouth pursed a little tighter. 'For a long time,' she added with a sigh. 'Passionately. They were cousins – and childhood sweethearts. When they quarreled, and she went to France, he truly thought it was over between them. And . . . You saw him.' Again her glance dodged from one to the other, then fled. 'Dam is . . . an ardent soul. He thinks with his heart. We knew each other as children, he and I. And he had always been a good friend to me.'

Her hands – small for her height, square-fingered and nervous

– pleated at the edge of her cloak. 'My . . . my father had just re-married then. My stepmother . . . She's a very kind, worthy person . . .'

This was not what January had heard about the second Madame Trepagier from Andy – 'snake-faced witch' was the nicest thing he'd had to say about her that afternoon – but since he could see Shaw didn't believe Olivia Aubin's polite excuse either he said nothing.

'But it's hard, you know, when a new stepmother comes into a household. And Damien asked me to marry him, to give me some-place else to . . . to go. I'd just come back from . . . from France. He said . . .' Blotches of unsightly red flared on her cheeks. 'It was never going to be anything but a nominal union. That I need have no fear. And of course my father, and my brother, were pleased. His brother too, because I knew about – well – of course my father is very wealthy. And I knew Damien had a . . . that there was a woman. He'd become furious with anyone who mentioned her. But it was meant in kindness – our marriage, I mean – and to help me. Please believe that.'

'I do believe it, ma'am.'

'Dam would never – not *ever* – have harmed anyone . . .'

'You think he loved his mistress?'

It was not a word that even a man of her own class – her own family – would have said to a planter's daughter, and January guessed that any of Olivia Aubin's cousins would have called Shaw out for speaking it in her presence. But though the crimson deep-ened in her cheeks she replied in a steady voice, 'I think he did, yes. He did when he married me. And I was glad, because . . .' She looked up into Shaw's face again. 'My husband needs someone he can love. Love passionately, I mean. *Be* in love *with*.' The tiniest ghost of a smile touched those tight-pinched lips. 'I'm not the best candidate for that.'

'Don't mean you can't be a good friend to him.'

'I try to be. He needs a friend. I know that everybody thinks I'm crazy. I'm not, really, you know. I walk sometimes in my sleep, and say and do things that I don't remember afterwards, but doesn't everybody? And I know that nobody believes that spirits really do talk to me . . .' She shook her head quickly. 'There are a lot of things I can't explain. Not to Damien, not to anyone. Like the fires, and – and why I hide. Why I cry. I cry a lot. It isn't because I'm sad. Or crazy.'

She managed another smile, though her gaze remained on the tops of the ship masts beyond the levee. 'I do try not to be the way I am. People just don't *understand*. Sometimes it's-it's as if I'm sitting in a chair in a little back room, watching me say and do things that . . . Sometimes I remember later. Sometimes I don't. Sometimes I dream about doing things that I don't know whether I did them or not. And the voices don't always tell me the truth. Damien – my husband,' she corrected herself quickly. 'He said he'd take care of me. And I think he meant to,' she went on. 'Even when he . . . when he realized that Mademoiselle Maginot still loved him, and he her.'

'Did she love him?'

'Oh, yes.' She looked at him at that, matter-of-fact as a child. 'She was a terrible little flirt, but she told me once – this summer, just before Damien came back from Washington – that he was the only man she'd ever loved. And I understand that. Damien is so handsome, and so strong . . .'

She sighed, and for a moment the thing she hadn't said – her own adoration – shone in her eyes. 'She said when they were in love before, he was just like an anchor chain, holding her steady when she'd have silly ideas. And I . . .' She stopped her next words, shook her head in quick denial. 'She said how she'd depended on his love. That she'd always wanted it all for herself. And I understand that. Anyone would. Which is why I don't think he'd really have been able to take care of me, after he married her. There simply wouldn't have been enough money. Not without my father's support, and his brother's.'

'Would you have let him go, ma'am? Signed whatever papers needed be signed?'

'I don't . . .' She looked away again. 'The voices told me I shouldn't.' Gulls circled, crying, through the clearing sky, and her eyes followed them, wistful and envious. 'But he was so unhappy, once he knew that it *could* have come true, for him and Mademoiselle Maginot. That they *could* have been happy. It's all he wanted,' she finished. 'To be free. To be happy.'

And she sighed again, a tiny sigh. 'Why can't they let people just do that?'

She pulled the hood of her cape over her head – despite the stifling heat of the afternoon – and darted down the slope of the levee again in a great billow of dark wool, disappearing into the old woodlot and, January guessed, beyond it into the cane. She'd have followed the field paths to intercept Shaw, he found himself thinking, away from Aurore until she'd been out of sight of her brother-in-law's overseer or work gangs, probably leaving long before the rain had ceased. Paths she could as easily have followed by moonlight, from Aurore to Duralde, Saturday night.

The clouds had broken. Afternoon sunlight streamed hot over the land.

It was time, thought January, to return to town, if he was going to get out to Milneburgh. He wanted to see Catherine at the jail, too.

'You think she was tellin' the truth?' Shaw glanced sidelong at him.

'I do, yes.'

'Me, too.' Shaw spit into the long grass. 'You notice anythin' funny 'bout Aubin's room, Maestro?'

January thought for a moment. 'I was by the door,' he said at last. 'And I couldn't look around much. I thought Monroe must have tidied the place up before they let anyone in, which is what you'd expect, from a man like Aubin. What are you thinking of?'

'Somethin' shoulda been there an' wasn't.' He chewed ruminatively for a time, gray eyes sweeping the flat horizon: river, batture, the low green snake of the levee and then the land flattening off away from the road, back to the green wall of the cane where the black speck of a sable cloak, a sable hood, could still be glimpsed. And beyond that, the darker wall of the ciprière. Downstream, faded splodges of color marked the second-gang men whose job it usually was to clear weeds or plant new cane while the main-gang men chopped wood in the swamp for the *roulaison*, the sugar rolling and grinding, come Christmas.

In his childhood, January remembered there had been whole villages of escaped Africans, living in the ciprière, before the slow expansion of the faubourgs, the spreading harvesting of wood. Was Akinto sheltering in some of those ruined huts? *I have to find Ti-Jon tomorrow. And talk to Bredon* – the man who acted as January's contact in the Underground Railroad – *about getting him north once we* do *find him, once we* can *talk to him . . .*

'You head on out to the lake, Maestro,' said Shaw after a time. 'I'm right curious as to what your mama an' Ma'am Dominique

got to say 'bout all these people. There's somethin' else down
here I want to have a look at.'

'Anything I can help with?'

Shaw shook his head. 'Findin' out where everybody's money
is, an' why Ma'am Aubin got packed off to France like she did.
Seven years sounds like a long time to me. Little Miss Maginot
didn't get sent for but one an' a few months.'

'Seven years is a long time,' returned January. 'It means the
family concluded they couldn't marry her off. I'm surprised she
didn't stay there.'

And in his mind he heard the clacking voices at the Democrat
Club reception: *Attacked some poor French girl with a pair of
scissors . . .*

'An' I'd purely like to know if'fn there's somebody in the
Trepagier family who left town sudden-like Sunday. Your mama'd
be the one to know about that. You come find me tomorrow at the
Cabildo an' we'll see what-all there is to be seen.'

FIFTEEN

The Pontchartrain Steam Railroad ran from the levee, first
through the Faubourg Marigny and then out past the
forlornly marked streets of prospective faubourgs to come
– cypress, oaks, crotch-high weeds and occasional piles of hopeful
bricks – to the shores of Lake Pontchartrain. Wind breathed across
the lake, inconveniencing if not eliminating mosquitoes, and even
in the wet heat of mid-afternoon the air felt freer and more open
than it did in town. Businessmen installed their families in cottages
and fishing camps, and took the steam train – or the horse-cars
that shared the track – to be with them at night . . . or every other
night. Or Saturdays and Sundays, depending on whether their
plaçées had lakeside cottages, too, or lived in town . . .

The grandly-named Washington Hotel was in fact a comfortable
boarding house that catered to plaçées and to those retired plaçées
– like January's mother, the beautiful Livia Levesque – who had
invested their money in town property, slaves, cotton presses and
shipping companies. Like the still-more-elegant establishments for

the whites, it boasted a terrace that overlooked the lake itself, cooled by the lake's damp breezes. In the afternoons, under green-striped awnings, the terrace was one of the most comfortable places in Milneburgh, and it was here that January found his mother, sipping lemonade with his sister Dominique – fresh as a pink-edged daisy in crisp white lawn – in company with two of Bernadette Metoyer's sisters, both of whom (so rumor went), like Bernadette herself, were former or current mistresses of Hubert Granville.

'Now, P'tit!' Minou reached across to clasp his hand once he had assured them that Zandrine seemed to be improving. 'Not a *word* will you get from *any* of us until you give us the *entire* account of what happened at Duralde Saturday night! I've heard *such* stories . . .'

'None of them true, Minou.' January bent to kiss her crème-café cheek.

'Have you been to see poor Catherine?' asked Virginie Metoyer, the tallest, slenderest sister, sensually pretty even at the age of fifty. 'I've heard *someone* arranged for her to have a private cell . . .'

January could only marvel at the speed with which things became known among the demi-monde.

Kindly Babette leaned forward in her chair. 'Is it true Zandrine tried to kill herself, Ben, for love of Michie Damien? I can under-stand her doing so . . .' She pressed plump, bejeweled hands to her plump, bejeweled bosom. '*Such* a handsome man! *So* dashing, and so in love with her—'

'So in love with Marie-Joyeuse Maginot,' retorted Virginie.

'Well, that's the issue, isn't it?' Livia Levesque, like a gorgeous dragonfly in her frock of blue-bronze silk, plied her fan. 'Was he sufficiently in love with Marie-Joyeuse Maginot to put aside that grass-biting idiot his brother tricked him into marrying? Or suffi-ciently in love that he'd rather see the girl dead than in another man's arms? Specifically,' she added, with a lift of her brows, 'James Clay's?'

'I gather he wasn't tricked, Maman,' contradicted January.

'Nonsense, Benjamin, of course he was.'

'And I'll be able to answer your questions better' – January took the chair to which Minou gestured invitingly – 'once I get a clearer idea of where the money is.'

Babette pouted protestingly at this preference for finance over romance, but the older women laughed, and Virginie tapped him on the arm with her fan. 'You are a cynic, Benjamin!'

'Where the money *isn't*' – January's mother snapped her own fan shut – 'is *chez* Maginot . . . Which I believe to be the answer to a lot of questions.'

After which the four women – three, actually, since Babette limited her contribution to tongue-cluckings and an occasional, 'Oh, the poor dear!' – proceeded to dissect the finances of the Trepagier, Maginot, Aubin, and LaFrennière families down to the last *sou* and sugarloaf.

January learned little that he didn't already know or suspect, and he wasn't surprised to have it confirmed that a great deal of the Trepagier money and political influence came from Charles-Louis's partnership with one of the largest slave traders in the Mississippi Valley. The fluid credit connected with the trade would give the man far more leverage in Washington than the mere ownership of land. *No wonder Brother Melchior was pleased with the marriage, however it was first arranged.* 'Trepagier's the one who backed that bill in the legislature – was it last year? – to outlaw renting rooms to bondsmen or allowing them to "sleep out",' supplied Virginie, and poked delicately at the raspberry ice that a hotel servant brought them.

From the nearby Hotel Pontchartrain, the strains of a piano, out of tune in the damp, drifted down the lakefront.

'And hired a couple of Kaintucks – like that friend of yours, Benjamin – to murder that fellow – what was his name? The abolitionist preacher who was killed back in February—'

'Hoff?' January had read the letter the man had written to the New Orleans *True American* about the recent efforts to forbid free men of color to enter Louisiana at all. Judas Bredon – of the Underground Railroad – had told him that Hoff had been found shot dead in an alley outside a saloon, despite the fact that the man didn't drink. 'I'd think Trepagier would have more sense than to put himself in the hands of a confederate.'

'Maybe he shot the man himself.' His mother shrugged. 'Or got that nasty stripe-eyed son of his to do it. I know he shot a Protestant preacher – one of those uptown freedmen' – she sneered as if she herself had not been born a slave, and owed her own freedom to a white man's largesse – 'who came around on his land one night, trying to get his cane hands to run off. Not that the man didn't deserve it. I don't know why these people never think that an overseer or a gang boss will tell the master when they see someone snooping. It's their job to do so, after all. I understand Trepagier and Aubin plan to run Damien for State Senator next year, and good luck to Trepagier if he thinks that daughter of his is going to make any kind of an impression as a political hostess.'

'At least she won't make a fuss about being left back on Aurore,' pointed out Virginie. 'Which you can be sure Marie-Joyeuse would. And you can imagine what a swathe *she'd* cut through Washington society . . .'

'Oh, they'd never have let Damien annul his marriage!' protested Babette.

'Damien was an imbecile to marry Olivia in the first place,' returned his mother crisply. 'He should never have put himself in that position.'

'I think it was a great act of kindness!'

'If you believe that story. I daresay Melchior pushed him into it. Damien's never had an idea of his own in his life.'

'It was a great act of stupidity.' Virginie toyed with the melting remains of her raspberry ice. 'I believe it. It's the kind of thing he's always done, on the spur of the moment, without thinking. He was like that from a child, you know. As for Olivia Trepagier, she was sent back from that convent in France last year because she tried to kill another boarder there with a pair of scissors.'

'Now,' cried Dominique reprovingly, 'that isn't fair! Phemie Miragouin says that was because the girl said she was possessed by the Devil.'

'Dearest, *please!*' The Widow Levesque rolled her beautiful eyes. 'I'm sure that's how Olivia tells the story. And of course Brother Melchior was absolutely beside himself, torn between the prospect of Trepagier support and terror at what Olivia was likely to do in public.'

'And she'll say anything, I hear!' Virginie tittered. 'Her father warned Melchior not to let the woman have her own maid, because when she was thirteen or fourteen she started telling her maid about how she was secretly engaged to an Indian sachem who'd visit her by coming through the wall of her bedroom, or how her brother could transform himself into a deer.'

'And *I* heard she told Marie-Solange Forstall – her second cousin, you know, on the other side of the family – that she saw her father shoot their butler, chop him up into pieces, and throw the pieces in the bayou,' reported Babette, round-eyed. 'And then when they brought the poor man in to see her, to prove he was really alive, she refused to believe that it was really him. She said they'd gone and gotten his twin brother from a dealer in Natchez.'

'Was she like that from a child?' asked January, and all four women nodded.

So much for the possibility that she might at some point have learned to use firearms . . . And how much of that tale of not being jealous of Mamzelle Maginot was true?

More from curiosity than anything else, he asked, 'If you had to choose someone, Maman, who would you pick, to have murdered Mademoiselle Maginot?'

'Melchior Aubin.'

'Laid up with a bullet-hole in his hip.'

'Bother.' She spoke as if he'd done it on purpose to trip her up. 'Charles-Louis Trepagier, then. Or that nasty son of his. And Melchior was an imbecile to get into a duel over *Napoleon*, of all people . . .'

'And just what was wrong with Napoleon?' demanded Virginie hotly. 'If it weren't for Napoleon . . .'

'Philippe Cournand,' offered Minou, with tactful promptness. 'Marie-Noel Pellicot tells me he was crazy in love with the girl, and didn't know who to be more jealous of: his brother Arnaud, who was also in love with her, or Mademoiselle Maginot herself, because Arnaud loved her more than he loved his brother. They'd always been close, you understand, Philippe and Arnaud. Arnaud tried to commit suicide over her – it's the real reason their father sent him to Cuba. And – what was it? Three weeks ago? Four weeks ago? – Philippe learned that Mademoiselle was trading love letters with Arnaud.'

January recalled the elder Cournand's face, ashen with grief and guilt, from the graveside. *Was that only this morning?* And Marie-Joyeuse's coquettish habit of sending one suitor off on an errand while she disappeared with another . . .

'According to Marie-Noel,' his sister went on, 'she'd promised to marry him when he got back.'

'That girl . . .' Livia Levesque made a gesture of exasperation, though whether the 'girl' referred to was Marie-Joyeuse or Marie-Noel Pellicot, January was unable to determine. Then his mother lifted her hand as Bernadette Metoyer, queenly in bronze-striped dimity, appeared in the hotel's doorway.

January rose at once to give her his chair; Minou motioned to a servant to bring him another, and to fetch more lemonade.

'I stopped at Zandrine's just now – oh, good, Benjamin's told you . . . *much* better. But someone at the shop' – to judge by her clothing she had spent the morning charming her customers at the chocolate shop – 'was saying today as how it was *Senator Clay* from Washington, that killed the Maginot girl, of all people! That he shot her to keep there from being a *scandal* between her and his son, who's engaged to someone else—'

'Damien Aubin is *married* to someone else,' retorted Virginie. 'And that doesn't seem to have stopped *him.*'

'Ginny!' protested the soft-hearted Babette. 'Damien was *frantic* with love for her!'

'Why else do you think people shoot people?' Livia regarded the girl with serpentine amusement. 'The man was jealous as a Turk. You all remember how he carried on when Zandrine Motet talked too long to Augustus Mayerling at the Orleans Ballroom last fall.'

'And he actually *called out* Yves Valcour,' added Minou. 'He got it into his head that Marie-Joyeuse was slipping away with him for lemonade at Madame Rost's ball back in July. According to Phemie Miragouin – well, according to her maid, anyway, who's Musette's cousin . . . my maid Musette – Damien actually *struck* Marie-Joyeuse, in the library at Destrehan, and called Yves out when Yves told him he was a scoundrel for doing so.'

Virginie sniffed. 'He'd have shot the girl quick enough if he found out she'd only been making up to him because she thought he'd get rich in Washington.'

Babette gave a dove-like squeak at this callous reading of the relationship.

'And Mr Clay's son outdoes a private secretary in the State Department any day of the week,' concluded Livia smugly. Feathers bobbed in five tignons as the women – even Babette – all nodded again. 'Particularly if Clay clears all the Democrats out of there when he takes over that department after the election.'

For a woman who would sooner have belched at the dinner

table than let anyone suspect her of reading a newspaper, reflected January, his mother was awfully well-informed. 'Senator Clay said Thursday night that if he was offered the position he'd turn it down.'

'And you believed him?' His mother raised elegant brows. 'Benjamin, I'm surprised at you. He's a politician. He'll say anything, that will get him votes.'

'Or in his case,' added Bernadette – who also pretended that she would never do such an unladylike thing as touch a journal – 'that will get votes for the man he's going to use as his puppet, to run the country for the next four years.'

'You notice' – Livia fixed her African-dark gaze on her son – 'that your Senator Clay has kept very quiet about that silly Colonization Society of his, unless he's actually talking to some American who thinks all the librés are trying to stir up slave rebellion, and should all be thrown out of the country. *Then* he'll open up.'

January opened his mouth to ask her where and under what circumstances she'd ever heard Henry Clay talk about anything, and then closed it. He only said, wearily, 'He isn't *my* Senator Clay.'

Nor will he ever be . . .

'In any case . . .' His mother plied her fan again, and glanced calculatingly across the terrace at a small party of well-dressed women – the former plaçée Agnes Pellicot and her daughters – who had just emerged from the hotel's door. 'General Harrison is an old man. Sixty-eight. He'll be in his seventies by the time his term is up, if he wins. And he's promised to serve only one term. And who's this Tyler who's running with him? A nobody. After four years as Secretary of State, of course Clay's going to run for president. And for that he's going to need money – and at least *one* son who hasn't caused a family scandal.'

Riding back to town on the horse-drawn railcar – there wouldn't be a steam train on the line for another hour – January turned what he had learned over in his mind, without coming to any real conclusion. It hadn't occurred to him that Olivia Aubin had lied to Shaw earlier that afternoon. Possibly, he reflected, because she believed her story herself . . .

And it might even be true.

And the tale Dominique (or Dominique's maid) had gotten from

Euphémie Miragouin's maid might well be a load of sour apples. *Olympe would know how reliable the woman is* . . .

He knew too well the lunatic illusions that made perfect sense to a man in the throes of jealousy. 'I had rather be a toad,' Othello had cried, 'and live upon the vapor of a dungeon, than keep a corner in the thing I love/ for another user . . .'

So where does that leave me? And what does the man with the rifle know? The man who was waiting for . . . someone . . . outside Granville's Monday night? The man who followed Marie-Joyeuse's coffin to her tomb, and took good care not to be seen?

SIXTEEN

He had come to no conclusion by the time he reached home. 'Rose went to Mama's,' Zizi-Marie informed him, as he came out onto the back gallery, having passed through the house and found Germaine and Cosette hard at work on their Latin in the parlor, but no sign of his bride. He was bound for the workshop above the laundry when his niece emerged from the kitchen, wiping flour from her hands. 'Cochon was here half an hour ago, saying as how Michie Griff came down sick – sick bad,' she added, her smooth young face contracting with concern.

Dammit . . . Virgin Mary, Mother of God, January prayed, *not yellow fever* . . .

Last week's outbreak still worried him, a dark undercurrent below the 'cancan and artillery' (as Zizi-Marie had put it) of rallies and musicales and missing runaways and giant balls of rawhide . . .

When it had appeared that he wouldn't – for a miracle! – be playing for either the Whigs or the Democrats this evening (*and how did* that *happen?*) he had gritted his teeth and sent a note to Dr Kerr, asking, could he be of help? To his everlasting gratitude he had received one back: No new cases yesterday, nor the day before. Lord bless you for asking, Ben.

While in the cathedral on Sunday, he had offered a rosary and burned a candle to the Virgin, in thanks . . . and another one, for Akinto, wherever he might be.

Now he turned back into the house, dashed tepid water on his face in the pantry and caught up his satchel. *Holy Mother of God please don't let it be an epidemic coming on after all . . .*

The words circled through his mind and his heart as he strode along the Rue Esplanade in the direction of the 'back of town'.

There was always fever in the summer, he reminded himself. Passing along the dirt streets of the Faubourg Tremé, he remembered them during the awful summers of 1833 and 1834. There hadn't been a house, it seemed – among those rickety shacks scattered between vacant lots still rank with swamp-laurel and elephant-ear – free of the silent miasma of fear.

Today children played in the smelly ditches, screaming when crayfish bit their bare toes. Between the houses, cypresses and palmettos still stood, ghosts of a silent past. The voices of women called from kitchens that were barely sheds, 'Bobby, you fetch me that kindlin' axe!' 'Corrie, get out here this minute, I need you . . .' The smell of cooking hung in the air.

He'd managed to miss the biggest epidemic, the year after he'd sailed for France. But the fever returned roughly every other year thereafter, and with each recurrence, the deaths increased.

A couple of young men wearing tin slave badges waved to him from across the street – possibly men owned by M'sieu Dessalines (*I have* got *to find Ti-Jon tomorrow . . .!*), possibly by his own mother, or Bernadette Metoyer. The young men were daubed with swamp-mud and running with sweat, but looked cheerful: the logging companies didn't generally rent slaves to do the really bad cutting in the swamps, standing crotch-deep in water to fell the big cypresses . . . Rentals were too expensive for work that dangerous. Cheaper to hire Irish from along Tchoupitoulas Street. Nobody would come around asking for reparation if *they* died.

Sally DeChaine owned a sprawling house on the Bayou Road which had started out small: as she'd taken in first one slave boarder, then another, she'd negotiated for rent in labor to add rooms, to build a bigger kitchen, to erect a long dining parlor, which had let her take in more boarders for hard money. As her own sons got old enough to lend a hand, she'd turned them into cooks and floor-swabbers and laundrymen, until now she had a thriving, if inelegant, boarding house for slaves 'sleeping-out' and two or three free laborers. Stout and blowzily pretty in

green-and-orange calico, she greeted January at the door with
a worried expression.

'I got him in the back,' she said. 'He was took bad last night
– shittin', pukin', shakin' all over like a hound-dog shittin'
peach-pits.'

'Blood in his puke?' January followed her around to the rear
wing of the house. Past a straggle of chicken coops, a rough outside
stair led up to a door on the second floor. There was another door
under the stair, and to this ground-floor room she led him; yet
another 'born an' dyin' room', usually, he guessed, used as a
storeroom. By the watermark on the walls, it flooded pretty
regularly.

'Not so far.'

'Face red?' Griff was sufficiently fair-skinned that the
characteristic brownish flush of yellow fever would show.

'Some. Nuthin' bad.'

He knew this woman had seen 'bad' and trusted her
judgement.

Hannibal rose from the goods' box he'd been sitting on when
they entered. A narrow cot beside him, barely a pallet, was the
only other furniture in the room. The fiddler's sleeves were rolled
to his armpits and a basin of water, ringed by a lake of drips, stood
on the floor beside his boots. He'd been sponging down Griff's
bare chest.

Griff turned his head as January's bulk darkened the door, and
managed a hazy smile. 'Mr J . . .' He had two quilts over him
and trembled like a man dying in a blizzard.

Hannibal yielded his place and stepped back. 'I think his fever's
down some.'

Griff whispered, 'Quinine,' and groped about towards the
spouted cup that rested on the floor by the basin. His hand was
so unsteady he couldn't have lifted it if he'd tried.

Hannibal shook his head, and moved the cup aside. 'I've already
given him two doses, dilute in water.' The fiddler picked up the
cup and measured three-quarters of an inch against its side with
his thumb. 'I have no idea how strong the stuff is. It smells like
the wrath of God. My Uncle Diogenes puts away quarts of it in
India but then, he puts away quarts of everything he can get his
hands on, from gin to Chinese *baijiu*, with no appreciable effects.'

January sniffed the nose of the bottle, remembered the bitter pong that had lingered in Zandrine's rooms. He took a seat on the goods' box. 'Malaria?'

'Fever.' Griff's slender, ivory hands made a fluttering gesture around his face. 'Doctor in Charleston gave me quinine. It's been years since it's come on this bad.'

Gently, January turned back the younger man's eyelids. The white of his eyes was clear. Only the lightest flush stained the creamy olive skin of his cheeks and chest. 'You've had this before?'

'I was a child.'

'You were a lucky child,' January said grimly.

'My mama had it.' Griff turned his head fitfully aside. 'My brother died of it. Raynard, his name was. Leave those,' he added, as one of Sally's teenaged sons came in, carrying Griff's folded-up shirts and waistcoats. 'I'll be fine tomorrow. Doctor said it was bad air in the swamps,' he added, to January, as the boy put the clothes – and the expensive, stylish boots he had in his other hand – on the floor by the door.

January poured water into the cup, and added two fingers of quinine. 'It's been years,' insisted Griff again, and again his fingers picked at the hem of the blanket. 'I just need rest. It passes off.'

Voices in the yard. January recognized Cochon's plummy baritone, and the sweet alto of Jacques Bichet's wife Jane. Quickly he scrambled in his pockets, brought out the yellow foolscap Shaw had handed him and tore it in half, keeping the portion with 'Margaret Blennerhassett' written on it and using the other to note the date, and the approximate times and amounts of quinine. 'You're playing at the Turkey Buzzard tonight, aren't you, Hannibal?'

'Old Hunks pays in actual money,' apologized the fiddler. 'Not that any of the gentlemen present will be listening to music. Jeff Butler is hosting a *symposion* on the subject of avenging the insult to President Van Buren by an assault on the parade Friday, though what they could possibly do to a six-foot ball of rawhide escapes me. Since about five militia companies are being called up to defend the cortege I suspect in the event, it will scarcely matter whether our clarionettist' – he gripped Griff's arm comfortingly – 'is on his feet by Friday or not, given how long the parade will be brought to a standstill in the middle of Nyades Street.'

'I'll be there,' insisted Griff again, as Cochon's comfortable width filled the door.

"Course you will.' The second fiddler looked around for another goods' box – there wasn't one – and the gawky shape of Jane Bichet slipped in around him, a towel-covered basket in her hands. Cochon took this from her and bent over the shivering young man in the bed, while January took Jane aside and explained his notes. No more than two more doses tonight, half an inch, dilute with water. 'If his chest starts to hurt, or he starts to itch, no more. I'm pretty sure it's malaria, not yellow fever.'

He saw her features relax. Like January, Jane Bichet had lived through bad fever summers in New Orleans. The pharmacies down-town would fill the big glass display retorts in their windows with red liquid, to warn visitors in the streets not to linger in the city.

'That's what we were mostly worried about,' said Jane softly. 'Sometimes it's hard to tell, an' Cochon wanted to make sure. I told him it looked like malaria to me. Cochon an' me' – she nodded to the fat man, daintily shedding his immense white linen jacket and rolling up his sleeves – 'we'll look after him 'til midnight. Jacques an' Uncle, they'll be along then. You make sure Hannibal gets fed, 'fore he has to go play in that pest hole bear pit tonight?'

'I'll make sure.' Even happily married women like Jane had a tenderness for the fiddler.

Jane tiptoed to kiss his cheek. 'You're a good man, Mr J.'

And that, January reflected, as he and Hannibal made their way down the Bayou Road again to Rue Esplanade, sufficiently answered a question that had returned to his mind, daily since he had gotten off the boat from France eight years ago. Many times a day lately, as he'd played interminable Vote For Harrison ditties and listened to blow-hard political speeches for an election he was forbidden to take part in . . .

Why the hell did I come back here? Maybe Henry Clay and the Colonizers are right. It was clear to him – clearer every year – that aside from a few men like Lieutenant Shaw, Hannibal, and Judas Bredon of the Underground Railroad, most white men, both in the North and in the South, didn't actually want free people of color in America at all. Slaves were fine – preferably ones who didn't rise up and kill their owners over being beaten and having their daughters raped. Free men of color just . . . didn't belong.

He could see it in so many faces: *Why don't you just go away, so we won't have to worry about all this?*

Clay at least – as a slaveowner himself – seemed to recognize the fact that there *was* a problem, and that the problem was going to get worse. He at least understood that slavery could not exist without arousing burning anger in its victims. It was the anger that the whites had feared from the start.

When he'd left for Paris in 1817, he had had no intention of ever coming back.

This, he realized, was why he had come back. When Ayasha had died, and the world had been to him only darkness . . . *This* was why he'd returned. This, and Olympe's garden that morning, and the soft voices of Rose and the girls on the gallery of an evening.

Because of the people he cared about.

The people who cared about one another. Catherine, Minou, Bernadette, Cochon, Ti-Jon . . . Who looked after one another – even Griff, a stranger newly come into their midst, but accepted as a brother.

Without this community of family and friends, with Ayasha gone he knew he would have been dead indeed.

Rose was sitting on one of the rough willow chairs on the gallery, a pot-bellied, pink-faced gentleman in black beside her, his few remaining whisps of silvery hair combed down over his shoulders. When Hannibal and January crossed Rue Burgundy, Rose turned her head as if she'd heard someone speak her name, and the old gentleman got to his feet. January recognized Francois Motet.

'Ben!' The old man hurried to meet him as he sprang up the gallery steps, clasped his hand. 'Thank you, thank you beyond what I can say!'

January so clearly remembered hating this man and could only shake his head at his younger self. *And that's what Damien Aubin felt . . .*

'I was telling Madame Janvier how indebted I am to you both. Afternoon, Sefton, afternoon!' He briefly clasped the fiddler's hand, but turned at once back to January. 'She tells me she's gone to see Catherine every day, taking her clean clothes and decent food . . .' His words caught, and his head twitched, just slightly, at the grief and anxiety that gripped him.

'Have you been to see her, sir?' asked January. 'What time did you arrive?'

'Just after noon, on the *Bonnets of Blue*. I went straight to

Marcel DuPage and then the two of us went to the Cabildo –
Tremouille's an imbecile and I will see Will Freret myself
tomorrow. And that scum in charge of the prisoners . . .! As if
Catherine would have been anyplace that night but at Zandrine's
side! The servants—'

'The servants had been awake all the night before, sir,' explained
January. 'I think she was letting them get a night's rest.'

'Of course she was!' Motet made a theatrical gesture with both
hands, like an actor playing Prospero and calling down lightning.
'The man's an idiot – and it's just like Catherine,' he added in a
softer tone. 'She always looks after her people. I went to Zandrine's
immediately from there – thank you, thank you! The poor child
. . . She told me to tell you that her eyes are much improved, and
she's even able to read a little now. I will personally horsewhip
that wretched puppy Aubin—'

'I don't think there'll be any call for punishing him, sir.' January
gestured the old man back to the chair, and glancing around, saw
that Rose and Hannibal had disappeared indoors. He heard the
clink of china carried from the pantry, and Rose emerged long
enough to bring another glass of ginger water for him, and – *Thank
God!* – a few more of Gabriel's beignets. 'I was at Aurore this
morning. I understand he is . . . is deeply affected with grief.'

Drinkin' heavy, he heard Shaw say again.

And Andy: He ain't been out of his room – keeps his door
locked . . .

Be a man, his brother had ordered.

'He was in love with the girl who was murdered – desperately,
I believe.'

Motet bridled. 'The man's married!'

Long used to the custom of the country and the vagaries of the
white outlook, January refrained from pointing out that Damien
Aubin had not let his marriage interfere with his relationship with
Zandrine. No more had Motet let his own status affect the long
and faithful shadow-marriage he'd shared with Zandrine's mother.
Any white Frenchman would have said the same. A free colored
mistress was not the same as an *affaire du coeur*.

The custom of the country . . .

Instead he said, 'There's a man in the City Guards who believes
as I do, sir, that Catherine had nothing to do with the killing. He's
enlisted my help in finding the true culprit. And indeed,' he added,

'there are a number of things about the whole affair that are . . . very odd. I'll see him in the morning, and I promise I'll keep you informed of anything we learn. At least Catherine has her own room at the jail—'

'I'll have her out tomorrow,' stated the old man stoutly, 'or know the reason why.'

January nodded as if he believed this – *I can* tell *you the reason why right now, sir!* – and molded his face into an expression of grave trust, like Oliver about to follow Roland down the pass at Roncevaux.

'And you let me know, if there's anything you need,' added Motet. 'I'll send you a draft on my bank tomorrow, for whatever expenses you've incurred so far on Catherine's behalf, or Zandrine's. And I'll send over Sippy and Alla – they're two of my most reliable women – to help out at Zandrine's house—'

'I think you going to see her, sir,' said January, 'letting her know she isn't alone – is already the greatest medicine you can give her. But extra hands will help.' And he remembered again, Hannibal sitting at Griff Paige's bedside, patiently sponging him to keep the fever down. Remembered how Jane Bichet and Cochon had appeared, to take over the task of nursing, when January knew the big man had to be as weary as he was himself. 'When Lieutenant Shaw gets here—'

'That's what I wanted to tell you, Ben.' Rose appeared in the French door of his study, a folded sheet of paper in her hand. 'Michie Shaw was here.'

'*Here?*'

She held the paper out to him. It wasn't sealed, but January guessed that Rose hadn't opened it: she never did. His name was scrawled across it in pencil.

He unfolded it.

woodlot landing byo wawaroon befor sunset dont let noon see you

'He waited half an hour for you,' said Rose, as January studied the message. 'When Cochon came with the news about Griff, I told him he could stay while I went to Olympe's – I knew you said you were short of willow bark . . .'

January thought about what the ciprière would be like in the hot twilight after the midday rain. Even walking along Bayou St John to Sally DeChaine's had been a species of clammy nightmare.

'Tell Hannibal to take my place at dinner,' he sighed. 'I suppose I'd better take a lantern. And get me another beignet to eat on the way, if you'd be so good. I knew I should have eaten lunch when I had a chance.'

SEVENTEEN

It was something over three miles to the old landing and woodlot on Bayou des Ouaouarons. Longer, had January followed the shell road along the levee, where the air was cooler off the river. But he went by the small streets at the back of Faubourg Marigny, and from there entered the half-remembered labyrinths of the ciprière: old oaks, a certain lie of the land, what had been small bayous thirty-five years ago when he was a child newly come to New Orleans. Seeing with changed eyes terrain with which he'd once been familiar. Recognizing it as the same and wondering at how different it was.

Like meeting Francois Motet as a man and not a jealous boy. Like his love for Catherine, changed and real and having nothing to do with the hot ardor of his adolescence – except that it was something they'd both been through together, like a scary adventure mutually survived. Something that they could both shake their heads over, and laugh.

As he'd feared, the wet heat trapped beneath the trees of the ciprière was nearly unbreathable. The air felt thick in his lungs, and the shadows lengthened without yielding one degree of temperature. Despite Olympe's mixture of grease and aromatics with which he'd liberally slathered his face and hands, mosquitoes swarmed.

Sunset, Shaw had written. *Let no one see you.*

The woodlot where the duel had been held, used when the little bayou had been deeper and had stretched all the way back to Bayou Gentilly, lay only twenty minutes' walk – if he remembered correctly – from the little headland at the back of the Duralde cane fields. The boot-prints in the cemetery mud returned to him, the long narrow foot and square-toed boot. Something else snagged at his memory, something . . .

After this long, was it possible Shaw had found tracks or signs of some kind there?

How easy it would be, for a man to hide in the trees at the site of the duel with a long rifle. He recalled again Charles Brunneau's state-wide reputation as a hopeless shot: *Did I really think he'd managed to hit Melchior Aubin at twenty paces?*

Had the shot that struck the elder brother actually been intended for someone else?

What is going on here? Was the note that summoned Marie-Joyeuse really meant to lure her suitor? And which suitor?

Damien was at the duel. His brother's second, as he'd always backed his brother in anything he did. He'd have been standing well clear of the line of fire, with the surgeon, the unknown Mr Bascomb.

Am I looking at one murder, or two . . . one of which hasn't been committed yet?

Although God knew, with Charles Brunneau pulling the trigger that ball could have gone anywhere.

Who else was there? And why should I care about any of them? And was this ground always this damn swampy?

His boots slurped in the morass, loosing clouds of stinging gnats. The shack Olympe had used as a girlhood hideout was barely visible as a building anymore, only a hump-backed snaggle of hackberry and wild jessamine, moated by sodden lakelets of reeds and mud. In his mind he could still hear his sister's voice, see the defiant glitter of her dark, furious eyes.

And now that angry girl was the mother of five children. The wife of a big, slow, faithful man who adored her. *Who did we all used to be?*

The clearing beyond, along the bayou's edge, was larger than he recalled. Two more ruined woodsheds, barely more than a few uprights under a bed-quilt of scuppernong vines. A moss-grown piling or two, that had been a landing. No sign of Shaw, who could vanish like an animal into undergrowth. *And who did* he *used to be?* January wondered. Back in the Kentucky hills, the 'dark and bloody ground' as the old tribes had called it.

With shocking suddenness, the Kentuckian's voice called out, 'Maestro, *run . . .*'

A rifle cracked. In the instant he'd called, January glimpsed him, a flicker of yellow shirt behind the green curtain of vine in one of the sheds, rifle in hands. In that same instant, it seemed, Shaw's body twisted half-around and crumpled forward . . .

January knew exactly how long it would take a marksman to switch guns. He threw himself forward into the tangle of hackberry, rolled and crawled to the shelter of a deadfall tree as another ball tore into the undergrowth where he'd been.

How many guns does he have? If I wait he can re-load . . . If I go now . . .

He lunged for the rifle Shaw had dropped, and a third shot barked. January flung himself backward.

More than one . . .? Shaw would have spotted a group.

A single killer, waiting . . . Waiting ahead of time to the place where he knew his quarry would come.

Thrashing somewhere in the woods. The last sunlight had vanished from the leaves; the shadows spread fast. January threw himself forward, grabbed Shaw's wrist and dragged him into cover; he came limp as a boned fish.

More thrashing – movement away to his left. January rolled, reached from cover. *How did they know to wait for him here . . .?* Another crash of gunfire and the ball stung his hand as he grabbed the Kentuckian's rifle, dragged it into the foliage with him. He didn't dare put his head up to see where his enemies were but he guessed now there had to be at least two of them. *Unless that second noise is someone else drawn to the shots . . .*

He pulled, got a better grip on Shaw's body; saw the blood on his temple and in his hair.

The blood still oozed. *It'll leave a trail . . .* There was a pulse in his wrist. January slithered back, into ground thick with palmettos and sodden with standing water. A broken branch gouged his back and something wriggled out from under him and fled.

Rustling and footfalls. *Hunting the thickets along the edge of the woodlot. If I move to bring up the rifle they'll find us . . .*

There was a pistol in Shaw's belt and he managed to get that without too much noise.

Stillness. *Waiting for us again?*

A rustle, softer. Cautious.

January lay where he was, among the mud and palmettos, barely daring to breathe. Twilight thickened.

Waiting? As he – or she? – had waited in the niprière, for Marie-Joyeuse to come hurrying along the path beside the cane.

Or was that rustling a retreat? Had the second person he'd heard been a stranger, whose approach chased the killer away?

Shaw's hand, when he touched it, was clammy and suddenly very cold.

Waiting . . .

No sound of the second man, if man there had been.

On the other side of the woodlot, a bird twittered, settling down for the night. Farther off the hoot of an owl. Beneath the trees it was hard to see now. Cautiously, January turned, felt the bloody gash along the Kentuckian's scalp.

Heard the faint gasp of his breath and felt for his pulse again, fast and thready now.

How close are they? After the killer had shot Marie-Joyeuse from cover, he – or she – had emerged from the woods, walked over to aim down at her . . .

Or have they been gone for an hour? He knew he'd have to get Shaw to someplace dry – and safe – soon, and have a look at the wound.

There probably wasn't a pebble closer than Faubourg Marigny in this flat, muddy land, but January slipped the stub of a candle from his pocket, threw it with a flick of his wrist away to his right. *And inside an hour I will almost certainly be imprisoned in a pitch-black dungeon and cursing myself for throwing a candle-end away . . .*

Nothing. No response, no rustle, no shot. Which didn't mean the killer – or killers – weren't still watching.

He rose to his knees. No shot. No movement. He bent, hoisted Shaw to his shoulder as gently as he could. Stood.

No shot.

The birds all stopped their night-calls, but he heard no movement in the woods.

Aurore.

That house was the closest. He had only to think of it to discard the idea at once.

Damien. Olivia. Tried to kill another girl at the convent . . .

Staggering a little under his lanky burden, he set off for Duralde.

The Big House at Duralde was dark when January emerged from the cane. Upstream, the yellow flicker of pine-knot torches moved around the quarters. Distantly he smelled congris, and greens cooking in pot-liquor. A child's squeal of laughter. A man called out, January didn't hear what. But there was laughter in the tone. If it had been roulaison – the sugar-grinding season – all would have been different, but this was late summer, and tasks were steady and unhurried. Get the corn in. Weed the cane. Cut wood – on a sugar plantation, it was always, *cut wood* – and weed the cane some more. Clear the ditches.

And come home at the end of the day to eat supper with your woman and tell your children stories. Or go with them to hear stories in somebody else's cabin, somebody who was a good teller of tales.

The overseer's cabin, as he recalled, stood on short stilts at the far end of the line of buildings beyond the kitchen, where the grim-faced Michie Carpenter could keep an eye on the quarters. There was a copse of oaks about thirty feet beyond it, and after that the beginning of the cane. Lanterns burned in one window, and beside the door. The other buildings in that line were dark: workshops; the jail; and the plantation infirmary. A woman crossed from the kitchen toward the overseer's house, carrying a wicker tray with a towel over it. January stepped out of the cane, called out, 'Ma'am!' and she stopped. It was Lottie Dupuy.

She startled, to see him carrying a wounded man over his shoulder, reached the bench beside the kitchen door again in two strides, the nearest place where she could set down her tray without putting it on the ground. Three more strides brought her to him. 'Mr J!'

'This man's been hurt,' said January. 'Shot in the woods by someone I didn't see.'

She had already caught his arm, led him to the cabin and up its steps. 'Mr Carpenter!' she called out, halfway up, then pounded at the door. Barely two knocks brought it open, to reveal the tough tall rangy man in shirtsleeves and braces, who'd sat his horse above him and Shaw only that morning.

'What the hell?' Carpenter stepped back at once, threw open the door to the cottage's bedroom and whipped back the sheet that covered the bed. 'Lottie, get hot water from the kitchen . . . He alive? Grab a blanket 'fore you go—'

He helped January lay Shaw down on the bed, felt his hands with the brisk competence of a man used to evaluating injuries in the field. 'Where'd this happen?'

'Out at the old woodlot on Bayou Ouaouarons, sir. He told me to meet him there—'

'I know you now,' said Carpenter. The only light in the tiny room was what came through the door from the candles in the front chamber, and that wasn't much. 'You were one of the musicians Saturday night. Piano player?'

'Ben January—'

'Gus told me you didn't find what you were lookin' for out past the cane this morning.'

'Maybe somebody thought we did.'

While they were speaking, settling Shaw on the narrow bed, Lottie brought in the lantern, then scrambled up a rickety ladder to what was probably only a few feet of attic. She came down with a quilt over one shoulder and a satchel wedged under one arm. Bandages, scissors, pins and a bottle of spirits of wine. The next second January heard the retreating clatter of her shoes going down the front steps.

There was an inch-long rip in Shaw's forehead, where the frontal bone of the skull curved around to the left side. January remembered how he'd barely seen him, a blink of yellow shirt in the green shadows of the overgrown shed. *He knew someone was watching him . . .*

His face was chalky in the dim light and his breath labored; sweat sheened his skin. 'Raise up his feet,' said January, and Carpenter looked around, grabbed about six inches off the top of the stack of old newspapers on a box in the corner, and put them under the wounded man's calves.

'Concussion?' he asked, took the lantern and held it close (*I knew I'd need that damn candle-end . . .*) as January opened Shaw's eyes.

January nodded.

The rat-trap mouth tightened. 'Whoever it was, maybe, that shot that girl Saturday night?'

At least the man didn't need things explained to him, or demand to see freedom papers, or ask what business January had roving around the countryside after dark. Compared with the average overseer, that was a lot.

'I think it was, sir, yes.' January unbuttoned Shaw's mud-soaked shirt, took scissors from the satchel and cut it down to the hemline, so that the wet garment could be drawn off him with the least possible disturbance. Together they pulled off his boots and trousers, covered him in the quilt Lottie had brought. His body was cold despite the heat of the evening. Gently, January dabbed the blood from the head wound.

'Graze,' he added. 'Deep, but it doesn't feel like the skull was cracked.'

The overseer tilted his head, studying Shaw's face, then January's, in the dim light. 'Why Bayou des Ouaouarons?'

January shook his head. 'I got a note this afternoon, asking me to meet him there. I've been helping him hunt for the killer, since neither of us believes it was the woman they arrested for it.'

Carpenter grinned, sidelong, like a man who hasn't truly smiled in years. 'The hands – and the town servants like Lottie – are talking how Damien Aubin turned out his plaçée and it was her mother who shot the Maginot girl, but that sounds like *blankitte* bullshit to me.' A gesture of his head in the direction of the Big House dismissed the whites he worked for. 'Any idea how your bird knew where to wait for . . . Shaw, he said his name was?'

'Not at the moment, no, sir. I'm coming into this in the middle.'

Lottie returned, carrying a gallon can of hot water and (*Smart woman!* approved January) another lantern.

Carpenter grunted, 'Thanks, Lottie,' and put the lantern where its feeble light would fall on the unconscious man. 'He have people in town?'

'His landlady.' January sponged, carefully, at the bleeding wound. 'Maggie Valentine – she runs a livery on Rue des Ursulines, and rents him a room in one of the lofts.'

'Takes good care of her stock,' approved the overseer. 'Can you write her a note? I'll have one of the boys take it tonight. He be all right here tonight? He don't look good, and I'd hate to try moving him.'

'Thank you,' said January. 'I admit I'd rather see him by daylight – and see how he does in the morning – rather than take him anywhere tonight.'

'Lottie, can you make me up a pallet in the attic?' Carpenter crossed through the door into the cabin's front room – it only took one of his long strides – and January saw him tear a blank back page from one of the ledgers on the fortress-neat desk. 'You need anything, Janvier? There coffee left, Lottie? Thanks . . .'

He came back into the bedroom. 'I'll have Teddy take a note to Michie Duralde in town as well, let him know what's happening.'

He shook his head. 'As much as any of us knows. Lottie,' he added, 'you make sure Mr Janvier has everything he needs? Thanks.'

Then his boots clunked on the steps outside, and he was gone. Presumably, thought January, to make a final patrol of the quarters for the night and make sure everyone was where they were supposed to be. January guessed nobody in the quarters wanted to be caught outside by this man.

With luck 'Teddy' would still be awake.

Carpenter had left the ledger-page and ink on the desk in the cabin's front room; Lottie brought January coffee there. 'You eaten, Mr J?'

'If it won't get you into trouble – and *only* if – I could do with something, M'am, thank you. You think Michie Carpenter would be willing to have your man take a note to my wife, on Rue Esplanade, as well? It's close to the livery . . .' He glanced back over his shoulder at the lantern-light of the bedroom door.

'He's a good sort,' allowed Lottie. 'A hard bastard, but fair down to the last half of a bean.'

'That's something you don't always see in the Man.'

Lottie sniffed her agreement, and went out. Through the open door January saw her retreat across the yard toward the kitchen. January thriftily tore the ledger-page in half, and wrote:

Duralde Plantation
9 pm
Sept 15, Tuesday . . .

He shook his head wonderingly: *Is it* still *Tuesday? Tuesday when I had breakfast with Olympe?*

My Nightingale,

Shaw was shot from ambush at the woodlot on B. des Ouaouarons. He is still unconscious, a deep concussion, and 'shock'. I think two attackers involved, tho' I saw neither. Connected with MJM's murder? I don't know. I'll be home tomorrow. Whole affair seems very strange. Vivamus, mea Lesbia, atque amemus.

B.

The second note he wrote in English.

> Duralde Plantation
> 9 pm
> Sept 15, Tuesday
> Miss Valentine,
>
> This is to let you know that Mr Shaw was shot from ambush in the course of investigation, at the old woodlot on Bayou Ouaouarons. He is alive but unconscious with what I believe to be a deep concussion, and what physicians call 'choc' or 'shock'. I will remain with him at Duralde tonight, and will do all that I can for him. I will bring him back to town tomorrow, but he will need careful nursing. Please believe that I stand ready to give you whatever assistance you may need.
>
> Your ob't sv't
> B. January, fmc

As he wrote, he could not help observing the darkness – and the different tint and consistency – of the ink.

Was there something about the paper he lifted, the ink at Aurore, that told Shaw . . . What? Did he go back to Aurore at all? Why return to the site of the duel?

Rising, he re-entered the tiny bedchamber, felt Shaw's pulse again. The Kaintuck's breathing was still rapid and unsteady. Times without number he'd seen the same – men who'd been accidentally cut with the huge cane knives in the fields, men in the medical tent after the battle at Chalmette. Men, and women, brought injured to the clinic at the Hôtel Dieu in Paris . . . The coldness and sweating and shortness of breath that could kill, even when the original injury wasn't fatal. Keep them warm, the British surgeon had said, of the men brought in from the battlefield – the surgeon himself having surrendered as a prisoner, so that he could look after the wounded. Raise up their feet if you can. Had January had his own medical kit with him, he'd have used the tiniest pinch of dried foxglove – Olympe's remedy – to slow and steady the fluttering of the heart.

From the bed he turned, and gathered up the Kentuckian's soaked clothing where it had left a great wet spot on the braided straw matting of the floor – and again, something tugged at his memory. Something he should have done. *Or checked*, he thought. *Or taken more notice of at the time . . .*

The wet clothing, the heavy Conestoga boots, made him aware, as he hadn't been before, of the soaked and muddy state of his own garments. As he hung the trousers and the cut remains of the shirt over the footboard of the bed, he fished in the pockets for the papers: Adrien LaFrennière's note to Marie-Joyeuse; Mrs Blennerhassett's to Henry Clay. The sheets he'd written on: sample paper, sample ink.

In addition, the garments contained about three dollars' worth of assorted coin, a small tin box of Lucifers, three candle stubs, a dry, brown twist of chewing tobacco much contaminated with pocket-lint, an unwashed and disgusting bandana, and four pistol balls.

Two were those Shaw had pinched from the gun-case at Aurore, neat and regular as if they'd just been dropped from a shot-tower. The others were deformed. Holding the larger of the two close to the candle, January could make out the faint traces of rifling, and guessed that it was the one that had killed Marie-Joyeuse Maginot.

So what is the fourth?

He weighed it in his hand. It was smaller than the other three, badly deformed, and bore no hint that the gun-barrel that had fired it had been grooved.

Which means what?

Lottie's footsteps creaked on the steps coming up to the open door. January slipped the four hunks of lead, the four pieces of paper, back into his pocket, walked back into the outer room to gather the folded notes from the desk.

So was Marie-Joyeuse the intended victim at all? And was there another note that we don't have yet?

EIGHTEEN

'There was a time when I hated Mr Clay enough to kill him.' Lottie Dupuy folded her hands on the worn surface of the overseer's front-room table, the lantern-light picking yellow specks in her eyes.

Nate Carpenter had returned to the cabin, and gone up to the attic loft. Through the open outside door, January heard the last bedding-down noises drift faintly from the quarters. A child's fretful sobs dwindled. A woman sang softly, '"Bye 'n bye, bye 'n bye/ Gonna lay down easy bye 'n bye . . ."' Cicadas drummed in the trees. The smell of the quarters – woodsmoke and privies and chickens – was oddly comforting, familiar as the childhood lullaby in the wet heat of the night. More distantly, the heavy green smell of the cane.

'Mostly he's like the others,' she added. 'He talks about how evil slavery is an' how slaves should be freed, but he'll have a man whipped – an' whipped bad – for back talk or comin' back late when he's sent on some errand . . . an' you can bet Teddy's gonna step out lively comin' home this evenin'. An' like the others, the senator'll take a girl to bed. There's sons of his live in the quarters, as well as in the Big House. It beats me, when I'd listen to him talk at dinner, about how slavery needs to be ended in Kentucky because of how bad it is for the *white* folks. How it makes them mean and immoral, oh dear. The poor things. But I don't notice him freein' nobody on Ashland.'

Old anger pulled for a moment at the corner of her mouth. 'My mama was freed, by her master Mr Condon, you see. He promised he'd free her in his will. But in spite of that I was sold when I was sixteen – Aaron, my husband, belonged to Mr Clay. We – my husband, my son Charles, my daughter Mary Ann, who's here with me – came to Washington City with Mr Clay when he was in the Congress, and we were in Washington, on and off, for twenty years. But when Mr Jackson took over as president and hated Mr Clay, Mr Clay broke up his household and said we were all goin' back to Kentucky for good. That's when I went to court, because my mama really was free. I guess you heard how that all played out.'

'I heard.'

'I hated him enough to kill him, then.' She turned the handle of the coffee cup she'd brought for herself when she'd brought in coffee for January – he noted that the chinaware was old and chipped, the sort of vessel that got passed along to the house servants when it was too worn to grace the white folks' table. *And God forbid she'd use a dish that Mr Carpenter would later put his lips to . . .*

'I haven't seen my husband in ten years,' Lottie went on after a time. 'I'll see Charlie when Mr Clay visits in town – he's Mr Clay's personal man. And he wants to go on thinkin' Mr Clay is the Angel Gabriel in a top hat. An' he reads the newspapers, an' he hears Mr Clay talk about how white men shouldn't have slaves, an' about how slavery has *got* to be dealt with before it tears this country apart . . . An' he'd rather not think about me bein' arrested an' sent down here to Mr Duralde, so Mr Clay won't feel itchy at the way I look at him, every time he comes into the room.'

'Or spit in his coffee,' added January, which got her to laugh.

'Yeah, well,' she agreed, and sobered again. 'But you can't hate somebody like that for years an' years. Least I can't. Christ Jesus prayed with his dyin' breath, for God to forgive the men who killed him.' She shook her head. 'I'd spit in Mr Clay's coffee in a minute. But I wouldn't kill him. Not if he was lyin' sick like your friend in there' – she nodded towards the lantern-lit door – 'an' nobody would know it, if I was to go in an' put a pillow over his face.'

'You know of anyone who would?' January returned to his original question, and Lottie sat silent for a long time, gazing into the dark beyond the glow of the lantern on the table between them. 'Or would hurt one of his children?'

'The boys . . .' She sighed, and for a moment the angry glint returned to her eyes. 'There's girls in the quarters who would probably have killed one or more of those boys, if they'd had a chance. Like most of 'em, Mr Clay didn't want to know about it. He'd always find some reason that the girl asked for it. They all do. Those boys had a bad streak, a crazy streak. Not Mr James,' she added. 'For all he's gone and made a fool of himself about that poor girl.'

'There's something about her death,' said January, 'that doesn't . . . doesn't *feel* right. Somebody lured Mr Clay away from that rally Saturday night, so he wasn't around for people to see him, at the time Mamzelle Maginot was murdered.'

'You believe that?'

'Yes, I do. Not just because the notes were forged with the same ink, and probably by the same hand. Killing her was stupid. Clay knew he'd been seen at the rally. Stupid and unnecessary. Whatever else he is, Mr Clay isn't stupid.'

'No.' Lottie sighed a little, and nodded. 'I figured that pamphlet was all humbug – though it's true Mr Clay does owe gamblin' money all over six states. An' Mr James—'

'People saw James Clay at times when it would have been hard for him to have done the shooting.'

'And why would he have shot her anyway?' The woman spread her hands.

'This is politics,' January reminded her. 'This is slinging mud in all directions. If a friend of mine wasn't being accused of the crime I wouldn't care who they hanged for it. But I have to care.'

'Politics.' She almost spit the word. 'I heard a hundred men say as how President Jackson said he wanted to have Mr Clay hanged for a traitor. Would he really have done it? Or sent him some fake note to get him out someplace and shot him himself? I don't know. Men say all kinds of stuff in politics. They really mean it at the time. Those Donaldsonville Boys, that came up carryin' a gallows with Mr Van Buren's image hangin' on it. Would they really hang him? He's a nice little man – I worked for him for a year an' a half. He fussed like a girl about did his tie match his hankie, but sharp? Lord, that man is bright. Men'll say anythin' in politics. Some of 'em are just blowin' smoke. Some aren't.'

'But nobody in particular.'

'Not that I know of.' She sipped at the now-tepid coffee, made a face. 'Doesn't mean there isn't somebody.'

January sighed. 'I just need to ask,' he said. 'Right now, anything that might help make sense of what seems . . . odd. There are things that don't make sense. And now . . .' He glanced back at the room behind them. The lantern had gone out. The dark smelled of burnt tallow, damp straw matting, and the green, thick odor of the cane.

'Thank you,' he added, and gathered the cups, and the gourd bowl in which she'd brought him congris and sausage, onto the wicker tray. The yard was silent as they crossed it to the kitchen, the quarters gone silent and dark, save for the incessant rattle of cicadas, the far-off barking of a dog.

'Talkin' about things that don't make sense,' she said. 'I don't know if this has anything to do with this or not. Night before last, late, my daughter Mary Ann'd been took sick with the grippe. Nuthin' bad, just bad food. I was comin' back from the infirmary, an' I saw a man walkin' around the house, a man with a rifle.'

'A rifle?' January glanced out towards the cane. The moon was waning, and had not yet risen. Under starlight everything seemed bleached and faint, as if scratched through black paint on a silver mirror. In his mind he saw a dark figure dart between two tombs. Saw a track in the mud . . .

'Just lookin' at the house in the moonlight,' said Lottie. 'Didn't act like a thief, and for sure wasn't a hunter. Not a patter-roller either.'

'White man or black?'

She shook her head. 'His face looked white enough, an' his hands. It's hard to tell, in moonlight. He was wearin' a hat, so I couldn't see his hair. Walked light, like a young man, kind of quick an' alert. Lookin' all around him. Went into the stables, then came out again. There was enough moon that I saw him pretty clear. An' he had a gun. There was no mistakin' that.'

Lottie had brought in a corn-shuck mattress – clean and stuffed fairly recently – a blanket and even a pillow and sheet, and had spread them out beside the overseer's bed where Shaw lay. The policeman had not stirred, and January still didn't like the sound of his breathing, or the coldness of his hands. He knew he needed sleep – he was teaching tomorrow afternoon and playing at the Democratic Planters' Club cotillion in Milneburgh – but what Lottie had told him kept his eyes open, staring up at the ceiling in the dark.

A man with a rifle.

A man who'd waited in the woodlot – who'd known Shaw would be coming . . . How? A man who'd waited in the ciprière, knowing Marie-Joyeuse Maginot would be coming . . .

One murder or two?

If it *was* a man. Olivia Aubin was tall and thin, wide-shouldered with narrow hips. Some women – Rose among them – dressed as men while traveling, especially if they traveled alone. At a distance, by moonlight, all a witness would be certain of would be trousers and the hat.

And spectacles. If Olivia was looking for something by moonlight, she'd be wearing her spectacles. *Wouldn't she?*

Rose certainly would.

Olivia Aubin was demonstrably mad – and apparently, on occasion, violent. And craziest, Andy had said, when the moon was full.

Had some mental shift on her way back to Aurore made it suddenly imperative that she kill the man to whom she'd just confided her secrets?

Had Shaw read something into her story that had turned him back to Aurore – if Aurore was where he'd meant to go after leaving the levee?

And what had he found – at Aurore or elsewhere – that led him to the Bayou of the Bullfrogs?

I'll have to go back to Aurore myself . . .

Sleep! he told himself firmly. *You'll need to get back out to the bayou tomorrow, if you can . . .*

And all that thought did was turn his mind back to Akinto, somewhere in the cyprière . . .

Lottie's words that evening made sense. Senator Clay spoke against slavery, but he had never freed his own slaves, not even when they'd sued him in court on the grounds that they had been promised freedom by a previous master.

He's a politician. He remembered his mother's jeering eyes. *None of them can be trusted.*

And glanced up at the bed beside him. He trusted Abishag Shaw, to the ends of the earth. Hannibal. People he'd known in Paris, old friends he'd lived with, side by side.

So where did that—?

A boot scrunched the weeds, outside the thin wall of the cabin. As January drew breath to call out, orange torchlight flared suddenly in the little window of the bedroom, and the next second, the glass exploded inward as a torch was thrown through it like a spear. January rolled to his feet, instants before the window of the outer room was likewise shattered, fire catching in the straw mat on the floor. He smelled oil, saw the long shaft of the torch rolling a few feet from him, the blazing cloth that wrapped it unraveling in a rush of flame.

From the loft ladder in the front room he heard the creak of feet, Nate Carpenter's voice yelled, 'Jesus!' And then: 'Janvier!'

'Here!' yelled January back. 'Don't go out the door! He's out there with a gun!' He knew this as clearly as he knew his name.

'Who is?' The overseer whipped around the doorframe into the bedroom, night-shirted and barefoot, bronze in the spreading glare.

'Hell if I know. Man who did this, I think.' January was already rolling up his pallet and quilts from the floor, lengthwise, into a long uneven bundle. And thanking God for the damp in the matting that held the flame momentarily at bay. 'There a window at the back of the attic?' He'd seen the one at the front, catching the torchlight as the procession passed it Saturday night. 'Rope,' he added, as Carpenter nodded, and the overseer plunged into the front room, leaped back in with a coil of it over his shoulder. The heat and smoke were already choking him – he could see through the doorway the fire spreading over the cabin's downstream wall and across the floor.

'There may be two of them—'

Who would Olivia trust to help her? If it is Olivia . . .

'If there was they'd have throwed fire in from both sides.' Carpenter's words were cut off in a paroxysm of coughing.

'You got a lot of trust in humankind, sir.'

The heat made him dizzy. As he rolled up the pallet he saw the other man already knotting the rope around Shaw's body. 'You need help getting him up that ladder?'

'You draw 'em off; I'll be fine.'

January scooped up his bundle, long and limp and, he hoped, of a size to pass for a man's body, in the glare of flame and darkness. *It'll go up like tinder if it catches . . .*

He plunged through the outer room, circling almost to the wall to avoid the flames, kicked open the door.

A rifle cracked in the darkness. January had made sure he burst out as far to one side of the opening as he could, and still felt the sting of the ball on his wrist. He threw up his arms and fell spectacularly backwards into the burning room, dropping his burden behind him and praying the flames hadn't advanced far enough for him to land in them. The pallet, a few feet to his right, blazed up like a torch, and January let out a scream of the worst agony he could conjure.

Nate Carpenter, in the act of shoving Shaw's unconscious body through the trap into the attic, leaned down and screamed helpfully. January screamed again, not entirely acting, as he dashed across the narrowing track of un-blazing floor to the ladder.

Through the bedroom doorway he could see the mattress on the bed had already caught, the dry portions of the matting on the floor ablaze.

The attic was a solid block of smoke, darkness, suffocating heat. His head swimming, January caught Shaw's knees, couldn't even see Carpenter ahead of him carrying the unconscious man's shoulders. *Thank God the room's small . . .*

Carpenter screamed again, in case their murderer was still listening. *Though if the man has any sense he's already back in the cane . . .* Through the thin walls of the cabin January could already hear men shouting as they ran from the quarters.

And well they might run, he thought, as he added his screams to the overseer's, then coughed so hard he thought he'd break a rib. They'd all be lucky if they weren't accused of a slave revolt.

Glass smashing. Air like the breath of life. It took both of their strength, to lower Shaw's body to the ground – the window was barely eighteen inches square, and set shoulder-high; flames were already licking through the floorboards, and up the rafters, when the Kentuckian's body reached the ground, far too close to the back wall of the cabin.

'Go,' gasped Carpenter – a voice out of the blackness and smoke behind him. January felt the rope twitch and jerk – being tied onto the bedframe, presumably. 'Oak trees about thirty foot back, then the cane beyond that—'

As he climbed down the rope January reflected that the overseer could just as easily have come this route the moment he, January, went into the front room to convince the arsonist that he'd killed his quarry, leaving Shaw – and probably January himself – to burn.

Gasping, coughing, and convinced that he couldn't even get himself thirty feet to the shelter of the oak trees, let alone carry another man's weight, January dragged Shaw away from the wall. Voices were shouting all around the front and sides of the house: he thought he could hear Lottie's, yelling, 'Ben! Ben!'

Then Carpenter was beside him. Together they carried Shaw into the darkness – the overseer, January guessed, knew as well as he did that Shaw's safety now – and January's – lay in their attacker thinking they were dead.

'There someplace I can hide him 'til morning?' January untied the makeshift rope sling, felt Shaw's wrist. The pulse was fast and weak – the fact that it was there at all astonished him. Or would have astonished him, in another man.

'Sugar mill. Keep him here for now. I'll send Lottie to you – I'll be back when this is under control.' The overseer gestured at the men now swarming around the cabin, hurling buckets of water into the blaze.

Men were shouting, 'Michie Carpenter! Michie Carpenter—'

Well, yes, reflected January, *nobody wanted what would happen, if they were accused of torching the overseer's cabin and killing an overseer . . .*

But he recalled what Lottie had said, that though a hard man – and as ready as any of them to enforce his commands with a lash – Nate Carpenter was fair down to the last half of a bean.

'Any idea who that was?'

January shook his head. 'Not the slightest. Thank you.'

But Carpenter had already turned and was running back toward the blazing cabin, still in his scorched nightshirt, calling out. From the shelter of the trees January saw him surrounded by servants and field hands, and two men, draped in dripping blankets, came crashing out the cabin door, having clearly rushed inside to help him, should he have been unconscious from the smoke.

Maybe they're just afraid of getting somebody worse.

He felt Shaw's pulse again – too faint to be read in his wrist, barely palpable in his throat. Sat in the darkness, watching through the tangle of palmetto and swamp laurel, the men moving around the burning house. Carpenter strode among them, taking his turn with the buckets, stopping to talk to this man or that.

Already the flames were lessening. Against their glow he saw Lottie approach, looking around her in the dark. He called her name softly, and was glad to see she had the sense to make sure she wasn't being observed, before she hurried to him, groped her way through the thicket around the oak trees' base.

'Ben?'

'We're all right.'

'He alive?' She knelt at Shaw's other side.

'For now. I think I convinced our friend he's dead. I'll have to get him back to town without anyone seeing. If they think he's still alive, they'll try again.'

'What the hell did he *find* out there?' The woman sat back on her heels. 'Or what the hell did our friend *think* he found, that it's worth killin' him – that's worth killin' you, an' a complete total stranger over it—'

'If he is a total stranger. I don't think he is.'

'You mean, it's somebody we know? The man with the gun?'

'I don't know.' The blaze was dying, the small house a burning skeleton, the air a fog of smoke. He fought not to cough.

Would the killer come back tomorrow and see the attic window? Guess what had really happened? He was fairly sure Carpenter had the sense to come up with a good yarn . . .

He heard the overseer now thanking the men and women who'd come running with buckets, sending them back to their own shabby dwellings. *Is he going to let them all sleep a few extra hours? Or will they still have to be up working in the fields at first light?*

Under his hand, Shaw's wrist moved. He bent down, touched the Kentuckian's face in the darkness. Felt the eyelids move.

He whispered, 'You're safe. Stay still.'

Like the thinnest rustle of grass, Shaw murmured, 'Maestro.'

'You'll be all right.'

'It wa'n't there,' Shaw breathed. 'It wa'n't noplace there.'

'Don't worry about it now.'

Under his light fingers, the Kentuckian's head moved, slightly. The skin of his forehead pinched.

'His eyes,' said Shaw.

NINETEEN

At first cock-crow, still dark and the sparrows in the cane fields just starting up their twittering, January – from his pallet in the deep shadows at the back of the sugar mill – heard voices in the yard. Wagon-traces rattled. The jingle of harness.

He felt Shaw's pulse, listened to his breathing, both still very weak but better than they had been last night. Then he rolled off the platform that contained the kettles – the old-style set-up that Melchior Aubin had decried – and crossed to the closed line of shutters that faced the yard. Threads of torchlight between the shutters guided him. Dry shards of last winter's stalks and leaves crunched under his boots.

He wondered if Rose had gotten his note.

He pushed one shutter gently, saw a man who was probably a

field-gang driver, and another who might have been the plantation 'mule boy', tacking up a small wagon, its bed filled with hay.

Lottie was with them. She'd changed her dress, re-wrapped her tignon, and sounded calm and brisk as ever. 'I told Mr Carpenter not to be a damn fool – that we could send for a damn doctor. But he insists. And lookin' at them burns he got, I can't really say I blame him.'

The driver – dressed as drivers often were, in a blue coat and the high-crowned hat that marked his office – shook his head. 'I seen that a dozen times. Man'll come out of a fight, or a scrape, just fine, not feelin' a thing. Only when he cools down it hits him. He all right to be moved?'

'He *says* he is.' Lottie sighed. 'I ain't gonna argue with him. You go on up an' fetch him out. I'll bring up the wagon. Go!' she added, when the mule boy seemed disposed to help her lead the team.

The two men crossed the yard, climbed the back steps of the Big House's gallery. Like Aurore – like most French Creole plantations – Duralde had wings that extended backward from the main block of the house, and in one of these, he guessed, Nate Carpenter had bedded down for what remained of last night. Distantly, January heard the man's knuckles on the jalousie, like the tap of a woodpecker in the darkness.

Presumably they were bidden inside. In any case, Lottie took the rein of the near mule, led the team – and the wagon – to the door of the mill. January was already striding back to the cold bank of kettles as she opened the shutter, held her lantern inside.

January whispered, 'Thank you!' as he carried Shaw – as gently as he could over his shoulder – to the opening, laid him in the wagon-bed and covered him with hay.

'I'll clear up your pallets in there,' whispered Lottie. 'Teddy says he got your notes to your lady, and to Miss Valentine at the livery. When I come into town tomorrow,' she added, 'I'll come by your house and you'd better tell me what this is all about.'

'I would if I knew.' January hopped up into the wagon-bed, squirmed down under the hay on the other side of the box, and Lottie scattered the copious fluffs of the stuff over him.

'You stay safe.' The wagon swayed as she sprang down. Feet scrunched the gravel of the yard – a blanket was spread on the hay: 'You all right there, Michie Nate?'

'Hell, no, I'm not all right! My back feels like a cooked pig—'

The chassis creaked as someone got onto the box. The jingle of bridle-bits. Then the dry clink of harness as the mules leaned into their collars. The wheels lurched.

The drive to the Duralde townhouse wasn't a long one. Nate Carpenter groaned every now and then for the benefit of the mule boy up on the wagon-box, and cursed the uneven surface of the shell road. Beneath the itchy blanket of hay, January was aware of light coming into the sky, and heard the birds in the cane fields. The smoke of cooking fires came to him, and the thick, moist smell of the ciprière. Hooves clattered as, presumably, another messenger from Duralde Plantation passed them ('Heya, Jimmy!' called the mule 'boy' (actually a man in his thirties), but for a short time there was only the stillness of early morning, the creak of leather and the grind of wheels on the shells.

Then the smell of coal fires from brickyards, the stink of tanneries. Rigging clinked by the wharves below the levee to their left. Men's voices called in German, English, Russian. Then town smells, town noises: the charcoal man's wailing song; the whistle of steamboats letting off pressure; a woman singing – doing what as she sang?

The streets of the French Town were still quiet as the driver drew rein. The man jumped down, led the mules around the sharp corner and into the semi-dark of a carriageway. January heard the clang of the gate into a courtyard, another man asking what the hell had happened? Both men came to help Carpenter down, the overseer giving a very good impression of pain stoically borne.

January wondered what Carpenter was going to do when someone asked to treat the supposed burns that had necessitated him to come into town in a wagon.

Bribe the doctor?

The gate creaked again, and instants later, light footfalls patted on the brick of the carriageway. 'Mr J?' whispered a girl's voice, young and rough.

And Rose's: 'Ben?'

Maggie Valentine was nineteen, red-haired, tall and thin. A few years ago, with her alcoholic father's disappearance, she'd masqueraded as a boy in order to keep running Valentine's Livery, periodically hiring Hannibal Sefton to dye his hair and pretend to be Tim Valentine whenever the man's creditors came around.

For a year now, January was aware that in addition to boarding in one of the attic rooms, Abishag Shaw had acted more and more as advisor and friend to Maggie, and surrogate uncle to her brothers and sisters. The most reticent of men, Shaw seldom spoke the young woman's name. But as Maggie and Rose helped him swiftly transfer Shaw from the bed of the Duralde wagon to the dray that stood waiting in Rue Chartres, January read in the girl's eyes that his own guess about what lay between Shaw and Maggie had been correct.

'I'm going to need to take him to my place,' he told her, with a glance at Rose, who nodded assent. 'We can keep him hidden in the storerooms on the ground floor.' In fact, in the hideout where he'd sheltered Akinto a week ago. 'I don't know who shot him, or why – but whoever it was tried to kill both of us, and Duralde's overseer, last night. He – or she – will certainly try to kill him again if he – or she – learns he's still above ground.'

He and Rose sprang up onto the dray's high plank seat beside Maggie, rattled away down the quiet street.

Damien? Olivia? The timing was rather fine Saturday night, but it could have been done.

Adrien LaFrennière? He'd been beside the coffin moments before January had seen – or thought he'd seen – the man with the rifle at the cemetery. Several of Shaw's contacts had seen him during the fireworks. The same went for James Clay.

But was the attack on Shaw connected to Marie-Joyeuse Maginot's death at all? And if not, what the hell *was* going on?

Where had Shaw gone yesterday, after they'd parted? To whom had he spoken?

Why Bayou des Ouaouarons, and what could he have found there that was worth . . . this?

It wa'n't there, Shaw had whispered.

But if 'it' wasn't at the bayou, why shoot him? Not only shoot him, but follow us back to Duralde to make sure of his death . . . The way he'd walked up close, to make sure of Marie-Joyeuse's.

And who was he looking for – waiting for – outside Granville's townhouse Monday night? Outside Duralde plantation by moonlight? Whose horse did he think would be in the stable there? Who did he think would be at the funeral?

Or do I only imagine I'm seeing a pattern?

He found himself looking back over his shoulder a dozen times, between Rue Chartres and Rue Esplanade. But there was more traffic on the streets now. More people who could have been the man – if it *was* a man – with the rifle.

Shaw had said, His eyes . . .

Whose eyes? One murder or two?

January only half-heard Maggie say, 'I'll send Emily over to help look after him,' naming her fifteen-year-old sister. 'To spare you trouble, Mrs J.'

In his pocket – along with the rosary of blue beads which never left him, the silver pocket watch and the Lucifer matches, which also never left him – he felt the solid little lumps of lead: two deformed, two unused.

I'll have to go back and retrieve Shaw's other rifle. And see what it is that I've missed. What it is that's there, that someone knew was there, and knew he'd look for.

But Shaw said it wasn't.

And talk to Ti-Jon. And Judas Bredon of the Underground Railroad.

And speak to Catherine, in the jail or out of it . . .

All he wanted to do was sleep.

After installing Shaw in the secret room downstairs, January slept for a few hours, dreaming tangled dreams of Charles-Louis Trepagier creeping up to the dark house on Aurore Plantation, to put sheets of foolscap and French laid notepaper in Melchior Aubin's desk, and pour out the contents of the inkwell and substitute the incriminating ink instead. The silence of the house was frightening. Through the open door he saw Melchior Aubin tossing in pain on the bed, the light of the fireworks glinting on the laudanum bottles that clustered the bedside table and intermittently outlining his profile in red and gold.

The images changed. Zandrine, lying in the dark of her room – alone. *Where the hell are Nessie and Gazoute?* The chair beside the bed was empty. Though he knew the fireworks were a half-mile up the river at Duralde, the light of them flared and died, flared and died in the slits of the jalousie shades, gaudy threads of color glinting on the rank of bottles on the table nearby . . . *They gave her laudanum so she wouldn't notice they were gone . . .*

Even asleep, he knew this wasn't true.

Briefly, he saw Olivia Aubin waking up in the darkness as a

giant ball of rawhide crashed through her bedroom wall, followed by the Shah of Persia's ambassador bearing the body of Martin Van Buren on a gallows.

Then he saw Catherine kneeling on her cot, the fireworks blazing as strong as ever through the window of her prison cell. The cell itself was dark, but he heard the nasal whine of the jailer Stookey, speaking to someone on the corridor. 'Well, 'course Clay killed the girl! But we can't put Henry Clay up for murder! Not with the election comin' up! Best for everybody, we let the woman hang.'

January yelled, '*No!*' and woke gasping.

Lay looking at the hot slits of daylight in the closed shutters of his room. Chou-Chou's voice, barely a whisper, reached him from the dining room. '*I* is the subject of the sentence, *remember* is the verb; *one morning* modifies the verb, and *when* begins a dependent clause . . .'

The smell of coffee blessed the hot air. By the angle of the light it was mid-morning.

Shaw, he thought.

Catherine.

And damn it, I have to teach the Jahnke boy out in Carrollton this afternoon, and *play the Democrat Planters' Club cotillion in Milneburgh tonight . . .*

Shaw had half-waked, Rose whispered, leading him out through the French doors onto the gallery so the girls wouldn't hear. Enough to drink some water, use the chamber pot, and ask, 'Did Ben find it?' before sliding again into sleep. He looked better, so far as January could tell by the light of a branch of candles, and his pulse was steady. The pupils of his eyes were dilated but that, January thought, could be only because the hidden room was dark.

'I don't know how long I'll be gone,' he murmured in an under-voice, returning to the bedroom to dress. 'Not long, I hope. Send for Olympe, if there's any change in his condition; if his pulse alters, or he becomes nauseated.'

'Did you find what?' whispered Rose. 'What did he mean?'

He shook his head. 'Whatever wasn't there?' Yet as he said the words something snagged in his mind.

Something about Nate Carpenter.

Something about his dream of Zandrine, lying alone in the darkness . . .

Rose returned to her pupils. January left by the French doors of the bedroom, taking Catherine the usual bundle of clean linen, ginger water, bread and butter, sausage and cheese and copies of the *New Orleans Bee* and the *Letters of St Simon* – which she had always said were far more entertaining and bizarre than any novel she'd ever read.

Her room on the prison's upper floor, though tiny, was reasonably clean – he assumed Francois Motet had arranged that – and the narrow bed boasted not only sheets but a mosquito-bar. Motet occupied the room's single wooden chair when Stookey let January in. *How much did Weasel-Puss charge him for that?*

But January knew he wouldn't have taken a second chair had one been provided. It was simply not something a black man would or could do in these circumstances.

Through the barred window that overlooked the Women's Yard, shrill voices drifted up: 'Move over, you stuck-up whore!' 'You'd be a whore your own self, bitch, if anybody'd pay for yours—'

'Tremouille's an idiot!' fumed Motet. 'Claims he has no jurisdiction – that we have to deal with that Royalist blockhead Barthelmy because the girl was killed in the Third Municipality.'

Some of the haggard look retreated from Catherine's face at his news that Zandrine was not only physically improving, but seemed calmer and in better spirits.

'That jailer said there was a fire out at Duralde last night,' said Motet. 'He said it was a slave revolt.'

'It wasn't.' January just stopped himself from making a comment about Mr Stookey that probably shouldn't have been shared with a white man, no matter how much that white man might agree with him.

'Did it have something to do with Mamzelle's death?' asked Catherine.

'I think so.' January was not at all sure of this himself. 'The problem is, at the moment, I can't figure out how.'

And he recalled the jailer's voice in his dream. *Best for everyone if we let the woman hang . . .*

His visit wasn't long, and he had seen, the moment he walked into the room, what he needed to see: that Catherine was being taken care of. That her spirits were better. That a man in a position better than his own was looking after her . . .

He was a few steps down Rue Orleans on his way to the wharves to look for Ti-Jon, when he heard running feet behind him. The jailer Stookey's whining voice called, 'You, Janvier!'

He was tempted to keep walking, but stopped, to let the man catch him up. *Now what?*

'It true what Sergeant Boechter says, that you's a surgeon?' The little man looked up at him as if trying to puzzle out how this was possible, for a man who by all rights should have been out chopping cane.

'I am, sir, yes. I trained in Paris.'

The jailer glanced around, and lowered his voice. 'I happen to have come,' he said, 'by a bag of sawbones' tools. I can let you have 'em, for five dollars.'

January opened his mouth to turn down this handsome offer – he had no desire to be arrested for receiving stolen goods, which these undoubtedly were. But if the parish jailer was peddling stolen property, it was just as well to get it and find the original owner, who – considering the cost of good-quality scalpels, forceps, probes and clamps – would be grateful to get them back.

And if the man had left the state already . . .

And then I really will *find Ti-Jon . . .*

'May I have a look at them?'

The leather satchel was cached behind boxes of soap, prisoners' clothing, and moldy public records in a corner of the storeroom next to Stookey's office. The jailer had to move two brooms and a mop bucket to retrieve it. 'It's on the up-an'-up,' the man said, a trifle defensively, as he brought it out. 'Jean Forstall's field hands pulled a deader outta Bayou Gentilly yesterday, an' I went back later, seein' as how he was dressed nice an' mighta had some other things go in the water with him, like a good cane or maybe a gun. This was 'bout a dozen feet along from where they found him.'

The satchel was nearly identical to the one January had been carrying on the night Akinto had attacked him. It was damp, but didn't look as if it had been in the water long. The contents seemed largely undamaged – forceps, fleam, scissors, lancet, and a couple of specula. Two scalpels – one straight, one curved, both carefully capped – and a small bone saw. A seton needle. The small, corked bottles of powders and medicine had all been contaminated with bayou water, the packet of plaisters and of bandages reduced to mush.

But the thing that drew – and held – January's attention was the name punched neatly into the inside of the bag's flap.

Bryant Bascomb, MRCS.

He had the sensation of having pitched a bucket of randomly colored pebbles into the air, and seen them fall into a perfect mosaic of Pompeiian dancing girls at his feet.

He said, very quietly, 'Oh.'

TWENTY

B ryant Bascomb's body was still in the small whitewashed room at Charity Hospital that the city used as a morgue. Like his surgical kit, he hadn't been in the water long. The crayfish had barely started on his eyes, earlobes, and lips. His clothing lay folded on one of the benches at the side of the room, clammy and already smelling moldy in the heat. The pockets had been emptied. January guessed that without Shaw to back him, he would have no access to their contents.

Not that it mattered. Had there been a folded sheet of coarse foolscap in one of them, it was unintelligible mush now.

And he had a good guess what it had said.

Bascomb had been shot through the body, with a second shot through the head.

He found Hannibal at the house on Rue Esplanade – correcting Latin exercises – when he returned there, walking swiftly through the forenoon's heat. 'Good. This saves me the trouble of tracking you down.'

'You have no idea, *amicus meus*, how many times I've been greeted with those words.' He wiped his pen. 'And it never ends well . . .'

When he told the fiddler where he wanted to go, Hannibal looked taken aback. 'I gather from Owl-Eyed Athene' – he nodded toward Rose's chemistry workroom across the yard – 'that's where someone attempted to make quietus for the good Lieutenant Shaw.'

'I suspect Shaw made his first attempt to reach the woodlot from the river road,' said January. 'I think he must have been turned back by Aubin's overseer, who would have reported the encounter. When he returned – just close enough to sunset that the work gangs had gone in from the field – the killer was already there, waiting for him. And then, he wouldn't have been hit if he hadn't called out to me. We can approach the place from Bayou Gentilly, through the ciprière.'

'Oh joy. "Thoro' brush, thoro' briar, thoro' flood, thoro' fire/ I do wander everywhere" . . .' He shuffled the foolscap sheets of Latin together and affixed them with a pin, pressed his hand to his side to still a cough. 'Please don't tell me we're to walk . . . What is it, three miles in from Bayou Gentilly to the woodlot on Bayou des Ouaouarons? If we can even find the place? Plus whatever it is, from here to Bayou Gentilly by way of the Faubourg Marigny brickyards . . .'

'I can get horses from Maggie Valentine,' said January. And then: 'I need you, Hannibal. Not just because of the chance of man-stealers in the ciprière. I think there were at least two of them, when I went out there after Shaw yesterday. I need someone to watch my back. And if I do find anything, I'll need a white witness.'

'*Certe*,' Hannibal said at once. '*Nullius boni sine sociis jucunde possessio est*, I suppose . . . I only hope the lovely Miss Valentine's steeds won't make us too conspicuous . . .'

'They won't,' said January. 'Because I will ask the lovely Miss Valentine to accompany us, and hold the horses beside Bayou Gentilly while you and I walk in to the woodlot . . . quietly.'

Hannibal sighed. 'I knew there had to be a catch.'

January wrote out a note to M'sieu and Madame Jahnke out in Carrollton – the parents of that afternoon's student – pleading a slight fever which he would hesitate, he said, to communicate to their son, a sturdy young Achilles whose mother cherished, to the boy's disgust, like a hothouse flower. This he dispatched via Ti-Gall, with steam-train fare courtesy of M'sieu Motet's bank draft. From the same source he was glad to be able to offer Maggie Valentine not only the rental of her horses, but the cost of her time.

'Hold onto it,' said the girl, as she waved the money aside. 'Pay me when this is all done. We don't know what else we'll need.'

And January smiled a little, at her readiness to include herself as 'we'.

She provided January with a large and sturdy riding-mule named Voltaire – many Americans who lived, or transported goods, along

Bayou Gentilly tended to take violent exception to the sight of a
black man on a horse – gave Hannibal an elderly dapple-gray
which had had, she said, a long career as a cavalry mount. She
herself, clothed in her boy-gear, rode a very pretty bay named
Lizzie, her long red hair bound up under a cap, and carried two
pistols and Shaw's rifle. From Shaw's attic room she produced
three other pistols – including a six-shot 'revolver' the Kentuckian
had acquired in Texas. These she handed to the men.

'You say there's nobody expectin' us out there,' she apologized.
'But it's just as well to have 'em on hand.'

In the event, the ride out Rue Esplanade to the head of Bayou
Gentilly – or Bayou Sauvage, as it was sometimes known – was
uneventful. They turned along the shell road that ran through the
rough fields that had once been viprière, some of them logged
over now, and dotted with the usual back-of-town straggle of cheap
'groceries', brickyards, and makeshift shacks half-hidden in the
trees. These grew more sparse, and the trees thicker, as the ground
got low and wet. Bayou Gentilly formed a sort of low ridge behind
New Orleans itself, but the land sloped away from it, both
toward the river and toward the marshy fastnesses of the genuine
viprière. To their left a slow, black whirlpool of ravens circled over
something dead out among the trees.

Once in the viprière, the air was deathly still. They left Maggie
with the horses, and – hoping he recalled the landmarks from his
childhood – January led the way into the squishy wilderness,
Hannibal dropping further and further behind him, and moving
off to his right, pistol in hand. Watching his back.

And like a man making a pebble mosaic of Pompeiian dancing
girls, January fit pieces together in his mind as he walked.

It wa'n't there, Shaw had whispered.

Other remembered phrases filled his mind. *A damn Democrat
who puts the government's money in his own pocket . . . You must
have heard how these new methods increase crop yield, if one
could only afford the equipment . . . You can bet every man, woman,
an' child . . . is gonna be here . . . The whole house was empty,
'ceptin' for Jerry . . .*

*Napoleon was a coward . . . I will never forgive him, for opening
the doors of this country . . .*

Why didn't I see that from the start?

Hannibal remained at a cautious distance ('It can't be too distant, *amicus meus*, I can't hit a church door with one of these things . . .') while January made a careful circuit of the woodlot, watching and listening for any sound. Any threat. He didn't really expect anyone to be there – at least he hoped his performance of falling backward into the blazing cabin with 'Shaw' over his shoulder had been convincing.

But he was dealing, he understood, with someone who now had everything at stake.

It had rained a number of times, since Melchior Aubin had met Charles Brunneau here to defend Napoleon's good name. Certainly the thick weeds retained no clear track of last night's events. January slipped into the ruin of the shed where Shaw had been hiding, found the Kentuckian's second long rifle there, and a number of rifle-balls on what remained of a bench. Set ready, presumably, for a quick re-load. His knife was there, too, and a couple of shards of wood, the largest only an inch or two in length. Carefully – the blade was razor-sharp – January stowed the weapon in his satchel, then slipped outside again.

They have to have faced off east to west. He gauged the shape of the lot. It was the only space where there was enough clear ground to pace off twenty steps. Cautiously, he began to examine the trees at the west end of the lot: bark, boughs, roots. *It could be anywhere, dammit . . .*

He moved deeper into the tangle of pickerel-weed and scuppernong, scanning the bark of every tree. Even if he found what he sought, he knew it would prove nothing in court . . .

A rustle, soft as the stroke of a bird-wing, immediately behind him.

He spun, and found himself face to face with Akinto.

Akinto, thin and muddy and scratched with twigs and cane. But relaxed, smiling to see him. '*Sadiq.*' The African held out his hand. January bowed.

Akinto pointed back through the trees, to where Hannibal was keeping anxious guard. Signed, *A man there*, then mimed pistols, with a soft pop of breath.

January made a gesture indicating a long queue of hair, then a mustache, and Akinto nodded.

He's my friend. January patted his own left arm, where a friend would stand, and the far traveler nodded approvingly.

'*Rafiki*,' the African said. He had acquired, January saw, a deadly-sharp cane knife, wrapped in what looked like the rags of a field hand's shirt and hanging from a rope belt at his waist; also a crude satchel wrought of squirrel-skins, rope, and the remains of an old towel. Though thin, he did not look starved, and January guessed he set snares wrought of kitchen string, and fished in the bayou. It was easy enough to make a spear out of a cane stalk.

By the look of him, too, he wasn't letting himself go dirty day to day, despite the mud on his clothes.

He hadn't given up his pride.

Akinto smiled a little, touched the grimed green calico shirt he wore, and pressed his hands in thanks to his breast, with January's earlier gesture: *Safe. Goodness. Peace.* '*Asante.*'

January grinned, and elaborately mimed handing him a gift.

Akinto grinned back, and repeated his gesture: '*Asante.*' Then with quick gestures, Akinto sketched Shaw: height, shaggy hair, touched the rifle January held, then mimed, *Someone shot him . . .* and January nodded.

'*Rafiki*,' he said.

This way.

The pistol ball had gone wildly awry – exactly as every shot ever fired by Charles Brunneau in his entire life had done. (*God only knows how many men on his own side he accidentally shot at Waterloo . . .*) The pale wood, where Shaw had cut it out of a tupelo tree, was about eight feet off the ground. Akinto mimed the Kentuckian searching, finding the place, taking the knife from his belt and cutting it out. Then he turned sharply, as if hearing some sound, and vanished – with a hunter's instant reflex for cover – into the near-by palmettos. A moment later he re-appeared, and gestured toward the ruin of the shed.

January nodded.

'*Rafiki – amekufa?*' The cut-throat gesture was unmistakable, and January shook his head.

He clutched his head and doubled over, then straightened up again, took several deep breaths. *Hurt, but lives.*

Will you come with me? he asked then, and Akinto shook his head, his dark eyes sad.

Will you be here?

The African nodded. *I will be here. Somewhere.* The gesture took in the still, brazen heat of the cyprière around them. *Here.* And reaching out, clasped January's hands.

'*Asante*,' he said softly. '*Asante. Rafiki.*'

Shaw opened his eyes, squinted against the single candle's light.

'How do you feel?' asked January softly, and the Kentuckian moved his head a little on the pillow.

'Like I been hit over the head with a church. Where am I?'

'In my storeroom.' Rose had greeted him, upon his return, with the news that Shaw was more or less awake, but at his request, only he had gone down to the ground-floor vaults to see him.

Hail Mary, full of grace, the Lord is with thee . . .

Thank you. Asante. Thank you.

'What happened?'

'Melchior Aubin shot you, snooping around the site of that duel.' January sat on the edge of the bed, held out the invalid's cup of broth that he'd brought down with him, and slid an arm behind his friend's shoulders. 'Can you manage this?'

'You know it was him?' Shaw took the cup in his own big hands, though January had to steady him as he drank.

'I have no proof, no. But that's what you meant when you said to me, It wasn't there. You meant there was no laudanum in his room.'

'I said that?' Shaw closed his eyes for a moment, as if the mere act of drinking had taken all his strength. 'Yeah.'

'I assumed he was drugged on it,' said January. 'The way he moved – he never caught himself with pain, except once or twice, I think now when he remembered he was supposed to have been shot.'

'Yeah, you was back by the door, wasn't you?' whispered Shaw. 'I was up next to him. The room was dim, an' his eyes was dilated, like a man's do in poor light. Laudanum, they'd be down to pinheads, whatever the light was. An' there wasn't no smell of it, anywheres.'

'You went out to the site of the duel,' said January, digging in his pocket, 'looking for Brunneau's pistol ball.' He brought out the four pellets of lead, dropped the smallest one – the odd one – onto the sheet beside Shaw's limp hand. 'You found it, too.'

Shaw's fingers moved towards it, but gave up on the effort. 'Can't prove it by me.'

'I found the place where you cut it out of the tree. And the splinters in that little shed in the woodlot, where you cut it away from the wood. It hit a tree eight feet high and yards away – which of course was the reason Aubin pushed Brunneau into challenging him in the first place. He knew he'd be safe.'

'It's a wonder Brunneau didn't hit one of the seconds.'

'I imagine,' said January, 'when the guns went off, they all dropped flat on the ground. I would have. Sorry,' he added, as Shaw chuckled, then grimaced with pain. 'And I expect the first thing Aubin did, after he was carried back to Aurore, was get rid of the trousers and the coat he was wearing. They found Bascomb's body yesterday.'

'Bascomb . . .?'

'The surgeon Aubin brought to the duel. I'm guessing Aubin had an old medicine bottle full of blood in the pocket of that baggy greatcoat I hear he wore to the duel, and gave Bryant Bascomb – and I've never heard of a surgeon in New Orleans by that name – instructions to make sure to be the first person to turn Aubin over after he fell. And to tell everyone to stay back while he pressed a dressing on the "wound".'

Shaw whispered, 'Cute.'

'Bascomb was shot, once through the body and again through the head. If there's someone in the Cabildo you trust with the job, it probably won't be too difficult to trace his movements after the duel. I think we'll find he left town right after the duel, then came back Sunday, as soon as he heard about Mamzelle Maginot's murder. He figured out why Aubin needed a cast-iron reason not to be suspected. And he figured it would be worth something. He hadn't been dead for more than forty-eight—'

January paused. Shaw was asleep.

TWENTY-ONE

At the Democratic Planters' Club cotillion that night at the Hotel Pontchartrain in Milneburgh, little else was talked of besides Friday's 'Great Procession' as the Great Natchez Ball would come rolling into New Orleans. Guiding his little orchestra through Rossini and Schubert at the reception – the guests of honor being former mayors Denis Prieur and the venerable old Augustin de Macarty, who was related to pretty much every French and Spanish Creole family in the southern part of the state – and later, through 'The Lancers Quadrille' and 'Napoleon's Retreat' for the dancing, January had little opportunity or inclination to follow what was being said.

Griff Paige, who had insisted on resuming his place among them, looked ashy and ill, and when an unguarded comment made it plain that Cochon had a bet with Jacques on whether the clarionettist would finish the evening on his feet, insisted on being cut into the wager. In addition to January's very real concern about the young man, the elaborately pillared and painted ballroom was extremely noisy. The men were mostly gathered around the punch-bowl at the far end of the ballroom, most of them looking as if they would far rather talk politics than dance with their wives.

And unlike the Orleans Ballroom in town, this room had no discreet hallway connecting it to a second festivity for the men's mistresses.

However, the women, grouped closer to the orchestra, agreed that the Ladies for Harrison who would be marching in the procession were a bunch of cheap, ostentatious busy-bodies who had no business pushing their way into men's affairs, and it would serve them right when 'our men' attacked the procession to rescue 'that horrible gallows thing' and teach them a lesson in respect.

January had, however, ample opportunity to observe how Charles-Louis Trepagier worked the room, moving from one group to another of the rougher-hewn men present: contractors; the captains of steamboats; and Jefferson Butler, who in addition to his shipping business owned two construction companies, commanded the Jefferson Parish militia, and exercised a sort of feudal dominion over a gang of ruffians – led by one Coal-Oil Billy – from the Jefferson Parish slaughterhouses. He was also, January knew from Ti-Jon, one of Trepagier's best customers for slaves and most reliable sources of credit.

'Trouble Friday, it looks like,' January opined, and deftly brought the sheet music for a Haydn quadrille to the forefront of his piano rack.

Griff jeered. 'Serve the bastards right.'

An older woman in the loud, flat voice of failing hearing said,

'Did you hear about what happened at Duralde? The overseer's house was burned, and a man – or maybe two – was killed. My maid tells me it was some of the field hands that did it—'

'Well, what do you expect, from a man who keeps all the hands stirred up about escaping, with all that fool talk about going to Africa and living like kings. Of course they're going to try to escape!'

'Beasts!' cried the white-haired Madame Mabillet. 'I tell my grandson, it's all of a piece! What happened in St Domingue will happen here, with all of them coming here and nobody making a move to stop them.'

'They don't know what's good for them, really,' stated the Widow Redfern, glorious in her usual deep mourning and aglitter with diamonds. 'You can't tell me the name of a single Negro in this parish who can make a decent living if there isn't a white man telling him what to do.'

January glided into the quadrille, his mind taking refuge, as it always did, in the beauty of the melody, the blended voices of Hannibal's and Cochon's violins, the light, conversational interchange of clarionet and flute. He would have done better, he reflected, that afternoon, to have slept again after talking to Shaw, instead of going down to the wharves. He had finally, for a wonder, encountered Ti-Jon there, off-loading crates of hemp sacking and 'Negro shoes' from the decks of the *Parnassus*. But when he'd asked his men, did any of them know the words *asante* or *rafiki* they had shaken their heads. Africa was a huge land of many hundreds of tongues. Even those men old enough to have been born there – and thanks to smuggling, a number of them had come to Louisiana long after the trade had been officially closed – none had heard the language that included such terms for 'thank you' and 'friend'.

However, Ti-Jon had told him two other things more encouraging. When at last the cotillion was over, and the musicians returned along Bayou St John to town in a rented wagon, January bade them goodbye where the road crossed Bayou Sauvage, and made his way, by the light of the late-rising gibbous moon, along the Gentilly Road. He was aware, as he walked, of movement in the ciprière to his left; cautious rustlings among the palmetto and swamp-laurel that crowded so close to the path, yet unseen in the gluey dark. Instinctive caution made his heart beat quicker, but he'd taken the precaution of bringing along the pistol he hadn't yet returned to Maggie Valentine. Had Hannibal, or any white man, been with him, his quarry would have melted into the swamp like a trick of the moonlight.

Gold light glimmered in the world of indigo and black. Something moved on the levee to his right, when he reached the little footbridge that crossed another bayou that fed into Sauvage: a dozen feet across, and probably not even half so deep. Frogs peeped, or boomed, or gulped; the cypresses were barely more than the whispers of ghosts guarding the night-shrouded bank.

He hoped the furtive stirrings glimpsed on the trace of pathway weren't gators.

Or were only little ones.

Then voices.

Muttering that paused – listened. Picked up again, softer.

'. . . coffee grounds. Smell 'em – only been run through once . . . Plenty of juice left in 'em . . .'

Had some sentry whispered, 'It's only Mr J . . .'?

'Think I might have what you're after, here . . . this'll snag anything short of Jonah's whale . . .' '. . . best quality linen. Michie Rost'll never miss it . . .' 'Tis good Massachusetts rum. There's whiskey, if you've got a thirst for something fancier. But if all you want is to get the job done . . .' 'You have any word from Baton Rouge for Allie? From someone named Ned?' . . . 'Indeed I do. I spoke to Ned only last week . . .'

The voices of the enslaved were half-whispers, tinged with the music of Africa and the cane patch. The white man's voice, soft as it was, bore the mellow accents of Wales.

When January stepped beyond the screen of palmetto-thicket that hid the pirogue from the path, three men and two women looked around at him, and seemed reassured. He guessed the stealthy rustle back on the levee had been a lookout. Sheriffs of the parishes from Belize to Natchez were keeping an eye out for False River Jones.

Andy the cook grinned at the sight of January and held out his hand. 'Michie J!'

Jones also rose from the bench on the bank to extend a welcome. 'A pleasure to see you again, sir. Is this visit concerning the African?'

'In part.' January gripped Andy's hand, then Jones's, in turn.

He wasn't at all surprised that the Welshman had heard of Akinto. False River Jones heard everything. 'Have you seen him?'

Jones shook his head. 'Well, once, maybe, at a distance. But the food I leave for him when I'm in these parts disappears. And he pays for it, he does, with things like squirrel-skins. Once I traded him some fish-hooks. They'll get him in the end, you know.'

January said, 'That's what I'm trying to prevent, sir. But that isn't my chief business here tonight. Please . . .' He gestured toward Andy and the other three, men and women who wore the neat garments of house servants. 'Don't let me keep any of you. I can wait.'

Andy waved aside the offer, though he and the others would all have been in for rough handling by parish patrols, or by their overseers, had they been caught night-walking at this hour, with or without kitchen spoils or the master's second-best linen shirts in hand. 'You go ahead, Michie J.'

After eight years back in New Orleans, January was known to many in the three black communities of the town: the enslaved; the uptown free blacks; and the 'downtown' free people of color, who regarded the uptown blacks, for the most part, as Protestants and Americans and 'uppity'. Active in the Church and in the Free Colored Militia and Burial Society – and, it was whispered, in other things besides – he had acquired a reputation as a man one could come to, in time of trouble. But it was also known that he was friends with one of the City Guard. And it was just as well not to take chances.

This, January understood – and recognized that there was nothing personal in their unwillingness to let him overhear the exact details of their dealings with False River Jones. They withdrew into the shadows, just beyond the circle of feeble light thrown by the pierced tin lantern on the prow of the little boat. The tall Welshman moved aside a little, to let January take a seat on the bench, and Jones's little black dog leaped off the pirogue, soundless as always, to sniff his boots.

'And what can I help you with, Mr J?'

False River Jones was perhaps fifty, long gray hair braided with blue ribbons, dark eyes very bright in the road-map of wrinkles that surrounded them. He was in shirtsleeves – as was January, with the night's thick heat – and across the purple brocade of an extremely fancy waistcoat at least four watch-chains dangled, glittering with keys, fobs, and seals. January wondered if this was a display of merchandise for sale, and if the Masonic arc and compass meant that the trader was in fact one of his Brothers in the Order (*God help us!*) or had merely 'acquired' it from someone else who was.

'I'm looking for a pair of trousers,' he said softly.

Jones's eyebrows went up, without the slightest trace of surprise in his eyes.

'Trousers, and an old-fashioned long greatcoat, or driving coat. These would have been found recently, probably here-abouts. This would be Friday or Saturday. They would have had blood on them.'

'Funny it is' – Jones tilted his head slightly – 'you should mention that.'

The blood itself had been washed out by the waters of the Bayou des Ouaouarons, where they'd been found, Jones said when he brought them out. The stains remained, discoloring the pale fawn of the trousers and even darkening the deep-blue silk lining of the coat.

January turned the fabric over in his hands. The trousers had been slashed open on the right hip, between the leg seam and the flies. When January lined up the edges of the gash, he found no evidence of a bullet-hole. Nor was there a hole anywhere in the coat.

'Andy,' he said, after he'd paid three dollars for the garments (and decided regretfully that he really shouldn't offer another dollar for the extremely fine cornet that hung temptingly from the pole framework fitted out on the pirogue – God knew who *that* had been stolen from). 'Do you recognize these?'

The cook stepped forward. January held up both trousers and coat – carefully, so that the faint bloodstains showed, but not the fact that there was no hole to go with them. 'Them's Michie Melchior's.' Andy reached to touch, but January moved the garments slightly but definitely out of his reach. 'That's what he was wearin' when he had that duel with Michie Charles Brunneau. There should be a bullet-hole—'

Again January moved the garments away from his hand.

'What was they doin'? Where'd they come from, Michie Jones? Bayou des Ouaouarons?' He turned back to January. 'Michie Melchior give 'em to that Dr Bascomb, 'cause they was spoilt.

Dr Bascomb took 'em away with him. Said he knew someone who could fix 'em up, almost good as new. Throwed 'em in the bayou?'

'So this Dr Bascomb came back to Aurore with him after the duel?'

'Oh, hell, yeah. Fixed him up good, an' left bandages an' basilicum powder an' what-all else with him, so's he could change the dressin's himself. Got behind Jerry somethin' fierce, that Michie Melchior wouldn't let him do it, but I don't blame him for that. Jerry's a good man, an' there ain't an ounce of harm in him. Me, I wouldn't want to depend on him for so much as a glass of water when he's been drinkin'. Monroe, or one of the housemaids, is always havin' to cover up for him when he's supposed to be ironin' the gentlemen's shirts.'

The cook grinned, and shook his head. 'I can't tell you how many of Michie Melchior's shirts – an' Michie Damien's – we had to sneak down here an' sell, 'cause they had brown burns on 'em the size of your hand.'

'Bayou des Ouaouarons,' said Shaw, when January – in between eating a much-belated lunch the following day and dressing for the piano lessons upriver in Jefferson Parish – gave him his report on the previous day's researches. Shaw had no recollection of their conversation of the previous day, nor of the brief words he'd exchanged with Zizi-Marie, when he'd wakened earlier that morning in the room to which they'd moved him, up in the main house. But this, January knew, was to be expected with a head injury, and he was encouraged to see his friend's eyes clearer, and to hear in his speech none of the muzziness of the day before. 'Closest spot he could dump his duds, once everybody in the house was asleep that night – barrin' the river, an' who knows who'd find 'em there. Wonder where he cached 'em when they brung him home from the duel?'

'If Bascomb was in on it,' said January, 'he could have just shoved them under the mattress of the bed, while Bascomb was "dressing" his "wound".'

'And then told Damien and Olivia that he'd given them to Bascomb,' agreed Hannibal, who had just arrived from Maggie Valentine's with a clean nightshirt and Shaw's shaving things. 'Why not simply actually *give* them to Bascomb to dispose of, by the way? Surely less dangerous – from the standpoint of being discovered – than having them on the premises for almost twenty-four hours. Almost as dangerous as chucking them in the river. Servants can be shockingly nosy.'

'Given what Bascomb already knew about him' – Shaw moved his hand to touch the folded greatcoat that lay on the bed beside him – 'namely that he was up to *somethin'*, fakin' bein' wounded in a duel – *I'd* sure be shy about handin' the man the evidence.'

'Witness,' said January, 'that he obviously *did* come back.'

'There is much,' agreed the fiddler, 'in what you say. *Ne scio quid curtae semper abest rei* has brought more than one man to a sticky end.'

Following January's return from Bayou Sauvage in the extremely small hours of the morning, he and Gabriel had moved Shaw out of the secret storeroom – which might at any time be needed to conceal a runaway – and up to the chamber that was officially January's 'bedroom', by the conventions of Spanish or French Creole domestic arrangements. In fact, January always slept in the room traditionally designated as belonging to the mistress of the house, with Rose. The little room behind his office, though it contained a bed, had become a sort of catch-all annex to the library. A haven – Rose had explained to her students, who had come down the attic stair, night-gowned and tousled, during the final stages of the transfer – for a family friend injured that night in an accident.

January didn't know if the girls believed her or not.

But if Melchior Aubin had faked both duel and injury, reasoned Rose later, with the intention of providing himself with the best of all possible reasons (short of being dead himself) why he could not have murdered Marie-Joyeuse Maginot, it would not be easy for him, once Shaw was back in New Orleans, to mount another attack on the policeman. 'It's one thing to lie in wait for someone and attempt to murder him half a mile from your own bedroom,' she said, and set down her tray of ginger water. 'Particularly if one's sickroom is at the back of the house and only a dozen feet from the cane rows. It's quite another to come up to town . . . even if he *hadn't* thought M'sieu Shaw was dead.'

January had drawn breath to agree, and then, after a moment, had nodded. The recollection of a shadow in the carriageway on Rue Conti, of a dark form stepping between tombs in the cemetery, returned to him.

He had a gun, Lottie had said. There was no mistakin' that.
If it wasn't Aubin, who, then?
And if the man – or woman – with the gun didn't know Aubin was the killer, who did that armed shadow pursue?
But from a purely practical standpoint, it would be easier to nurse a man with a concussion on the main floor of the house than in a secret storeroom that had to be reached from the back gallery and through the yard – to say nothing of whatever the girls might observe, or what Shaw might remember about where he'd been, when his mind cleared a little.

January had just enough uneasiness about the figure with the rifle not to place their guest out in one of the three rooms in the rear yard above the kitchen. ('I doubt he'd have slept comfortably,' had commented Hannibal, 'once he knew our Athene's chemical workshop was next door, anyway.')

Shaw asked now, 'Got any idea where this Bascomb jasper was stayin' in town? Not a local man. Wonder where Aubin met him?'

'Democrat Club meeting?' suggested Rose.

'I'll tell Boechter to look up an' ask Jeff Butler, or Jed Burton. They'd know. An' they found him where? Bayou Gentilly? If'fn you'd be so good, Maestro, as to bring me paper an' pen – consarn it, I'm weak as a cat . . .'

'I can write for you,' offered Hannibal.

Shaw shook his head. 'Needs to be a official request to Captain Tremouille, not to bury the poor bastard's body 'til somebody can have a look at it an' be sure.'

'I can write it for you in your handwriting.'

'You gonna get yourself in real trouble one of these days, fiddler.'

'The captain won't be able to read it otherwise,' pointed out January. 'I doubt you can hold a pen, sir.'

'Well, you's prob'ly right.' Shaw sighed. 'How'd he get out there that time of the night, anyways? Has to been when all the Aubin house servants was asleep—'

'Apparently' – January took from his pocket the list of names Ti-Jon had given him – 'there are three men one can contact in town, if one needs to hire a horse – and a vehicle, evidently – for . . . er . . . night work.'

'Ah,' said Shaw, perusing the list. 'I knowed about Django Mercer . . .'

'There's two others,' said January. 'And one of the two advertised on Tuesday morning, for the return of a liver-bay gelding with a white nose and an off-hind white stocking, with saddle and bridle. For ten dollars, courtesy of M'sieu Motet, I was able to get the direction Bascomb gave. A Madame Schaellert, on Tchoupitoulas Street. Hannibal's on his way over there this afternoon' – he nodded to his friend – 'to learn what he can about Mr Bascomb's visit – or visits – to this city. If you could write . . .'

He stopped. Shaw had fallen asleep again.

TWENTY-TWO

January returned from instructing little Susie Taylor and the Walters children in Carrollton – a small American enclave a few miles downstream of Nine-Mile Point – through the last of the thinning afternoon rain, to find a blue-uniformed City Guardsman standing on the gallery of his house. The man knew him, by sight at least, and nodded as he came up the steps. From within, January heard the voice of Captain Tremouille boom, 'That's ridiculous.'

Dammit . . .

Two strides took him across his office, to the door of the room where Shaw lay.

Captain Robert Tremouille was a tall man, dark-haired and sturdy and related to half the old French Creole families in town. Like January, he had served under Jackson at the Battle of Chalmette, though he'd been half a dozen years younger: not one of the old aristocracy of sugar planters, but born when New Orleans had been still under the French flag, of parents who had come from France in their youth. Six years ago he had pooh-poohed the rumors that Delphine LaLaurie – formerly married to Jean Blanque, merchant, lawyer, legislator, and possibly slave dealer, herself a daughter of the very respected Macarty family – would do something as frightful as torture slaves in her attic (January himself had barely gotten out of the place alive). He was not a man, reflected January, to easily contemplate hanging a prominent French Creole planter for murder when he had a perfectly good black woman to take the blame instead.

'I ain't so sure of that, sir.' Shaw's voice was barely a scrape, like a clamshell grating on stone. 'I think it's worth goin' down to Aurore an' askin'—'

'Asking a man who's been flat on his back for almost a week with a pistol ball through his hip whether he was actually shot?'

'We only got his word for it, sir.'

'It should be Barthelmy handling this anyway,' added the captain pettishly. 'The crime took place in the Third Municipality—'

'An' Barthelmy couldn't figure out the winner of a cock fight if'fn he was eatin' the loser for Sunday dinner. Senator Clay asked me to look into this hisself . . . sir.'

'I expect,' said Tremouille frostily, 'that among your own acquaintances – and among the men with whom you're accustomed to dealing, and dealing very well, I might add – it's both customary and wise to doubt every word they say.'

He glanced meaningfully across the small room to where Hannibal Sefton stood by the door that led into the back gallery, and his lips compressed. For years a well-known drunkard, Hannibal was still regarded as degenerate by the respectable of New Orleans, both French and American. One of the very few white men who performed with the black orchestras of the town, even after giving up both drink and laudanum he was almost completely indigent, living where he could, and making what money he could, as he could.

'M'sieu Janvier . . .' Tremouille turned, and extended his hand as January came into the room. 'My deepest thanks are owed you, for your service to a valued member of the First Municipality Guards—'

'Mr J will back me up,' persisted Shaw, 'that there was somethin' fishy 'bout that duel, Captain. Seein' as how it was worth somebody's while to shoot me when I started pokin' around the site—'

'Good God, man, that part of the ciprière is alive with smugglers and slave stealers. From what you've told me, that woodlot is a known landmark. You doubtless interfered with a rendezvous of some sort—'

'If you'll excuse me, sir . . .' January put all the diffidence he could muster into his voice, and bent his shoulders slightly, in an attitude of deference. He knew the police captain wasn't a man to slap a free man of color for being 'uppity', but he knew also that no white man could stand being corrected by a black one.

To judge by Tremouille's expression, the police captain was no different from the rest.

'I was there when it happened, sir,' he went on. 'And my impression was that the attacker had arrived at the woodlot before Michie Shaw did, and was waiting for him.'

Tremouille's brows lifted, as if at the assertion of a child that yes, there had been a platt-eye devil under the bed, and he turned to Shaw. 'And was that *your* impression, M'sieu Shaw?'

'Only impression I got of that whole day's the one on my skull.' He turned his head slightly on the pillow, face gray with fatigue in the silvery afternoon light. 'I don't even remember wakin' up that mornin', much less talkin' to Aubin like Ma'am Janvier tells me I told her yesterday I did. Pieces of it,' he added, his brow furrowing with pain. 'Like there bein' no laudanum in the room nor no smell of it neither . . .'

'That hardly sounds like grounds for breaking into a sick man's room and arresting him for the murder of a young girl in his own family, when we already have the true culprit in custody. Particularly since, as you say, your recollections of the day are unreliable at best.'

'What isn't unreliable' – Hannibal gestured with a much-tattered memorandum book – 'is the fact that we have the garments M'sieu Aubin was wearing for the duel – well, the trousers and greatcoat, at any rate – and neither of them has a hole in it, despite copious bloodstains. A cork, and the medicine bottle that undoubtedly contained the blood, were still in the coat's pocket. The cork was bloodstained as well.'

Tremouille looked down his nose at him. 'And where did you come by these garments, M'sieu – uh – Sefton?'

'They were found in the Bayou des Ouaouarons.'

'By whom? An acquaintance of Madame Clisson's?'

Clearly seeing that any provenance originating with False River Jones would not help the situation, Hannibal made a gesture like a fencer conceding a hit.

'A surgeon attended the man at the duel, and I'm sure he would have noticed had his patient been unwounded.'

'Not necessarily.' The fiddler opened the little booklet, flicked through the pages with spidery fingers. 'The attending surgeon was an Englishman named Bryant Bascomb, passing through New Orleans the week of September seventh to twelfth. He boarded with a Mrs Schaellert on Tchoupitoulas Street, but spent most of his evenings at the Salle d'Orléans. I'm sure Mr Davis there will remember him, since I found some two thousand dollars' worth of markers from the Salle in his rooms. Mrs Schaellert had some understandable concerns about payment of her rent and board, but in fact, Mr Bascomb paid – in Bank of Louisiana notes – on Saturday, the day after he served as surgeon in the Brunneau-Aubin duel.'

'That's a damn fair price to pay,' murmured Shaw, 'for a surgeon.'

'Having never had the money to hire one in this country—'

'The cost of six nights' lodging,' said January. 'It's about four times what—' He stopped himself from saying, *even a white man.* 'What even the best men in New Orleans would charge.' He had found that there were whites who didn't care to be reminded that free black men could be professionals, and charge professional fees, albeit lower ones than a man of the preferred ancestry and hue.

'And I have already ascertained,' Hannibal continued, 'that Melchior Aubin deals exclusively with the Bank of Louisiana. By all accounts – viz. Brunneau's second Hercule LaFrennière, and Brunneau's valet Elkin – and M'sieu Brunneau himself – Mr Bascomb was the first to reach Aubin's side. I expect everyone else was too stunned that Brunneau had managed to hit his target. Bascomb already had bandages pressed over the site of the wound, and there was blood splashed about everywhere. Aubin was carried back to Aurore – the woodlot on Bayou des Ouaouarons where this all took place was less than a mile from the plantation house – and put to bed. According to the Aubin cook, Aubin insisted that only he himself was to change the dressings, and he seems to have refused all help in doing so. Bascomb evidently left him Saturday morning with bandages and the wherewithal to doctor his own wounds. I don't know how much Aubin paid him, but that afternoon Bascomb paid up all his debts about town – except his gambling ones – and left New Orleans.'

'Which is what he might have been expected to do,' retorted the captain irritably, 'after he made sure his patient had what was needful for healing. One can't—'

'Bryant Bascomb returned to New Orleans,' Hannibal continued, 'on the following afternoon, Sunday . . . with about three dollars in his pocket, according to the good Mrs Schaellert, who evidently searched his room. He left her house at two o'clock Tuesday morning, the fifteenth. She heard him let himself out with his own key. He then . . .' He licked his finger, flicked a few more pages. 'Rented himself a saddle-horse through the offices of one M'sieu Hache, who evidently knows people who'll hire their cattle out in the middle of the night, for sufficient fee—'

'Hire them out my bottom.' Tremouille caught the notebook from Hannibal's slight grip, glanced at it, and threw it to the floor. 'Rey Hache has been fired from four liveries that I know about, for stealing horses in the middle of the night and hiring them out. Bringing them back wet and fatigued—'

'Only this one – a liver bay with one white stocking – was found stray later Tuesday morning along Bayou Gentilly – out past the old Gemme Plantation – and returned.' Hannibal stooped, to retrieve his memorandum book. 'Later that same morning, Bryant Bascomb's body was found in the Bayou des Ouaouarons – which is the nearest body of water to the back of Aurore Plantation.'

'A body was found,' Tremouille corrected him acidly. 'I hardly consider that grounds for disturbing a wounded man by accusing him of killing his own cousin, of bringing grief to his own kin, out of *your* personal conviction that a woman who cannot account for her movements that night, a woman who had good reason to hold a grudge against that poor girl—'

Through his words, January had half-heard, half-felt the tread of someone ascending the steps of the gallery from the street. Had heard Rose's voice, and a man's – familiar footsteps on the floorboards . . .

'Robert,' said Francois Motet's voice from the door. 'I understand that one of your men may have found the true culprit in this terrible affair.'

Tremouille turned, harassed. 'We have done nothing of the kind. That is, we have a . . . The idea that Melchior Aubin, of all people, would have . . . have counterfeited injury in an affair of honor, in order to murder his own cousin—'

January moved his startled gaze from Motet to Rose, who stood just behind him, looking suspiciously innocent . . . then on to Chou-Chou, who gazed about her with an expression more innocent still. With difficulty he restrained himself from going over and embracing them both.

Motet frowned angrily, but kept his voice level as he said, 'Would not the reasonable thing be to go see if his injury is genuine?'

The captain drew himself up. 'How you can have the . . . the *face* to suggest—'

'A woman's life is at stake here, sir.' The old man met the younger one's eyes, daring him to say the words 'black', or 'mistress'. Daring him to bring out phrases about 'one of the most respectable men in this town . . .'

Every plaçée in town, reflected January, knew about the woman Captain Tremouille kept on the Street of Great Men in Marigny.

'I think we owe it to the public – and to our own consciences – to make sure there is no mistake.'

'Of course.' Tremouille spoke as if his mouth hurt him to say the words. 'Salazar!' he called, stepping through January's office to address the officer on the gallery. 'Would you be so good as to step around to Dr Lemonnier on Rue St Louis, and say that we'll need his services this afternoon? Get Barnard on Rue Royale if Lemonnier isn't available.' He turned back to Motet. 'Shall we meet at the Cabildo at five, sir? M'sieu Sefton,' he went on stiffly, 'I shall expect you to accompany us, with those "proofs" of yours.'

He said the word as he would have referred to the 'proofs' offered a few years ago by the *New York Morning Sun* that civilizations of winged beavers had been seen on the moon by means of a giant telescope.

'M'sieu Shaw . . .'

But Shaw had faded into uneasy sleep.

As the men were taking their punctilious leave of Rose and January – with renewed thanks for their civic-mindedness in caring for a wounded member of the City Guards – January heard the clatter of Zizi-Marie's steps on the gallery. The girl whipped in through the French doors of Rose's room, pulled up short in the doorway at the sight of the men in the parlor, and curtsied. Chou-Chou hurried to her and January heard her whisper, 'He was at Zandrine's . . .'

Rose must have dispatched duplicate notes the minute Tremouille had appeared on her front gallery.

The last one out the door – save for Hannibal, who had disappeared back into the sickroom and would undoubtedly be at the dinner-table – Motet turned, shook Rose's hand and then January's. 'You'll join us?' he said. 'Going out to Aurore? Oh, I expect Lemonnier can tell whether a man has a gunshot wound or not – even that charlatan Barnard can't miss *that*. But I'd rather have someone present who knows what he's looking at. Robert . . .' He shook his head. 'Robert's still looking for a reason why it couldn't be his wife's second-cousin . . .'

'I'll be there.'

January set the table, Hannibal and Zizi brought cold grits and tepid gumbo across from the kitchen – suspecting that everybody involved was going to miss supper – and over that sketchy repast, Hannibal recapitulated his day's researches into the surgeon Bryant Bascomb's movements during his last twenty-four hours on earth. 'When he didn't come home Monday night, Mrs Schaellert – a most formidable lady with blonde sausage-curls and a stock of profanity that would put a sergeant of the Marines to the blush – searched his room very thoroughly. She found another pile of markers – I expect we can trace down eventually who they were from, but they amounted to nearly a thousand dollars, in addition to what he owed from his first visit. I expect' – the fiddler scratched the side of his mustache a little self-consciously – 'Bascomb heard about the murder on Sunday. At church, perhaps, wherever he was . . . God knows it's where *I* always picked up the best bits of gossip in my youth. It doesn't sound like it was far. And he realized just exactly why Aubin needed to accomplish his hoax.'

'Silly of him.' Rose spooned a little gumbo over the grits – they were that morning's, and solid as an iron skillet. 'I suppose he thought if he carried a pistol to the rendezvous with Aubin he'd be quite safe.'

'And I suppose,' finished January, 'that Aubin never even met him. Just waited for him at the appointed spot. As he'd waited for Marie-Joyeuse, and later for Shaw.'

'One can't think of everything.' She propped her spectacles more firmly onto her nose. 'And on the subject of not thinking of everything, while I was sitting with Zandrine yesterday, I had a look through the day-books of the house she kept for Damien Aubin in Washington. They were on a shelf in the kitchen. I remembered what you told me, of Nessie's description of the little *ménage* on Judiciary Square.'

January raised his brows. Of course Catherine would have trained her daughter in that simplest and most necessary routine of housekeeping.

'Evidently she was in charge of entertaining, not only her beloved, but quite a number of his political cronies as well.'

'I remember Nessie said that.'

'My mama says,' ventured Cosette, 'that you should never trust a housekeeper, because they always take a little for themselves out of every sum you give them.'

'And were his political cronies impressed?' inquired Hannibal.

'I hope so. French champagne at a dollar the bottle – and not just a few bottles of it, either. Potted foie gras and pâté de Strasbourg – and a set of mother-of-pearl knives so as not to contaminate the taste of the pâté. The hire of a chef named Aristide Sorrell, at a dollar-fifty, on six different occasions, each of them coinciding with the aforesaid champagne and pâté and quantities of French mustard . . . and incidentally with purchases of new waistcoats for m'sieu and new frocks and earrings for Zandrine.'

'And how much does the secretary of a secretary make in the State Department?'

January said, 'Somehow I can't see Brother Melchior sending his vacuum-pan fund to spend on pâté.'

'Quite the contrary, I suspect. If we check his bank accounts, I think we'll find the money went from Damien to Melchior—'

'With a bit subtracted,' murmured Hannibal, 'for champagne and new frocks.'

'When our housekeeper was stealing from *us*,' provided Germaine helpfully, 'she never took a lot of money at a time. Not a hundred dollars or fifty dollars – not enough to be missed unless you were looking closely. But, mama said, it adds up.'

'So it does,' agreed Rose judiciously. 'And in a department like that of the Secretary of State – in fact in any department – that sort of bloodletting would be grounds for dismissal. It certainly would if the secretary were someone like Senator Clay.'

'And if the secretary *isn't* Senator Clay,' said January, 'Brother Melchior would more than ever need Trepagier's support in Washington. Preferably if Harrison lost the election altogether, owing to a scandal over Clay being accused of murder.'

Footfalls on the gallery steps, and a moment later the tall shape of a man glimpsed passing the French doors of the parlor. A man who halted as if startled, turned quickly to scan the trees of the wide strip of empty ground up the middle of Rue Esplanade, searching for . . .

What?

Then he turned back to rap, very properly for the French Town, on the door of January's office – and January saw that it was Henry Clay.

TWENTY-THREE

'**M**onsieur Janvier.' The senator held out his hand as January, startled, opened the door. 'I pray you'll forgive the intrusion.' Hand shaken, he produced a card, which January took, wondering how to say politely, Good God, I know who you are, sir . . .!

'We haven't been introduced, but I've seen you at Granville's and my son-in-law's . . . and didn't you play at President Adams's evening reception in Washington in the spring of '38?'

'I'm flattered you remember me, sir.' January stepped aside. 'Please come in. Won't you join us – for coffee, if you don't care for anything else? We're having supper early because I have to be at the Cabildo at five. I assume you know all about that.' It was one of the peculiarities of America, which had always entertained and baffled his Paris friends, that it was perfectly acceptable for a white man to sit at table with blacks in their home – white gentlemen dined with their quadroon plaçées as a matter of course, for instance – but under no circumstances would a free black man or woman, no matter how fair of complexion or what the connection was, be tolerated at the same board as whites in *their* home, or in any café or restaurant catering to whites.

Because any white is assumed to be the guest of honor in any black person's house? January had only shaken his head when asked.

'Thank you,' Clay said, 'that's very kind,' in his flawless diplomat's French, and followed January through to the back gallery, to bow over Rose's hand. 'Please forgive this unpardonable intrusion, ma'am. I would not have come at this time – and unannounced at that – were the matter not urgent.' And he bowed to Zizi-Marie and the girls, and shook Hannibal's hand.

Turning back to January, he said, 'Captain Tremouille of the City Guard tells me that Mr Shaw is here, convalescent—'

'This way, sir. I warn you, he suffered a deep concussion and might not be able to speak to you. If you'll excuse us, ladies.'

He opened the door of the sickroom, stepped aside to let the senator precede him in. And, seeing in the dimness that Shaw was asleep, he said in an under-voice, 'I take it this concerns the death of Miss Maginot?'

For almost forty years it had been Senator Clay's job not to appear startled or put out by anything, so he simply tilted his head, and January went on.

'I've been working with M'sieu Shaw on the matter – we've worked together on similar affairs for years. I'm personally interested because the woman accused of the crime is an old friend of mine.'

Clay said, 'Ah,' and January could almost see the oiled steel wheels of his mind click the information into place: that January could go places, and ask questions, almost invisibly in New Orleans, where Shaw, a white man, would meet only prevarication or silence. He could see also, in those sharp hazel eyes, a recognition that this was an exception to his general rule that free white men and free black ones were necessarily incompatible. Like many men, January guessed that his visitor perceived individual relationships in a completely different category from those of men – and women – in the abstract.

'Mr Shaw told me the case against Madame Clisson.' The old man shook his head. 'I must say it didn't sound terribly convincing to me, and I could tell Shaw didn't think much of it, either.' He hesitated, looked down at Shaw again.

January said, just as softly, 'M'sieu Shaw showed me the note you received the day of the rally.'

Clay glanced up, and said, 'Ah,' again. And waited.

'I understand why you kept the rendezvous, sir. And why you would want to keep the number of people who know about it to a minimum.'

'Damn it.' His breath blew out in a sigh. 'Shaw's the only one – besides my son-in-law, and yourself, I assume – who's seen that note. I gave Tremouille some cock-and-bull story about being taken ill at the rally, and the truth is that I haven't been well. It's this damned heat.'

He shook his head, impatient at the slow encroachment of age. 'You never know where a story's going to end up. Particularly in an election year. My involvement with Burr is something I can't have dragged out now – not with me carrying the flag for the General from Richmond to Nashville and all stops between. It's something the whole Whig movement can't afford, if we're to correct the wrongs in this country, and move America forward out of Jackson's shadow. I took the note to Shaw to ask as a personal favor – I knew him as a boy, back in Kentucky. I know he's as true as daylight.'

'He is,' said January quietly. 'I have cause to know it.'

'I have to know if there's anything to it,' said Clay simply. 'Anything besides that note. I have to know if, God forbid, Blennerhassett's wife really *is* here in New Orleans; if someone has gotten hold of some of my papers from the Burr business and put them in a context that can be used against me and against the Whigs.'

'I doubt that's the case, sir,' said January. 'The one other person I've shown that note to – at M'sieu Shaw's suggestion – was an acquaintance of ours, an expatriate Irish scholar . . .'

Better, perhaps, he reflected, not to mention that the man referred to was the shabby gentleman at the dining table whom half the town remembered puking his heart out in the gutters of Rue Bourbon.

'He's an expert on handwriting, and it's his opinion that the note is a forgery. That it was written by the same hand as the note that summoned Marie-Joyeuse Maginot to the place where her body was found. The paper, and the ink, are very common, but M'sieu Shaw found samples of both in the desk at Aurore.'

Clay's eyebrows went up. 'Did he, now?'

'And the ink, at least, seems identical to that which was used on the note that brought Mamzelle Maginot to the place where she was killed. It proves nothing in itself, but it's one reason,' he concluded, 'that Captain Tremouille is going out to Aurore this afternoon. He'll be bringing a physician, to see whether, in fact, M'sieu Melchior Aubin does or does not have a hole in his hip.'

'So he informs me.' Clay's voice turned grim, and he touched his breast pocket, indicating the missive that had clearly brought him here. 'I don't suppose he can have any objection to my making up one of the party. It was' – his brows pulled sharply together – 'a dastardly crime. No, I wouldn't have wanted James offering to marry the young lady, for reasons that have nothing to do with what that villainous Democrat handbill insinuates . . .'

January looked solemn and said nothing, and Clay shot him another swift look from under those faded red eyebrows. And indeed, thought January, even if it was fairly certain that

Marie-Joyeuse Maginot would have betrayed a husband with every man in Washington, these were still not sins demanding the girl's death.

But he understood that for a young man with a political future to make – whether Whig or Democrat – a headstrong and roman-tically-inclined wife was not what a father, or a brother, would want to see.

The senator stood for a moment longer, looking down into Shaw's face. January found himself wondering what his friend had been like when first he'd met the then-congressman: the best killer on the mountain, January had heard him called. *I was awful old, he'd said once, 'fore I knew what a sheriff was . . . We looked after our own.*

Very quietly, he said, 'So long as it doesn't jeopardize Madame Clisson's case, sir, you can count on my help.'

Clay regarded him again, sizing him up, as years in the govern-ment had taught him to appraise the loyalty of men. 'Thank you,' he said. 'Given what's at stake for Aubin, I suspect your help is going to be very much appreciated.'

Clay and January left the house together a few minutes later, the post-rainstorm heat of the New Orleans afternoon heavy in the air. When they came out onto the gallery the senator paused, barely perceptibly, on the threshold, and January saw him again scan the tree-lined Esplanade up the center of the avenue, and this time the look in his eyes was unmistakable.

He was watching for something. Looking for something.

When January paused, inquiring, at the top of the steps down to the street, Clay shook his head, hesitated. 'What have you learned about Damien Aubin during all this?' he asked abruptly. 'I understand he was passionate about the young lady – that night at my son-in-law's wasn't the only occasion upon which I had to step in to prevent a challenge. Given the circumstances of the crime, do you think it possible that Damien Aubin still believes my son James had something to do with it? Or that he actually believes that-that farrago of lies on the handbill, and thinks I'd actually kill a girl that age to keep my son from marrying her?'

January started to disclaim this theory, then closed his mouth again. *The man ain't been out of his room*, Andy had said. *Ain't changed his clothes, keeps his door locked – cussed like a crazy*

man when . . . his valet tried to go in an' get him a clean shirt or shave him . . .
    Trying to fit times and distances together in his mind. *Burnin' up inside . . . Drinkin' heavy . . .*
    'Why do you ask, sir?'
    It was Clay's turn to pause. 'Do you think he's dangerous? To me? To my son?'
    A man with a rifle, half-glimpsed in the shadows of Rue Conti. A dark form darting between the tombs.
    A footprint in graveyard earth . . .
    Wait, what is it I should have looked at and didn't . . .?
    January said, 'I don't know, sir. Maybe he doesn't know.'

Sunlight smote the river like a hammer of burning diamonds as the little party turned from the shell road onto the drive of Aurore. At the sight of the house, more than ever like a grounded steamboat among the crowding green of the cane fields, January's nape prickled, and he drew rein. 'Something's wrong . . .'
    Clay halted beside him. 'Where is everybody?'
    Tremouille's eyes narrowed, scanning the gallery – where there should have been movement at this pre-supper hour – then the pathway that led around towards the kitchens and the quarters . . .
    It's summer. The women and children should be coming and going from the provision grounds, no matter what the men are doing . . . The men should be coming in from working in the corn-field, or the ciprière.
    A second glance showed him that the French doors on the gallery were shuttered.
    'Damn it,' muttered the captain of the Guards. 'I told him we'd be coming at this hour—'
    'You *told him*?' Clay and Motet demanded in unison, as January nearly bit his own tongue out not to join the chorus in the same disbelieving tone of voice.
    Dr Emil Barnard – the first physician Tremouille had been able to locate, above Motet's objections that the man still thought sliced onions and honey would cure yellow fever – sniffed, 'One owes it to a gentleman to send him a card before one descends upon him . . .'
    'We are investigating murder, sir.' Clay's voice was like the slap of a leather whipping-paddle on flesh, an echo of years as a lawyer.

'We're not coming uninvited to tea.' And without another word
– not, reflected January, that Tremouille or his constable, or the
socially prominent physician, would have gone up against Henry
Clay in any case – Clay spurred his horse to a gallop up the drive,
the other riders stringing behind.

Tremouille dismounted before the gallery steps, and January's
glance confirmed his first impression. The house was closed up.
Before the captain of the Guards could hand January the reins and
make him hold everybody's horse, Clay sprang from his own
saddle with the lightness of a man of thirty, called, 'Janvier, with
me,' and strode off in the direction of the overseer's cottage.
January wrapped his mule's reins and those of Clay's horse around
the newel at the bottom of the steps, and followed the senator. He
was only halfway to the cottage when Clay reached it, pounded
on the door.

Behind him, January could hear Tremouille knocking – first
politely, then more firmly – on the shutters of the upriver French
doors. 'Is anyone there? M'sieu Aubin? Monroe?'

January reached Clay's side, said, 'Sugar mill.' The senator, he
had observed, had brought a pistol with him. So had January, but
he wasn't about to display it unless the matter were one of life
and death. Clay looked sharply inland, to the gaggle of half-
crumbled brick buildings beyond the lifeless quarters. With family
in New Orleans, he would know that on any plantation, the sugar
mill was the largest and strongest structure, and deserted for three-
quarters of the year.

'Now where have they gone?' he heard Tremouille demand,
still up on the gallery. 'He must have gotten my note. Tallien,' he
called to the stout young guard who had accompanied them. 'Go
round the back and see if anyone is there—'

'Like anyone is going to shut up the front of the house and not
notice riders coming up the drive,' fumed Clay, starting for the
path to the sugar mill as Motet hurried to join them.

'I don't see a soul in the quarters,' panted Motet. 'But the doors
are all open. Why would anyone—?'

A gunshot split the air to their left – *Quarters? Barns?* – and
January grabbed the startled Motet by the arm and dragged him
into the first of the cane that surrounded the house, pulling
him down low. Clay, a few paces in front of them, had already
vanished like a fox going into a burrow.

Another shot, from a different direction, January thought. He heard the rifle-ball *hrush* through the cane.

'What on earth . . .?' Motet tried to crawl to the edge of the cane to see what was going on, and January pulled him back.

'Looks to me like somebody doesn't think he's going to talk his way out of arrest.' Still holding the old man's sleeve, January retreated backwards – carefully, knowing there were snakes in the cane – until he emerged onto one of the narrow ridges between the wet cane furrows. The cane was barely shoulder-high, and this field was nearly impenetrable with weeds and maiden-cane, thin growths of useless stalks that sprouted around the main crop. As a sugar planter, Motet at least had experience with the environment, and knew how to weave and wriggle through the thick dark-green wall of leaves that hemmed the two men in like a coffin.

Damn Tremouille for not bringing more men . . .

Another shot, within a yard of them. *With the cane this short, of course he can see movement . . .*

Then the sharper bark of a revolver. *Clay . . .?*

'He'll have herded the men into the sugar mill,' whispered January. 'Keep them out of the way.'

'Damien?'

'I think it has to be. God knows what his brother told him about what's going on.'

The younger man, January guessed, wouldn't be thinking straight. In any case, for most of his life he'd done as he was told.

Except for falling in love . . .

Another shot, and then a second, so quick that it had to be a second gun-man, somewhere to their right.

'All he has to do is hold us here,' said January, 'until it gets dark.'

'And Melchior can get away,' said Motet grimly. 'And the good Lord only knows what kind of tale he'll come up with, given breathing space.'

Rustling in the cane. January turned, his hand going to the pistol hidden under his jacket. Fortunately he didn't produce it, because he glimpsed the black of Henry Clay's coat moments before the senator shoved his way clumsily through the last thicket, soaked to the knees from the water in the furrows. Another rifle-ball tore through the cane only feet away, and Clay swore.

'Two of them, I'd say.'

'At least,' whispered January. 'Maybe three, if the overseer's been enlisted – or if Madame Olivia can shoot.'

'Which means one of them can double back to town, if he can get to the horses.'

'Exactly my thought, sir.'

Shaw, lying unconscious at the house on Rue Esplanade. Rose, and Zizi . . .

'He can't hope to get away with it!' protested Motet.

'I'm sure he'll do exactly that,' returned Clay grimly. 'He was dragged out of his bedroom blindfolded – forced by some threat or other to order the overseers to lock up the servants and field hands, or to have Damien do it. We'll find him somewhere in a day or two, and by that time he'll certainly have a small hole in him somewhere convenient. A bit fresh, but who's to know? He had no idea, start to finish, who his attackers were or what it all meant . . .'

If he can get back to town and dispose of Shaw . . .

'He's somewhere among the barns.' January mentally summoned the layout of the yard behind the house. Half-guessed territory he had only seen by moonlight.

'Behind the mule shed,' provided Clay. 'If he's still there.'

'Good,' said January. 'If I draw his fire' – he knew he could not ask either of the white men – *old* white men – to do the deed – 'the pair of you can rush him from the sides.'

'Classic pincer movement!' cried Motet enthusiastically. 'Just like the Parthians at the Battle of Carrhae.'

'Tremouille and Constable Tallien should be moving in on him—'

'For a man of your experience, January, you're certainly an optimist,' remarked Clay. 'M'sieu Motet, have you a pistol? Here.' He withdrew a second weapon from under his coat-tails. 'You probably won't have time to re-load—'

'Senator Clay . . .' The old planter drew himself up with exaggerated dignity. 'I am proud to say I served with de Crillon fighting the Spanish at Gibraltar. I know to hold my shot 'til it's needed.'

'Good man,' grinned Clay. 'Now you can tell your grandchildren that you fought beside Clay at New Orleans! I trust you are a Whig, sir?'

'Depends on how this turns out.'

The two old men parted, moved, crouching, along the edge of

the field, and January was spared the task he'd assigned himself. Each of the attackers (*And I hope to God there's only two of them!*) fired at the movement in the cane, and January, well aware of how quickly a good marksman could re-load, burst from the cane and raced for all he was worth toward the mule shed. Tiny instants evaporated like sand going through an hourglass – he veered toward one of the open ends of the shed. *Where the hell are my re-enforcements?*

He was almost at the shed when a pistol cracked – through the gaps in the shed he could see the gun-flash, only feet away. The ball tore past his head – he could hear it whine – and at the same instant a man in the shed screamed in agony. A thrashing movement in the shadows, and the man cried out again, and January whipped around the door of the shed in time to see Damien Aubin, sprawled on the ground among the soiled straw, grabbing for his rifle, which lay close by.

He couldn't reach it, because Akinto had tromped on his wrist with great violence.

Aubin was lying on the ground, because there was a makeshift – but thoroughly effective looking – cane-stalk spear skewering his right shoulder.

Footfalls – *finally!* – on the earth outside. Akinto met January's eyes, made a sign of greeting, bolted out of the mule shed and vaulted over the side of the pigsty just opposite, then a moment later leaped out and disappeared around the nearest cabin in the quarters.

January hoped he'd been able to dig up a few yams or rob a hen's-nest or two before the excitement started.

Clay gasped, 'That was a—' as he dashed into the long shed, pointing – then saw Aubin, sprawled on the ground.

January said, 'It wasn't one of the hands, sir. He was dressed in rags – I think he has to have been a runaway—'

'Must be the one Charlie told me about.' Clay reached down and picked up Aubin's gun. Glancing around, January saw Aubin's pistol lying near the wall, fetched that, too. The barrel still whiffed smoke. 'Charlie my valet. His mother's one of my son-in-law's house servants at Duralde. Charlie says Lottie tells him there's been a runaway hiding out hereabouts for the past week.'

More running footfalls. Instants later Motet, Captain Tremouille, and the constable Tallien crowded into the wide doorway of the shed. (*And presumably Dr Barnard is back holding the horses where it's safe . . .*)

Clay walked over to Aubin, knelt beside him to check the spear, which pinned his shoulder rather than through his chest, then rose, and pulled the weapon free. Aubin cried out, and January stepped quickly forward, tearing from his pocket the bandanna he usually carried.

'We need something to bandage this. It doesn't look like it went through.'

'I never shot to hit any of you,' gasped Aubin, as January stripped the steel-buttoned jacket from his shoulders, wadded his bandanna into the wound. The young man was visibly unwashed and unshaven, as Andy had said. His eyes were bloodshot, his shirt, breath, and sweat reeking of liquor. The smell of his clothing (. . . *and him so pernikkity*, Andy had said) confirmed the cook's account of self-imprisonment and self-neglect.

Clay took the bloodied jacket and went briskly through its pockets, yielding a handkerchief. Motet handed him another, and while January packed the cloth against the hole, Clay untied and pulled free Aubin's soiled cravat.

'I only meant to hold you off . . . until my brother could get away. Said . . . you'd been lied to. Said . . . he'd be killed in the jail . . .'

'That's balderdash!' Tremouille bristled.

Blood oozed to soak the cloth as January knotted the makeshift dressing in place. As he'd guessed, the spear hadn't gone through. *Cephalic vein?*

Aubin shook his head. 'Conspiracy,' he whispered. 'Vengeance—'

'Conspiracy by who?' demanded the captain of the Guards. 'Vengeance for what?'

Aubin shook his head. 'A Whig plot. They want to destroy us, Melchior said—'

It always came back to that, January understood. *Melchior said* . . . 'We need to get him in the house. That wound needs to be cleaned.'

'Constable.' Clay got to his feet with the brisk decisiveness of a man who's stood up to everybody from John Randolph to Andrew Jackson, and gotten the better of them. 'Run get that clown Barnard and bring whatever you can from the house – one of the shutters should do it – for us to carry this man on. Tremouille, everybody'll be in the sugar mill – better take this.' He tossed the captain Aubin's rifle, and when Tremouille started to turn towards the door, added, 'He didn't finish loading.'

Tremouille bent, and gathered up the shot-pouch and powder-flask from the ground. January wondered whether the captain was one who would have voted for Clay, had the senator won his party's nomination. Clay, he suspected, would have had nothing to do with fireworks, hard cider, or songs about his prowess to the tune of 'Little Pigs'.

'And watch out. Melchior's probably out there in the cane and he's had time to re-load.'

'Can't be . . . Melchior . . .' Aubin whispered, as Motet took off his own coat, to lay under him as they eased him back down to the ground. 'Can't . . . walk . . .'

'Who, then?'

The young man shook his head. 'I think . . . must be Pernet. Overseer . . . Melchior talked to him while I was saddling the horses . . . I don't know. He just said . . . it was vengeance. A Whig conspiracy to convict him of murder. "They're all in it together," he said. He said, they planned to kill him in the jail.'

'He never spoke to you of this "conspiracy" before today?' Clay knelt again beside him, and Aubin shook his head.

'Conspiracy . . .'

'Tell me, Aubin,' said the senator. 'Did you ever see the wound in your brother's hip? Ever help him dress it?'

Again Damien Aubin shook his head. 'Always dressed it himself. And I . . . Since the murder I . . .' He turned his face aside then, and January saw tears swim in his eyes.

Wondering why the hell this had all happened to him.

While his brother – if he watched his times carefully, and knew where the work gangs would be – could slip out as he pleased.

TWENTY-FOUR

In the house they found two supper-trays half prepared in the pantry, but no evidence that the dining table would be used. 'The bed in Madame Aubin's room has been stripped,' reported

Motet, coming in as January and Captain Tremouille were laying
Damien Aubin on the bed in his room in the main house. 'No
clothing in the wardrobe—'

'In town,' whispered Aubin, through desperately clenched teeth.
'Miragouin's. Said – fire at Duralde – spirits told her . . .'

Constable Tallien returned from the kitchen with a jug of water
in either hand. 'The boiler fire was out, so this isn't as hot as it
could be . . .'

'No matter,' sniffed Dr Barnard – who had, as January suspected,
remained with the horses by the front gallery of the house during
all the shooting. 'All this fuss about boiling water and alcohol is
just a silly fad, and there's no proof that it does anything except
waste time. A little dirt never hurt anyone.'

Having dealt with Barnard before – and knowing what the result
of an offer to help would be – January walked down the men's
wing of the house, to the end chamber where Melchior Aubin had
lain. From the gallery he could see the field hands, the house
servants, and a short, barrel-chested black-haired man whom he
recognized as Pernet the overseer, all emerging from the sugar
mill. He wondered what Melchior Aubin had told the man.

*Conspiracy of our enemies? Vague threats of melodramatic
vengeance?*

A complex Whig conspiracy didn't sound like anything a man
who wasn't half-drunk, grief-stricken – and used from boyhood
to believing whatever his brother told him – would believe.

How about, 'I'm not paying you to ask questions'? That would
have done for most overseers January had ever met.

There was a small bottle of laudanum at the back of a drawer
in the 'born an' dyin' room' about half empty, its cork crusted
from age. No bandages. No pins. No spirits of wine or basilicum
powder, such as would be used to clean a healing wound.

Not even a sickroom smell.

Nor was there, on the floor under the bed, even the tiniest
dusting of basilicum powder, or a single dropped pin. There was,
however, plenty of floor dust.

Two household ledgers had been pitched in the fireplace, but so
carelessly lit – with only a hasty crumple of business correspond-
ence around them – that they'd failed to burn effectively. Presumably
there had been too little lapse of time between Melchior's receipt
of Tremouille's 'We're coming to visit you' note and the appearance

of the posse on the river road to make a decent job of it. The flames had consumed the outer edges of what was intended to be kindling, leaving the leather-bound ledgers mostly unharmed.

These January set aside in the armoire, went out to intercept Pernet, and followed the overseer to the plantation infirmary for the medical kit. Knowing overseers as he did, January decided to leave it to Senator Clay to question him.

'"Conspiracy of our enemies" my grandmother's left hind foot,' grumbled Clay, when January returned to the house. Dusk was gathering – at such an hour, January knew, the quarters would have been stirring, children playing, women calling to one another as they prepared supper. Without the deadness of an hour ago, the shabby dog-trots were still very quiet. A half-grown girl fed chickens; a woman walked quickly back from the provision grounds, a basket of greens on her hip. Clearly, the families there had been told to get in their homes and stay there.

'Ledgers, you say? Didn't you tell me on the way here this young plaçée of his had day-books for their stay in Washington City? Now, I wonder whether those sudden spurts of cash you spoke of in those, might coincide with similar inputs of funds here.'

'It wouldn't be my place to say, sir,' responded January, leading him down the gallery to Melchior's room. The senator glanced sharply at him, sidelong.

'You're as bad as my man Charlie,' he said.

January bowed. 'While you're looking at those,' he suggested, 'I'm going to go have a look down the outhouse, to see if anyone has ever thrown away any empty laudanum bottles – or if, with a wound in his hip that I know has to have been excruciating, Michie Aubin managed to do without. The same way he did without changing the dressings.'

The senator grinned. 'I'll be very curious to learn.'

Men emerged from the cane, ran towards the house. January recognized the blue work-coats, the plug-hats of gang drivers, the stocky M'sieu Pernet striding before them. Clay walked to the edge of the gallery and the men came running up to him, as Tremouille came out of the main house, hastened to join the group.

Pernet pulled off his hat, dipped a bow to Clay. 'We found M'sieu Aubin, sir.' His voice was flatly matter-of-fact. 'Dead, out in the cane.'

*   *   *

January helped one of the drivers carry the shutter on which they'd borne Damien Aubin to the house. Melchior Aubin lay, grotesquely, on the little headland between the cane field and the ciprière, the twin of the spot only half a mile upriver where Marie-Joyeuse Maginot had died. A small caliber pistol lay close beside his body, smoke still in the barrel when January sniffed it. Traces of back-blown gunpowder stained his fingers. He had what could have been intended for a blindfold, tied around his head and pushed up out of his way. *To be pulled down later, presumably.* His hands were full of bloodied bandages – more lay near him, and a few clean ones trailed from his pockets. He lay on his back, having pulled down his trousers to his knees, and carefully turned coat and shirt up beneath him, presumably so they wouldn't pick up tell-tale bloodstains.

He might, January thought, *just as well have saved himself trouble.*

Beneath him, blood soaked into the weedy ground, spattered his stringy belly and hairy thighs. Constable Tallien and one of the field hands, who'd been watching over the body, stood back, uncomfortable and a little shocked, not understanding the sight.

The gunshot wound in his hip was fresh. *One of the last shots we heard when we were in the mule shed.*

The ball had gone through the femoral artery. *He must have bled out in minutes.*

'No other wound?' asked Clay.

January shook his head. 'No other wound.'

'Trying to make it look good?' Clay fell back a few paces, to speak quietly to January as the drivers carried their master's body back to the Big House. Dark had gathered on the land, the great chicken of night tucking all her offspring to sleep beneath her feathers. Nobody had brought a torch or a lantern, but the field hand who'd helped Tallien watch over the body had run ahead to get two flaming brands from somebody's supper fire. January was aware of everyone in the quarters, crowding at the edge of the cabins to watch. The firelight glimmered in their eyes.

What happens to us now? What if Michie Damien dies, too?

They would all know, January guessed, that the plantation was deep in debt.

'I think he thought he could stop the bleeding quickly,' he

replied. 'Adjust his clothes, and be found, blindfolded and helpless and convincingly wounded. Who was going to check the age of the wound, or compare it with the hole a dueling-pistol would have left?'

'Me, for one,' said Clay. 'The same way I'm going to go over every single entry in those ledgers and every piece of paper we can retrieve out of that fireplace . . . And we'll see what we'll see.'

And none of it, thought January, *will bring back Marie-Joyeuse Maginot. Or Zandrine's child. Or the happiness Damien Aubin had so desperately – so clumsily – struggled for. At least he'd be able to give up his hunt for the murderer of the girl he loved. If he lives . . .*

As they mounted the back gallery steps, he glanced through the half-open door of Damien's room. The young man lay face-down on his bed in the glimmer of candlelight, his political career well and truly over.

The young man who'd married a madwoman because he pitied her. Because, his own heart broken by the girl he truly loved, he could give her 'someplace to go'. And who then had left her on his brother's plantation, to go to Washington. To improve the family fortunes, to give expensive dinners to men of power, just as his brother told him to do.

Michie Damien's a fine figure of a man, Solla had said, compassion in her dark eyes. *But inside he's still a little boy. A little boy who wants to be happy.*

And if he does live, what will become of Olivia? Or if he doesn't?

Old Basile Aubin would probably take over Aurore. Would he find somewhere in the family organization for a woman who spoke to spirits and sometimes lit things on fire?

What will become of Zandrine?

Damien's breath dragged, stertorous with laudanum. His muddied clothes lay in a heap beside the door, and January paused, something snagging at his mind.

Something not right.

He stepped back, and looked at them again.

His boots lay beside the bloodied shirt and coat, clotted with straw and wet dirt and mule shit.

Wide soles. Round toes.

Nothing like the prints he'd seen in the cemetery mud.

*   *   *

'The prints – and in fact the man – you saw may have nothing to
do with Mamzelle Maginot's death, you know,' pointed out
Hannibal, the following day, as the musicians were herded into
the (thankfully shaded) area behind the gargantuan log cabin,
which had been set up in Tivoli Circle. Beside it were ranged the
bandstand, a stage (likewise shaded), a podium for orators, and,
at the center of the circle, a small platform complete with ramp,
upon which the Great Natchez Rolling Ball with its thousands of
signatures would be triumphantly displayed.

Gaily uniformed militiamen were already beginning to gather,
hot sunlight glinting on the bullion of sleeves and epaulets. From
the cabin roof, the tethered eagle screamed defiance at the crowd
already thick below. The two raccoons attempted to conceal themselves in the chimney at the ends of their leads. A man serving
hard cider out of one of the many open barrels threw a tin cup at
the terrified beasts. The militiamen cheered and laughed.

'He could be a smuggler out to eliminate someone he suspects
knows about a choice shipment of contraband slaves from Cuba,
who happened to be lurking about at the same place and time. It
would account for poor Shaw being targeted . . . Thank you,
acushla,' he added, as Lottie emerged from the log cabin with a
tray of lemonade. '*Acceptissima semper munera sunt*, as Ovid
says, *auctor quae pretiosa facit.*' The day was already growing
hot.

'I don't think so.' January polished a speck of dust from the
bell of his cornet – a piano being out of the question in the circumstances – and scanned the growing crowd gathered in the circle,
and already beginning to string out along Nyades Street in the
direction of Carrollton and the river road. 'After Shaw and I talked
to Melchior, Shaw turned back to look at the woodlot where
Melchior's duel with Brunneau took place. Pernet headed him off,
and according to Andy – the cook on Aurore – sent word back to
Aubin about it. Aubin had plenty of time to get out to the woodlot
with a rifle before Shaw had another try at it, just before sunset.'

'And did the ledgers Aubin tried to burn turn up anything
interesting?'

'Senator Clay carried them off in his saddlebags last night,' said
January. 'I sent Zandrine's day-books over to him early this
morning.' The prickly sensation that there was something he hadn't
seen, something else going on, tugged at him, and his eyes returned

again to the growing crowd in the square. 'If there's any correlation of dates between those unexplained influxes of cash to Zandrine, and similar windfalls to Aurore Plantation, Senator Clay will find them. He's been a lawyer for over forty years, and a Washington politician for nearly that long. What he doesn't know about chicanery you could write on the back of a business card, and still have room there for a couple of sonnets.'

'*Probitas laudatur et alget*,' agreed the fiddler, and retired with Cochon to the concealment of the log cabin, to make sure their fiddles were in tune. Not, January reflected, that it would matter in the least, given the rising din around them.

Will McCullen hurried around the corner of the cabin then, one of the few members of the New Orleans Whig Club not out at the upriver end of Carrollton, waiting for the Grand Procession from Natchez – Great Natchez Ball, brass bands, and all – to come into view. 'You boys all right?' he asked. His broad pink face beamed. 'Got everythin' you need? Now, Ben, the Adams County militia has instructions that they'll be playin' "Tippecanoe and Tyler, Too" as they're passin' Felicity Street; you'll be able to hear 'em in the distance. You think you can chime in the same music, match it up so it's comin' from both directions? Up the street an' down?'

'I think we can do that, sir, yes.' January glanced around him at the others: Jacques blowing experimental trills on his flute; Philippe adjusting the set of the bow on his cravat; Uncle Bichet . . .

'Is Griff all right?' he asked, after McCullen darted away in pursuit of Mrs Farmer of the Refreshments Committee. 'I should have sent him home Wednesday night – and to hell with your twenty-five cents, Cochon . . .'

The men looked at each other. The two fiddlers, returning to the shaded 'green room', shook their heads. Close by the bandstand a green-coated man of the Jefferson Parish militia – half-strangling, it seemed on his high leather collar – was shouting at the constables of the First and Second Municipalities over who would get to stand where. Jefferson Butler's deep voice boomed, 'I didn't bring my boys out here for you to use 'em as constables, Tremouille!'

More quietly, January added, 'Or has he decided he's had enough of playing "Little Pigs" for white folks to argue about voting?'

'I think it may be that,' agreed Hannibal, after long hesitation. 'He seemed – angry.'

January himself – between cooked account books, attempts at slander and libel, lies, half-truths, forged threats, unspecified 'Whig conspiracies' and the poisonous scramble for votes and power – felt angry as Achilles on a bad day and only wanted the whole thing to be over.

Senator Clay's sincerity and charm notwithstanding.

After another silence, Jacques asked, 'You know what it is, that he got, Ben? It ain't yellow fever, but he sure didn't look well yesterday.'

'Malaria, I think,' said January slowly. 'It's common in the bayou country, and there's marshes all around Charleston.'

'I thought that might have been it.' Uncle Bichet carefully lifted his bass fiddle from its case, turned an ear to it as he plucked a string. 'And worse, for them as goes there from America, not livin' with the disease from childhood. Him bein' mostly white, it's worse, of course.'

'*There?*'

'Africa.' The old man looked up. 'His wife died of it, an' his children, back in Africa.'

'*Africa?*' The name struck January like the tap of a small hammer on his back.

'Monrovia,' agreed Uncle Bichet. 'Only by time he an' his family got there, all the good pieces of farmland had already been taken, not that Griff had the slightest idea how to be a farmer. Nor most of the others sent out by the Colonization Society, either, from what I heard. Society said they'd all get land, see, an' be able to vote an' hold office an' all them things.' He nodded slightly, toward the jostling groups along Nyades Street. Men waiting to cheer on their candidate for president. Their party to exercise power through the will of the people . . . or some of the people, anyway.

'He told you this?'

'When I sat up with him Tuesday night.' The sensitive fingers adjusted another key. 'He was a little off his head. He'd been dreamin' about his wife – Mary, her name was – an' his children. Said how the folks from the society told them, how good it would be. Showed 'em letters from those who'd gone, sayin' how happy they was an' what a beautiful place Africa is. Showed 'em pledges from supporters sayin' as how they'd send 'em what-all they needed to live 'til their colony was set up strong an' independent.'

Those old, dark eyes blinked at him, from behind the

thick-lensed spectacles. White brows and wrinkled lids surrounded by the tribal scars of his own village, his own people . . . the first of the old man's several varied lives. 'Only somebody sort of forgot to tell them that the Africans already *livin'* in Africa weren't any happier about a bunch of foreigners movin' into their lands, than the Houmas or the Chickasaw or the Cherokee were here, no matter what color they were. An' they forgot to tell 'em that some of those Africans are still makin' a livin' tradin' slaves from the interior to the smugglers an' the Portuguese, an' didn't want that trade messed with. Didn't tell 'em about the fevers, neither.'

Very quietly, January said, 'Shit.'

'Griff worked harder'n any dog, he said, to come up with the money he needed to buy his wife an' their two babies free, from the gentleman what owned 'em in Philadelphia. The children was Ellie an' Will. All three of 'em, dead within six months of goin' ashore at Monrovia.'

January felt sick with shock. Remembered Ayasha dead in the suffocating heat of the cholera summer. 'He never said a word about it,' he said after a time. 'Not to me – not to anybody, I don't think. No wonder he called me a fool.'

'Called you worse than that,' said the old man mildly. 'He called you a dupe, like the men who betrayed Denmark Vesey an' Gabriel Prosser. Black men, who should have joined them in their fight for freedom, rather'n runnin' tellin' their masters of what they knew. He has hate in him, Ben.'

A tight little smile puckered his lips, and he nodded toward the stout figure of Will McCullen, very red in the face now, hurrying toward them through the thickening crowd. 'Now, money's money. Givin' Jane what I make, so's I can live comfortable in my age – I like bein' able to do that. Some days I don't even miss Timbuktu, an' those I left there. Jane and my boy work hard, an' I've lived a long time. But I understand Griff havin' no use for Henry Clay, an' sayin' as how it was him, who murdered his Mary an' his children. I understand him wantin' no part of playin' for him to ride down the street in a open carriage with everybody cheerin' his name.'

Hannibal said quietly, 'No.'

And January asked, 'He said that?' Another mosaic, forming up from pieces thrown into the sky . . .

One murder or two?

'That he wanted no part of playin' for Henry Clay?'

'That it was Henry Clay who murdered his wife and his children.'

Uncle Bichet nodded. 'A man speaks wild sometimes when he's fevered.'

And sometimes he speaks truth. 'He said, "murdered"?'

A boot-print in cemetery mud.

A shadow in a dark carriageway.

A boy at Sally DeChaine's boarding house, carrying a pair of boots into the sickroom. January saw them clearly now in his mind, as he'd seen them then. Stylish boots with long, stylish square toes . . .

'Dammit!' Will McCullen flustered back into the little circle of chairs behind the log cabin. 'Ben . . .' His voice was coaxing. 'I've asked so much of you, and I'm afraid I'm going to have to ask more! And you will be paid extra, I promise you, if I have to take up a subscription myself. It's Coal-Oil Billy and those damn Jefferson Parish Democrats.'

Where Nyades Street debouched into the Circle, Tremouille, Butler, and Captain Barthelmy of the Third Municipality City Guards waved and shouted in what had escalated into a three-way argument. Further down Nyades, January saw very few blue uniforms in the crowd.

'Going to try to rescue the president?' he asked, and McCullen flung up his hands.

'We didn't think they'd really—'

A boy came running, dressed like a drummer for the Orleans Parish militia. 'The ball's just passed the Jefferson Parish line, sir!' He was so winded he could barely get the words out. 'It'll be here in twenty minutes!'

'I hate to tell you this, sir' – January tried to sound both respectful and rueful – 'but it's been all over town all week.' And inside him his mind was screaming. Conti Street, where Clay could have been expected to be. The cemetery . . . Duralde . . .

The way Clay had looked over his shoulder on the gallery, as if in the recent past he'd seen someone – maybe – following him . . .

McCullen made a noise usually written as *Aaargh!* 'Start up playing now,' he said. 'Make it jolly! Make it fun! The last thing we need is a riot tying up the parade at Thalia Street.'

'Is that where they're coming in from, sir?' asked Cochon, seeing January stand without speaking – almost without seeing . . .

'I heard it was Melpomene,' put in Jacques helpfully. Like most New Orleaneans, he pronounced the Muse's name as Mel-puh-meen.

'Ten cents says it's Erato.' Hannibal produced a thin coin. 'I'll always back love poetry over tragedy . . . They can come in almost to Nyades through the waste ground back of Dryades.'

The Orleans Parish drummer looked interested and fished in his pocket. 'I'd say it's Melpomene. There's more of a show in front of Butler's store.'

'You can count on us, sir.' January dragged his thoughts back, as one of Hubert Granville's bank clerks came running up, gorgeous in a yellow militia uniform, half a dozen others in like attire and about forty club-wielding gentlemen in shirtsleeves thundering in his wake.

'Oh, good,' said Hannibal drily. 'Let's have a riot, just to make a dull day interesting.'

'Lottie!' McCullen raised his hand to catch the woman's attention. 'Lottie, you can tell Schurtz he can broach the cider barrels . . . Oh, I see he has. Well . . . Let's get people in a good mood here, draw them away from whatever trouble there's going to be.'

'Yes, sir.' Lottie kept her face expressionless, but January caught a glimpse of her true thought – *And you think gettin' everybody drunk gonna help?* – in her eyes.

'I knew I should have put the senator up toward the front of the procession, instead of following the ball. If there's trouble God only knows how long it'll take him to get here. You have to keep people smiling, Ben. Get them clapping their hands.'

A boy on a pony came galloping down Nyades Street, waving his hand. The crowd – and it was a crowd now – beneath the galleries of the tall brick shops began to jostle and cheer.

'Good Lord, and they're in sight now!' McCullen cried. More militiamen – in the red uniforms of Plaquemines Parish – raced by, rifles on shoulders and shakos askew. 'May Flora stay here with you here, boys, out of the crowd? She's going to present the senator with flowers . . . I daresay his carriage will be full of them. Like it was Mardi Gras . . . Effie? Effie! Over here in the shade . . . Lottie, can you get . . .? Yes, lemonade. You stay here with Mama, sweetheart . . .'

He dashed away.

January's heart was pounding.

Jacques remarked, 'Senator gonna be lucky somebody don't pitch dog-crap at him from one of those balconies, while he's stopped there sittin' in the street when the fightin' starts.'

And duCoudreau laughed. 'Well, Griff sure would, if he was here.'

Damn it . . .

'How much you bet that's where he is?' Cochon produced a ten-cent piece from his pocket. 'Bet he really ain't sick at all.'

Damn it . . .

'He sure wasn't there when I stopped by his place early this mornin' with beignets . . .'

Lottie, stepping back from the joking group that suddenly formed around the porcine fiddler, touched January's sleeve.

'The man with the rifle,' she said softly. 'I seen him.'

Someone in the cabin yelled, 'Lottie!' and she made a step towards its door, then turned back.

'Back of the crowd, goin' up Triton Walk. Just as the Plaquemines militia was comin' down. He was trailin' after 'em in militia uniform,' she said, 'but seein' him now in daylight, I'll swear he was a man of color.'

TWENTY-FIVE

The streets behind Nyades – Bacchus and Apollo – were also crowded now, white men and women trooping out of the big American-style houses there, with their wide yards and tidy coach houses. House servants followed more slowly, not averse to cheering and crowds and the music of bands, even if the whole matter didn't concern them in the slightest. They knew perfectly well that whoever got elected, he wasn't going to do a damn thing to keep them from being sold away from their families to cover debts when their owners died, or give them the right to protest in court if they were sent down to the parish prison to be whipped without cause. As he moved through the crowds, January asked himself what the hell he cared whether Henry Clay, riding in his open carriage, got shot from the top of one of those tall brick store-buildings or not.

His own disillusion still stung – and the bitter reflection that his belief that Clay would actually do anything to help either the enslaved or the free colored in America had been, as Catherine had said, a child's fairy-tale hope.

He liked the man personally, but as his mother had pointed out, it was the votes that mattered. And none of them could vote.

But at least he's talking about the problem, thought January. *At least he's looking at it clearly, and coming out and saying, clearly, that there is a problem, even if he knows himself to be part of that problem. At least he knows that slavery will lead to disaster, and that the majority of white men simply don't want free blacks in this country of theirs. At all. And just turning slaves loose doesn't mean most of them have anything to look forward to. Only illiterate poverty and the same dirty jobs that the white men don't want to do themselves.*

And talking about it is exactly what pretty much nobody else is doing.

And talking about it, January was well aware, was the reason that Henry Clay was riding down Nyades Street in an open carriage, trying to get votes for another man. Showing his wounds to the people, as Shakespeare's Coriolanus had refused to do, to 'beg their stinking breaths'.

To elect in his place a man who keeps his mouth shut and doesn't say what *he's in favor of. Tippecanoe and Tyler, too!*

He stopped in front of a very handsome new house on Apollo Street: fancy-work shingles, iron fence cast in flamboyant Gothic frills. A gaggle of his own militia company – the Faubourg Tremé Free Colored Militia and Burial Society – strode past, unarmed, as was deemed proper for a man of color, even if free. Looking up Clio Street he could see men coming in from the long, narrow stretch of weedy ground that extended swamp-ward, the remains of one of the plantations that had been close to the town walls, when he was a child . . . Arcadie, it had been called. There'd been two brothers named Parrot and Jemmy that his mother had thrashed him for playing with, because he was now free. A brushy ruin of maiden-cane, palmetto, pickerel-weed and swamp-laurel was all that remained of those exhausted cane fields, where the boys' father – and later Parrot and Jemmy themselves – had sweated and bled. He wondered where they were now.

The men were moving cautiously across the tangled ground, emerging a few at a time to cross Dryades Street. Like McCullen's militiamen, most were armed with clubs, some with cutlasses. He guessed there were over fifty of them. *More on the other side of Nyades?* They'd have slung shot in their pockets, and knuckle-dusters. Drovers, laborers, Salt-River roarers, half-horse half-alligator . . .

But there were more respectable types among them, too: coats and waistcoats and beaver hats.

Contractors, some of them – men Charles-Louis Trepagier had been chatting up at the cotillion Wednesday night. Men who owned cotton presses and the wagons that hauled freight along Rue Esplanade back to the lake. Men who worked the slave gangs that cut timber in the ciprière or ran the Jefferson Parish cattle yards. Jackson men, Democrats who distrusted banks and blamed the bank failure on everyone but their blockheaded hero. Men who thought that driving tens of thousands of Creek and Cherokee and Chickasaw families out of their homes was a perfectly good idea, since white men wanted the land and the Creek and Cherokee and Chickasaw were only savages anyway.

They'll stop that parade dead in its tracks.

And give Griff a clear shot at the vengeance he craves.

January slipped his hand under his jacket, to where a pistol dug into his back. He hadn't dared bring his own to Tivoli Circle. Not with all those militiamen milling around, and the members of the Free Colored Militia – unarmed though they'd be until the last possible minute – in their uniforms practically inviting any white man to be watching for the slightest hint of that white nightmare of nightmares, a black man bearing arms.

But a crowd this size – confusion this pervasive – would also draw the man-stealers, the blackbirders, professional kidnappers who lurked around the wharves. Profit could be made, when everyone's attention was elsewhere, and he did not believe in taking chances. Hannibal might flinch at the thought of pulling the trigger on a fellow human being, but when January had handed him a pistol at his house that morning and murmured, 'Hold this for me, would you?' the fiddler had obediently pocketed the weapon.

Music boomed joyfully from Nyades Street – 'Little Pigs' yet again for the millionth time:

Like the rushing of mighty waters, waters, waters,
On it will go,
And in its course will clear the way
For Tippecanoe and Tyler, too,
For Tippecanoe and Tyler, too . . .

The voices of a chorus of women lifted. January wondered whether
Mrs McCullen was leading it, with little Flora marching proudly
at her side in her colorful, miniature sash.

Can grateful freemen slight his claims
Who bravely did defend
Their lives and fortunes on the Thames
The farmer from North Bend . . .

He winced at the mangling of 'Auld Lang Syne', but the Tippecanoe
version of Scott Key's 'Defense of Fort M'Henry' – also known
as the melodically impossible drinking song 'To Anacreon in
Heaven' – was infinitely worse.

Oh, say, have you heard how in days that are past
Bold sons of the West with brave Harrison leading . . .

Paused on the corner of Erato Street, watching which street the
Democrats would choose for their ambuscade, he whispered,
'Ouch.' Anacreon himself – that sweetest singer of ancient Greece
– was doubtless turning in his grave . . .

The Democratic ambushers divided themselves, some going
down Thalia Street, others down Melpomene. *How far behind
the Van Buren gallows is Clay's carriage?* He scanned the backs
of the buildings that faced Nyades: flat brick American-style
buildings from this angle, shops below, flats above, with galleries
front and back to catch the river breeze. Slate-tiled roofs, dormer
windows . . .

He walked quickly along Apollo Street, scanning the pavements
inland. *He's light enough to pass at first glance*, he thought as he
walked. *But he can't risk anyone stopping him and getting a clearer
look. Not in daylight. That means he'll have to be on this side of
Nyades.*

His eye passed over the crowd, looking for the red of a

Plaquemines Parish militia coat. *A rifle means distance, from above, over the heads of the crowd. It's what I'd do*, he reflected. *At ground level, he can't be sure of getting close to the carriage.*

Only a few months previously, an assassin in a London crowd had attempted to shoot England's young queen and had been immediately overpowered by bystanders. All the buildings along this block of Nyades were two or three stories in height, with courtyards behind them. Small service buildings in the courtyards, workshops, woodstores, kitchens. Stairs going up to the galleries above. On a day as hot as this one the doors would be open and everybody living in those upper apartments would be on the front galleries. If they weren't now, they'd be out there once the fighting started in the street. Every attic would have a service hatch leading up to the roof.

He crossed Melpomene. Men crowded under the shop galleries there, and he hung back, listening.

> Should good old cider be despised
> And ne'er regarded more?
> Should old log cabins be despised,
> Our fathers built of yore . . .?

Then people yelling, scorn and anger. Chanting. 'Van, Van, he's a used-up man . . .'

Not remembering that it was their hero Jackson's policies, that had brought all the banks in the country crashing down four years ago. Blaming his successor for four agonizing years of hard times.

Here comes the gallows. January turned down Terpsichore, scanning the roof-lines.

Van, Van, he's a used-up man . . .

Yes. One building in the middle of the block, very much in the American style. Three stories, and a sort of false front on the Nyades side, to make it appear taller yet. Jefferson Butler's Dry Merchandise Emporium. Exactly the place a man could shoot from, if he didn't want to risk going inside a dwelling and firing from somebody's dormer.

The building on the corner of Nyades and Terpsichore was a shop selling tea and coffee, and as he heard the sudden swell of shouting, presumably signaling the Democratic attack on the Donaldsonville Boys at the corner of Thalia (*I guess Hannibal loses ten cents . . .)*. Two men came running out of the shop in waistcoats, aprons, and shirtsleeves. January stepped quickly into the building, looked around him to make sure there was no one there, then passed through the back room and into the courtyard behind.

Deserted, as he'd guessed. The courtyard itself – like most New Orleans courts – was walled ten-feet high, its only openings either into the shop, or out through a gated passageway to the street. Any slave belonging to the shop owners or those who dwelled in the rooms above would have to pass their masters on their way out. January could move very silently, for a man his size – he climbed the steps to the second-floor gallery, hearing the voices of the upstairs' inhabitants through the French doors. He glimpsed them in passing, visible through the open doors of interior rooms. Men, women, children – and probably all of their friends as well who didn't live on the parade route – clustered along the rail of the front gallery above the street.

There was no access from the back gallery to the roof. But through a French door at the end of the building he saw a ladder going into the attic. By the sound of it the fracas in the street had reached a level somewhere between the Fall of Troy and the Battle of Waterloo. Nobody on the front gallery so much as turned a head as he slipped in through the French door, two steps across the little chamber that doubled as a storeroom and a nursery – a baby in a crib, solemnly playing with her own feet, turned her head to watch him pass. He clambered up the ladder, opened the trap at the top, and debouched into the attic: dust, old newspapers, trunk after trunk of clothing. Dismantled bedsteads and an overwhelming smell of mold and rat piss. Another, shorter ladder – the ceiling was barely six feet at the center – led to another trap, to the roof.

The heat glaring from the slate roof-tiles was overwhelming. January edged across them, bent low and keeping to the courtyard edge, the height of the roof-ridge concealing him from the street. The marks where boots had scraped and skidded in the soot and birds-mess made a clear track in front of him, nearly obliterated by half a dozen rains. A few yards along, the resurrection fern growing between tiles had been pulled loose, as if someone had lost his balance and caught at it . . .

Reconnaissance. The minute Griff overheard Jed Burton and Jefferson Butler discuss the plan to rescue Van Buren's dummy.

That would have been Sunday at the musicale . . .

The minute he heard from Lottie that the senator's carriage would be close behind the effigy.

That was why he came to New Orleans in the first place, January realized. *Why he turned up in town only days before the senator's announced arrival. He heard he'd be here. Campaigning for Harrison . . .*

The tracks weren't fresh. *Does that mean he's not up here yet? Or just that he explored this way once, and maybe found a better one from another direction?*

The passageway into the courtyard ran from Terpsichore Street. It was a jump of barely a yard to the roof of the next building, but it froze January's heart to do it: it was a good thirty feet to the pavement, and the next building along was both slightly higher and more steeply roofed. Just before he made the short run to leap, he thought, *Let him die. Who knows how many other women – children – and men believed Colonization Society clap-trap, and laid their bones in African soil because white men don't like the idea of sharing freedom with black ones?*

But he knew that killing Clay wasn't the answer. That it would only make the situation worse.

He suspected, *much* worse.

On the other side of the jump he found where tiles had been dislodged, again, only a few days before.

The gap was narrower at the far end of the building but the next building along was the one he was aiming for – Butler's Emporium. The Emporium building was one story taller than the one on which he stood, so he was forced to go down to the gallery below him – the attic trap here was bolted from the inside – a heart-stopping grope with feet and fingers for the dirty, rusty iron of the gallery pilasters, and then a leap across to the second-floor gallery of the taller building . . .

A barbershop run by a man named Mueller, he recalled, on the ground floor. And next to it Butler's. Fine chinaware, silks, pianofortes and Dutch crystal wine glasses.

Stairs up to the third-floor gallery. More open French doors – the noise blowing through the house louder as the rioting spread. An attic where the air was nearly unbreathable from the rising heat. Mattresses and pallets among the trunks. Children or slaves or both slept up here.

The roof of the taller building was more shallowly pitched. The front wall on Nyades Street some five feet tall at the center, a little over three at each end. January saw in his mind the blue-and-white lettering painted on that façade: Butler's, in fancy letters, with stars and flowers. Crouching, he made his way to the wall, looked over.

Griff Paige had laid his plan well. January felt he could have tossed a half-dollar forty feet straight down onto Henry Clay's hat. The senator sat in an open barouche, his son beside him. The driver's box was empty, the coachman at the team's heads, struggling to keep them quiet in the face of the jostling, shouting mob that blocked the street from wall to wall before them. Martin Duralde, attired like the two Clays in morning coat and dove-gray trousers, stood on one of the wheel-spokes to speak to his guests of honor, gesturing . . .

As McCullen had predicted, the carriage was filled with flowers.

Men surged around the vehicle, pushing from further down the parade to go to the aid of the Donaldsonville Boys. Men poured from Terpsichore Street, either with the same intention or with that of aiding in the rescue of Van Buren's threatened effigy – the fighting was clearly spreading up Nyades and among the carriages. Clay started to his feet and his son pushed him back into the carriage seat – twenty years previously, January guessed, the man would have been in the thick of the fray, trying to subdue his opponents and get them to listen to reason.

That was what the man did, thought January. *Gets people to listen to reason.* He'd kept the Southern states from pulling out of the Union in 1820 over Missouri's statehood and again in 1832 over tariffs; he was one of the few politicians who saw, clearly, that there would be plenty of countries in Europe which would be only too happy to step in and 'help' one side or the other, if it came to bloodshed, in exchange for the resources of North America.

Does that pay for men lied to? Does that pay for a woman and her children dead, and a man left desolate to face his own country that shoves him away?

He didn't know.

Rose dead, my boys dead . . . myself betrayed to a foreign and hostile land . . .? The way Lottie had been betrayed, jailed, dragged fifteen hundred miles to a strange city and new masters . . . *Would I seek revenge?*

He thought that he would.

Movement in the corner of his eye. January slipped backwards immediately so that the low slope of the roof hid him. *All I need is for the head clerk at Butler's to come asking me what I'm doing up here . . . Oh, I just came up here, sir, with this pistol, to watch the parade . . .*

But it was Griff Paige, still in his scarlet militia uniform, though he'd discarded the silly shako. He had two rifles, slung on his back. *Two shots to my one.*

This'll have to be fast . . .

The younger man had come from the opposite end of the building. Further reconnaissance must have showed him a better way to get up here . . . *Does this building have two attics?* As January watched, Griff came to the wall – cautiously, keeping low – and looked over. Moved a few feet further towards the higher projection in the middle of the wall.

I have to catch him. Just driving him away will only postpone murder.

There were about forty feet between them. *If I call out something stupid like, Stop! he'll either shoot me – and then Clay – or flee.*

He has to keep still while he aims.

Griff set one rifle down, checked the other one, turned toward the street.

And knowing that he'd have a much better chance if he simply shot the young man in cold blood, January stood up, pointed his pistol, and called out, 'Put it down!'

Griff swung around, startled, and January strode towards him, pistol still leveled at his chest. 'Drop it!' he ordered again, and ducked aside as Griff brought up the rifle and fired.

January knew he couldn't aim with single-shot accuracy and dodged again, but Griff scooped up his second weapon and lunged for him, dodging also, striking at him with the butt. January twisted, tried to bring his pistol around, and Griff smote him in the knee, slashed at his head with vicious strength, then slammed the butt down on his elbow. The pistol went skidding away and January dived for it (*I should have shot the bastard in cold blood and to hell with scruples . . .*), rolled out of the way of Griff's kick. Caught the ankle, knocked him sprawling backwards.

Griff rolled, slithered from January's grabbing hand, fired the

rifle at a distance of a yard and missed (*Virgin Mary thank you
. . .*) and then reversed the weapon in his hands and snapped the
butt at January's head. The blow caught him glancing, knocked
him dizzy. He lunged for Griff's knees, caught them as the younger
man grabbed for the pistol, thrashing and struggling on the hot
slates of the roof. Griff struck him twice, three times with the rifle
butt, clumsy blows in his panic, overhand swats like a housewife
beating a carpet, agonizing on the unhealed knife-gash from last
week where January curled his back to take them on the muscle
of his shoulders. He grabbed for Griff's belt, to pull him closer
to grapple, and Griff writhed around to drive his knee into January's
chin.

January's grip broke and the young man lunged for the pistol,
seized it.

At the crack of the gunshot – with the muzzle only feet from
his face – January thought for a moment that, impossibly, the
young musician had missed again. As if in the same instant of
time he saw the bloody exit-wound explode out of Griff's throat
and flung himself aside, as Griff's hand, convulsing on the trigger,
fired a second shot.

And January found himself facing Jefferson Butler, three other
white men in shirtsleeves, and a blonde woman in a calico dress
and a VOTE FOR HARRISON sash. All five had pistols. Smoke
curled from the barrel of the woman's.

Butler said, 'You better stand up real slow, boy. Then maybe
you'd like to tell us what you and this other fella was doin' up
here on my roof with all these guns.'

TWENTY-SIX

Sergeant Boechter – one of the few men left at the desk in
the Cabildo watch room – identified January immediately as
a free man and a respected member of *libré* society, notwithstanding the moss- and soot-stains all over his clothing. Nevertheless,
it was the following morning – Saturday, the 19th of September
– before Captain Tremouille had him brought into that dingy little
chamber in the prison.

Henry Clay occupied the chair that Rose had sat in when they'd first visited Catherine a week ago. Francois Motet perched, as January himself had, on the corner of the desk. Will McCullen hovered in the background. Hannibal later told January that between no cornet to lead the melody, and the much inferior Laurent Lamartine on the clarionet in place of Griff Paige, the music, when it finally got started, had been very poor indeed. *Not that anyone was listening much by that time, mind you*, the fiddler added.

'Mr Butler tells us they found you and your clarionettist up on his roof with two rifles and a pistol,' said McCullen, when two guards led January in. 'I must say—'

'Lottie tells me,' Clay interrupted him, 'that this man Paige was attempting to kill me. And that you went to stop him.'

'I did, sir.' January inclined his head, and tried to think of a way to tell the truth without enraging every white man in the room. 'Paige . . . had a grievance against the Colonization Society, over the deaths of his wife and children in Africa.'

McCullen opened his mouth to protest that Africa was a perfectly healthy and wholesome country – not that he'd ever been there – but the senator lifted his hand for the man's silence. 'Go on.'

'The night of Mayor Freret's dinner I saw a man that I think now must have been he, waiting in the carriageway across Rue Conti from M'sieu Granville's townhouse. I think he was waiting for you, sir. I saw him again the following morning at the cemetery, on the day of Marie-Joyeuse Maginot's funeral. Again, he had a reasonable expectation of your presence. I have good reason to believe he came at least once to Duralde, late at night, to see if you were there. At the time I thought it had something to do with Mamzelle Maginot's murder.'

McCullen again looked as if he would argue, but Clay only said, softly, 'Ah,' and looked for a moment aside at the corner of the desk. Then he met January's eyes again. 'The Society does warn its emigrants that they are likely to face the same hardships faced by any pilgrims setting forth to settle new lands.' It was not said in the tone of an argument.

'I know that, sir. I've read their literature.'

Clay's quick glance asked, *So you thought about it?*

And January's eyes returned a stony, *No.*

Not ever.

'It is a grievous thing,' Clay said, after long silence, 'nonetheless.'

He, too, January remembered, had lost children.

'That's still no excuse—' McCullen began indignantly, and again Clay gestured him quiet.

'Is there ever excuse for murder?' Those sharp bright eyes moved to Francois Motet. 'I am glad and grateful that your friend Madame Clisson has been exonerated, but I don't think there's a man in this city, who didn't find the motive attributed to her unreasonable.'

Motet said quietly, 'No.'

'I spoke with Madame Aubin this morning.' The senator's tone was that of a man who seeks to turn the subject. 'She confirms that her brother-in-law would lock himself in the sickroom for hours at a time, and that no one – not her husband, not any of the servants – were permitted to go near that wing of the house when he did so. His valet was supposedly posted outside his door, but most afternoons he was asleep, and nobody cared to risk Melchior Aubin's wrath by asking questions. After Miss Maginot's death Damien Aubin barely left his own rooms.'

Motet turned his head to the captain of the Guards. 'You haven't dragged poor Damien all the way here . . .?' and Tremouille shook his head.

January bit his lip to keep from saying – and Henry Clay *did* say – 'Well, shooting at one's visitors *is* against the law . . .'

Tremouille frowned as he nodded, and January felt himself reminded that the Aubins were his cousins. 'I've sent a man out to keep an eye on him, yesterday and today. His wound looks to be suppurating . . .'

A little dirt never hurt anyone . . .

But it was like looking at a beautiful, high-couraged stallion lying broken on the ground.

'And of course Madame Aubin – and her friend Madame Miragouin – have been there with him as well.'

As a doctor – or simply as a human being – January had to agree that the parish prison was no place for a man who'd been pinned through the shoulder with a cane-stalk spear, with or without Dr Emil Barnard's views on cleanliness. As a former potential target he wanted to point out that given the size of the crowds that everyone in town knew would be on hand for the parade – and given the fact that everyone in town had also known that the Democrats were arming for an attack on the Donaldsonville Boys – sending one of the thirty-six First Municipality Guards a mile and a half downriver to watch over a single prisoner was probably not the best use of available manpower . . .

And he asked instead, 'Does he know his brother is dead?'

'I think so.' Clay sighed. 'When I talked to him this morning he was pretty well dosed with opium, but he spoke of it. And Madame Miragouin can be counted on, to break it to him again gently, if he . . . if he thinks it was all part of dreams.'

Motet asked, 'What did he say?'

'That he was sorry.' Clay shook his head. 'That he didn't rightly know what he was doing – which I believe. He confessed that yes, he's been sending State Department money to his brother for the past two years. It's all there in the ledgers, but I don't think he knows we have them or even that records were kept. You saw what kind of a state the plantation is in. It isn't as if Brother Melchior were spending it on foie gras and champagne.'

'And since you announced that you wouldn't accept the position of Secretary of State,' said January, 'M'sieu Melchior knew he would have no leverage to keep his brother in that position. From that point on, his goal was to keep Harrison from winning, if he could. He *had* to keep his brother from divorcing Trepagier's daughter, and the only way to do that was to lure Mamzelle Maginot to a place where she could be killed with impunity.'

'And putting it on me' – Henry Clay raised an eyebrow – 'for what you gentlemen here refer to as lagniappe?'

'He didn't really need you to be convicted,' pointed out January. 'Though obviously he knew that Blennerhassett's name would bring you, and force you to keep the meeting secret. But all he really needed was the scandal.'

'Can it be hushed up?' asked Motet. 'The . . . defalcation, I mean. As well as . . .' He glanced apologetically at Tremouille. 'For the sake of the family. Old Jules Maginot doesn't deserve this kind of disgrace, nor does poor Madame Olivia.'

'They're Martin's cousins, too,' added Clay. 'And yours, I'll wager, as well, Robert.' He glanced at Tremouille. 'I'll do what I can in the department. I've worked with Secretary Forsyth on and off for years, and I think he's not a man to press the point, if restitution is made.'

His mouth hardened, as if remembering – as January remembered – that brilliant girl in her bird-of-paradise dress, and the way her father's eyes had followed her. The four black coaches, that only the very rich could afford. The broken sound of the man's tears. The knowledge of what such an equipage cost and where the money for it had to have come from . . .

'I'm sure something can be worked out,' said Motet.

Voices in the corridor. January heard someone speak the senator's name, and the jailer say, 'He'll be out presently—'

'Well, they're waitin' on him at the Exchange.' January recognized the slurring American accents of the journalist Hector Blodgett, of the *New Orleans True American*. 'How the hell long does it take for him to vouch for a nigger?'

'Hey, fat-head,' retorted Stookey, 'you just tell 'em to hold their water. And you hold yours. The man saved his life.'

Clay turned his head slightly, listening, then sighed, as his eyes went back to the men gathered before him. 'Damien says he never much cared for Washington,' the senator went on after a moment. 'But after marrying the Trepagier girl – out of kindness for her situation, but that doesn't make her any easier to live with – and getting tangled with the Trepagiers, *père et fils*, all he wanted to be was out of New Orleans. Poor silly pup. He says he never meant to hurt that poor plaçée of his.' The sharp glance went again to Motet, acknowledging what neither would speak aloud. 'He says he'll take care of her, as well as he can, now the plantation is his to manage – and whatever happens, I'll talk to Basile Aubin about doing the right thing. Damien says the girl Zandrine doesn't have to see him, if she doesn't want to.'

Quietly, Motet said, 'Thank you. I'll . . . tell Madame Clisson that. *Will* he live?'

'That I don't know.' Clay sighed again. 'Barnard's bled him four times already, and he did not look good. He's strong as Hercules . . .'

January thought, into the ensuing silence, *Only on the outside. Poor pup indeed.*

'Some people want to have power.' The senator shook his head, as if he still saw that strong young Adonis before him, like a war-horse broken on the field of battle, bleeding in the mud and waiting for the knacker's cart to arrive. 'To change the country, to pull all the levers. Or just to own all the steamboats and railroads and get rich. I really think all he wanted to do was be happy.'

Something both Melchior, and Marie-Joyeuse Maginot, knew better than anyone. Again January said nothing.

Stiffly, Tremouille said to January, 'Well, M'sieu Janvier, you're free to go. We – the Whig Party – owe you thanks, not only for solving a despicable crime, but for averting a scandal. I believe M'sieu Aubin will be appearing before Judge Canonge on charges of reckless endangerment, as soon as he's well enough. If you would be so kind as to come in on Monday to give a statement . . .?'

'Of course, sir.'

Blodgett's voice bawled in the corridor about the constitutional rights of the Fourth Estate.

'Needless to say,' Tremouille added, 'I trust we can all rely on you to let none of this go any further . . .'

'Of course.' *I get shot at, locked in a burning house, and almost thrown off a roof, and I get to give a statement . . .*

'The First Amendment to the Constitution guarantees—'

Old M'sieu Motet asked Clay in a polite whisper, 'You want me to go out there and kick him in the pants?'

''Twere it not an election year . . .' sighed Clay, with comic regret.

Motet bowed acquiescence.

'Indeed the Whig Party thanks you. M'sieu Janvier,' Clay added, as Tremouille opened the door for them all to leave. 'A word in private?'

Blodgett was already trying to crowd into the little office. January tried not to look pleased as the jailer, McCullen, and Tremouille all shoved him down the corridor to the street door.

Clay closed the door behind them. 'January,' he said, 'thank you. I am truly sorry I couldn't get here last night. There's not a lot a man can give in thanks for having his life saved,' he went on quietly. 'If there's anything in my power . . .?'

The right to vote? The assurance that I or my wife won't be kidnapped and sold to pick cotton in Missouri?

He regarded the tall white man before him: more haggard than he looked on the campaign posters, red hair fading to gray. The marks of illness on his face – and sorrow, too. The eyes bright with energy, as if he were ready to wade in and keep the Union from breaking up once or twice again.

'*Anything in my power.*'
Those things are not within his power to give. Nor would they be, he knew, even were Clay to be elected President himself.

January said, 'Two things, sir – if it doesn't sound greedy of me to ask.'

'I think I'm worth two – or three – or five . . .' And he grinned like a schoolboy. 'Name them.'

'The runaway who speared Damien Aubin so he wouldn't shoot us,' said January. 'He's an African, smuggled into this country illegally – I think what your Society calls a re-captive.'

Clay nodded. 'There's a case in the courts now, about the Africans taken from the Spanish vessel *La Amistad*.'

'As President of the Board of the American Colonization Society, I'd like you to write up letters of introduction, and arrange for passage for this man – I believe his name is Akinto – on the first Society ship back to Africa. I have an acquaintance who can escort him to Philadelphia – or wherever the next ship leaves from. And I think I can find him and convince him to go. As far as I know,' added January, 'there's nobody suing for his return, so you won't need to worry about the courts.'

With luck, he thought, Akinto would believe that *rafiki* – in whatever language it was – would cover the pale-eyed Judas Bredon enough to get him to travel with him. Whether Akinto's home was anywhere near the settlement of Liberia was another story – or whether Akinto could find his way back to his wife and his children from there.

But at least he'll no longer have an ocean to cross. And like Henry Clay's attempts to get Americans to at least address the problem of slavery, it was the best he could do.

'I'll have the papers sent to your house tomorrow,' said Clay. 'James and I are off to Natchez on the *Vermillion* on Tuesday. It will be good, beyond words, just to go home.'

For a moment he closed his eyes, and January felt, in that moment, compassion for him. A warrior coming to the end of his strength, and knowing it. Knowing, too, that the worst of the battle lay ahead.

Then his eyes opened and he grinned. 'I am truly sorry I missed that giant rawhide ball . . .'

'I'm sure Michie McCullen will send you a scrap of it, sir,' said January. 'If they don't roll it on to Mobile to raise more votes for General Harrison, I'd be willing to bet they'll take it apart and sell the pieces to pay for hard cider on election day.'

Clay's grin widened, and he raised both hands in surrender. 'No bets,' he said. 'I think you're absolutely right, Mr J. What's the second thing?'

'Free Lottie.'

The smile faded. Clay looked aside.

January went on: 'If it wasn't for Lottie, I wouldn't have known Griff Paige was there. If it wasn't for Lottie, I'd probably be dead myself. It was Lottie who recognized Paige yesterday, when all of us thought he was home sick. Who sent me after him. She's the one who saved your life, sir. And you're not running for President now.'

The senator glanced quickly at him, a sharp glance like the one that had passed between him and Francois Motet on the subject of Motet's free colored daughter, admitting what he'd never speak.

'That was the reason you never freed her, wasn't it, sir?' he continued quietly. 'Because you were running for President in '32, and didn't want voters in the South to see you as a man who would let a black woman win over him in a court of law.'

Clay sighed again, and rubbed the side of his nose. 'On that,' he said ruefully, 'I fear I must refer you to the Fifth Amendment of the Constitution of the United States.'

'It has been ten years, sir.'

'Aye.' The old man nodded. 'That it has.'

He went to the door, and as he laid his hand on the handle he straightened his shoulders, as he had done at his son-in-law's reception, returning to greet his constituents, witty and cheerful after his fight with his son.

Like a Spartan adjusting his crimson cloak before battle, so that the enemy would not see him bleed.

Then Clay opened the door and went out, to be caught by Blodgett, McCullen, and a dozen other journalists from the New Orleans papers, who surrounded the tall figure as they moved off down the corridor and into Rue Orleans. January followed, and when the mob around Clay had boiled away, saw, waiting for him, Rose, and Hannibal, and Catherine.

'I get to give a statement,' he reported drily, as his friends surrounded him. 'I may faint with joy.'

Hannibal mimed exaggerated surprise. '*Ecce miraculum mundi!* We all bet that the whole affair would simply be dropped.'

'*You* didn't.' Catherine regarded him accusingly, as she slid an arm around January's waist. '*You* bet they'd accuse Ben of not only killing that poor girl, but of murdering Melchior Aubin as well.'

'*Bella Caterina*, I was only playing the odds . . .'

Rose's arm circled January's waist from the other side and they started down Rue Orleans in the wake of the growing crowd of Whigs clustered around Senator Clay. Laughing at his jokes. Charmed by his brilliance. Ready to be guided by his wisdom.

Tippecanoe and Tyler, too . . .

'Cheer up,' she said gently. 'At least you don't have to spend the next three days in jail.'

January sighed. '"A plague on both your houses".' As Mr Clay had said, it would be good beyond words, just to go home.

EPILOGUE

The coroner's inquest on the death of Marie-Joyeuse Maginot returned a verdict of murder by person or persons unknown, exonerating both James Clay and Catherine Clisson. The New Orleans Whig Club made sure that every newspaper in South Louisiana carried the story, and proclaimed the Democratic pamphlet to be demonstrably a tissue of lies.

In October of 1840, upon his return to Kentucky, Henry Clay took out manumission papers to free both Charlotte Dupuy and her daughter Mary Ann.

James Clay went on to marry the daughter of the wealthiest man in Kentucky, and to himself become a lawyer and eventually a congressman for his state.

Old Tippecanoe – William Henry Harrison – was elected ninth President of the United States that November, and offered Henry Clay the position of Secretary of State, an honor which Clay declined. Clay was later elected to the US Senate – for the fourth time – and managed – for the third time – to prevent the Southern states from withdrawing from the Union in 1850. Not many years after Clay's death they did, finally, secede, resulting in the bloody horror of the US Civil War. But the reprieve of some thirty years which Clay's expertise with politics and compromise bought for the Union enabled the North to build up the industrial and technological advantages which resulted in Union victory.

After the first presidential election to rely on songs, rallies, and publicity stunts – changing the nature of American presidential elections forever – President William Henry Harrison delivered the longest inaugural address on record (nearly two hours), on a chill and drizzly day. Three weeks later he developed pneumonia and died, exactly thirty days after his inauguration.

He was the first US President to die in office. His Vice President, John Tyler, established the precedent that a Vice President who inherits the office is the actual – not merely an 'acting' or place-holding – President of the United States, with full presidential powers. Tyler holds the record as the president who fathered the most (legitimate) children: fifteen, by two wives. He is also the first (and so far, the only) US President to so thoroughly alienate his own supporters that he was thrown out of his own party while in office.

He later supported the Confederacy, was elected to the provisional Confederate Congress, and is the only US President (so far) to be buried under a flag other than that of the United States.